Vice and Vengeance

Dennis Zigrang

DEDICATION

This book is dedicated to the memory of,
Detective Daryle Wayne Black.
You were taken from us too soon but will never be
forgotten.
E.O.W. April 30, 2000

CONTENTS

Cover graphics by Steve Zabel

www.montagephotooc.com

I would like to thank my wife Marcia and our three beautiful children, Richard, Melissa, and Allison. Being married to, or the child of a police officer, has its price. Missed parties, birthdays, holidays and more. Through it all, good and bad, they have been nothing but supportive and proud.

All characters and events in this novel are fictional.

Chapter One

The Outcall

Waiting. Oh, how he hated the waiting. Patrick Sullivan paced back and forth in his hotel room, his arms folded, just waiting. He was a nice looking guy in his early 40s with brown hair and frosted tips of blonde. His mustache and goatee had a natural red tint thanks to his Irish roots. The room was as handsome as he was, $380 a night for a ninth floor view of the ocean and the old majestic cruise ship the Queen Mary. He lay on the huge bed watching the television but not really paying attention. During a commercial he began gazing out the window to see the sunset paint the horizon with pinks and reds. This wasn't his first time calling a girl to his room, but he was still nervous. He began to fidget with the cufflinks on his tuxedo shirt and the gold band on his finger. He looked back at the clock and mumbled aloud, "Shit, she's forty-five minutes late." He opened another beer and took a sip, thinking, *I wonder if she'll be good looking or some nasty skank.* He hated it when they showed up and they were nothing you would take a second look at on the street. He'd just be glad if she showed up at this point.

He was startled by the loud knock at the door. A quick check of the room to make sure everything was in order and he made his way to the door. Peering through the peephole he saw a distorted view of a woman in a short black skirt and white blouse. Patrick

1

took the chain off the door and opened it to greet his companion for the evening. The woman looked up with deep blue eyes and in a voice as soft as velvet asked, "Patrick?"

Taken by her beauty, all he could say was, "Yeah. Summer?" She flashed a smile that a cover girl would kill for. "I'm glad we finally get to meet, Patrick. Are we gonna just stand here or may I come in?"

He stepped aside and motioned with his left arm for her to enter the room. She strolled in with confidence, as if it were her own house. As she passed Patrick, she lifted her hand to his face and gently stroked his cheek. "You're cute," she whispered.

Feeling the warmth of her soft palm he said, "And you're more beautiful than your pictures." He looked at her backside as she sauntered on by. She had flowing blonde hair with a thick inward curl at the end – the kind of hairstyle you would see on pinup girls from the '40s, but it fit her sophistication well. The blouse was silk. He could make out the lines of a bra, but it could not hide the fact that it was cold outside. The skirt fit tight and short, short enough that the tops of her black stockings were visible. Four-inch heels, so pointed they could puncture the skin, finished her ensemble.

He shut the door behind her and asked, "Would you like a drink?"

"No thank you, darling."

"How do we get started?" he asked like a schoolboy.

"Well, you could start by paying me."

Patrick asked, "Ah, eight hundred, right?" as he pulled a gold money clip from his tuxedo trousers and began to peel off the bills one at a time.

"That's for two hours, sweetheart, but I never really watch the clock." She took the bills that he held out and put the money into a small pocket of the large black shoulder bag she had set on the dresser. She made her way over and lay down on the bed diagonally, propping her head up with her left hand and patting the mattress with her right. "Come sit with me, Patrick, and get comfortable."

He sat down next to her and her hand quickly made its way to his thigh. She stroked his leg and made eye contact as if to say, *I am going to rock your world.* And there was no doubt in his mind that she could.

"You're so tense. Would you like a rubdown first?" she offered.

"Sure, that would be great."

She began to give him instructions. "Go ahead and get undressed and I'll be right back." She hopped from the bed, took her purse and dashed off to the bathroom.

Pulling off his slacks, Patrick called out, "I must say, when I found your website I thought it was phony, or maybe you wouldn't be the girl in the pictures. But now that you're here, I'm so glad I sent you that email."

"I'm glad you did too, Patrick. You seem really sweet," she said from the other side of the closed bathroom door. Down to just his underwear, he noticed that Summer had placed the chain lock back on the door. He walked over and quietly removed it, then returned to the bed and lay on his stomach. She returned wearing a bra and matching white thong panties. The brightness of the lingerie amplified her perfect tan. He was stirring with excitement. Never before had he seen a body so perfect, so warm and she was so close. Summer held up a plastic bottle in each hand and asked, "Lotion or oil?"

He smiled and said, "Oil."

She walked over to the dresser and set down the lotion. Patrick could now see a tattoo on the small of her back. It was of a peacock with its tail curling under its feet. It was as beautiful and graceful as she was. While at the dresser, she picked up an airline ticket printout that was among Patrick's things. She examined it and said, "You flew in from Houston? I thought you said in your email that you're from Palo Alto?"

"I am," he replied. "I was in Houston on business and flew here for a good friend's wedding before I head home."

"Just checking. I have to be careful, you know. The police sometimes pose as businessmen or travelers and will try to bust ya," she said in defense of her nosiness. She climbed onto the bed and straddled him while he was face down. Gently kissing his ear, she whispered, "I know you're not a cop. You turn me on, and cops, well, they don't turn me on." Then he felt the warm oil in her soft hands stroking his back. She rubbed his shoulders and asked him questions about his work and where he lived. Within just a few minutes he was drenched in oil and she was lying on top of him sliding her body up and down his back. Although he could not see it, he knew that her bra was off because he could feel her nipples on his shoulder blades. More kissing of his neck and ears was followed by her hypnotic voice: "Do you want to see me play with myself?"

"Oh yeah," he replied.

She slid down his body and off of the bed, and in the same motion she stripped away his underwear like a magician pulling a tablecloth out from under a candelabra. She said, "I'm not gonna be the only one naked, silly." He rolled over as she climbed back onto the bed and walked on her knees to the middle. He looked at her and thought, *Oh God, she's perfect.* Her breasts were glistening from the oil, and she began to rub them with both hands, pausing only to pinch a nipple now and again. Her right hand slid down her flat stomach and slipped into her panties. "Feel free to masturbate, Patrick."

"No, I'll cum too quick. I'm enjoying myself just watching," he said.

She arched her back as the hand in her panties slowly moved in little circles. "Take my panties off, Patrick," she said in a half-moaning voice. He slid them off carefully by holding the straps on the sides of her hips. Her tan body was broken up only by a thin bikini line that covered that special place on every woman's body that controls most men, and will ruin others. Her well-manicured fingers were busy pleasing herself as she was now on her back, sliding her finger in and out. "Do you want to fuck me?" she questioned.

"Of course I do. Is that extra?"

"No, silly. Eight hundred dollars for two hours, all the fucking and sucking you can handle. I put some condoms on the dresser for you." She pointed to the dresser with her left hand as her right continued its pleasurable work.

He walked over to the dresser, picked up a condom and said, "I have to take a piss or I won't be able to get off. I'll be quick, so don't finish without me." He quickly slipped into the bathroom, shutting the door behind him. A few seconds later she heard the click of the entry door latch. She looked up to see not Patrick, but four men with badges around their necks. A few wore black raid jackets with POLICE written across the back.

"Long Beach Vice Squad," a voice called out. Then a few flashes from a camera blinded her.

"What the hell is going on?" she yelled at the top of her lungs as she grabbed a pillow and tried to hide her nude body.

"You're under arrest for prostitution," Patrick explained as he stepped out from the bathroom, now wearing a pair of boxers.

"Patrick, you're a cop?" she said with a hint of confusion. They were always a bit confused at this point, when they found that Patrick was really an undercover detective.

"Yes, Summer, I'm a cop, and my name's not Patrick, it's Travis, Travis Jensen. I'm a vice detective, and you're under arrest. Now put your clothes on and please be quiet or someone's gonna call 9-1-1 if you keep yelling like that."

The boys chuckled at his comment because the last time they had a screamer some good citizen had called in a possible rape in progress. Summer didn't seem to think it was so funny. She slipped back into her clothes, never taking her eyes off of Travis, who was getting dressed on the other side of the bed. She had *You bastard* written all over her face. He never could understand that kind of hate. The girls he encountered all knew what they were getting into when they decided to be an escort, or hooker, or call girl; whatever they called it, they were still prostitutes. The California Penal Code made it clear: Any sexual act for any form of compensation is prostitution. All the courts wanted to see was that the perpetrator had done some independent act of furtherance to show they were going to go through with the arrangement. Summer's little strip show and the condoms would easily convince a jury she was willing to consummate their little illicit tryst.

The team of long-haired, unshaven detectives packed up quickly and moved to another room. Ben Hutchens, another member of the squad, began to set up his things in the room. He'd brought along travel brochures and timeshare literature to support his cover as a travel agent. He had a girl due any minute who he'd landed on Craigslist. Summer's show had been so much fun to watch that it had taken Travis a little longer than usual to give the hit sign indicating he had enough for the arrest.

Once they were all in a room across the hall, Summer sat on the edge of a large bed as some of the team sat next to her watching a Lakers game. The room was a few doors down the hall from where the arrest had been made. It was like a mini command post for the night's operation. A laptop computer for some last-minute emails sat on the desk. Next to it was a charging bank for six police radios. Jack Barnes was sitting at the desk listening to a receiver with headphones. The transmitter was hidden in the arrest room with

Ben. It was Jack's turn to listen for the hit sign, but more importantly it was up to him to decide whether there was any type of emergency situation that needed a response. The laptop was also hooked up to a miniature camera that was hidden on a room service tray in the hallway. The team could see if there were any thugs in the hall before the undercover operator answered the door. A setup or rip-off was always a possibility when doing this type of operation.

There was another girl sitting on the edge of the bed. She was barely 18 years old, with strawberry-colored hair and pale skin. Her eyes were bloodshot from crying, but she had finally calmed down. Her boyfriend sat in handcuffs as well but he was on the floor between the bed and the wall. He was supposed to be her "protection", now he sat there in his urine-soaked pants. The experience of four burly cops swiftly snatching him from the hallway was a little much for this 19-year-old political science major.

Detective Jesse Guerra took care of filling out Summer's booking slip. Jesse and Travis had become good friends over the last few years. Jesse, or Jesus as his mother called him, was 38 years old and, like Travis, he had joined the Army right out of high school. A short but stocky man, he came from a traditional Mexican family in East Los Angeles, and had helped Travis a lot with his Spanish. Being able to speak Spanish in Long Beach was a real plus for police officers. Even though the Vice Squad worked as a team, Jesse and Travis had become more like partners. They each knew how the other thought and how they would react to different situations. They even spent their time away from work together with their families.

While Jesse took care of Summer, Joe Marino pulled Travis into the bathroom area to hear how things went and to determine whether Travis had all of the elements of the crime. Joe was the sergeant of the team, a great guy, and of pure Italian blood. Just under six feet tall, he had a wide frame that still resembled the high school football star he had been some 30 years ago. He was one of a handful of guys who hadn't forgotten what police work was like when he got his stripes. He and Travis had worked together for several years in another unit before both of them had gone to vice.

Joe asked, "Did you get everything?"

"Yeah, it was eight hundred dollars for 'all the fucking and

6

sucking I could handle,' and she brought the condoms."

"Cool," Joe replied as he nodded his head. "She's pretty hot, T.J. Did she put on a good show?"

Travis gave him a devilish smile and said, "This was a tough one, bro. I thought I might never give the hit, and I'd have to go to the ATM to reimburse the city funds. I've never seen a hooker this smokin' hot before."

"I'm not a hooker!" Summer yelled from around the wall.

"Hey, speaking of the city's money," Joe said with an inquisitive tone.

"It's in her bag, outside pocket."

"I got it," Jesse answered and held it out for Joe. Travis confirmed the amount as Joe counted it. You could always see the relief in Joe's face when he had all of the city funds back in his own pocket. You couldn't blame the guy, though; he would be in a world of shit if they were short a few hundred bucks.

Travis took a few minutes to write out some notes of what had gone down in the room while it was still fresh in his mind. The story would later be dictated on tape when they got back to the office at the end of the night. After he completed his notes, he jumped into the shower to get the oil off of his body.

Now wearing jeans and a USC T-shirt, he asked Summer to come over and talk with him. She still looked pissed off. "Have a seat." He motioned to an ice chest that was in the vanity area of the bathroom. "You want a soda or water?"

"Actually I could use a water, thanks," she replied in a quiet, sad voice. He opened the cooler he'd been sitting on, pulled out a bottle of water, opened it and handed it to her.

"You've never been arrested before, have you?" he asked. She gazed at the floor and shook her head no. "Who do you work for?" Travis asked, even though he figured she was probably an independent.

"No one. I just started doing this a few months ago. I need the money to pay off my student loans, and I didn't know what else to do. A girlfriend of mine that I used to dance with told me about it and helped me set up my website."

By this time she had tears on her face and was shaking. She was mentally a wreck, but she still looked stunning, and the image of her naked body kept popping into his head. He said, "Look, Summer."

7

She interrupted him and said, "It's Jennifer. My name's Jennifer Bennett, but I go by Jen."

He continued, "Jen, I want you to read something." He reached into his backpack and pulled out a newspaper clipping. It was yellowing and wrinkled from continuous folding and unfolding. Handing it to her he said, "This could have been you." The article told about an escort who had been called to a house in Orange County that turned out to be a vacant foreclosure. She was met by two men who held her at gunpoint and raped her repeatedly. As she read on, Jen began to cry more. When she finished the article she handed it back to Travis. He told her, "I don't want to see something like that happen to you. Get out of this business while you can. You're beautiful and you seem intelligent, it would be a shame to see you waste your life like this. You got lucky. I turned out to be a cop and not a nut like these guys." He pointed to the story. Now he was preaching, trying to save her from herself just like he did with all the others, but something told him he could make a difference with this one.

"I don't know what I can do," she said, sobbing.

Jesse walked over and said, "She's all set." He was holding her bag and her booking paperwork; it was time to take her to the jail. The three of them quietly walked down to Travis's undercover car in the hotel parking structure. Travis opened the front passenger door for Jen and said, "You're not gonna like this, but now I have to put handcuffs on ya."

She gave him a goofy smile and said, "Like I'm going to hurt you guys."

"It's department policy, dear, gotta do it." He cuffed her and sat her in the front seat. Travis drove while Jesse rode in the back seat. The five-block ride to the station was quiet; she never spoke a word.

While they were in the booking area in the basement of the police station, some patrol guys kept checking Jennifer out. One young officer with curly dark hair and a toothpick in his mouth came up to the vice cops and said, "Why the hell did you arrest her?"

"'Cause she was eight hundred dollars for two hours," Travis said. The cop looked at Jen again, then at Travis with a shocked look on his face, and said, "Wish I had eight hundred dollars."

8

Travis sat next to her on the bench for a few minutes as they waited for the paperwork to be processed by the civilian employees behind the bulletproof glass. There were a few male prisoners on the bench, too. A drunk sat at the far left mumbling to himself, and in the middle were two tatted-up Mexican gang members who had their eyes locked on Jen. She was way out of her element, so Travis moved her to a holding cell nearby to spare her from the lowlifes. Separated from the main booking room, the cell normally was used for prisoners on misdemeanor charges who were waiting to bail out, or prisoners who were waiting to be picked up by other agencies. There was no one in it at the time, so he figured she would be a little more comfortable in there.

"Thanks. Those guys are real creepy," she said.

"She speaks," Travis joked. "Hey, I have to go up to the office now. Jesse will take you up to the jail when your paperwork is finished. Once your fingerprints clear records you can bail out. Do you have someone who can get you out?"

"Yeah, my girlfriend will come get me," she said. "Hey, what about my car? It's at the hotel."

"Don't worry, it will be there when you get out." He turned his head over his shoulder and asked, "Hey, Jess. Are her keys in her property?"

Over at the workstation Jesse held up a plastic bag and said, "Yeah, there's a set for a Mercedes in here."

She nodded and said, "Yeah, that's my car. Thanks."

Travis said goodbye and walked to the elevator just a few feet away. As he was waiting she said, "Travis." She paused for a moment. "Thank you." He looked back in disbelief and asked, "Thanks for what?"

"You're the first guy to treat me with any respect after finding out what I do for a living. Whether it's this or dancing, it's difficult. So thanks, you're a sweet guy, whether you're Travis or Patrick." She began to smile for the first time since she'd been arrested, and her face regained that beautiful warm look it had when he'd first answered the door at the hotel. It was kind of odd; he'd never had a call girl thank him before. They were usually so pissed that he'd fooled them into believing he was someone else that being civil during the arrest and booking process was not the norm. He turned away without saying a word and walked into the elevator. As the doors of that old box closed behind him, he thought, *Shit, a Mercedes. I'm in the wrong business.*

He unlocked the vice office located on the third floor of the station and let himself in. He wanted to get the report done because it was close to midnight and the rest of the guys would be on their way in soon. It was hard to dictate reports on tape in that office when all the boys were in there shooting the shit. The office sat in the center of the building so it had no windows and only one door. It was all of 30 feet long and 12 feet wide. Crammed into this space were six desks, eight file cabinets and a wall locker. Put the six-man team in there and it looked like Chinese refugees packed into a cargo container, nothing but the best accommodations for the misdemeanor squad.

Travis pulled his notes from his pants pocket. More like chicken scratch recollections on a hotel note pad that only he could understand. He also had the three condoms that Jen had brought with her. He put them on his desk and popped a cassette tape into the dictation machine. What a lifesaver it was to have this machine in the office. It had to have been dreamed up by a cop because they were the worst spellers, and their poor handwriting was rivaled only by doctors. In the top drawer he found the printout he had made of Jen's website and attached it to the evidence sheet. He began dictating the story into the microphone. Jesse walked in and set Travis's cuffs and booking face sheet on the desk quietly so as not to disturb him in midsentence. A few minutes later Travis was done with his report and ejected the tape and placed it in a plastic bag with all of the paperwork.

The Vice Detail secretary, Debbie, would type up the finished product in the morning. She was a quiet lady in her late 50s, kind of an introvert, but Travis could not help but think she got a kick out of all of the sex talk in the arrest reports.

After setting the bag in the inbox on Joe's desk, he sealed the condoms in an evidence envelope with Jen's booking number on it. On the way out of the station he would drop it in the evidence lockers in the basement.

Travis plopped down in his worn chair, exhausted from all the fun. This was only Thursday, the second day of their four-day work schedule, and it felt like the end of the week. The team normally started work on Wednesday, but they called it Monday. Their last day was Saturday, and they called it Friday. Even they got confused sometimes.

Jesse looked up from his newspaper and said, "Dude, she was hot. When I got her up to jail she told me you were sweet." He had this grin like the Cheshire Cat. Playing it off, Travis said,

"Gee, a hooker thinks I'm sweet. The keyword here being 'hooker.' Come on, Jess, she's still a pro."

"I know, but what a body. Dude, did your dick get hard?"

"No," snapped Travis. Relaxing his response, he added, "But it sure was getting there." They both burst into laughter, leaning back in their old desk chairs and at that moment the rest of the guys walked into the office. As it turned out, Ben's girl had never showed up, which was typical for escorts. So Jen brought the total number of arrests to six for the night, not bad numbers for an outcall operation. An outcall was when the girl came to you at a hotel or your home. An incall was when you went to her. The best part of both operations was that the girls tended to be much better looking than street prostitutes, and it broke up the day-in, day-out routine of nasty street whores, dope fiends and the boys in the toilets looking to pleasure a total stranger. Tomorrow the team was headed back to the streets.

They put all of the electronic equipment away in the cabinets and straightened up the broom closet they called an office. Travis pulled his airline printout out of his backpack and handed it to Jesse.

"Here's that boarding pass, she bought it hook, line and sinker," Travis said.

"Good. I have to give it back to my cousin Enrique. It's for a real ticket so he has to take it out of the system."

"Is he a ticket agent?"

"No, he works as a manager at the FedEx terminal, but he's nailin' the counter manager at the airline so she printed it for me," Jesse said.

"Well, tell him thanks, and let her know it worked like a charm."

The team left the office together and walked down the hall. "Travis, you coming to have a beer with us?" asked Ben as they all stepped onto the elevator.

"Not tonight, I'll catch you guys tomorrow," Travis said. He was wiped out and could hardly stay awake. He knew one beer would soon be three, and he would have trouble keeping it between the lines on the drive home. It was 33 miles from work to his home. His car still had the scrape marks on the fender from when his luck had almost run out a year before on the 405 Freeway. Besides, tomorrow was "Friday debriefing," and that meant they would all go to the local cop bar and tell stories, curse the department brass for screwing someone over on a job selection, or just catch up with friends they didn't get to see that often. It was a police ritual that had been going on ever since there had been police officers. They needed an escape and time to be with the only people who truly understood them. People unfamiliar with law enforcement often believed cops felt that only other cops were good enough to be their friends. That wasn't the case at all. Sometimes, cops were the only ones sick enough to understand each other.

Travis started driving home, keeping a keen eye out for all of the drunks on the Long Beach Freeway. He popped in a CD and listened as The Plimsouls began to play "Zero Hour." Travis enjoyed the drive home; there was a sense of evolution in the miles between work and his house. He drove past the rundown apartments and vacant lots that were once businesses before the riots of '92. Some of them were finally making a comeback after all these years. The wealthy professionals who worked in the high-rises downtown saw the same things Travis did on his drive, with one difference. To them it was just an old, rundown part of the city they had to pass through in order to get home. To the officers who worked there, each building, street corner, or vacant lot was etched in their minds, each a page telling a story, like the blue three-story apartment on Tenth Street at Locust. That's where Travis had caught his first rapist. A little farther north on Anaheim, his friend had gotten into a shooting in a hotel stairwell – a terrifying night Travis would never forget.

There were thousands of people down there, and he saw them, too. He saw them trying to make a better life for themselves through hard work only to have some hype take their worldly possessions so he could pump the love of his miserable life into his arm. He saw the kids who didn't stand a chance, with no father and a mom turning tricks in their one-room apartment. Tweekers, whores and hoods, all intertwined within the fragile society of downtown; this was Travis' world.

Soon the scene from the elevated freeway changed to the

single-family homes on the east side, built in the '50s when Long Beach was growing rapidly. Most were still the same as they were back then. A lot of newer families got started out there, as did Travis's, yet some of the homes still had their original owners. Travis used to live out there when he first started on the job. His wife and he had a cute little place they fixed up, but it was too close to work. Travis would see people he had arrested in the market or at the mall. When you were alone it was no big deal, but with your wife and a little one in a stroller, you were vulnerable. So they moved out to Irvine about five years back. It offered all new homes, twice as much room and beautiful Spanish architecture. Irvine was so new there were no run-down areas, not much crime to speak of and great schools. It was an easy choice.

As he crossed the LA / Orange County line he began to think about the night. What a bizarre scene; she really thought he was Patrick Sullivan. The scary thing was, he wanted to be Patrick, if only for one night. He was envisioning himself in the same situation but never making the arrest. Travis said to himself, "My God. I'm fantasizing about a hooker. What the hell am I doing?" This was strange for him. He'd never thought like this about a woman he had arrested, but it was over with now. He knew he would probably never see her again. Most escorts didn't fight it in court because juries were not sympathetic when you were naked within 10 minutes of meeting someone after they gave you hundreds of dollars to do it. The best chance the escorts had was to plea bargain to a lesser charge or no jail time. A lot of folks, including some cops, thought it was a waste of time, all this work for a little misdemeanor with no victim. Travis didn't mind, though. To him it was a nice break from real police work, and besides, being proactive with vice made it harder for organized crime to become established in the city.

Rolling into his driveway, he looked up at his bedroom window hoping the light would be on. The darkness told him that his wife, Sarah, was asleep and the chances of getting some lovin' were just about nil. He was disappointed, because the night's events had made him horny. After taking the dog out to leave his mark on the lawn, he stripped down and slid under the covers.

He reached over and felt her warm body barely covered by a T-shirt. As she was lying on her stomach, he caressed and massaged her smooth butt. He pulled down the covers to reveal the most

13

beautiful shape God ever put on this earth, a woman's body. The work of his hands drew moans of enjoyment from her, so he slid his hand down between her legs. Now awake, she slowly opened herself to him and softly said, "You sure know how to get me." She rolled over and he quietly crawled above her. They made love there in the quiet darkness. Wrapped in each other's arms, he kissed her forehead and told her how much he loved her. The job had put quite a strain on their marriage and it had been quite some time since they'd been this close, but tonight they drifted off to sleep together.

Chapter Two

Boys and Girls

Friday brought beautiful summer-like weather to the city. The thermometer on Travis's rearview mirror said it was 88 degrees. This was a nice change as there had been a lot of fog and drizzle for the last few weeks. The bad thing was this meant Beach Day. No doubt that when the team got into the office Joe would want them to go work the boys at the beach. This was the only part of vice investigation that Travis didn't like. It was a whole new world he'd never known existed, an entire society of men who loved to engage in lurid, anonymous sex with other men in public places like bathrooms and parks. Although it was only about 10 percent of their job, it accounted for the most headaches and controversy.

Some local liberal do-gooders were convinced that the Vice Detail targeted and entrapped members of the gay community. A few made it sound like all police officers were homophobic gay bashers from the 1960s. They just couldn't believe that grown men had sex in public bathrooms with total strangers.

***

About a year back, two gay candidates ran for the City Council. One was a lesbian who worked as a defense attorney, and she specialized in defending lewd conduct cases. The other was a

15

retired businessman named Paul Wise. The Second District, where they were running, had a large gay community. After Wise won the election, he made it a point to ensure that his office looked into his opponents' claims of entrapment by the Vice Squad.

Joe agreed to show Wise the daily routine of the squad. He followed in Joe's car on whore runs, watched a John sting, and even went on a warrant service. Finally, he asked about the infamous Junipero Ave. parking lot toilets at the beach. So Joe had Travis drive him down there one warm fall Tuesday around 2:00 p.m., and they parked in the west end of the lot. At first the politician didn't see anything unusual, just a few cars in the lot, a few sunbathers on the beach, and a lifeguard truck parked at the lifeguard headquarters. He said to Travis, "I don't see anything goin' on."

"Keep looking sir," Travis instructed. "There's a difference between observation and perception. We are seeing the same things, but they mean different things to me because of my training and experience. How many cars do you see at this end of the lot?"

"Not counting us and the lifeguard truck, four. Why?"

"How many have men sitting in them?"

"Three. I don't see your point."

Travis explained, "The empty one is probably the lifeguard's personal car, so don't you think it's odd that all the others have guys sittin' in them? Why haven't any of them gotten out and headed to the sand? We've been here for five minutes and not one has moved."

"OK, that's strange. So what are they doing?"

"Well, they may be waiting for someone to make a move and go to the bathroom first. Let's just wait a bit."

About seven minutes passed, and the conversation had turned to families and work, that's when Travis spotted a young Hispanic man walking down the iceplant-covered bluff. He was dressed in a maroon T-shirt that was cut off above his navel. His jeans were so tight over his skinny legs he looked fragile, and they were tattered at the cuffs from the man walking in bare feet everywhere. He had an earring in one lobe that had a long feather dangling to his collar. This guy's appearance just screamed feminine. What happened next couldn't have been better if Travis had planned it himself. The young Latino reached the doorway of the public restroom, looked around and walked inside. One of the men in the parked cars got out and followed him in a few moments later.

"What was that?" Wise asked in an elevated tone.

"You're pickin' this stuff up pretty quick, sir."

"So, then, how do you know if they commit a lewd act?"

"Ya gotta go in and see it." And that's when Travis's brilliance kicked in. "Go ahead, I'll be about five seconds behind you."

Initially there was no reaction from Wise but a chuckle. Then he looked at Travis and said, "You're not serious?" Travis had Wise's balls between two rocks. If Wise didn't go in, he was basically conceding that there was some sort of unacceptable activity going on inside. If he went in, he would have a good chance of catching them spanking the monkey and thus proving the Vice Detail's claims of lewd sex acts being committed in the bathroom on a regular basis.

"OK, I'll go. But what if they're doing something?"

"I'll just badge 'em and tell 'em to take off. We don't have any backup."

Wise got out and slowly walked the 60 feet or so across the lot. Reaching the door, he looked back to make sure Travis was behind him. He turned in the doorway and went out of view. Travis counted in his head to five and was holding back the laughter, hoping the worst was going on inside. Rounding the threshold, Travis was hit with a blur of red and blue and long hair. As he gained his balance he could make out the back of the Hispanic guy running to the bluff. Fearing that the guy had assaulted Wise, Travis ran to the south end of the bathroom, where he heard a commotion. There was Wise standing in front of three open stalls. Cowering in the corner of one stall was the guy they had watched get out of the car. He was facing the cold block wall and was tucking his shirt into his open pants. Wise just lost it. "You fuckin' sick bastard! What the Hell are you thinkin'? I should kick your fuckin' ass right here!" Travis was thinking how priceless this was as Wise continued. "What if a kid came in here?"

The poor guy tried to answer him. "I, I'm…"

"Shut the fuck up before I smack the stupid out of you, bitch!"

Travis quickly realized that now was not the time to pull out his badge. He grabbed the councilman by the arm and yelled, "Dad, let's go!"

Wise immediately caught on to the detective's cue. "OK, son," he said as he calmed down. They both walked out the door and then jogged back to their car, hopped in and headed for higher ground. Driving up the access road to Ocean Boulevard, they saw the Latino kid, still running north through Bixby Park toward First Street. Travis began laughing hysterically, but Wise sat there in the passenger seat, stunned, his face beet red, staring at the dashboard.

"Bitch. You called that guy 'bitch.' Where did that come from?" Travis asked.

Wise snapped out of it and began laughing as well. "I have no idea. I mean, those guys … right there." Then a complete thought came to him. Turning to face Travis, he said, "We're not like that. I mean, gay people, we're not like that. Shit, I never knew…"

Travis interrupted him. "I know that, sir. I know a lot of gay guys and gals, and they aren't like that either. What you just saw is not what I would call mainstream behavior."

Wise never told Travis exactly what he saw that day, but he did thank the veteran detective for not letting the pervert know who they were. Wise's little motivational speech in the toilet would not have gone over well printed in the local paper. Since then, the team had never been hassled about its tactics combating the "lewds" in the toilets.

***

Travis parked his Suburban next to his undercover car and unlocked the rundown '93 Chevrolet Beretta, with a cheap after market paint job in a dark gray and a cracked windshield. Some crazy hooker had kicked it a few months back after he'd arrested her. He had planned to fix it, but it made the car look more like all the other piece-of-crap cars along Pacific Coast Highway, so he figured it helped him to fit in better. Travis put a change of clothes in the trunk for when the sun went down and they worked the highway. For now, shorts and a T-shirt would be the uniform of the day.

Walking into the station, Travis saw a few friends on the back steps. They were dressed in the dark blue wool uniform that most people associated with the police. When you combined the Sam Browne gun belt, weapon, magazines and vest, you added nearly 20 pounds to your weight. And then there was the heat.

"Must be hot in them uniforms, boys," Travis joked.

"Kiss my ass, Jensen," one of them yelled back with a smile. A lot of guys were envious of the Vice Detail because of the freedom they had. But if they knew the fact that Travis was wearing shorts meant he might have his testicles grabbed by some sleaze-bag pervert in the next few hours, they might not want his job as much as they thought they did.

Travis made his way through the station's rear door and walked onto the elevator. Once inside, he stood next to a rookie who looked to him to be high school age. Travis could see out of the corner of his eye that the young officer was trying to figure out who he was. Travis still had his badge inside of his shirt, and with his bleached hair and goatee he sure didn't look like a cop. He could tell the rookie was contemplating challenging him about who he was and why he didn't have a visitor's pass, when the doors opened on the second floor and Lieutenant Prescott walked into the elevator. He was a nice old-timer with more than 30 years on the job, smoky gray hair and eyes to match. The small ruby in the city seal of his badge signified the three-decade milestone few cops ever reached. He could retire at any time, but stayed on thinking he might actually make commander one day. He probably never would, though; he never went in for being an administration man, and that's why all the guys liked him.

"Jensen," he belted out. "You look like shit, boy. Are you still workin' vice?" He asked the question even though he knew the answer.

"Yes sir, and lovin' every minute of it!"

A big smile came over Prescott's wrinkled face and he said, "Vice is the best job on the department, boys. I had so much fun there."

Travis looked over at the rookie, who was now smiling as he said to Travis, "Hi, sir." He had finally figured out who Jensen was, and Travis could see the relief on his face.

"How are you doing, bud?" Travis said, realizing he had forgotten the young officer's name. Travis had taught at the academy, but all of the recruits looked the same with their shaved heads, so that when they hit the street and grew some hair back he had no idea who they were.

The doors opened and Travis quickly walked to his office. The Chief of Police's office was on the same floor as the squad's, and the chief didn't like the vice guys wearing shorts to work. He just didn't understand that if you were at the beach at high noon in hot weather and you were wearing pants, you stuck out like a cat at a dog show.

As Travis got to the door, he pulled his badge out from his shirt. It hung around his neck on a chain along with a handcuff key and the key to the office. This way the key chain for his undercover car didn't have any "cop" keys on it. With one quick motion he put the key in, turned the knob and dashed inside. Letting the door close behind him, he was greeted by Jesse, who was sitting at the computer. "Dude, come look at this," Jesse muttered.

Throwing his backpack onto the desk, Travis asked, "What's up?"

"I looked up Summer's website, and take a look." Jesse pointed to the screen and said, "She's completely deleted her web page. I guess your little talk got through to her."

Sitting down next to him, Travis said, "Looks like it. Or her attorney told her to shit can it right away, hoping I never downloaded it."

"Did you?"

"Of course I did, my little propeller head," Travis said with a smile as he rubbed Jesse's head, messing up his hair. Jesse was the team's unofficial technology guru. He knew stuff about computers that the department's civilian experts didn't even know. When the bookmaking guys did search warrants they always included Jesse because the modern bookie always had a computer, smart phones or Ipads.

They heard a knock on the door and both detectives yelled out, "Password." To them, if someone didn't have a key to the office then they didn't belong in there. They liked to keep it locked because sometimes when they were online looking for hookers there was nudity on the screen, or they might have a confiscated porno video playing on the TV. God forbid a female employee saw that; they would probably all end up in a federal sexual harassment lawsuit.

"It's Debbie," was the reply from the other side of the locked door. Travis reached over, never getting out of his chair, and opened the door. She stood in the doorway and said, "Is Ben in yet?"

"No, just us," Jesse told her.

"OK. When he gets in have him come see me. Oh, and Travis, nice report from last night, sounds like you had a hot one," she said, letting the door close automatically as she walked back down the hall.

When the door closed Jesse turned from the computer and said, "Oh yeah, Joe called. He can't make it in tonight cause his kid's sick and his wife's out of town, so you're in charge. He wants us to do a beach run then, after dinner, hit the highway." Tonight, they were going to work boys and girls.

"OK, when the other guys get in we'll head out right away. I don't want to hang out around here without Joe to intercept the brass." Technically, Travis was in charge because he was the next senior guy, but they were all equals and everyone knew the job.

The rest of the guys all walked in together about 10 minutes later, and Travis told Ben to go see Debbie. She worked in an office across the hall with the lieutenant and the permit staff that regulated things like entertainment, alcohol licenses and massage therapists. Travis was in the process of telling the guys what the evening's plans were when Commander Baker walked into the office. He was in charge of a few specialized sections including vice. "Where's Marino?" he asked.

"He had to take a sick day, sir, his kid is sick and his wife is out of town," Jesse informed him.

"Hey, I saw the numbers from last night, you guys did a good job."

Then Jesse said, "Did you read Jensen's report, sir?" All the boys began to chuckle, cautiously waiting to see if the commander laughed.

He smiled and nodded, then shook his head as if to say, *You guys are going to be the death of me*. He walked into the office and sat in one of the chairs. He'd never noticed it was a chair from his own waiting room. The team had snatched it months ago. Looking up at the ceiling in reflection, he said, "Yeah, I read it, and it reminds me of when I was in Narco back in the '80s." All the guys looked at each other; they knew what this meant. The commander was about to take a walk down memory lane and they were all going with him, whether they wanted to or not. Travis thought, *Crap, this is what I wanted to avoid. Now it will be an hour before we get out of here.*

Baker was an old-timer like Prescott. A big guy standing six foot two with fists the size of grapefruits. He'd shaved his head when his hairline left him, but his mustache was as thick as a forest. He was the last of the guys who'd patrolled the Pike on foot. A mix between amusement park and red light district, the Pike, from what Travis had been told, was kind of like that island Pinocchio ended

21

up on with all of the tough boys. The cops had to be tough too, and Baker had put those big fists to work a lot. Now Baker was a commander who wanted to be an officer again, and talking to the guys was as close as he could get.

He began telling a story about the time he had made a dope deal in a restaurant on the fly. He'd been with a date who had no clue he was a cop, when he saw this black guy who he suspected of being a dealer. He'd actually made a dope buy from the guy while on the date without a backup team or anything. He later got an arrest warrant for the dealer. Well, when his date got a subpoena to appear in court, she didn't understand it but showed up anyway. He said, "When I told her who I was and what I had done, she flipped out. Boy, I knew that was the end of that pussy."

Ben came back in and Jensen told the team, "You guys better get down to the beach to catch the lunch crowd." They all knew he was getting them out of a long "back in the day" session. They cleared that office like cockroaches when the lights came on. Travis stayed back to check the complaint log. Besides, he always liked hearing the old stories.

Commander Baker and Travis's dad had worked patrol as partners for four years. The older Jensen was killed in the line of duty when his patrol car hit a box truck that turned in front of him at an intersection. He had been in pursuit of a murder suspect who was never caught. Travis was just a little kid at the time, so listening to the old salt made him somehow feel closer to the dad he'd barely known.

Baker hung out for about 30 minutes telling him stories about what police work was like before racial profiling and civilian complaint commissions. The old man sure missed making a good felony pinch. As Baker talked about the past, Travis thought about his future. Some of his classmates were now sergeants and one was even a lieutenant. If he had any aspiration of promoting he should do it now, because not too many sergeants or lieutenants were positioned to retire. That could stall promotions for a few years, and depending on any future raises, that could keep guys hanging on an extra year or two to spike their pensions. The next test was just a few weeks away. The more he tried to convince himself he should promote, the more he told himself, *I'm not done having fun yet.* Sitting in front of him was the reason he wasn't hot on climbing the ladder. He'd joined the department to catch crooks and help people, not to manage a budget and analyze crime statistics. Perhaps someday when he was slower and the job didn't thrill him like it did now he would promote, but not now, not today.

After Baker's secretary came in and dragged him off to a meeting, Travis began to sift through the complaint log. It was a book kept in the office in which the Vice Squad kept track of complaints from the public related to vice issues. Travis went back about two weeks and started reading the entries that did not have dispositions written next to them.

There were several complaints about whores working on Pacific Coast Highway near Lemon Avenue. This has always been a problem. Travis called that stretch of road "The Valley of the Dolls." As far back as any Long Beach cop could remember, that was where the street trade had thrived in the city. Men would come from all over the Los Angeles basin to this area looking for quick sex. Travis just couldn't understand the risks these guys would take to get their rocks off. Most of them were married men from middle-class neighborhoods, and they had no idea about the dangers they were venturing into. Some ended up getting robbed by pimps or ripped off by the whores. If they didn't end up a victim of a crime, they ran the chance of getting AIDS, the clap or some other God-awful disease. All for the chance to get a blowjob at bargain prices.

Most of the girls out there were drug addicts and would sell themselves to score a rock of cocaine. They had to chase the dragon at all costs – the dragon being the euphoric high one gets from smoking rock cocaine. Smoking coke gave a much quicker and potent high than snorting it. The drug hit the lungs and was directly sent to the bloodstream, one hit was all some people needed to get hooked. The high was so good and fast you wanted more. The problem was your first high would be the best. Then you needed to do more crack more often, trying to reach the same level of nirvana as the first time. That was chasing the dragon, and the dragon always won.

Most of the white girls were tweekers. Their drug of choice was meth – crystal methamphetamine, which had exploded in popularity in recent years. The tweek made many users drop their sexual inhibitions, leading to dangerous unprotected liaisons. In the gay community, meth use had been blamed as a major contributing factor to the continued spread of the AIDS virus.

23

Street prostitution was a very tragic scene. The hookers who lost control of their lives for whatever reason and found this to be the only way of surviving, and the Johns who were driven to satisfy their sexual needs, came together for a clandestine union. The true victims were the people who lived in the neighborhoods where these street urchins consummated their deals in cars and discarded used condoms on the sidewalk where children could find them the next day. That's why Travis did this job. Not because he thought prostitution was wrong; he didn't really care what two adults did behind closed doors. He worked vice because the fallout of prostitution adversely affected the good people in this city.

After he was done with the complaint log he started putting the file together from the previous night's operation at the hotel. Arrest reports, receipts, advertisements and booking photos. As he looked at Jennifer's photo, he couldn't help but wonder how she was doing. He hoped she could understand how dangerous it really was to do what she had done. Even in her booking photo she looked beautiful, perfect hair and makeup, a sweet smile and soft eyes. This was not your typical hooker. Travis wished he could have talked to her more. She probably had quite a tale to tell of how she'd found her way into this business.

When he was finished, he put the file in the old brown cabinet that was a surplus item from when the Navy left the base. The Navy had left behind a huge office building full of furniture for the department to use. Well, in typical Long Beach style, the city went through there like tweekers through the trash looking for anything that was useful. Even Joe's desk had a USN serial number on it.

He couldn't stand being in the office alone; he just kept thinking about Jennifer. So he headed out to the beach to see if he could catch up with the guys. As he drove down Ocean Boulevard past the high-rise condos, the sound of laughter could be heard over the radio. He was now within range of the other detectives' car-to-car radios and could hear the guys chatting. Ben was saying, "That guy is staring at you, Jack. He wants you in a bad way!" Jack Barnes was a good-looking guy, and the men at the beach just loved him.

Travis called out to Ben on the radio, "Hey, you guys get anything yet?"

"Not yet, but there are four guys down here sitting in their cars. One of them is just staring at Jack. I bet he's strokin' himself right now."

"Is Jack out of his car?"

"Not yet, he's waiting for this chick to leave. Her son is in the bathroom and he doesn't want to freak her out."

As Travis pulled into the parking lot for the beach he asked, "What about Jesse, is he out?"

"Yeah, but I think he's scaring them off." Jesse wasn't the most attractive man. Plus he was wearing jeans on the beach. No one wears jeans on the beach.

Jensen pulled into a parking stall about 70 feet from the bathroom. It was a typical city beach bathroom with five urinals side by side and three toilets each separated by a four-foot block wall. Above the door as you walked in was a sign stating that it was a violation of law to engage in, or loiter about for the purposes of committing, lewd acts in public. In other words: "Piss at your own risk, sometimes men jerk off in here."

The little boy came out of the bathroom after a few minutes and his mother took him by the hand. She rushed him off to their spot on the beach while she looked back at the parking lot with disgust on her face. She'd kind of figured out what all the single men sitting in the cars were up to. Travis hopped out and walked over to the pay phone next to the bathroom door. He put a quarter in and dialed an 800 number. That way it looked as if he was really using the phone, but he would get his quarter back. Jesse walked by and Travis said to him, "Go back to your car, you're scaring off the boys." Jess took a sip from the drinking fountain and headed to the parking lot.

By this time Jack was almost to the bathroom dressed in a bathing suit and a tight T-shirt that showed off his bodybuilding physique. As he passed through the doorway it was like the Pied Piper leading the children out of the village. In this case it was two of the four guys who'd been in their cars. They got out and made their way straight to the head. The first was a young black guy with a muscular build and a pencil-thin mustache. The second guy was about 55 years old white dude with grey hair, in a dress shirt and tie. He'd driven up in a BMW, and not a cheap one – it was a nice 700 series. Travis followed the second guy into the cinderblock building. A turn to the right, then back to the left, and the room opened up with the urinals on one wall and the toilets on the opposite one.

Jack was already standing at the middle toilet as if he were taking a piss. The black dude was washing his hands and looking over his shoulder at Jack. This guy was excited; he was washing his hands like he had wiped his ass with them, scrubbing and lathering up. He never noticed that the old guy and Travis had walked in just behind him. Travis went to the far urinal and stood at an angle like he was hiding his "stuff." The old guy pulled down his pants and sat on the toilet to Jack's left.

Now the black guy was in heaven. He walked to the stall to Jack's right and stood next to him. He looked over the wall toward Jack's crotch, then he looked at Travis. Travis moved to the sink and began to wash his hands, taking his time about it and watching the black guy the whole time. The black dude lost interest in Jack and moved to the urinals, which were closer to Travis. It went on like this for about five minutes. They were doing the dance, the dance of toilet love, each man getting a vibe off of the others, but the detectives were restricted. They couldn't start conversations or act as if they were committing a lewd act. These were the rules of engagement.

Then it started in earnest. The black guy turned so Travis could see his penis in his hand. He was slowly stroking it with his right hand. *Holy shit*, Travis thought. It was the biggest dick he'd ever seen, and the bastard was growing. It got hard fast, and he was now whacking it pretty quickly. Travis didn't hesitate long and gave the hit sign to Jack by pulling out a bandana and pretended to blow his nose into it. Jack took one last look at the old man and went out to give the signal to the other guys.

To buy some time, Travis acted as if he was not interested in the black dude and walked over to the old man and stood in front of his door-less stall. The old guy was sitting with his pants down at his ankles and was bent forward looking at the floor. He looked up at Travis, smiled, sat back and said, "I want you to suck me off." He was holding his penis in his hand and it had a leather cock ring around the base. Travis was caught off guard. He hadn't thought the old guy was a player, and if he was, Travis thought for sure he would have gone for Jack by now. Apparently Jack wasn't his type.

Travis said, "What did you say?" even though he had heard the man clearly. Then a deep voice over his shoulder said,

"He wants to know if you'll give him head." Travis turned to see the black guy walking toward him still smacking his huge rod.

He said, "And I want to give you some *Greek*."

This guy wanted to do Travis in the ass and the guys were not in the bathroom yet. The shock must have been showing on Travis's face because the black guy said, "Don't worry, I have lube." That statement actually made Travis more worried.

Behind the black guy to the left Travis saw Jack, Jesse and Ben walk through the door. They had their badges out and tapped the salami-slinging black guy on the shoulder.

"Put that thing away," Jesse said quietly, thinking that the old man wasn't involved and not wanting to freak him out. As the guys were walking the black guy to the sink to wash up the old man said, "Come on, come on." The guy was so hard of hearing he didn't hear the arrest being made just a few feet away, and the stall was blocking his view. Travis looked over and saw the old man laying back on the toilet masturbating. He was really going to town, so Travis yelled, "Stop that, I'm a…"

It was too late. The pervert started cuming right there, all over the stall like a 12-year-old schoolboy discovering his pecker for the first time. Travis jumped back to avoid getting any on him and yelled, "Holy shit!" When the old guy was done, Travis told him, "Look, pal, I'm a cop. Get cleaned up and go wash your hands at the sink, you're under arrest."

The old guy sat there like a sad puppy and said, "You're not gonna tell my wife, are ya?"

"No, we don't do that. Come on, let's go."

The guy pulled up his pants, then slowly made his way over to the sink and washed his hands. The other cops had already left the bathroom with the first guy. When the old man was done, Travis took hold of his left hand and clicked cuffs on his wrist. As Travis reached for the guy's right arm, he was caught off guard once again. The old fart was pulling the arm away and across his chest, out of Travis's reach. It was like slow motion. Travis thought, *What's this guy thinking? He's like 60 and dressed in a nice suit.* These were the ones you never expected to put up a fight. When the old guy's head came back at Travis's face, it drove the point home that he wanted to go the hard way. The guy was shorter by about four inches, so the back of his head caught Travis on the chin. It stung a little, but it pissed Travis off more than anything. Still holding the jerk's left hand, Travis grabbed the man's left elbow with his right hand and spun him to the left. At the same time, Travis went up with the elbow then down to the floor, performing a perfect arm-bar takedown. Perhaps too good of a takedown as the knucklehead's feet came completely off of the ground as his face headed for the concrete floor. He went down like a lawn dart, landing on his head with his body in the air for about a full second. Then he went completely limp and fell on his belly. Travis thought for a second he'd killed the old guy, but then the guy moaned. Travis hadn't meant to do him so hard, but the guy was like a rag doll when he got spun. Quickly the suspect was cuffed behind his back.

Hearing the smack of the old man's face on the floor, Jesse ran in and said, "What the hell happened?"

"The asshole head-butted me," Travis said with amazement.

Then Jesse pointed at the ground and said, "Do you want me to call for paramedics?"

A pool of blood was forming under the face of the poor fool. Travis rolled the man over and sat him up. He had a split over his left eye that ran the length of the brow. The blood was all over his face and he was crying like a baby saying, "I'm sorry, I didn't want my wife to find out."

Jesse replied, "Well, now she's gonna know you've been up to something today."

In about 30 seconds a goose egg had developed over the guy's eye. "Yeah, let's get him patched up, and then we'll take him to the hospital and get him stitched," Travis told Jesse.

The paramedics responded and did their thing, then Jesse had a patrol unit take the guy to the ER. He didn't want blood all over the inside of his undercover car, and besides, the rear seat of a black-and-white was hard plastic so back at the station the seat could be wiped clean. Travis went straight in to file his report and notify the watch commander about the use of force. He finished up in about an hour, but Jess was still at the hospital and the other guys wanted to go eat. "Ben and I are going to head out and get some pasta, you comin' Travis?" Jack asked.

"No, you guys go on ahead. I'm gonna wait for Jess and eat with him. I'll get you guys on your phone when we're done."

Jack grabbed his jacket and radio and asked, "Whore run after dinner?"

"Yeah, I don't have any city money to do any bar checks, but if we need I can use my money and get Joe to pay me back tomorrow." The team took off. Travis waited for about 30 minutes, and then called Jesse to see how long he would be. Jesse answered the phone in Spanish: "*Bueno.*" The vice guys always answered in their undercover personas because they didn't know who might be calling as they used the phones to set up call girls.

Travis purposely replied like a first semester Spanish student butchering Jess' native tongue: "*Hola, como-usta-usted?*"

Jesse laughed and said, "What's up, dude?"

"Nothing, the guys went to eat. When will you be done? I'm starving." Travis could hear Jess saying something to someone there at the hospital.

He came back on the phone and said, "The patrol guys said they'll book this guy. I already did the paperwork so they just need to transport him. Where do you want to eat?"

"Pico's," Travis suggested.

"Sounds good, bro. I'll meet you there in 10 minutes."

"Cool, see ya there," Travis said and then hung up his phone.

Pico's was a small Mexican place on Seventh Street run by Jose and Maria Campos, a husband and wife team. They had been feeding the locals and the boys in blue for the last 20 years. They were nice folks and the perfect example of the American Dream. They'd become citizens last year on June 14th, Flag Day. The American flag displayed in front of their small establishment was a gift from the Vice Squad commemorating the occasion.

Travis parked his car in a vacant lot down the alley. This way he could enter through the kitchen and say hello to Fred, the cook. Fred wasn't his real name; he had a long Spanish name that began with the letter "F". No way in Hell could Travis pronounce it, so he just called him Fred. Fred thought it was funny, and the name stuck. While Travis said hello, he could see Jess was already at the table. In his thick accent and raspy voice, Fred asked, "*Dos tacos con todo?*"

"*Si, con todo.*"

Travis slipped through the narrow kitchen. He sneaked up behind Maria and gave her a quick peck on her round cheek. She jumped a little and said, "Oh, Travis, you're terrible."

He told her how good it was to see her, as it had been a few weeks since they had eaten there. Travis plopped down in the booth across from Jess. "Did you order, or did you wait for me?" he asked Jesse.

"Yeah, I ordered. You eat like a starving dog. I need a head start."

Within seconds, Fred was at the table with a large plate topped with a cheese quesadilla smothered in red enchilada sauce and melted cheese. As he set it down, he said, *"Muy caliente."* Amazingly, Fred never used a potholder, just his bare hands even though the plates were on fire. The quesadilla was a tradition at Pico's, not on the menu and reserved only for the cops. They had never ordered it, but it was included with the meal every time free of charge. Some called it a gratuity, but it was simply Maria and Jose's way of saying thank you for the job they did. Either way, the police loved eating there, and the Composes loved feeding them.

"What's up for tonight?" Jesse asked.

Travis took a bite of the cheese and tortilla dish, thought for a minute while he ate, and said, "Well, let's do a whore run after we eat so we have some numbers on the books. Then I want to check on that old bar at Fourth and Alamitos. There was a complaint about over-serving and gambling there."

"Do we have money?"

"Yeah, I have enough, and I'll just have Joe pay me back tomorrow."

Jesse had a big smile on his face. Travis thought it was because they were going to have a few beers after the run, but it was because Fred was approaching the table with his burrito. It was the *El Rey*. Spanish for "The King," it was the king of burritos, some two and a half pounds of beef, beans and rice, all wrapped up in a tortilla the size of a small blanket. As they ate their dinner, there wasn't much talking except for the occasional moans of delight. Just before they finished, Travis's phone began to vibrate. He pulled it out to find a text message from Ben and Jack. It read, *We are back from dinner. We will see you on the highway in about 10 minutes.* "Perfect", he thought, they would catch them on the run.

Travis showed Maria some pictures of his kids before they headed out. She only got to see the kids about once a year, now that Travis no longer lived in the city. She looked at his daughter Tara and said with admiration, "Travis, she is you and you are her."

"She does look exactly like me, doesn't she?"

"Poor kid," Jesse said.

They said their goodbyes and headed out. Travis said to Jess, "I'm out back. Go to channel one on the car-to-car, we'll head up to Anaheim Street and see if we can hook up with the boys."

Jess responded by giving Travis a thumbs-up over his head while he walked out the front door. He was too full to speak.

Travis headed down the alley to his car and saw an old man pulling aluminum cans from a dumpster. He looked 70 years old but he was probably only 50. You could see the homeless life had been hard on him. Looking at him made Travis think about the guy from the beach toilet. He felt bad that the guy had gotten hurt, but it had been his decision to go the hard way. Too bad for him he'd realized his stupidity three seconds too late. Oh well, that was just part of the job, and you couldn't dwell on things that had already passed. You needed to move on and prepare for the things that were yet to be.

Travis pulled in behind Jesse as they drove north on Alamitos Avenue. Almost immediately they could hear the guys over the radio. It was scratchy, so they were not yet in range. Through the static they heard "Magnolia."

"Travis, you hear that?" Jesse said.

Travis grabbed the little radio and spoke into it. "Yeah, let's head west." Magnolia Avenue was about two miles west of Alamitos. When they got to within four blocks it was clear by the radio traffic that someone had a hooker in their car.

"OK, I got him, I got him. We are westbound Fourteenth from Mag," the voice said. It was Terry Knight, the sixth member of the squad and the newest. He'd come in late because he'd been watching his kids. Terry came back on the air.

"Still westbound coming up to Daisy. I need to pull off, can you get it, Ben?" He was following Jack but didn't want the girl to make him as a cop so he was passing off the follow.

Ben said, "Yeah, I'll get him at Daisy, you pull off."

Travis jumped in and said, "We're in the area."

Ben responded, "Ten-four, Jack has one on board and Terry's here. OK, OK! He's parking on Daisy north of Fourteenth, stay back."

Jesse asked, "Ben, do you need me to take the eye?"

"No, I got it. I was already parked when they turned the corner," Ben said in a faint whisper because he was holding the radio low and out of sight. He continued, "He pulled over right in front of me."

They all waited for the hit, the signal each guy used to indicate it was time to make the arrest. They all had different variations of the arrest signal. They did this because they arrested the same girls over and over. Soon the girls would start to catch on to what the cops were doing, so this way each time a girl got busted she wouldn't know it was coming. Jack would put a piece of gum in his mouth and throw the wrapper out the window. When the eye saw the wrapper, it was time. Ben's voice pierced the silence of the radio. "She laid the seat back, and, what the hell? Jack is getting out of the car, but no signal yet. Wait. OK, it's a go!"

Travis turned the corner and saw Jack standing behind his car. He motioned for everyone to move up and put his index finger to his lips to tell them to be quiet. He walked up to the passenger door and opened it. Travis looked through the rear passenger window and could see a woman all spread out. She was almost completely naked. Her pants were off and her shirt was up over her saggy tits. Her crotch was a big bush of hair and there were sores all over her legs and arms. She couldn't see Travis because he was standing in the blind spot of the car. She said to Jack, "Come on, fuck me, fuck me!"

Travis, laughing inside, couldn't help himself. He stuck his badge in the car right over her face and said, "OK, you're fucked!"

She jumped like she'd been zapped by the electric paddles paramedics used to revive dead people. "God damn it, Jensen!" she yelled. "You're such an asshole!"

It was the Bird Lady. Her real name was Cynthia, but her hideous pockmarked face and long beak made her look like a bird. She was an old, nasty street whore who'd chemically fried her mind in the '80s and had been pulling down tricks ever since.

While the bird was getting dressed, Travis pulled Jack aside and said, "You sick bastard, why did you let her get naked in your car? No one will ever want to ride in the passenger seat now." Jack smiled at Travis like Jack had done something bad but was proud of it. Travis looked at the car again and realized it wasn't Jack's car. It was Sergeant Atkins's car – the same model and color, but two years newer than Jack's ride. "Oh, Jack, Atkins is gonna shit!"

Atkins's first name was Jerry. They called him "Jerry-Atricks" because he was so old and a total goofball. That wasn't the worst of it; he was also a clean freak. He hated it when the field team borrowed his car, and he absolutely lost it when they picked up hookers in it. He was the administrative sergeant for vice, but for some reason the department's old policy authorized him for an undercover car. He only used it to go to lunch, so the team took it sometimes when one of theirs was in the shop.

Jack said, "Don't worry, she didn't piss or anything. Well, at least not 'till you scared the crap out of her."

Travis turned to the Bird Lady. "Hey, did you piss in the car?"

"Sorry Jensen, I couldn't help it," she said with a sheepish look on her face.

"Great. Joe takes one night off of work and I split some poor bastard's head open, now a nasty whore lets loose in Jerry-Atricks's car. Hell, we haven't even gone to a bar yet." The rest of the team just kept laughing.

Ben had already made an arrest about 10 minutes earlier, and his girl was sitting in the passenger seat of his car. Travis told Jack, Terry and Ben to take the two streetwalkers in and book them. "Jack, see if you can get a trusty to wipe that seat and dry it. Jesse and I will continue the run on our own."

Jesse and Travis drove up to the highway in their separate cars and headed west over the flood control channel. The setting sun was in their eyes as it sat just above the Palos Verdes Peninsula. "Travis, let's go south on Santa Fe, then back east on Anaheim. This sun is killing me," Jesse said over the radio.

Travis replied, "Better yet, let's flip a bitch and head back toward Cherry. Dispatch just sent me a text about a car date on Nineteenth at MLK Park."

A citizen had called in about a couple having sex in a parked car. Normally this kind of call would go to a beat car, but the communications supervisor figured a plain-clothes officer stood a better chance of catching them in the act. She'd paged Travis first to see if the team was in the field.

"David-Victor-Thirteen," Travis said into his portable radio on the patrol frequency.

The dispatcher repeated his call sign: "David-Victor-Thirteen, go ahead."

"Please show me and David-Victor-Ten en route to the six-forty-seven-A in beat five."

"Ten-four," she replied.

It took about five minutes for the unmarked cars to make their way through traffic to Orange Avenue. Turning north, they slowed down and notified dispatch they were on scene. Nineteenth Street was just one block north of the highway and a favorite place for prostitutes to take their customers for a quickie. So this was probably a good deal.

Travis spotted the car first. It was facing west against the north curb. He drove past Nineteenth and parked on Orange. He could see the car clearly through the corner of the park. Travis called on the radio, "Hey, Jess, I've got an eye on it. You wanna get out on foot and do a walk by?"

"Sure thing. With your blond hair someone might rob your white ass in this neighborhood."

Jesse parked south of Nineteenth got out. He walked past on the south side of the street and went all the way to the next intersection. About 30 seconds later he came back into view, now heading east on the north sidewalk. He was walking right past the passenger side of the car when he waved to Travis to come over. It was not an inconspicuous hit sign but a "get here now" kind of motion. Travis got his car turned around and shot over there as quickly as he could. As he turned the corner he saw Jess pulling a very large black woman out of the passenger seat by the arm.

Travis pulled in behind with his headlights on, helping to illuminate the scene now that the sun was almost down. Out of the driver's side emerged a black man in his mid-40s. He stood about six feet tall with short hair and big arms. He wore a blue work shirt with an oval nametag. He was calm and cooperative, but the woman was another story. She was yelling at him something awful. The only words Travis could make out were "motherfucker," with a few "punk asses" thrown in here and there. Travis, holding up his badge, told the man to stay where he was, then asked Jess if he was all right.

"Dude, I walked by and this chick was kickin' his ass."

"Who's that?" Travis asked, pointing at the woman as he walked toward the black guy.

"She's my wife, sir."

By now Jesse had her sitting on the curb. A black-and-white patrol unit rolled up because they could see Travis's car in the middle of the road and they figured something was happening. "Hey, you guys mind hangin' around while we sort this out?" Jesse asked.

"No problem," the Field Training Officer said as he pointed to

34

the woman and looked at his recruit. The new officer walked over and began to fill out a field interview card on the woman. Travis looked at the nametag on the black man's shirt. It read, "Gus."

"Gus. Is that your name, Gus?"

"Yeah, kind of a nickname, sir."

"Well, Gus, you want to tell me why she was smackin' ya?"

"Look, officer, she didn't do no harm. She just gets like that."

When the 230-pound princess heard that, she spoke up. "You're right, cause if I wanted to hurt you you'd be out, motherfucker."

Jesse leaned over and asked her, "What the hell did he do to piss you off so bad?"

"It's not what he did, it's what he won't do. The man won't eat the trash. I just want him to eat the trash once in a while."

"Why on earth would you want him to eat the garbage?" the rookie officer asked.

"Not the garbage, the *trash*, the *trash!*" she said as she pointed with both hands to her crotch. "You know, like mugambo, pussy. He won't eat my pussy!"

The four officers all looked at each other in amazement. None of them had ever heard it called "the trash" before. Trying to keep a straight face, Travis walked Gus to the police car so they could talk privately. "Gus, am I getting this right? She's pissed because you won't go down on her?"

"Yes, sir."

"What's the problem, Gus? Just do it if that's what she wants."

"No way, man, that's nasty."

"Gus, I do it all the time."

"That's fine for you white guys, but the brothers, we don't go in for that shit."

Travis didn't know what to say except, "Really? I didn't know that."

"Yeah, this black man ain't goin' down on no nasty pussy."

Travis took a few more minutes and tried to explain the benefit of pleasing her in the manner she desired, and said the possibility of a return favor was very likely. Gus started to come around after a while and agreed to give it a try when the couple got to the privacy of their own home. The two were advised about the legal implications of having sex in their car and were sent on their way.

Travis shook the hand of the training officer and thanked them both for stopping. As he stood in the door of the cruiser, the rookie said to Travis, "Sir, did she call it 'the trash'?"

Travis said, "Yeah, rook, she sure did." He looked at Jess and then at the FTO. They were still amazed by what they had just heard. Travis said to them all, "Only in the L.B.C. boys"

Travis pulled out a little notebook from his back pocket and started jotting down the phrase he'd just heard. He kept notes on the strange and funny things he'd heard and seen over the years. It was something he'd picked up from an old-timer he'd worked with long ago.

They made it through the rest of the night without any more vocabulary discoveries or unexpected disasters. The team got back together around 9:00 p.m., and they had a few beers on the city dime while looking for alcohol violations at the bar on Alamitos. The rest of the week was fairly uneventful, but Monday was going to change the squads' and Travis' lives and careers forever.

Chapter Three

Snitches and Stitches

The sun was blistering as it burned through Travis's window, hitting his face from the side as he drove west on the Garden Grove Freeway. He had the air conditioning on full blast, and he was feeling hot and irritable. When you're hung over your senses are amplified; the bumps in the road bounced the car and made his head pound like a drum. Last night was a mistake, but he wasn't going to sit at home and listen to his wife complain anymore. After all these years, the passion had just died for some reason. She said he didn't do the right things, but when he did the things she wanted, he always seemed to do them wrong. He wanted it to be the way it was before, but feared their marriage was nearing the end. Travis did not want to fight so he ventured into the city and met some of the boys at the club.

***

He went to The Tube, a local hangout on the east end of town. It attracted surfers during the day and cops at night. An old local named Tommy owned the place. He'd been a fairly good surfer in his day, but he was really known for making great long boards. In the early '70s he opened a warehouse, employed some high school kids and taught them how to shape boards. His shop became the spot for the locals to hang out and have a beer while they swapped stories after a day at the beach. Tommy's place was so popular that when long boards were no longer the hot stick in the water he applied for a beer and wine license from Alcohol Beverage Control. Amazingly, he got it, and the old warehouse was converted into a bar. He still shaped boards in the back room during the day and served cold beer at night.

The bar was simple and long like the building itself. Against one wall was a shuffleboard table so massive it must have been built in place. Most of the seating was on stools, except for a few booths. The Tube was a real dive, complete with peanut shells on the floor and near-frozen 28-ounce schooners of beer. It made the perfect cop bar: It was secluded and cheap, and they had it all to themselves. The surfers still came in, but they all got along. There were a lot of cops, like Ben Hutchens, who were among the ranks of the local beach crowds from Huntington to Redondo. The main room was decorated with old photos of the city and the beach before the breakwater was built. In one corner there were some framed pictures of eight police officers. They were all gone now, but would never be forgotten. Two of them had been Travis's friends, and they'd shared more than a few beers at The Tube together. One was killed in a car accident and the other was shot. They were the only two on the wall Travis had known personally, except, of course, for his father.

When Travis walked in there were a few young guys throwing pucks on the shuffleboard table. They couldn't have been more than 23 or so, Travis figured by the pimply faces and the young girls they were with. The girls were cute, with tight clothes and thin little bodies. They wore tight miniskirts that they both kept tugging down while they sat in a booth. The blonde had a waist you could put handcuffs around, and her friend was a brunette but had a tint of red coloring. She was a little shorter and about five pounds heavier, but she was the wilder of the two by far. Her blouse was a black lace number with a body-toned liner. It was completely backless, showing off the sunshine tattoo just above the crack of her ass. She was all over her date, sticking her tongue down his throat and stroking his leg, but he wasn't that into her. He was into his game of shuffleboard, too much to pay any attention to her.

Tommy brought Travis his usual beer before Travis had even ordered. He saw Travis looking at the girl and said, leaning over the bar, "Quite a little hottie, isn't she, Travis?"

"No shit!" he said. "Looks like homeboy is gay the way he's blowing her off."

"He's an asshole. Comes in here on Saturdays usually and always has a cute girl with him because he's a good-looking kid. He nails 'em, then treats 'em like shit and moves on."

"Sounds like you're jealous, Tommy."

"Fuck him," Tommy belted out loudly. He walked away with Travis's $20 bill to get change. Tommy didn't even turn around when he asked, "What are you doing here on a Tuesday, Travis? Did the wife piss you off again?"

Bartenders can read their customers like a good book, and Tommy was no exception. Travis thought that if psychiatrists worked as bartenders while they went to school, they would learn how to actually listen to people's problems. Tommy had known Travis for about eleven years, and Travis told him everything.

"Yeah, she just isn't there anymore like she used to be. I don't know what I'm gonna do." Travis looked over and caught the eye of the young gal with the lace top. She had overheard their conversation about Travis's wife, and she seemed amused by it. Travis gave her a smile. She turned her head away but looked back, smiled and gave him a little wave. He thought how unfair life was sometimes. His wife was at home and had almost no interest in sex anymore, at least not like she used to. Then here was this cute young nymph who couldn't get enough, and her date had no clue that he should take her home now or risk not getting it at all.

The metallic clicking sound Travis heard behind him told him the front door was opening. There'd once been a bell hanging on a swivel, but it had gotten knocked off during a fight between some homicide guys and some gang detectives. They'd been arguing over how a case should be handled, and it got a little out of hand. When the dust had settled, all that was left was the swivel that now clicked whenever the door opened.

It was some patrol guys from the swing shift. They had taken an early out to get there at 11:00 p.m. "Jensen!" they called out at the same time. Tommy was already pouring the schooners. He knew what everyone in the place drank. Fred Crackers came up to Travis first and greeted him with a handshake. His name really was Crackers. He and Travis had gone through the academy together, and the staff didn't let up on him because of the funny name until the last week. Besides the name, he was a tall, lanky guy with reddish hair and freckles. It was like having Richie Cunningham next to you during inspection and while you were getting yelled at by the T.A.C. officers. As it turned out, he became one of the toughest street cops around. He'd stayed in patrol to share his experience with rookies, and he was also on the SWAT team. He was a well-respected straight shooter who told it like it was.

The patrol group had all just been in a 30-minute pursuit of a shooting suspect that had led them through three other cities. *Real cops and robbers shit*, Travis thought to himself. He missed the wild action you got in patrol.

They all drank until Tommy kicked them out at 2:20 a.m., well after the bar should have been closed. Travis and Fred got a six-pack to go and went to the park down the street. The two friends sat on the tailgate of Fred's truck in the shadows of 50-year-old eucalyptus and pine trees. Fred told Travis how he had been studying for the next sergeant's exam and how he thought Travis should also take it.

"I'm not ready for that kind of responsibility," Travis said.

"Sure you are."

"The money would be nice, and you know Sarah has been bugging me about it too, but I don't know."

"I know. She told Stacey she wants you to take it."

"Well, we'll see, bro. Hey, I gotta go, I have to work tomorrow." Travis pulled one last can of beer from its plastic ring and took the *flyer* for the ride home.

When he woke up in the morning his wife was at work and the kids were off to school. He figured getting in at nearly 3:30 a.m. hadn't helped matters much.

***

As he pulled into the back of the station the headache was starting to go away, but he was still dragging ass. What he needed was food – Mexican food. The best cure for a hangover he had found was a good cup of salsa and a basket of warm tortilla chips. He started salivating just thinking about it. He made his way into the building and quickly onto the elevator. There were the usual people milling about doing their respective work, but Travis was still buzzing from the night before and it almost felt surreal to him, as though he were out of his body. He walked through the busy atmosphere as if he wasn't even there. He rode the elevator alone, leaning against the back wall thinking of how long it would take to get the boys out of the office and off to dinner.

When the doors opened he saw Jimmy Parks sitting at the reception desk for the Detective Bureau. He was a criminal justice major at Long Beach City College, and he interned at the station a few hours a week. To the side of his desk was a couch for the public to use while they waited to meet with investigators. Jimmy looked up at Travis, smiled and pointed to his right by tipping his head. As Travis stepped out he looked to the couch, wondering who it could be. Vice detectives didn't have victims, so who would be there to see him?

It was her, there in the police station, and she looked up at him with a sad face. "Jennifer?" Travis said in amazement. "What are *you* doing here?"

"Travis, I need your help. I didn't know who to turn to." Her voice cracked and trembled, and she sounded like a terrified child. She was scared.

"Well, Jennifer, you should talk to your lawyer first. We have an open case on you, and I shouldn't even be talking to you without your attorney."

"My case is over. I went to court today and asked the prosecutor what he would give me if I just pled guilty. He let me plea to ... I guess it's called loitering? I got a fine and a year of probation."

Travis had never heard of someone going in and pleading out just a few days after their arrest, but he figured it was possible.

"So, can you help me, Travis?"

"What's the matter?"

Cautiously, she looked around the lobby. There were a few detectives from auto theft at the copier, and Jimmy was just a few feet away. She said in a low voice, "Can we go somewhere a little more private? I have some information for you." The way she said "private" stirred him, and he began to think of the last time they'd been in a private place. The moment was so seductive, so dangerous – and then his stomach started talking to him. "Would you like to grab a bite to eat?" he asked.

She beamed a relaxed smile and said, "Sure, that would be great."

"Give me a few minutes, and I'll be right out. Oh, and my partner Jesse will probably come with us." He needed another officer with them. Although she was so sweet and beautiful, he had to be careful. All it took was one allegation of an improper relationship with a female defendant or a snitch, and you were screwed. He had heard about a narcotics detective from long ago who had started to see an informant on the side. It was a consensual relationship and all went well until she got busted for drunk driving in Orange County. She felt her cop boyfriend should be able to get her out of it. When he couldn't, she told Internal Affairs that he had coerced her into sex to work off her case. Needles to say, that guy was no longer a cop.

Travis passed through the gate that separated the waiting area from the hall that led to the detectives' offices. He glanced back and looked at Jen as she sat back down. She was dressed in a tan business suit with a white linen blouse. Obviously they were the clothes she'd worn to court, but she even looked sexy in that. Across the room he could see the auto theft guys drooling over her. He didn't think they had a clue she was a hooker. Hell, he'd arrested her and he was starting to forget what she had done.

Travis walked around the corner and opened the door of his office only to see the stares of the entire team fixed on him. "What, what did I do?" he said jokingly.

"What's she doing here, T.J.?" Joe asked, sounding more like a sergeant than an old friend.

"I'm not sure, Joe. She says she needs my help, says she has information for me. Don't worry, she already pled out on her case."

Joe paused for a bit. Looking down at his desk, he said, "Help with what?"

"I have no clue."

"OK. See what she wants, and let me know what you've got."

"Thanks, Joe. We'll be at Super Mex if you need me, and I need Jess to go with us if that's cool." Joe understood Travis's thinking because he had worked many informants before. He nodded at Jess to go along. Travis said, "First, I need to call the city prosecutor and confirm that her case is closed." A quick call to one of the prosecutor's stenos verified that she had indeed pled out earlier in the day. Jess and Travis grabbed their kit bags, and they started for the door.

Jesse's kit was an Army flight bag he'd picked up when he was a crew chief on a Black Hawk helicopter in Germany. Travis's was a backpack, the kind a college kid would use to carry his books. Instead of books, his had a few extra magazines of ammo, his radio with an extra battery, a ticket book and handcuffs. With his kit and the change of clothes he kept in his undercover car, he was ready for just about anything, although he wasn't sure if he was ready for her.

They walked out to the lobby to find two more guys loitering around the copy machine trying to make it look like they were actually doing something important. What they were doing was checking out Jennifer as she sat patiently waiting. She stood up as she saw Travis and Jess turn the corner. "Jennifer, do you remember Detective Guerra?" Travis asked as Jesse put his hand out to shake hers.

She smiled and said, "Oh yes, I remember. You were very nice." They shook hands and the three of them waited in silence for the elevator. Travis looked over at the guys standing at the copier. He could tell by the look of shock on their faces that they were putting two and two together. Who else, other than a hooker, would come to see two vice cops? The doors opened slowly on that old box made by the Otis Company. The elevator was on its last leg, and you were always taking a chance on getting stuck or visiting every floor before reaching your destination. They all stepped on and were greeted by Frank Tillbak.

Frank was a nice guy and did all right in the field, but he was kind of a geek. He had a computer repair business on the side, so when the department started up the Computer Crimes Unit, he was a natural choice. With the evolution of modern crime going hi-tech, just about every investigative detail needed the unit's services. Every time you served a search warrant you found a computer, smart phones, tablets and surveillance cameras. The only way to find out what was in there was with the help of the computer guys. They could even find crap that the crook had erased, or thought he'd erased. Jesse struck up a technical conversation right away with Frank. His goal was to get into the unit after he left vice. The two techno-nerds were really getting into it. Travis looked at Jen and she looked at him with an expression that said, *I have no idea what they are saying*. They both quietly chuckled, and she was fighting back a smile. When the doors opened they all stepped out into the lobby on the first floor. Jess said goodbye to Frank, who stayed on to go to his office in the basement.

"Jess, why don't you follow us to Super Mex? That way Jennifer doesn't have to come back here when we're done."

Jess nodded. "OK. What kind of car are you in?"

Jennifer said, "An Explorer."

"What's the color?"

"Red. I'm out front on Broadway." She pointed to the front door of the police station. Travis headed for the door and opened it for Jennifer. After she passed though it to the lobby, Jesse looked at Travis meaningfully. "Don't get lost, bro."

"Don't worry, we'll see you there," Travis replied.

Travis and Jen were silent as they walked across the street to her car. It was a nice 2WD model with a tan leather interior and all of the amenities. She unlocked the doors with the remote, and they got in. Travis told her to wait for Jess to come around from the back of the station. As Jess appeared in his Pontiac Grand Am, Travis directed her to head east. They only had to go about 10 blocks to get to the restaurant, so he didn't expect much conversation. She reached over with her right hand and put it on his thigh, and he almost jumped right out of the car. She spoke before he could say anything. "I want you to know, I am very grateful that you're at least willing to listen to me. You're the first guy in a long time to see me as a person and not some piece of meat to be bought and sold. What you said the night you arrested me made me think, you know, that I can get out of this life and be respectable."

"You can do anything you want to, Jen. All you have to do is believe in yourself and not in what people tell you."

He placed his hand on hers while it was still resting there on his leg. It was warm and beautiful, with long, slender fingers and well-manicured nails. He squeezed her hand gently, and then let go. She put her hand back on the wheel and asked for more directions. He didn't even hear her at first. He was still thinking how cool it was that what he'd said might actually save one of these girls.

"Travis. Travis, where do I turn?"

"Oh, right. Turn right at Lime, it's the next light down. Then go one block to First Street, it's to the left."

Travis looked over his shoulder to make sure Jesse was still with them. Although Jesse had been to the Mex a hundred times, Travis wanted to be sure he could see them. Jesse was there when they pulled up to the curb. Travis and Jen entered through the bar side of the restaurant. It was still early for the dinner crowd, but there were quite a few folks in the dining area, including four motor officers, so they took a table in the bar. They were the only ones in there, and Travis thought that would make Jen feel more comfortable to talk. Jesse hadn't come in yet when the waiter came to the table.

"Good evening. Can I get you something to drink?" He handed a menu to Jen and set Travis's on the table. The waiter knew Travis, and knew that he always ordered a number thirteen. Jennifer asked for a Corona, and the waiter pointed to Travis and said, "Diet Coke?"

"Yeah, and Jess is on his way in, so an iced tea for him."

"I forgot you're on duty," Jennifer said.

Jesse slid onto his stool as the waiter brought their drinks to the table. He took their orders by confirming with Jess and Travis that they would be having their usual orders. Then he asked, "And for the lady?"

Jennifer looked at the menu one last time and handed it to the waiter. "Just one taco would be fine, thanks."

Travis thought she must really have something bothering her. She hadn't even read the menu. After the waiter walked off, Travis didn't waste any time finding out what kind of help she needed. "So what's up? What do you need help with, Jen?"

"It's my boyfriend, ex-boyfriend. He won't let me out of this, this life."

"What do you mean? The call girl life?"

"Yes."

"Are you saying he's also your pimp?"

"I guess that's what you'd call it. It didn't start that way, though. I met him while I was dancing at the Tropicana. I was in school back then and was trying to pay for my tuition. He was a customer that came in now and again, and a lot of the girls seemed to know him. One night he told me he knew some businessmen that would pay a ton of money for private shows when they were in town. It sounded real good, twice the money in half the time, no drunks, and I wouldn't have to wait on tables between shows."

"But they wanted more after the shows, didn't they?"

She looked at Jess, then at Travis, and shook her head in disbelief. "I can't believe I fell into that trap. It wasn't like that at first, and I was actually having fun. I was making good money and had more time to finish school. Then one of the guys wanted to have sex with me. At first I didn't want to, but he was an all-right kind of guy and real cute, so I told him it would be extra. He pulled out a wad of cash and handed me five hundred bucks and asked if that would cover it. It wasn't until later that I felt totally cheap about the whole thing, but still, it wasn't that awful either. My boyfriend said he was OK with it, in fact he said he could hook me up with some real high paying customers who would 'treat me right.' That's when things got sick."

"What's his name, your boyfriend?"

"Peter."

"Peter what?"

"Peter Mullen," she said, and then came the bombshell: "Everyone calls him Snake."

Jesse and Travis nearly pissed in their pants. For the last six months, they had been hearing about a guy named Snake who was running girls on the highway. All the black girls would tell them about a guy who would drop off two or three girls for the night or a weekend then come back and get them. They were always white girls and much better looking than the regular streetwalkers. Travis and Jess had even arrested a few of them, but the girls always claimed to be independent. Travis had never dreamed the guy also had high-class call girls. Now he had a name and a place to start.

"Why do you want to give him up? That's why you're here, right?" Travis asked. A snitch's motivation was a very important factor in an investigation. She got very quiet, looking shameful. Then she spoke in a soft whisper, careful not to be overheard.

"A few weeks ago, before I met you, he sent me to LAX to see a date at the Marriott. Everything went fine like normal at first, but then the guy started getting kinky."

"Like what?" Jesse inquired.

"He was pinching my nipples real hard. Now, normally I don't mind but this was hurting. Then he tells me to get on all fours. Well, while I'm doing this he goes to the bathroom and gets a tube of KY jelly. He's standing there wiping it on his penis, and I told him he didn't need it because he got me all wet. It was bullshit, of course, but that's what guys like to hear. So, he gets behind me and says, 'You're not wet in your ass.' I told him I didn't do that, and he still tried it. I rolled over and told him there was no way I was going to let him do that to me. I was so scared. He finally agreed not to put it in there, and I took care of him quick and got the hell out of there."

Travis pushed for more. "That's it? That's why you want to roll over on Snake?"

"No! Let me finish. I was totally freaked out by this creep, so I went straight to Snake's house to tell him about it. I guess the asshole called him before I got there because Snake was furious. He told me that when I see a 'customer,' the customer's always right. I told him that I had never had anal sex before and I was scared. That's when he did it."

She stopped talking. It was like a power outage during the Super Bowl in overtime; the suspense was killing them both. "What did he do, Jen?" Travis asked. He took her hand and could feel her trembling.

"He began yelling at me and made me get undressed. I thought he was going to hit me. He grabbed me by my hair and pulled me into the living room, bent me over the couch and began to rape me. He stuck it up my ass. God, it fucking hurt, that fucking bastard raped me. I just wanted to die. When he was done he said, 'There, now your asshole isn't a virgin anymore, don't let this shit happen again.' I got dressed and left. I haven't seen him since." Jen just sat there staring at the table, and a tear slid down her cheek.

Both Jesse and Travis were speechless. What could you say to woman who had been violated like that? Some cops would call it an "occupational hazard" or a "business dispute" when a hooker was raped, but no one deserved that. This was a sick bastard, and somehow they were going to get him.

They spent the rest of dinner talking about how Snake had a stable of street girls and a handful of call girls. His bread and butter, though, was drug trafficking. Jennifer thought he could move one to two kilos of meth a week. He supplied drugs to his girls, too, if that's what they wanted. She said that, because she wasn't a meth head, Snake kept her close to him. She also knew where he kept the money and the product. One night while they'd been drinking wine and fooling around he showed her.

"I think he was showing off," she said. "In his office he has phony panels behind the stereo speakers. One hides his stash and the other hides his cash. Real simple – so simple no one would look there."

Travis took down the information on Snake and some of

Jennifer's information. He told her they would get back to her in a day or so when they had a plan for how they would handle the case. He assured her that somehow they would be able to help her. He gave her his cell phone number and told her if she needed anything to call him. When they left the restaurant she turned to Travis at the curb and said, "I'm staying at my girlfriend's house in the 310 for now, so if you see that area code you'll know it's me." She was smiling.

They stood outside the restaurant in silence for a few seconds until she wrapped her arms around his neck and hugged him so tight he could feel her take a breath. Over her shoulder, Travis could see Jesse sitting in his car quietly laughing at them. Then she kissed him on the lips and said thank you.

"Jen, you can't do that. I'm a cop and you're, well, you're like my informant now. It's just not right."

"I'm sorry, you're just so nice. You're not like other guys."

She walked away and got in her car. She drove off with a smile and a wave. Travis got into Jesse's car, and Jesse was now jiggling his plump belly with laughter. Travis didn't say a word, but Jesse wasn't so kind. "Dude, what the fuck do you think you're doing?"

"I didn't do anything, *she* kissed me."

"That's not how Internal Affairs would see it."

"And how would they know she kissed me?"

"You know I'd never say anything, but you don't know about her." Jess was right. Travis didn't know thing one about her except that she was now consuming his thoughts.

When they got back to the office, the other guys were gone on a dinner run and then, according to the note on the white board, a whore run. Travis started to do some records checks on the computer while Jess went to get a second booking photo of Jennifer from her last arrest. In order to use her as a snitch, they had to have a file on her including a detailed record of her criminal background and a log of the meetings they'd had with her. She had no criminal background in California except for her arrest in Long Beach. Her driver's license had only been issued about six years ago, and her Social Security number was from out of state, so Travis checked the FBI database but found no additional arrest records. The Department of Motor Vehicles record did reveal something interesting, though. It showed her address in Hollywood, and then about six months ago it was changed to an address on Naples Island.

Naples was a well-to-do neighborhood in east Long Beach. It was built on landfill with canals and arched bridges like in Venice, Italy. Luxury boats lined the waterways waiting for the wealthy homeowners to take them out on the weekends. The streets were narrow and filled with expensive cars. By far, it was the most exclusive neighborhood in the city, with some homes costing six to seven million dollars. Travis figured it must be Snake's address. A quick check of the utility billing for the address showed that Peter Mullen indeed owned the property.

They couldn't find much more information on him other than a DUI conviction five years earlier. A business license check revealed four car washes and five laundromats in Long Beach alone. They were all cash businesses, so if he was dealing dope he had the perfect setup for laundering the money.

Jesse got on his computer to complete the background work. Jess ran Mullen's name through a few search engines. What he found didn't say drug dealer. One hit was an article in the local paper covering the grand opening of a community theater in the downtown area. Mullen was the lead benefactor. The article referred to him as the son of Senator Jerry Mullen, who was also Long Beach's former mayor. There was also a picture of Peter Mullen with the theater manager and City Councilman Paul Wise. Was Mullen a philanthropist or a sick, perverted criminal?

When Joe and the crew got back to the office, Travis briefed them on what they had learned. Joe was excited to hear they were after Snake. The guy was like a ghost figure on the highway, a rumor, more fiction than fact, but that was until now. Joe gave them the green light to do what was needed to get it going. He even authorized them to go the narcotics angle if needed. A good sales case could carry a lot more weight than a pimping pinch. "Make sure Narco isn't working him first," he warned. It was good advice. Parallel undercover operations had ended up with terrible results before, including dead cops.

They got started on the case on Friday, after Travis received a call from the Narcotics Detail lieutenant. He told Travis that he had checked Mullen's name against a special database that the narco detectives used to ensure they didn't run into other agencies that were investigating the same person. There were no hits for Mullen by name or address, so they were clear to begin their investigation.

Jesse and Travis went out to the island to get some pictures of the house and any cars Snake might have. Naples Island wasn't a place where you could just snoop around without being noticed by the neighbors. Even though they were the good guys, they didn't want anyone to know who they were. So on the way there, they went by the city yard and traded their car for a public service truck and two city work shirts.

They acted like a survey crew, measuring the street and marking it in spots with spray paint. When they were in front of Snake's house, Jesse snapped away with his camera. It was a digital camera with a special pinhole lens on the end of a four-foot cord. The camera itself was strapped to Jess's body under his work vest. He just held the little lens in his hands and clicked the shutter with a remote button in his pocket. Jess had built the device himself.

Snake's house was a large Tudor-style home with stone walls and a slate roof that had a steep pitch. Tall leaded glass windows broke up the ivy that covered the brick walls. The driveway was made from cobblestone-like pavers. It was a pull-through with a gate at the main road and another at the alleyway. The place looked more like London than Long Beach. Parked out front were two cars, a black Mercedes 500 and a red Hummer. There was no telling what he had in the three-car garage. The house looked like a royal palace; there were even peacocks milling about on the front lawn. Jesse said, "Look, this guy has pet turkeys." There obviously weren't many peacocks where he'd grown up in East LA.

"They're peacocks, Jess, not turkeys, you silly Mexican."

"What's the difference?" he asked.

Travis thought for a minute and all he could come up with was, "They're like turkeys, but from the good side of the tracks."

Jess nodded his head and said, "I see," as if what Travis said had made perfect sense to him. Jesse said, "You know we're going to have to follow this guy, right?"

"Yeah, I figured that would have to be our next move. We'll also have to watch this place and see who comes and goes, and it looks like it backs up to one of the canals. I want to get a look from the water or the air. We need to know what we're in for if we have to serve paper here."

Jess took a few more photos, looked at Travis and said, "They look like turkeys to me."

Travis laughed and said, "OK, let's go, bud. It's going to be a long night and I want to try to get out on time for once."

They packed up the truck and headed back west. During the drive back Jess asked, "So, how are things going at home?" He knew all about the problems between Travis and Sarah.

"I don't know, dude. The spark for her is just gone. I try to do everything she wants, but it isn't good enough. She almost never wants to be romantic, although we had sex the other night when I got home from the outcall; it was the first time in more than two months. She hates my job and complains about the hours and... well, and the drinking."

"What are you going to do?"

"I don't know, bro. If we didn't have the kids I would have been gone long ago. Now even that might not keep me there."

There was a strange silence in the cab of the truck. It was odd for them not to be joking around, but on the other hand Jess and Travis shared everything with each other, the good and the bad. They had a bond that was closer than brothers.

They dropped the truck off at the city yard well after the staff had gone home, so they left the shirts in the truck and the keys on the visor. Jesse was still untangling himself from the hidden camera when Joe called for them on the radio.

"Hey, T.J., are you and the Jess going to join us anytime soon?"

Travis pulled his radio from the car and called back, "Where you at?"

"We're on the road, headed out east to get pizza. Are you two going to join us?" He could hear the other guys in the background. They were all joking around.

"Yeah, we'll be en route in a minute unless Jesse hangs himself with the cords from the camera."

On the way to dinner Jess said, "You know if you and Sarah need a break from each other or whatever, you could stay with us for a while."

"Thanks, buddy, I really appreciate that. We'll see. I don't wanna be a bother, especially with you having the kids at home. Plus with Sandra's cooking I would get as big as you in a week!" Travis jabbed Jess's gut with his radio antenna. Travis loved Sandra's cooking. He and Sarah would go to the Guerra house on weekends and the kids would swim all day while Sandra would make tacos, burritos and enchiladas. She would keep the food

51

coming to the back yard all afternoon. They hadn't done that in quite a while; Sarah just didn't want to do anything that was related to Travis's job anymore.

"I appreciate that, my brother," Travis said. Then they both said at the same time, "My brother, from another mother!" They started laughing, and the seriousness of the moment was gone.

Dinner in the Vice Unit was always a fun time. On this night they had pasta and pizza around a large family style table. Joe sat at the head like the father, and they all discussed their cases like kids telling their parents about their day at school. The Lakers were on, so they stayed until the game was over. Then Joe handed out the night's assignments. They were all going to be doing bar investigations stemming from various complaints. That meant following Snake would have to wait one more night.

Ben and Terry were going to a dance club way out east that had a history of violations. The place had changed hands at least three times in the last 10 years, but the crowd never changed: young kids looking for a hookup or just blowing off the pressures of college for a night. They drank too much, acted like idiots in the parking lot and made a lot of noise, waking up the neighbors. Ben and Terry were the logical choice for the assignment because they were the youngest-looking ones on the team.

Everyone else was heading to The Dugout up on Willow west of Magnolia. It used to be a neighborhood sports bar owned by a local guy named Barber who'd almost made it to the majors as a catcher. The bar turned out to be his only real success. It was a great place for many years until Barber was diagnosed with cancer; he was dead a month later. It all happened so fast he never made plans for the bar after his death. With no will or wife, his two sons inherited it. Both of them were in their early 20s and were already on the revolving door plan at County Jail for such things as theft and narcotics.

Having no business training, they were doomed from the start. It quickly became a hangout for tweekers and hypes. The bands that played there brought in their own crowds, who sometimes didn't get along with the local trash. The place quickly became a problem in the middle of a quiet part of the central area. That night the headliner was a grunge band called FUSION. The marquee said they were from Hollywood. It was probably more like Burbank, but Hollywood sounded a lot better.

52

When the team pulled up, there was already a line outside, and some more folks were in the parking lot smoking. Joe arrived first and parked in the bank parking lot west of the bar. Jack parked with Joe so they could walk over together. Jesse and Travis pulled down Daisy to park in the neighborhood. While Jess was getting his car parked, Travis could see Joe and Jack walking toward the front of the bar and out of sight. About five seconds later, he saw them walking back to their cars. Travis's phone rang, and it was Joe.

Travis answered "What's up?"

"They have a security guard at the door with a metal detector. He's wanding everyone, so we have to go in sterile."

"Ten-four, thanks for the heads-up."

They had to leave everything that was police-related in the car: gun, badge, cuffs – anything that might set off the detector and let the door guy know who they were.

Travis and Jess let Joe and Jack go in first, and waited about five minutes before they headed to the door. The door guy was a fat biker type, a white guy about 40 with a dirty beard and dirtier denim clothes. He probably worked the door for a cut of the gate money and a few bindles of crank. He was thorough with the wand, checking everyone closely, even girls with tight clothes. Travis thought it was strange; the guy looked as if he needed to be checked for weapons himself. When Travis got inside he understood why the door guy was being so diligent.

The band was onstage and they were blasting the place. They had their own following all right – a group of about 20 hardcore punk youngsters, half of whom were Black or Latino. They were decked out in studded jackets, piercings and funky hairstyles. A few speed freaks sat in a booth in a dark corner, and some muscle-head biker types at the bar represented the resident white trash. The two groups were looking at each other like lions and hyenas. Travis could feel the tension in the air.

The bar sat in middle of the original establishment, while the band and dance floor were in another room that used to be a flower shop next door. Shortly after Barber died, the boys had leased out the space and knocked a 10-foot opening between the two storefronts.

The daytime Administrative Vice detectives had been putting together a package on The Dugout's many violations. They wanted to get the place's entertainment permit revoked, or get the Department of Alcoholic Beverage Control to take away the bar's alcohol license altogether. Any violations seen would be mentally noted by the team and then forwarded to the admin guys in the morning. They already had several municipal code and A.B.C. violations such as smoking, band noise outside the business, and no uniform for the security guard. A bunch of ticky-tack things, but when combined with everything else the unit had already compiled, it would give the chief the ammo he needed to rid the city of this piss pot.

Other than the terrible music and smoke, everything was going fine until five skinheads walked through the door. Even the bouncer knew this could be trouble, as he moved his stool from the sidewalk to just inside the door so he could keep an eye on the place. Three of the five walked to the bar, stood next to Travis and ordered beers. Two stood just a few feet inside the door and stared at the band.

Travis tried to listen to the guy next to him. It was almost impossible to hear anything over the band, but he did make out one word: "Niggers." Travis leaned over and told Jess what he'd heard.

Jesse said, "When they start talking about 'spics' you better get ready, cause they know we're together."

After getting their beers, the white pride group went into the dance room and stood against the back wall listening to the band. Everyone on the team kept an eye on them, but they didn't bother anyone. When the band took a break the musicians mingled with the crowd. The drummer walked over to the skinheads and shook hands with them like they were about to arm wrestle; he even embraced one of them.

As they all talked, a black kid dressed in all black walked over and started talking with the drummer. For some unknown reason, he and one of the skinheads began wrestling on their feet, knocking over a table, each trying to put the other in a headlock. The crashing of beer bottles caught the attention of the rest of the bar. Now the Nazi wannabe had the black guy pinned against a wall and was pounding him viciously in the face with his fist. Within seconds, 15 or so punks and skinheads were pushing and shoving each other. The group was a big mass of fists and kicks moving from one end of the dance room through the opening to the bar.

Travis and Jess grabbed their beers and moved down the bar away from the fight. Jess asked Travis, "What do you want to do?"

Travis looked over at Joe and Jack, who were sitting in a booth. Joe waved his hand back and forth in front of his neck, signaling for Travis to just observe. There wasn't a lot the detectives could do with their tools tucked away in their cars. Joe tried calling the dispatch center, but his phone wasn't working in the bar.

The bouncer rushed to the crowd to do what he could to break up the madness. He put the main skinhead in a headlock and started dragging him toward the door. To his credit, the short skinhead still had a grip on the black kid's collar and was throwing punches even though he was being dragged himself. The rowdy group all followed the combatants outside.

Joe got up, walked past Jess and Travis and told them what to do. "Get to your car and get your shit, I'm goin' to call for patrol. Don't ID yourself, just be ready if it gets out of hand."

Jess and Travis left the bar and headed down the street to their car. The sound of arguing could be heard on the other side of the building in the parking lot. Travis popped open the trunk with the remote as they got close. He grabbed his gun and slid it into his rear pocket, and put some handcuffs in the other. Jesse grabbed a radio, his five shot revolver and his cuffs. Jesse handed Travis his badge, and Travis put it around his neck and tucked it into his shirt as they made their way back toward the excitement.

By now Joe and Jack were back with the crowd, watching as the main combatants were being pulled apart by friends and the two brother bar owners. Several girls were screaming, causing more confusion than was necessary and adding to the tension. Travis and Jess got to the lot just as the group was splitting into two factions. On Joe's side of the lot, the racist peckerhead was walking to his car when Joe heard him say to a friend, "I'm getting' my knife and cuttin' that fuckin' porch monkey."

As three of the skinheads passed him, Joe grabbed the leader by the wrist and elbow. He arm-barred him onto the hood of a car and held him there. Jack stood between his sergeant and the other two guys, showed them his badge and told them to back off, and the two guys complied. Travis and Jesse could see the altercation involving their teammates, so they started to make their way through the crowd, most of whom were still yelling insults back and forth.

As Jess got close, one of the detainee's girlfriends saw what was happening but probably didn't know Joe was a cop. She ran toward him yelling, "Get off him, it's not his fault!"

As she ran by Jess he reached out and grabbed her shirt collar, causing the 100-pound tweeker's feet to fly out from under her. Landing flat on her back, she let out a blood-curdling scream. Jess bent over her to tell her who he was. A fourth skinhead who didn't know any of them were the police ran over and kicked Jess square in the face. Detective Guerra went tumbling backward into Travis's legs. Blood flew from his mouth into Travis's face. As the young supremacist with the thick goatee and Army jacket headed toward the downed officer, Jack lunged at him from behind, putting the suspect in a full nelson and halting the asshole's advance. Travis jumped over Jess, who was rolling on the ground holding his face. Travis threw a punch into the young guy's stomach. This kid was a stud with rock-hard abs, and the punch had much less effect than desired. So Travis drew back and spun a right-handed uppercut to a part of the body no man can ready for a punch. It wasn't because he knew it would hurt more, but because Jack was lifting the guy too high for Travis to hit his face. The blow below the belt proved very effective.

Travis pulled back and hurled one more shot, then noticed a flash of movement to his right. He turned to see a uniformed patrol officer coming at him with his baton in full backswing. Travis couldn't move, he couldn't speak, he just braced himself, and it came. The laminated bloodwood stick hit its mark just above his knee with a *THWAK!* In excruciating pain, all Travis Jensen could yell was, "Vice!" as he fell to the ground. This stopped the patrol officer before his next swing.

"Shit, dude, I'm sorry, I didn't know, I didn't know!" the young officer said.

"Oh, fuck, that hurt. God damn, good hit, kid," Travis said, holding his knee. Travis was rolling on the ground next to his partner, who was bleeding from his mouth and nose. Seeing the rush of blue-suits fill the lot, Travis rolled over to Jess and said, "Don't worry, bro, it can't make you any uglier."

The fighting had come to a quick halt with the arrival of the patrol officers. Travis had never heard the sirens coming, and he hadn't noticed the headlights of the first unit that pulled into the lot. When his best friend went down he got tunnel vision, a phenomenon common in stressful situations when adrenaline caused the loss of peripheral vision. Travis hadn't heard the officer coming, and he'd never heard him yelling, "Stop."

The guy who took Travis's two shots to the nuts was on the ground throwing up. Jack had him handcuffed and was holding him up out of his vomit. The parking lot was a mess of blood, vomit and flashing red and blue lights. Someone got Jesse a towel and Travis a bag of ice from the bar.

About that time Lieutenant Walls showed up. Betty Walls had never been respected by the troops. She'd promoted very quickly because she was a good test taker, and she'd hardly spent any time in patrol. How the hell she'd made lieutenant was still a mystery. She walked right past Guerra and Jensen and asked Jack Barnes, "What's wrong with him?" as she pointed at his prisoner spitting out the last of his lunch.

"He kicked Guerra in the face with a steel toe boot, ma'am," Jack said.

"I didn't ask what he did, I asked what happened to him."

Joe came over and said, "Hey, he got what was coming to him. He kicked Jesse in the face and probably broke his nose. Detectives Jensen and Barnes jumped in and stopped him from doing it again. We tried to stay out of it, but we had to act before the black and whites could get here."

The arrestee yelled, "He fuckin' hit me in the balls!"

That was all she needed. She pulled out her Blackberry and started looking for a phone number. "This is an IA callout," she said.

"What! My guys didn't do anything wrong. Jensen was protecting Guerra, who was on the ground and about to get stomped on by that jackass. Besides, it doesn't fit the criteria."

"Yes, it does."

"How?"

"He struck him in an unapproved area of the body."

"That's horse crap, Betty, and you know it. That's not part of the call out criteria. You just can't stomach this happening on your turn as the watch commander so you want to pass it off to IA."

"It's not my fault your guys can't use proper tactics."

"Tactics?" Joe was really getting lit. "This was a street fight. The only tactic in a street fight is to win."

"Why didn't he use a baton or a Taser?"

"You're fuckin' kidding me, right? We're undercover; we don't carry those things on us. Perhaps if you did more than just pass out stickers to kids in the DARE program when you were an officer you'd know this." By now everyone was watching them, including the prisoners.

"Watch your tone, sergeant."

Joe leaned in close and spoke softly so only she could hear it. "Make that call and I may have to report how I caught you fuckin' that DA in your car after the Christmas party."

"You wouldn't. Besides, that was four years ago."

"Yeah I would. Remember, it was your city take-home car, and that's a violation of department policy. Hey, don't you still have the same husband now that you had back then? I bet he'd love to hear about it too."

Walls looked around the lot at the crowd looking at her. She drew a deep breath through her nose, flaring her nostrils, and said, "Fine. Get me the use of force reports before EOW." She then turned and stomped off to her car. Pulling out onto Willow, she sped off heading west, probably to go hide in her office at the west substation.

For the next 30 minutes Joe and some patrol guys took statements from the patrons and other witnesses. The paramedics from Fire Station thirteen responded and took a look at Jesse. They packed a crap load of gauze up his nose and taped it in place, as blood was already beginning to pool under both his eyes. As a precaution they took him to Long Beach Memorial Hospital to get a CAT scan. Joe called Ben and Terry and told them to cut what they were doing out east and meet Jesse at the ER. After the fire rig left, Joe noticed Travis sitting on the curb alone nursing his leg. He walked over and asked, "You OK, T.J.?"

"Yeah, I'll be all right, I was just thinking."

"Don't worry 'bout Jess, he'll be OK."

"Oh, I know. I wasn't thinking about that. I was just lookin' at the intersection. Did you know that's where my dad died?"

"No shit? I knew he died in a pursuit but I didn't know where."

"Yeah, he was headed eastbound and a truck pulled out in front of him. I'm sure my dad was probably goin' way too fast. When I got out of the Army, Commander Baker took me on a ride-along back when he was a sergeant. He brought me here and told me the story about that night. How they looked for hours for the guy my pop was chasing, how the watch commander that night asked Baker to break the news to my mom since they had been partners. He told me about all kinds of stuff I never knew, stuff my mom wouldn't talk about. All she told me when I was growing up was how he was going to be promoted to sergeant the very next week and how glad she'd been that he would be a little safer."

"Wow, I never knew all that, Travis."

Travis looked up at his boss and asked, "Joe, what's the last day to sign up for the sergeant's exam?"

"It was supposed to be today, but they extended it to Tuesday because some folks were on long vacations and couldn't get to City Hall on time. The test is in a week and a half. If you're thinking of taking it you'd better get studying."

"I will," Travis said as he tried to bend his knee. He looked back at the intersection and said, "Besides, I think it's about time for me. I can't work vice forever."

Chapter Four

Surveillance

Travis woke to the sound of his kids playing in the back yard. At first it didn't make sense to him, but then he realized it was Saturday. He looked over at the clock and turned it so he could see the blue numbers: 10:12 a.m. *Wow, she really let me sleep in*, he thought. He just lay there daydreaming for a while, watching the ceiling fan. One of the lights was out on the fan, so he added that to his mental list of crap to be done. Then he rolled over, felt the pain, and realized he couldn't bend his knee. Sarah walked through the door holding a stack of folded laundry. "Good morning, sleepy head." She smiled as she saw he was awake. She set the clothes down on the blanket chest at the foot of the bed and sat next to him. "We need to talk," she said. It translated to him as, *I'm pissed at you*. This was never a good start to any conversation in a marriage. He didn't answer her but sat up and scooted back so he could lean on the headboard. She looked down as if to find the courage to say what was on her mind. Looking back up she said, "I want you to get help for your drinking."

"I don't have a problem."

"Travis, you go out almost every night after work and drink." She was starting to get louder. "You're hung over in the morning, which makes you cranky so I don't even want to be around you."

Travis wasn't taking too kindly to this attack. "Maybe I go out and drink with my friends because there's nothing here for me.

You lost all interest in me a few years ago. You never want to be with me and you're always too tired." Then he threw a verbal hand grenade into the dialogue. "If it wasn't for the kids I probably would have left by now." He didn't know why he'd said it or what reaction he was looking for, but it was in the open now. "Do you love me?" he asked.

She said with tears forming in her eyes, "Yes. I just don't know if I'm *in* love with you anymore."

"Why? What have I done? It's like I'm just a roommate now."

She had no answer and just sat there with her head down. Travis got up and walked to the bathroom with a terrible limp. Sarah saw the swollen knee with the eight-inch bruise in the perfect shape of a police baton.

"Oh my God, what happened to you?"

"We got into a bar fight last night. Well, more like a parking lot fight at a bar."

"Who hit you?"

"A patrol guy."

"Another officer?"

"Yeah, the poor kid didn't know who I was until it was too late. He came up from behind me while Jack Barnes and I were giving the business to a skinhead. The asshole had just kicked Jesse in the face."

"Oh my God, is Jesse OK?"

"He broke his nose. The ER doctor took him off of work for at least a week."

"How about you?"

"No, I'm just light duty, but that's OK cause I'm signing up to take the sergeant's test and Joe's going to let me stay in the office and study all week."

Sarah walked over to Travis and wrapped her arms around his neck. "Is it what you want? Do you really want to promote?"

"Yeah. I've been giving it some thought, and yeah, it is."

"Good. Um, back to what we were talking about. I was thinking that we might look at some time apart for a while."

"Apart?"

"Just to see if it helps us. Let's talk after your shower." She kissed him on the cheek and walked out of the room.

The hot water of the shower felt so good that he didn't want to get out. He wasn't sure if he didn't want to get out because of the water or because he didn't want to face the reality that lay beyond the shower door. Here he was 42 years old and the woman with whom he had shared almost half his life thought they should split up. When they'd gotten married it had been so wonderful. All newlyweds were like that, but they generally felt they were different. After seven, eight, even nine years, people commented on how much Travis and Sarah loved each other. He knew this was going to be more painful than his knee.

Travis stepped out of his watery retreat and there she was, sitting on the blanket chest next to the neatly folded laundry. She was looking right at him and had a much more determined look on her face. He could tell she had been formulating her words – something he wasn't good at when it came to relationships. "I can't live like this anymore, Travis. You're married to your job, not me."

He wanted to hear it all before he spoke. "Go on," he said.

"You get calls at all hours, day and night. If it's not your boss it's one of your snitches. When you're with the family I don't want some dope fiend interrupting our time. Vice is consuming you. You just can't leave it alone when you're not on the clock. It wasn't like this when you were in patrol or special enforcement. Do you know I can't even tell my friends what you do? How do I explain to them that my husband drinks beer at work and has call girls give him naked massages?"

"What do you tell them?"

"I just tell them you work narcotics, just like we tell the girls. Look, I'm alone four nights a week and we can't have a regular social life because you work the oddest hours and weekends. At least when you were in patrol you had the seniority to get the weekends off. The undercover work scares me too. The people you deal with are dangerous, and I worry that you'll end up in the hospital or worse. Last night proves that it is a real possibility." He felt like shit now, like a gangster getting jumped on by his homies. Then came the crushing blow, the words he'd tried to avoid for the last 19 years as a cop. "But worst of all, you've changed." She said it with a hint of pain in her voice. "Vice has changed you. You want sex constantly, always pawing at me, grabbing me. It's a real turn off. You weren't like that before, before you went to vice."

He couldn't tell what hurt more – the fact that she felt that way, or the fact that she was right. He didn't have a retort to the thrashing she gave him so he simply asked, "Now what?"

"Leave vice or move out."

They left it at that and went about their Saturday routine. He got the light changed above the bed and attended to a few other chores in the yard, but he had to put off the weeding in the dog run because he couldn't bend his knee. As he was heading back to the garage she met him in the doorway with a bottle of cold water. Even though she felt she couldn't live with him it was clear she still cared. "Thanks for the water," he said. "I need to get washed up before I head in."

When Travis got in to work there was no one in the office. He looked at his email and found the reading list that was suggested for the upcoming sergeant's exam. Some of the titles were obvious, like the department manual, training bulletins, and the search warrant manual. But some of the items were a surprise to him, like the current labor contract between the city and the civilian employees. He called Fred Crackers to ask him about the importance of this stuff as it related to the test. Fred's wife answered the phone. "Hello?"

"Hi Stacey, Travis here."

"Hi Travis, I heard you and Jesse got roughed up last night."

"Boy, the good news travels fast. It wasn't as bad as it sounds. Hey, is the biggest mistake of your life home?"

"Yeah, let me get him. Hey, are you guys up for dinner tomorrow?"

"You'd have to call Sarah and ask her, but I don't think we're doing anything."

"OK, here's Fred."

Fred greeted Travis with, "Hey, dude, I heard you made a nice piñata last night."

"Very funny. Hey, are you coming in to work tonight?"

"Yep."

"Can you bring in the sergeant's test study materials? I'm going to be in the office all night and some of the books on the list are in Baker's office, so the earliest I can get to them is Monday."

"Sure. So are you actually going to take it or just read it for fun?"

"I'm gonna take it, and I'm gonna outscore you. But seriously, do I really need to read all that crap on the list?"

"You kinda need to know the main points of all of it."

"That's what I was afraid of. I'll be in the vice office when you get in, see ya then?"

Fred answered with "Ten-four," and hung up.

Travis went back to reading and broke only when the team came into the office. After about half an hour of teasing the gimpy detective and calling Jess at home to see how he was doing, the boys left and Travis got back to the books. The constant reading of police manuals written in a way that only attorneys could understand was driving him nuts. Joe had given him a list of sample questions he and other sergeants had put together over the last few years. They wouldn't be on the current test, but they were a good example of what to expect. Travis couldn't give a crap about things like the city's mission statement or its guiding principals, but he knew it would matter to those in charge of the test, so he studied them. The more he read, the more he could see how non-leaders like Lieutenant Walls could get promoted. If they didn't have baggage and were good test takers, they could do well.

Fred came in a few hours later with his rookie, Kevin Sharp. Kevin was a well-built young black man with a light complexion. His father was a fire captain with Los Angeles City Fire, and his mom was a dispatcher in El Segundo, a small city near L.A. International Airport. Fred said that Kevin was doing great with his training. No doubt having parents in the public safety business had rubbed off on him a little.

"Hey, thanks for bringing this stuff in for me. I've got some catching up to do."

Fred set a stack of books on the desk and stared at his old academy buddy. "You're really gonna do this, aren't you?"

"Don't give me a hard time, it's your first time, too."

"Yeah, but everyone pegged you as a detective for life. Have you practiced any tactical exercises?"

"No. I didn't know it was such a big part of it."

"Stacey said you guys are coming over tomorrow night for dinner. We can run through a few scenarios to get you back in the patrol state of mind."

Travis looked at Sharp and said, "He knows my schedule better than I do."

Fred and Kevin left with the respectful rookie having never said a word, only nodding his head to indicate hello and goodbye. Travis studied for about four more hours and couldn't take it anymore. So he went home for the night.

The next day Travis's family went to the Crackers' for an early dinner. After the meal, the kids played in the bonus room while the wives chatted over a few glasses of merlot in the kitchen. Travis and Fred went into the garage, where Fred had a large map of the city's south division mounted on a board with clear plastic over it.

"Dude, this thing is huge. Where'd you get it?"

"Off of the SWAT truck. It's an old one that they were throwing out last year so I nabbed it."

"What's the matter? Stacey won't let you hang it in the living room?"

"I took it to study for the test. OK, here's how it works. I'll be the proctor and give you a scenario for you to manage. If you need something just ask me, and I'll also be the dispatcher. Don't say things like 'Well, now I would do this.' Just do it, because that's what they'll expect."

"So it's kind of like the practical exams we do with the recruits at the academy, right?"

"Yeah, but it's at the supervisor level. It's to test your decision making skills, crisis management, and tactical thinking."

Fred started the scenario: "One-Charlie-Six has just checked on a scene at a domestic disturbance call at 412 Cedar when he comes on the radio calling for backup. He is in a foot pursuit northbound Cedar from Fourth Street and describes the suspect as being the suspect in his dispatch, and said the guy took off from the corner when he pulled up. Your call sign is One-Sam-Ninety-Nine. What do you do?"

Travis thought for a second and said: "One-Sam-Ninetynine have two units roll code three to assist."

"Two units are rolling and One-Charlie-Six broadcasts a change in direction to west in the alley south of Fifth Street."

Without looking at the map Travis said, "If the responding units are close have them go to the area of Chestnut and Fifth, if they are further out go to Magnolia."

"OK, good thinking. Just remember that during the test, look at the map just in case you need the name of an alley or something. They don't mark you off for it, and if you call out an incorrect street it could bite you later."

This went on for about 12 minutes and developed into an officer-involved shooting when the suspect barricaded himself in a trash yard and shot at One-Charlie-Six. Travis was doing a terrific job with the perimeter and use of resources like the helicopter and K-9 units. Fred played it out until the suspect finally gave up. Travis was feeling confident and wanted to do another scenario when Fred said, "So who's with your victim?"

"What victim? You said he didn't hit One-Charlie-Six." Then Travis realized he'd been so focused on the chase and shooting that no one had ever made contact with the other half of the domestic call. Travis was so frustrated he dropped his head and said, "Fuck."

"She bled out from a gunshot wound. If you found her in time she could have been saved."

"I didn't even think of that," Travis said.

"That's because you're thinking like a cop and not a quarterback. That's what a good sergeant is. He doesn't tell the troops how to do something but supports them while they do it and stands back to get the big picture. Make sure they're in the right position to take action and ensure they have the right tools. You were so intent on getting the bad guy that you missed the whole mission."

The point was not lost on Travis. He told Fred, "You're going to make a great sergeant, bud. I'd work for you any day."

"We'll both make good sergeants. Now let's do another one."

On Monday Travis Jensen signed up for the test at City Hall. After that was done, he went to see Commander Baker to get more study materials. Baker invited him into his office and told him to have a seat. "Take a load off, Travis. Here, let me get another chair to put your leg up." Baker went into the waiting room and brought back another chair. "I had to put one of my office chairs out there. Someone stole my waiting room chairs."

Travis tried not to break a smile and said, "No shit, thieves in the police station, go figure."

"Heck you guys probably get more use out of them than I do anyway." Travis couldn't believe it; the old bastard had known all along where his chairs went. Baker continued with a big smile, "Besides, I got to order new ones."

Travis filled him in on the brawl, Jesse's nose, and the run-in with Lieutenant Walls. Baker's response was harsh and to the point: "Fuck that bitch. Between you and me, I don't think they should let split-tails become police officers, let alone lieutenants." Baker was a true chauvinist at heart and was having a hard time giving in to all the changes that came with modern police work.

They talked for an hour about work and their families, especially Baker's son, David. He had died in a helicopter crash during the first Gulf War. With Travis fatherless and Baker heartbroken at the loss of his only son, they found a lot of comfort in their talks. As they wrapped it up, Baker said, "Let's go fishing again up at Bishop when the weather gets better."

"OK, boss, just let me know when and I'll put in for the time off."

Travis spent the next week cramming for the test and going to Fred's house on his days off. Sometimes they had four or five guys in the study group. When the test finally came, he actually felt he was ready for it. After it was over, the group got together and discussed the questions and their answers. From what he could make of everyone's input, Travis could only think of about nine or ten questions that he had missed. Now he had to tackle the oral interview and tactical exercise. He wasn't worried about his assessment of promotability – the portion of the process in which candidates' career records were evaluated. Having been in detectives, and having taught at the academy, he figured he was a cinch to max out those points. But that was a week away, so it was time for a break. Jesse was due back at work, and Travis had made arrangements with Jennifer to follow Snake.

On his drive into the city, Travis got a call from Jesse saying he would be a little late. His son's baseball team was in an extra-inning game. Jensen told him it was no big deal because they were going to work the boys at the beach toilet, and Jesse was so ugly he would just scare them off.

As it turned out, there was no action at the beach or at any of the parks they checked. They all went back to the office, and Joe pulled Travis aside. "Hey, we all have to go work in north town tonight. Can you and Jess handle the surveillance of Snake alone?" He asked. Joe had a lot of faith in T.J., but he was a sergeant and ultimately responsible for the team.

"Yeah, we can handle it. I don't even know if he's gonna move or not."

"What does your snitch say?"

"She thinks he'll go to some spots and pick up money from some girls. We'll try to get it on video."

Joe looked over at the guys who were now playing a video

gambling game that the bookmaking team had confiscated and asked, "Is she going with you?"

"Yeah, we might need her to identify people or explain what he's doing."

Joe looked back quickly, putting his hand over his mouth. In a petting motion he stroked his goatee. "Make sure Jess is there at all times. At least in radio contact, if not visual."

Travis knew what he was getting at, but thought he would tease Joe a little. "What do you think, she might try to hurt me, Joe?"

"Shut the fuck up. You know what I mean." He didn't talk to the team like that too often.

Travis assured him, "OK, Joe. It'll be fine."

Shortly after the boys left the office, Jess showed up dressed in a San Francisco Giants jersey. Travis asked, "What's with the shirt, dude? Wait, don't tell me your kid's Little League team is the Giants?" Jess just dropped his head; he knew where Travis was taking this. "What Mexican from East L.A. would be caught dead in a Giants uniform? The archenemy of the Dodgers! Dude, I hope you call your mother tonight and beg for forgiveness."

Jess sat down and said, "That's not the worst of it. My son roots for the real Giants now because that's *his* team. Now he wants me to take him to a game when they play at Chavez Ravine."

"You can't let him wear his uniform. You'll be kicked out of the bleachers."

"I know, and that's like my second home. I grew up in those bleachers."

"Let me look at your nose," Travis said. Jess stuck his face into Travis's. "Not bad, just a little black and blue under the eyes."

"Yeah, it doesn't hurt anymore except when I bend over. Hey, are we on for tonight?"

"Yep, it's just us though."

"What's the plan, then?"

Travis grabbed his kit and looked at his watch. "Well, it's 5:30 now. We're supposed to meet Jennifer at the café in Belmont Shore at six. Do you want to go now and get a bite?"

With a big smile Jess said, "Yeah. I couldn't eat at the game I was so nerve-wracked."

"I almost forgot about the game. Who won?" Jesse's son was a good pitcher. Only 12 years old, he could strike out most 15-year-olds.

"Well, he had a one-hit shutout into the tenth. Remember, it's only a seven-inning game for his age. Then he hit a batter, which must have messed him up because the very next batter took him yard."

"Ouch. Was that the game?"

"Yep."

Travis placed his hand on Jesse's shoulder to console him and said, "Well, what do you expect? He plays for the Giants."

While they headed out to the meeting spot in their separate cars, Jesse continued to fill Travis in via the radio on the game and how his boy was doing so well at pitching. Travis was only getting about half of it. He kept thinking about Jennifer and how he was actually excited to see her again. She had been on his mind the last few days. The brake light came at him fast. "Shit!" he yelled as he slammed on the brakes of the old Beretta. The radio flew off his lap and onto the floor. He'd just missed the car in front of him. He could hear Jesse's muffled voice saying, "Nice one." The traffic had caught him off guard; it wasn't usually this packed in the Shore area of town.

When they got to the café it was no different, with patrons spilling out onto the sidewalk, but they had an ace in the hole. The hostess was Lisa O'Riley, a cute redheaded Irish girl with fair skin and a love of Art Deco jewelry. She was finishing her master's degree at Long Beach State after spending a few years traveling the world. Travis had first met her four years back at a beach party.

She saw them come through the door, and her eyes met with Travis's. She didn't say anything to them at first. She seated a couple and returned to the podium, looked on the sheet, put her finger on a name and called out, "Travis party?" When Travis acknowledged her she said, "Oh, you're back just in time," as if they had put their names in ahead of everyone and had walked around the shops for a while. You had to love service like that. After they sat in the booth she handed them menus and said, "I haven't seen you in a long time, Travis."

"I don't get out to the good part of town too much anymore. Have you met my partner, Jesse?" She hadn't, so Travis made the proper introductions. After she walked away, Jesse said, "Dude, how do you know her?" He was like a puberty stricken teenager.

"I never told you? Oh, this is a good one. We met at a beach party down at Bolsa Chica State Beach. She was probably twenty-one at the time. We had been talking, and she was kind of flirting with me. Well, her friend got tossed, absolutely passed-out drunk, and she was Lisa's ride home but had a Jetta with a standard transmission. Lisa couldn't drive a stick, so I gave her my car to drive and I drove her friend home to Huntington Beach in the Jetta while Lisa followed. It took the two of us to get her friend up the stairs and into bed. After that I drove Lisa home, which was only about another mile. When we got there she invited me in for a beer. I knew I shouldn't have, but I accepted. She was really grateful to me for helping her friend. She went on about how the guys her age wouldn't have been so kind and yada yada. I think she had a father figure thing goin' on. Then she began kissing my neck and worked her way down, tore open my pants and began blowing me. Dude, she totally knew I was married. We had talked about Sarah earlier at the beach. I couldn't believe this was happening. I had never cheated before, but it was a rush, and shit, look at her – she's so frickin' hot. When she finished, she said, 'That's for being such a sweetheart.' I saw her about a week later and I returned the favor, but I felt so guilty about being unfaithful that we decided to just be friends."

"Dude, I can't believe you never told me," Jesse said in amazement.

"I know, I sometimes have a hard time believing it ever happened. It's not my greatest moment, you know?"

Just as they were finishing with that tantalizing subject, Jen walked through the door. Travis watched her look around for them. She was wrapped in a loose black turtleneck sweater and tight jeans. Even when she didn't dress up, she was still the most beautiful thing wherever she went. He could see her asking Lisa if she knew where they were seated. Lisa pointed to their table and watched inquisitively as Jennifer walked over. Travis could see Lisa looking at him for an explanation. He just shrugged his shoulders and gave her a smirk. Jennifer had to walk through most of the café to get to the table. The detectives could see several heads turning as she passed each table. The amazing thing was she was oblivious to the attention she was given, or at least she gave the impression she didn't know she was being watched. When she reached the table she held her purse behind her back with both hands like a schoolgirl at a dance. "Hello, Travis." Her voice was happy and uplifting. It was quite an improvement from their last meeting.

70

Travis stood and asked her to join them. She remembered Jesse and said hello to him by name. She wasted no time in asking what the game plan was for the night.

Travis said, "Well, we're going to see if Snake rolls tonight. If he does, we're going to follow him in separate cars and see what he does. I want you to fill in any questions we might have as we go along. You know, like who he's seeing or what he might be doing at different places. What do you think?"

"No problem, it sounds fun."

Travis didn't want to disappoint her, but he had to prepare her for what surveillance was really like. "It's not as exciting as on TV, Jen. We might just sit in the car for a few hours and see nothing."

"Will I ride with you?"

"Ah, yeah."

She put her hand on his and said, "That could be fun, too."

Jesse looked down at his lap and was trying to keep a straight face. T.J. was caught of guard, but was flattered by her gesture. She sat next to him, and the waitress came over to take their orders. Jess and Travis both ordered the special: a third-pound burger, fries and a soda. Jennifer only wanted an iced tea. As the waitress left for the kitchen, Jen turned to Travis and said, "I'll just pick at your fries if that's OK." Before he could answer she said, "Hey how come every time I see you guys you're eating?"

Jesse answered, "A good cop never goes hungry or gets wet."

"Never gets wet?"

"Yeah. When you're on patrol and it rains, you do what you've got to do to stay dry," he said as he slid back into a reclining position on his side of the booth.

"Where's the rest of the famous Vice Squad?" Jennifer asked.

"Well, what ya see is what ya get. The rest of the guys are off doing other assignments. Normally we would have like four guys on this, but we should be OK," Travis said.

"Good. Your boss kinda scares me. Is he a mean guy?"

As Travis was telling her no, Jess was nodding his head saying, "Oh, he's an ass!"

"Don't listen to him. Joe's a good guy, he just has a lot of responsibility and we kinda push the envelope sometimes out here. So it can be real stressful for him."

"Pushing the envelope? Is that what you call it when a girl is dancing above you while you're both naked?"

71

"Well, it's a big envelope," Travis said.

Jess jumped in, saying to Travis, "It has to be a big envelope with your fat ass."

"This, coming from a guy who has at least 30 pounds on me?"

Jen came to Travis's defense. "Well, I've seen his ass, and I think it looks good." This was strange for Travis. With every word she spoke, with every action, she was eroding the barrier between cop and informant. Sitting there eating his dinner, all Travis could think was how much he wanted to be with her, kiss her, make love to her. He just had to keep those thoughts to himself, although he figured Jess could see it. There was a sharp street cop inside that jolly frame, and not much got by him.

They finished with dinner and they all walked outside. Travis told Jennifer that they could leave her car there. She said, "I don't have a car. My roommate dropped me off. Can you take me by her work when we're done?"

"No problem."

Jess started toward his car, and Jen and T.J. waited to cross the street. Jess yelled back, "I'll be on the car-to-car, channel two. Joe's crew is on one."

Knowing she was going to ask, Travis told her, "The car-to-car radio is like a walkie-talkie."

They crossed Second Street and got into Travis's car. Jen was looking around the interior like a mother looking at her son's college dorm room. "Pardon the mess. We live out of our cars, and all this crap makes it look more like a ghetto car."

She laughed as Travis pulled away from the curb heading east. Snake's place was just over the next bridge in Naples. The radio crackled, "Travis, I'll take the house if you want to stay out on Second Street."

"Good call. I don't want her getting spotted by a neighbor or something," Travis replied, holding his radio in his lap to keep it out of sight. They only had to go about a mile and took up a position in a bank parking lot. It was a good spot, allowing them to go in either direction on Second Street if they had to. Jess drove by them, and about 45 seconds later let them know he was sitting right outside the gate at Snake's place.

"Do you see anything?" Travis asked.

"Well, the Hummer is there, and there are a few lights on in the house."

"Ten-four. Let us know if anything moves."

Travis looked over at Jen, and she had a smirk on her face.

"What?" Travis asked.

"Nothing. I just think it's cute how you're so laid back and fun, but when you talk on the radio you're all business, like, 'Ten-four, ten-four good buddy.'"

"No mocking the tour guide, ma'am."

They sat, and sat. About an hour had passed and nothing was going on. The lights in the house stayed the same. No cars in or out. Jess kept them updated on the movements of the peacocks, and he even gave them names. It got boring on surveillance when you were solo. Luckily for Travis, he had Jen to talk with. She began to open up about her life. There was no hint of an accent, so Travis was shocked to hear she had grown up all over the Midwest. It turned out her father was a wildcat oil rig worker, so he would move the family every couple of years depending on where the oil was being pumped. She'd even lived in Lake Charles, Louisiana, while Travis was stationed about sixty miles away at Ft. Polk. Of course, she was five and he was twenty at the time.

"So, how did you end up out here, and how did you end up with Snake?" This question had been gnawing at Travis for some time. Her face changed slowly to a somber, sunken look. He'd hit on something bad, for sure.

"Well, it's kinda long."

"We have all night and I'm a good listener." That was kind of an ironic statement, because poor listening was one of his wife's chief complaints.

"When I was 14 my dad was killed in an industrial explosion in Sulfur, Texas. We had some insurance, so we were OK for a while. After about a year, my mom started dating this guy who seemed nice at the time. We moved in with him, and it wasn't long before he started hitting her. Eventually she just wasn't attractive enough for him anymore. That's when … " She paused, and Travis could see she was looking for the courage to say the next words. Words he had heard way too often in patrol. So he helped her to get it out.

"Is that when he turned to you?"

She began to shake slightly, and a tear rolled off the tip of her nose. He forgot all about what they were there to do and placed his hand on hers. She turned her hand so their palms met, and she squeezed with the force of a man.

"I was only 16!" she yelled. "That motherfucker took it from me."

She was looking straight at the dash. Travis had no idea what to say, so he asked the typical cop question. "Did he get arrested?"

"No. I told my mom and she wouldn't let me call the police. She said, 'It's not his fault, and can you blame him considering the way you dress?'"

Being the father of two daughters, Travis couldn't fathom the lack of instinctual protection on her mother's part. "What did you do?"

"I ran away from home. First I went to a friend's house, then to my grandma's house in Tulsa where my older sister was living. My mom gave up custody, and I stayed with my grandmother until I came out here for college when I was twenty."

Before she could go on, Jess came over the radio: "Heads up, he's rolling, he's driving a black Mercedes. He's the only occupant, and he's on his way out to you."

As Jess gave the play-by-play, Jennifer wiped the tears from her face and perked up. "That's Snake's car," she told Travis.

"Thanks for the warning, bro!" Travis said sarcastically over the radio.

"Sorry, I was concentrating on the Hummer and the house. Then all of a sudden the side gate opened and he was already driving out."

"No problem, I got him now. Looks like he's going to go east." Travis started his engine and drove to the exit of the lot, pulling onto Second Street about a block west of Snake. "I've got a good position to follow and two blockers."

"What are blockers?" Jen asked.

"Cars between us and the target, we call them blockers. If we have blockers and stay on a main street, we will stay as the eye a lot longer. If he turns off or we loose our blockers, we'll pull off and let Jess take over. That's why we like to have the rest of the team. The more cars to pass off the eye to, the less chance we have of getting burned."

Snake drove to Pacific Coast Highway and turned left. They stayed with him through the turn and could see that Jesse couldn't make the light. They continued up to Anaheim Boulevard, where they stopped at a red light. Jess caught up and called them off, so Travis pulled into a liquor store parking lot. Jess stayed with Snake until he got to a laundromat in the central area of town. "The Central" was the lower-income area of Long Beach, and geographically it was located where the west and south divisions met.

Jesse called to Travis, "I'm rolling past. You got it?" They were just five cars behind him.

"No problem," Travis responded as they pulled into a motel across the street. They could see the entire laundromat through the big front windows. Snake was just getting out of his car when Travis parked. Snake was a tall guy, six foot two or better, Travis figured, but he was skinny. He wore a black leather coat and black pants. He dressed nice, and expensive. His dark hair and bushy goatee reminded Travis of an East Coast mobster. He headed into the business holding a bank bag and walked to the back.

"Hey, Jen, under your seat there's a pair of binoculars. Can you get them for me?" Travis asked. Jennifer reached under and pulled out a small pair of camouflaged binoculars. Travis took them and glassed the shop. As Snake walked to the back, a Mexican guy who'd been reading the paper began to follow him. Snake opened a door to the back room with a key. The Mexican followed him in, and the door closed behind them. Jennifer thought the guy who went in with Snake worked at the laundry. She said, "Every time we've been here, that guy has been here, and Snake would talk with him in the office."

"What does he do?"

"I'm not sure, but I think he takes care of the machines and takes the coins out." They waited about three minutes, and the Mexican came out of the office. He walked to his car with a peppy step, looking around the parking lot. He got into a sharp-looking late '80s maroon Chevy Monte Carlo and drove east on the highway.

"Jess, did you see that?" Travis squawked quickly over the radio.

"Yeah. He sure looked like he had the happy walk." Just then Jesse's car passed in front of Travis and Jen. "I'll get his plate and come right back," Jesse said.

"What's the happy walk?" Jennifer asked.

"When someone is holding drugs they tend to walk quicker than normal due to their excitement. They also give themselves away by looking around a lot. They don't want us to spoil their fun."

While Jess was following that guy, Snake came out of the office. He went to the cash machine and opened it. After a quick inspection he went and opened the change boxes on a few washers. He took the quarters out of the machines and used them to fill the change machine. "Have you ever seen him do that? Fill the machines, that is."

She nodded and said, "Yeah, a few times."

"If Snake changes the machines, then what does the Mexican guy do?"

You could see the light go on above her head. "I bet Snake just sold to him!" she blurted out.

"You would make a fine detective, Jen. I doubt he's a user; the car he was driving was too nice to belong to a meth head."

When Jess got back they met him behind a closed-down, boarded-up McDonald's three properties over. The two detectives parked their cars with the drivers' windows next to each other about a foot apart. Jesse filled them in on where the guy went. "I followed him only about three blocks to the Gold Rush Motel. He parked and went into room six. I watched for about fifteen minutes, and four different tweekers came and went."

"That guy's a dealer! Isn't he?" Jen interjected. She was getting pretty good at this detective thing.

"Yeah, he probably is, but we'll let him slide for now. I don't want to spook Snake. I want the case on him tight, air tight."

Jess added, "Machu Picchu tight!"

Travis held out his fist and tapped Jess's. They both repeated, "Machu Picchu tight."

Just then they could see the lights of Snake's car turn on. The game was afoot once more. Jess took the first tail as it led to the Long Beach Freeway. "Seven-ten north, and I've got blockers," Jess belted over the car to car. He stayed about three cars back for the trip north.

When there was a lag in the radio chatter Jen asked, "OK, I give. What the hell is 'Machu Picchu tight'?"

"It's kinda a long story."

"I think we have the time, isn't that what you told me?"

"OK. About a year ago we arrested this street hooker who was looking real bad. She was around 40 but she looked 55 in street years, similar to dog years but a different formula for street people.

Anyhow, she was nasty and was pissing off this detective we had back then. She was telling him he couldn't get laid and all that good stuff. He got so hot under the collar that he said, 'Well, at least my girl doesn't have a worn-out loose pussy.' The booking room went silent and she lit into him. 'My pussy might be old, but it's still as tight as the first day it was laid. Just like the stones of Machu Picchu!' The laughter was deafening."

"But what is Machu Picchu?"

"It's an ancient city built by the Incas in Peru. It's, like, 500 years old and so high up in the mountains it's a marvel of engineering. But the funny thing was, she was totally accurate about the stones. You see, with only stones to cut stones, the Incas made walls with joints so tight that till this day you can't stick a butter knife in between them."

"And she knew that?"

"Yep. It turns out she had a master's degree in anthropology and was a professor at one point. Then she tried crack at a party. She said it only took about two years for her to end up selling herself."

Travis wasn't thinking when he said that. He could see Jen didn't like how he trivialized a woman being desperate enough to turn to prostitution. His last statement really put a damper on the moment, so he finished the story. "Jess and I made a deal to someday travel there together and hike the ruins, just the two of us."

She smiled and asked, "No wives?"

Travis said, "Looks like I won't have one when we finally get to go." He turned his head to see her reaction. She was now sitting sideways in her seat with her left leg tucked up under her. With her left hand she reached over and stroked his hair back from his face. He got one of those stunning chills, the kind that goes from your head to your feet.

"She'll be losing a great guy." Her voice had become soft and seductive. There was an odd silence in the car. Her hand was still on the back of his neck when the radio broke. She quickly pulled her hand away as Jesse spoke: "Dude, I'm off. I lost my blockers. I'm getting off at Atlantic-Bandini."

"Yeah, I see you, we got it. Just pull in when you can." They followed him up the 710 Freeway to the northbound Interstate 5. From there they transitioned to the 101 Ventura Freeway.

77

"Hollywood, he's going to Hollywood," Jennifer said with confidence. "He met me there. I bet he knows other girls up there."

She was right. He exited and headed to the heart of West Hollywood. They watched as he met with three separate streetwalkers. Two of them, after sitting in his car, made trips to their motel rooms and back to the car. They never stayed longer than three or four minutes, then got back out and headed to their rooms. "OK, Jess, what do you make of that?"

He broke the squelch on his radio but there was nothing. Finally, Jess spoke. "You think he's collecting taxes, Travis?"

"Probably. I don't think he would sell on a street level."

Then a tough-looking black dude walked out of the shadows and up to the car. The guy was yoked up. No doubt a parolee or an ex-con at best. Snake got out and greeted him like a lifelong friend. Jen didn't know any of these people he was seeing. Snake and the black dude talked for about 10 minutes, and then Snake slipped the guy a wad of cash. Jesse had the best eye on the duo. "Was that a drug transaction, Jess?"

"Nope, he just gave him money. I bet he's the stable master for this area. If Snake's their pimp, he can't keep them safe and in line from Long Beach."

"I think you're right. That would explain what we just saw."

Travis looked over at Jen and could see she was starting to get bored. He held the radio up to his mouth and told Jesse, "I think we can call it, bud. Let's head in."

Jen asked, "Did this help? I mean, is this what you wanted?"

"Sure. We learned a lot about his habits, and perhaps a few ways to get to him." Time had slipped by without him knowing it. When Travis's phone vibrated, he knew it was a text from Joe. Almost like a date's father turning on and off the porch light. The message said that he and the rest of the guys were done for the night and they were going home. Jess let Travis know that he had received the text on his phone also.

"Jess, I have to drop Jennifer off at her friend's work. Go on ahead."

"Are you sure?"

"Yeah, I'll see you tomorrow." That was the last transmission for the night. Jesse never responded.

"Where can I take you tonight?"

"Las Vegas," She said giggling. With the way his life was going, it sounded like a nice diversion. She must have been thinking the same thing. "Well, maybe if things were different," she added. She had a sweet, soft look to her face, warm and glowing and a bit flushed. "My girlfriend works at The Powder Room by the airport," she said. Travis gave the comment a little chuckle and headed for the San Diego Freeway.

"Have you heard of it?"

"Are you serious? Of course I have. I'm a vice cop."

The Powder Room was a two-story gentleman's club down by Los Angeles International Airport. Now, Travis always called a titty bar a titty bar, but this place was different. The cover charge alone was never less than $25, and the women were first-class beauties. Hell, with the piece of shit car Travis was driving, he wasn't sure they would even let him park in their lot.

When they pulled up to the club, the parking lot was full. Jen directed him to the employee parking lot in the back. There was a brick wall with arms sitting on a stool at the gate. He was a nearly 300-pound black guy wearing a security T-shirt. His hair was a bushy Afro from the '70s, and he had a few days growth of beard. He began to walk over to the car as they drove by, and when he got about five steps away he recognized Jennifer. "Hi, Summer!" he said, waving his hand.

"Well now, there's a name from the past," Travis joked. She must have thought it was funny too, because she introduced him to the monster as Patrick. He parked, got out and walked around to her side to open her door. The engine was still running, and she asked,

"Aren't you coming in? Just for a minute. I want you to meet my friend. Come on, I get free drinks."

He couldn't say no to her big eyes. He walked back over to the driver's side and pulled his Walther PPK out from under the seat and stuffed it into the front of his pants. As they walked toward the building Jen let her hair down and it fell into place perfectly. As she took Travis by the arm, he said, "Jennifer, don't ever say 'free drinks' to a cop."

They walked in through the dancers' entrance and went through the dressing room on their way to the main hall. Jennifer knew quite a few of the girls and gave several hugs as they walked through. When they got to their table and sat down, an older man came over to them. He had dark hair and a lot of jewelry on his wrists and fingers. Travis could smell the cigar smoke and cologne mixture coming from the man's shirt. The man said with a deep Armenian accent, "It's so good to see you, Summer, are you back for dance?"

"No, Antranig, I'm here to see Cheryl."

"And who is your friend?"

"This is Travis."

"Travis, you be good to Summer, she is best girl."

"Yes sir," Travis replied.

"Drinks on me. You best girl, Summer," Antranig belted out as he walked off.

Travis said, "Who's that guy?"

"He's the owner, Antranig Petrossian. He came here from Soviet Armenia in the '80s. He's a great guy, he watches out for all the girls and pays well."

"He sure likes you, he calls you the best girl."

"He calls every girl the best girl. It's kinda funny."

They sat there and watched the show for a few minutes. Then a redheaded beauty came onto the stage in a plaid skirted schoolgirl uniform. She wasted no time in getting into her routine. The DJ played "Welcome to the Jungle" by Guns N' Roses, and she gyrated perfectly to the tune. Travis had seen his share of topless dancers, but this one treated it like a sport, and she was going to be the winner at all costs. Her body was a powdery white, but it was perfect. Travis thought, *It's sure a good night for redheads.*

Jennifer leaned over to Travis and asked, "Do you like her?"

"Well, she's definitely a trooper."

"That's my best friend, Cheryl."

He watched as she swung around the brass pole and worked the rail. When she went topless she had to be six feet back according to ABC rules, but there was still plenty to see even from the back row. Travis could tell that Antranig ran a straight house. When Cheryl was down to just her G-string, the place was hopping. Several guys from tables farther back made their way to the rail seats and began tossing dollar bills on stage. When she was done, she put her bra on and began collecting the tips. Each guy she'd seen throwing money onto the stage got a kiss on the cheek. The DJ said, "Let's hear it for Bunny!"

Travis turned to Jennifer and said, "Bunny? Does everyone

have a stage name?"

"You have Patrick Sullivan, I'm sometimes Summer. Aren't we all trying to be someone else if only for a little while?"

"Who do you want to be? Summer or Jennifer?"

"I just want you to be Patrick for a while." She placed her hand around his neck and leaned toward him. Travis was frozen, confused and aroused. As she came toward him he didn't try to pull away although he knew he should. She kissed him softly at first and then deeper. For a moment, they were all alone in the middle of the nightclub with a hundred people around them, neither hearing nor seeing anything but each other. They paused and looked into each other's eyes to see if it was real. The moment was broken by a woman's voice saying, "Who's the cutie?"

Travis turned to see Cheryl standing there with her schoolgirl outfit on.

"This is Travis. He's the one I told you about."

Travis stood up and shook her hand. Cheryl smiled and said, "Carry on, Detective, it looked like you were onto a good lead there."

Travis was blushing now and lowering his face to avoid eye contact. "Hey, I've gotta go. Thanks again for all your help, Jen." He turned to Cheryl who was now sitting at the table. "Cheryl, that was a great show. I hope to see you again." He looked around, confused because he hadn't come through the front door. When he found it, he was on his way. As he walked out to the sidewalk, it took him a second to find his bearings. He turned to the left and headed for the parking lot. As he passed the stage door, it opened and Jen came running out and made her way over to him.

"I'm so sorry. I didn't mean to embarrass you," she said as she grabbed his arm.

"You didn't embarrass me. Who would be embarrassed to be with you?"

"Then why did you take off like that?"

"Jen, I'm married."

"You said yourself you think it's over."

"Yeah, but I'm also a cop – a cop who arrested you, and now you're my informant. It's just not right, and I could get fired."

"No one here knows who you are, but I understand how that scares you."

"That's not what scares me. What scares me is how much I was hoping you would kiss me, and how I didn't care that I was married. That could lead to a place I've never been, and to tell you the truth, the only scary thing is that I don't care about what could happen to me."

They grabbed each other and began kissing with a passion he'd only seen in the movies. This went on for several minutes until he pulled himself away and said, "I have to go. I need to do some thinking. I'll call you, OK? Just stay away from Long Beach right now."

"OK. Take care of yourself, Travis," she said as she stroked his cheek with the backs of her fingers.

She stood there and watched as he drove out of the lot and out of sight. He was flushed with emotions as he drove south toward his city by the sea. A thousand thoughts ran through his head, mostly about the consequences but a few about the possibilities.

Chapter Five

Party Guest

The day after they followed Snake, Travis was in the office briefing Joe about the night's events and what he and Jesse interpreted them to mean. Travis left out the part about dropping Jen off at The Powder Room and the kiss. As long as no one knew, he figured it would be all right.

"So is this guy a true pimp or a meth dealer?" Joe asked Travis.

"He's both, I think. We saw him make a delivery here in town to a Mexican guy. Jess got his plate, and it turns out the guy has a record for weapons, drug possession and trafficking. His name is Raymundo Flores, he goes by Araña, it's Spanish for spider. It looks like he's staying at the Gold Rush on PCH and selling out of there. Then we followed Snake to Hollywood and watched him meet with three hookers and what looked to be his muscle up there. He's way frickin' dirty."

"Boy, he had a busy night for an upstanding business man. What's your plan?"

"Well, I'm not sure about how to get him on pimping because he's got insulation between him and the girls we saw, so I was thinking about developing the drug angle and getting a warrant for his house."

"How about Jennifer? Can you set up a date with her and send her back to him with a wire?"

83

"I was thinking about that, but I found her on her own independent site. I don't have an in with Snake to set up the date."

Just then Ben Hutchens spoke up from behind the newspaper he was reading. "You might be able to get yourself invited to his party."

Joe asked, "What party?"

"Look here in the *Business Journal*. He's hosting an AIDS benefit at his estate a week from Saturday. The benefit is being put on by none other than our very own councilman, Paul Wise."

Joe asked, "Wait a minute. Two things, how is he supposed to get on the guest list by then and when did you start reading the *Business Journal?*"

"Wise owes me, Joe. He'll do it," Travis assured him. "Jesse, I'm going to need a wire on me that can't be detected. Can you see what Tillbak has down in the computer lab?"

"Yeah, he's got a cool one that looks just like a cell phone."

Travis started for the door and Joe asked, "Where are you going?"

"I'm going to City Hall to speak with Wise. I'm not going through his office to arrange this."

Travis walked across the bricks between the station and City Hall. It was a single tower consisting of four columns of concrete on each corner with brown metal and glass between them. At the thirteenth floor he introduced himself to Wise's secretary.

"Hi there, is Mr. Wise in?"

"Yes, but he's busy right now, do you have an appointment?"

"No ma'am, I don't. I was just in town for business and thought I would see if he was available. Can you have him call Patrick Sullivan when he gets a chance? Here's my number." Travis wrote down the number to the office cold phone that all of the detectives used to make undercover calls. He was banking on the fact that Wise would remember his undercover name from their day at the beach and make the call. About 30 minutes after Travis got back to the office the phone rang. Travis answered it, "Patrick here."

"This is Paul Wise. Is this Patrick Sullivan, or should I say Travis?"

"Ah, you did remember. It's Travis, sir. Sorry for the cloak and dagger stuff but I need a favor. I need an invite to your AIDS benefit next Saturday."

"I didn't know you were such a charitable man, detective."

"I'm not. I need to be there as part of an undercover investigation. I assure you, though, no one there will know who I am or what I do."

"I don't understand, Travis."

"I can't fully explain it right now but there will be someone there that I'm investigating. Getting into the party would be a perfect opportunity to make contact, but you're the only one who can know who I am."

"OK. What do you need me to do?"

"I am going to send you an email from P. Sullivan at Trinity Shipping telling you where you can send the invite."

"What's that company?"

"It's a high school friend's company in Palo Alto, and he set me up with a phony email account and business cards for my undercover identity. Just have your secretary send the invite there overnight and he'll forward it to me."

"OK, Travis, consider it done."

"Thank you, sir. I won't do anything to tip anyone off that you were in on it."

When Travis hung up the phone Joe asked him, "OK, you're in the party, so now what?"

"One thing at a time, Joe, one thing at a time. Where's Jess?"

"At Tillbak's lab."

Travis headed down to the computer lab in the basement of the building. It used to be part of the locker room, but when the department decentralized patrol into three substations it freed up space. The door was controlled with an electronic combination lock that only the computer guys and the chief knew. Travis knocked on the door and said his name. Jesse opened it. "Dude, you gotta see this thing," Jesse said.

Tillbak spun around in his chair holding a phone. "Here it is, Travis, a continuous broadcasting wire in an iPhone body. But here's the best part. It's actually a working phone."

"How does it work?"

"You wear this plastic holster on your belt. When the phone is in the holster this little nipple in the plastic pushes into a button on the back of the phone. That turns on the wire. When you take it out of the holster the wire turns off and you can use it as a phone.

We can record from up to a half-mile away, but I would recommend more like 400 yards or closer."

"Will it ring while in the holster?"

"Yep, you just pop it out to answer it. You can get voice and text but no Internet or apps."

"Fuck, this is great. How long will it work?"

"About two to three hours on a charge, or if you use the phone a lot, about an hour and a half. Unfortunately, the battery is built in so you can't change them out in the middle of an operation. It has to be plugged into an outlet for 30 minutes."

"Hopefully this won't take longer than an hour."

"Can I come, Travis?" Tillbak asked with a boyish excitement.

"You bet. You and Jess can be my support and feed me info as I need it."

Jesse asked, "So what are you going to do once you're at the party?"

"I'm working on that," Travis answered.

Now it was time for Travis to build his image so he could pass as a solvent businessman. His first stop was a car rental place the team used from time to time when the undercover cars were in the shop. He booked a Cadillac, as it was the nicest car they had. Driving a rental was perfect because Patrick Sullivan was from Palo Alto, California, 400 miles away. Next he drove up Long Beach Boulevard to a pawnshop near Del Amo Boulevard. He knew the owner from some cases he had worked back in patrol. He often stopped in and chatted with the man over lunch. The owner of the pawnshop, like many in Southern California, was a Russian immigrant and his name was Lazar. Ever since Travis and his old partner caught a tagger etching the shops windows, Lazar has been very eager to help the police.

Travis walked in, and it took Lazar a minute to recognize him. He had never seen Travis with the goatee and definitely not with the bleached hair. "Detective Travis, is that you? You look so different with this faggot hair."

"For your information, Lazar, chicks dig this hair."

"You look like faggot to me, but that's OK, I still like you. So how you been?"

"I'm good my friend, but I do need a favor."

"Anything for you, Travis."

"I need to borrow a watch."

"You don't know time? I can sell you a nice Tag Heuer at my cost."

"No, I have a watch. I need to borrow a real nice one to impress someone."

"Ah, you looking to make good impression on girl?"

"No, it's for an undercover operation, and I need to look like a well-to-do importer."

"I have what you need, a fine Rolex, 18 karat gold. It worth about twelve thousand dollar."

"That would be fine. Can I pick it up next week?"

"Anything for you, Detective Travis."

Everything was set for the party, but that was in a week. Travis had his tactical exam for the sergeant's test in two days, so he stayed in while the guys worked the highway for streetwalkers. While he was studying, he received a call from Jennifer. She told Travis that she was sorry for kissing him.

"Look, Jennifer, don't be sorry. We're both adults. It wasn't like I pushed you away."

"Thanks, Travis. I thought you were mad at me."

"No, not at all. I was just scared, scared of pushing the envelope too far. Hey, are you going to Snake's big shindig next week?"

"I don't know. He did mention it a while back."

"If you can swing it, I want you to be there. I'll be going as Patrick."

"You're kidding me. How did you pull that off?"

"Long story, but I have an invite and everything. Do your best but don't push the issue. If you make it to the party, don't let on that you know me."

"OK, Travis. I guess I'll see you next week then."

After she hung up, Travis got back to preparing for his exam. It was going to be held in the chief's conference room and would include sergeants and lieutenants from other departments. That way the grading would be impartial. He was relentless on his studies and practicing right up to the exam. When the test day came Travis was a nervous wreck. He wore his class-A uniform complete with a tie. He knew he looked odd with his surfer hair and goatee, but he hoped the proctors could see past that. He sat in the hall and waited to be called into the room. A lieutenant from the nearby city of Torrance came out and told him to come inside.

There was a large map similar to the one that he had practiced on at Fred's house and a table with five proctors, all from other agencies. Sitting in the back of the room was Commander Baker and a few other members of the Long Beach brass. Baker stood and told the panel, "Pardon Detective Jensen's grooming, he's working undercover on a case that precludes him from changing his appearance at this time."

A few in the group nodded that they had heard the old timer, and then the test began. The scenario ran just like they had practiced in Fred's garage. Travis felt more and more comfortable as he progressed. When finished he was asked if there was anything he would have done differently. He had a few things in mind but didn't want to appear to be self-conscious, so he said, "No sir, if I did, then I would have done them differently to begin with." This impressed the panel, and his oral interview afterward went well too. Later, when he was changing in the locker room, Commander Baker walked in and said, "Shit, boy, you nailed it! Everyone else, with the exception of a few, changed their minds and began to sound unsure of themselves. I'm so proud of you."

"I haven't made it yet, sir."

"But you passed, and that means you'll make the list. It may be a few weeks before we know where, but you'll be on it. Oh, and that's not official, so you didn't hear it from me." Baker patted him on the back and walked out. Travis couldn't believe it. He might actually promote. The list would be good for two years, so it would depend on where he landed as to how fast a promotion would happen. The first few promotions would be within a few weeks to fill vacancies. The further down the list he was, the longer it would take. Too far down and you could "die" on the list and have to do it all over again in two years. But for now, Travis was satisfied that he had done the best he could.

***

The night of the AIDS benefit came quickly, and Travis got to break out his tuxedo for the second time in a month. As he buttoned up his shirt, Jesse and Frank Tillbak came into the office. They had just come back from Naples, where they had parked the computer crime detail's van before the neighborhood got full. "The van's in place, and we're connected to the net through an unsecured network," Frank told him. "We're within 300 yards of Snake's place on the next street over."

88

Travis asked, "Jess, help me with these cufflinks, would ya?" He was getting frustrated with them, as he was a bit nervous. Jesse took one in his hand and noticed that it was real gold and had the initials P.S. engraved on it. He asked, "You got cufflinks with your undercover initials?"

"No, they were my grandfather's. My mom's dad is named Patrick Sullivan, that's where I got my U.C. name. He gave them to me for my wedding. He was a cop in Ireland, you gotta meet him someday."

The trio left the office at 8:00 p.m. and all headed for Naples Island in the rented Cadillac. As they drove, Jesse filled Travis in on the backup they had in place. "Joe and the rest of the guys are hanging out at Fire Station Eight just over the Second Street Bridge. They're in raid jackets and have squad cars. Now, if for some reason you're in trouble and can't get out through the front of the house, bail to the canal behind the house. Ben is on the lifeguard boat, and they'll be in the area just for us 'till you're done."

"Wow, you sure got it covered, Jess."

"So what's your plan?"

"I figure I'll just get friendly with Mullen and see where it goes."

"That's it? That's your big plan?" Travis never answered him, he just smiled because this is where he shined. Thinking on his feet and making something out of nothing.

Travis drove down Second Street and dropped Frank and Jess at the Rite-Aid in the center of the island. He waited a few minutes as they walked into the darkness of the neighborhood, soon they called his phone and said they were in the van and set. Travis turned on the wire and put it in the holster. Frank let him know that they could hear it fine and that both Joe and Ben were being advised that he was going to the house.

Travis pulled up to Mullen's estate, and there were valets running back and forth in the street. They were parking cars all over the crowded beach community. At the gate was a black man dressed in a dark blue suit. He was checking invitations and opening the gate for the guests and closing it after them to keep the peacocks inside the yard. Travis handed him the invitation that his friend had forwarded to him from Palo Alto. He was let in, and as he walked toward the front door he found himself alone, so Travis took the opportunity to check the wire. "Jess, send me a text to see how quick it is." It took about fifteen seconds for the phone on his hip to vibrate. He took it out of the holder and tapped the screen to bring up the message. It read, *How are the turkeys doing?* Travis snapped it back on his waist and said, "Peacocks, you knucklehead, peacocks."

The main entry had a large solid wood door that must have been eight feet tall and was decorated with metal adornments and a large Gothic-looking knocker. It opened to a grand foyer that was twenty feet in diameter and two stories tall. A round gold-leafed table sat in the middle with a gorgeous flower arrangement. Like any good cop, Travis made his way directly to the bar and ordered bourbon on the rocks. As the bartender was making the libation, Travis studied the room. Everyone was in his or her evening finery. The men were all in tuxedos, and most of the women were wearing black evening gowns, with the exception of a few old bags trying to recapture their youth by dressing in sexy outfits of gold or red.

Taking his drink, he noticed a glass enclosure behind the bar that had a snake inside it. He asked the bartender about it, and he told Travis that it was a python. He explained that Mr. Mullen loved snakes. Now it was clear to Travis where the nickname had come from. Near the fireplace was a group of men listening to a story. Travis made his way to the group, and there he was, sitting in a leather chair. Peter Mullen was telling the group of his latest adventure aboard his fishing boat, The Cottonmouth. As he finished the story one of the guests asked, "Where did you come up with the name for your boat?"

Travis jumped in before Mullen could answer. "I bet it comes from the Cottonmouth Water Moccasin."

Mullen looked over his brandy snifter and said, "Correct, but can you tell them why?"

"Well, from what the bartender told me, you love snakes, so the perfect snake name for a boat would be The Cottonmouth. It's the only poisonous water snake in North America."

"Bravo, sir. I don't think we've been introduced." Mullen stood up and stuck out his hand to shake.

Travis took it and said, "I'm Patrick Sullivan, and I've gotta tell you, I love your home."

"Thanks. I inherited it from my folks a few years back."

Something over Travis's shoulder caught Mullen's attention, and he excused himself from the conversation. He walked away from the group toward a curving staircase. At the top stood Jennifer in a long black sequined dress. She looked as beautiful as ever. When she made it to the first floor, Mullen took her hand and leaned in to kiss her. She turned her head and the kiss landed on her cheek. Travis figured that wasn't Peter's intended target. He led her over to the group of men and introduced her.

"Gentlemen, this is my girlfriend, Jennifer." She began shaking hands, and when she got to Travis, Mullen said, "This is Patrick Sullivan, he knows his snakes."

"Oh, it was luck. When I was stationed in Louisiana the first thing they told us was to look out for the gators and cottonmouths."

Peter and Jennifer walked off, and Travis felt his phone vibrate. He pulled it out to read the message. *Dude, you're like a James Bond with blonde hair.* He put it back and had a little laugh to himself. He was relieved to know they could hear him from inside the house. He began walking around the grand home to get the layout. In the hallway he noticed several paintings from the same artist. He talked into the wire: "Jess, what can you tell me about Diego Rivera? He's a painter." He continued down the hall and opened a door that led into the garage. The floor was painted white, and in the middle was the black Mercedes they had followed around Hollywood. The garage was well kept and had nice white cabinets and a workbench. The only mess was a few rags and tools on the bench. One tool caught Travis's attention: a two-inch-long cylindrical bristle brush made from brass.

In the van, Jesse was busy looking up Diego Rivera on the Internet. He typed to Travis a quick version of what he had read. *He was a Mexican born painter who studied in France. He died in 1957. Some of his work was controversial because he was a communist.* Travis read the text and went back into the house. Mullen was standing in the hallway. "Are you lost, Mr. Sullivan?"

"I was looking for the bathroom, and please, call me Patrick."

"You missed it by one door, Patrick." Peter pointed to the door five feet from the garage door.

"I love your Diego Rivera collection. Are they originals?"

"No, all reproductions I had commissioned. Are you a fan of his work?"

"I like his stuff. I think he would have been more popular in America if he weren't a communist."

"Not many people know that about him. Why haven't we met before, Patrick?"

"I'm not from Long Beach, I'm just here for business. Excuse me." Travis darted into the men's room. He waited a minute and called Jesse's phone as he turned on the water to hide his voice. Jesse answered, "*Bueno.*"

"Hey, are you getting all this?"

"Yeah, we're recording. You're doing great, man."

"Got any suggestions?" Travis asked.

"Lead on how you're a *lonely* businessman. If he's pimping he should bite on that."

"OK, thanks buddy. Oh, and he must have guns in the house. I saw a barrel brush in the garage."

Travis left the bathroom. Peter was no longer in the hallway, so he went out onto the patio and began looking at all of the items going up for auction. There were sports items signed by star athletes, vacation packages, and a lot of artwork. Peter walked up and said, "There's something here I want you to see." He took Travis to a painting on an easel. It was a nude woman with her arms around a large basket of flowers. "This is a reproduction, but it's one of the best I've ever seen," Peter said. "It's called *Nude With Calla Lilies*. It is by far Rivera's best-known work. I think Mr. Wise got it for the auction knowing I would buy it."

"Perhaps I'll bid on it. It would be the first woman I've taken home in some time," Travis said.

"Come on, a guy like you without a lady?"

"I travel a lot for work."

"What do you do?"

"I work for a shipping company based in Palo Alto, but I travel constantly. Los Angeles, Shanghai, Houston, just about anywhere there's a port. So I don't have the time for a relationship. Now, when I go to China everything is taken care of for me, and I mean *everything*, but back here in the states it's too much of a headache." Travis took a drink from his glass with his left hand to be sure Peter would see the gold Rolex.

"You just don't know the right people," Peter said.

"Yeah, but it's not like the right people are in the Yellow Pages."

Peter led Travis away from the auction items and down the gangway to his boat. "Patrick, one of the things I do is to make sure my clients and friends have a good time. I'm like a party host every day of the year." It was working. Mullen bought into the story. He continued, "If you want some company while you are in town or even tonight, I can make it happen." Travis didn't plan on it going so well that it would happen tonight. He needed to stall.

"Well, you certainly have my interest. Can you give me a minute to think about it, Peter?"

"No problem. I'll get you another drink while you think it over." Peter headed back up the gangway while Travis walked a little farther out to the channel and spoke into the wire. "I need a room, tonight, under the name Sullivan. Try the Westin or the Hyatt, and let me know if you have any luck."

Jesse got on the radio to Joe. "We need to book a room under Patrick Sullivan quick. Can you do that?"

"Ten-four, give me a minute," Joe said. He grabbed his cell phone and scrolled through his list of contacts. He called the security manager at the Westin Hotel. He still had the number from the operation they did when they'd arrested Jennifer. Within three minutes there was a room booked under the name Patrick Sullivan. Joe told Jess the news and he relayed it to Travis in a text message. As Peter handed Travis a fresh bourbon, the phone vibrated. Taking the drink in his left hand, Travis looked at the message with his right, *It's a go, Westin Hotel.*

"You know, Peter, I think I'll take you up on that offer. What kind of arrangement are we talking?"

"Talk to Jennifer when she comes over tonight. Everything is between you two."

"Jennifer? Your girlfriend?" Travis asked.

"She's not really my girlfriend, but more like an employee. But first I want you to enjoy the party."

"Well, tell her I'm at the Westin downtown." Travis held out his glass and said, "To new friends." Peter tapped his glass to Travis's and the two headed back to the party.

On the way up, Travis saw Councilman Wise looking at them. When they passed, Peter introduced them. "Patrick, I want you to meet Councilman Paul Wise, this is his party. Councilman, Patrick Sullivan."

Before Wise could say anything Travis spoke up. "Ah, Mr. Wise, it's a pleasure to finally meet you. I must say, your Harbor Commission and the Port Authority are by far the easiest to do business with compared to Los Angeles and Houston." Wise just nodded and said thank you with a confused look on his face, but never let on that he knew Travis.

Travis hung out for about 30 more minutes, then looked for Peter again and let him know he was going to his hotel for the night. The two shook hands, and Peter saw him to the door. No mention was made of their arrangement, except Peter said, "I sincerely hope you enjoy the rest of the evening."

Travis made his way back to the gate and gave the valet his claim ticket. While he waited, he looked at the gate guard in the suit. The guy had taken his jacket off, and Travis could see how tight the sleeves were around his huge biceps. Then he realized it was the same black guy Mullen had met up with in Hollywood. Once in his car, Travis spoke into the wire. "Jess, have everyone hook up in the Vons parking lot at Ocean and Livingston." As Travis drove over the bridge into Belmont Shore, he could see Joe and the others leaving the old brick fire station in their black-and-whites. Once at the Vons, Travis told Joe what had transpired at the party. "Now Peter and I..."

"Peter?" Joe asked.

"Yeah, Peter, my new best friend. Peter and I never spoke about sex for money, so when Jennifer comes to the hotel we'll have to send her back wired with some recorded funds."

"OK, I'll go to the office and get some cash," Joe said.

"I'm gonna need over a grand, perhaps two if we have it, and Joe, thanks for the room, that was quick."

Joe got back in his black-and-white with Jack Barnes and headed back to the station. Terry was in another squad car and had his raid jacket on. Travis instructed him to go get Ben from the lifeguard boat and get into plain clothes. He said they only had about a half an hour to get set in the hotel lobby. He explained how he wanted to treat it like a regular outcall in case Jennifer was followed or if Mullen sent a different girl. Jesse and Frank were getting out of the van as Terry took off for the lifeguard station.

"Frank, I've got to hand it to you, this wire is the best thing I've ever seen," Travis said.

"Thanks, Travis."

"Do you have the regular wire in there?" Travis asked.

"Yeah."

"OK, we'll need it at the hotel. Give it to me and I'll wire up

Jennifer."

Frank lifted the lid to a footlocker in the van and took out a hard plastic case the size of a cigar box and handed it to Travis. He explained that the range was about the same as the iPhone wire and that it turned on automatically when the battery was placed in it. Travis opened the box and examined the contents to see that the batteries were inside.

"Jess, you got my gat?" Travis asked.

Jesse reached into his kit bag and pulled out Travis's holster with the Colt Government .45 and his badge. He handed them to Travis, who tossed them in the window of the Cadillac.

"How did the recorder work?" Travis asked Frank.

"Perfect. It's digital, so when we get back I'll put it on a disc for you."

"Great. I'll need you to record Jennifer too. Can you do that?"

"Yeah, it's the same frequency."

Travis sent the two of them back to the Naples neighborhood to reset in a place close enough to pick up the signal. Hopefully they wouldn't lose the parking spot they had just left. Travis then headed west on Ocean toward downtown to check in to his room. While at a red light, he stuffed his gun into his trousers and put his badge in his jacket pocket. After giving his car keys to the valet, he made his way to the reception desk. He placed his undercover driver's license and credit card on the counter and said, "Hi, I'm Patrick Sullivan. I would like to check in."

The lady behind the counter took both cards and began looking up his name. She handed Travis his ID and credit card back and said, "Yes sir, no need for the card. According to the computer the room is complimentary, sir."

"Oh, well, thank you."

He signed in and was given the key for room 712. He called Joe on his cell and gave him the room number. Joe was in the office getting the money. All he could get from the office safe was $1,500. He told Travis that he and Jack would be at the hotel in 10 minutes. Travis told Joe to have Terry bring up the money as he was in plain clothes. Once in the room, Travis took his gun out of his waistband and put it on the bed. He tossed the box that contained the wire next to it and took off his jacket. He turned on the television, not to watch anything in particular but to break up the monotony of the silence. The waiting always made him nervous.

***

Back at the party, Mullen asked Jennifer to follow him into his office. She walked in and sat in one of the plush leather chairs. Peter shut the door and began to talk. "I need you to go entertain a new friend tonight."

"Who's that?" she asked.

"Mr. Sullivan, the fella with the frosted hair. He's from Northern California and is staying at the Westin."

"And you want me to show him a good time?"

"Of course. I'll have Lawrence drive you."

"I can drive my car, Peter."

"Lawrence will drive you there and he will bring you back. I just met this guy so I want Lawrence nearby." While she sat in the chair, Peter stroked her hair like a master and his dog. Jennifer just sat there with no reaction. She was repulsed that he was touching her but she knew she needed to go along with it. While Peter was doing this, he called the hotel. When the operator answered he asked to be put through to Patrick Sullivan's room. When the phone rang Travis answered, "Hello."

"Patrick, Peter Mullen here. I wanted to let you know everything we talked about is all set. What's your room number?"

"I'm in seven-twelve."

"Great, Jennifer will be on her way in a few minutes."

Travis responded like a real John would: "Thanks, Peter, I'm excited to see her."

Peter hung up the phone and said to Jennifer, "Show him a good time, and don't fuck it up. He works for an importer and that could be very helpful in the future."

"How can that be helpful?" she asked.

"That's none of your concern. You just keep my friends and clients happy and I'll make sure you have the nice things you crave. You see how simple it is? I'll take care of everything, so don't ever try to go independent again. You're just not smart enough, Jennifer." She just sat there and held in her rage. She hated his controlling personality. When they'd first met, she mistook it for confidence, but she was too deeply involved by the time she learned just how domineering he was. She was hoping that it was all coming to an end with tonight's operation. She got up and went to get her coat while Peter went out the front door. "Lawrence, come here please," he yelled toward the main gate.

Lawrence Washington was a monster of a man. He had been a local hero when he'd played as a defensive lineman for UCLA, but that had all ended when he blew out his knee during his senior year. Dropping out of school, he worked as a doorman at several clubs until Snake employed him as his enforcer. His ghetto vocabulary made him difficult to understand at times and hid his actual intelligence.

"Lawrence, I want you to take Jennifer to the Westin on Ocean. She has a date. Take my Hummer and wait while she's inside, OK?"

"Got it, boss. Do you needs me to go in wit' her?"

"No. This guy's OK, I think."

Jennifer came out and the two of them loaded up in the Hummer. As they drove out the gate, Peter turned around and headed back into the party.

***

Travis heard a knock on the door. He looked through the peephole and saw Terry Knight standing in the hallway. He opened the door and Terry handed him an envelope. "There's nineteen hundred in there. Joe and I got two hundred each out of the ATM. He wanted to be sure you had enough."

"Thanks, Terry. Is it recorded?"

"Yeah, we have the numbers. Ben and I are in the lobby so we'll call ya when she comes in."

"Great. Snake just called, she's leaving Naples now."

With that, Terry headed for the elevator and back to his spot.

***

While they drove toward downtown, Lawrence began to talk. "My name's Lawrence, ma'am. If you needs anythang, call dis number." He handed her a card with his cell phone number on it. She took it and put it in her purse. She asked him, "So, do you work for Peter? I've never seen you before."

"Yes, I watch after his girls in Hollywood. They not as pretty as you though, ma'am."

Reaching the hotel, they pulled into the circular driveway and up to the valet station. Jennifer was waiting for the valet to open the door, but Lawrence got out and quickly made his way to her side. He stared down the valet who was about to open the door

97

and said, "Dat's my job." The young kid in the vest stepped back when he saw the size of her driver. Lawrence opened the door and took Jennifer by the hand as she stepped down from the tall SUV. He whispered in her ear, "You be careful. Call and let me know dat you're fine up there, OK, Miss Jennifer?" She was touched by his kindness and flashed him a big smile to let him know she would be fine. He stayed with the Hummer, and she headed inside to the lobby. It was strange to her as she walked through the great entry. The last time she was there Travis had arrested her. This time he was there to help save her.

***

Travis got the call from Terry letting him know she was on her way up alone. A few minutes later he heard her knock. He opened the door, and she walked in quickly. Travis looked up and down the hallway to make sure Snake hadn't sent a rip-off crew. He closed the door and turned around to see Jennifer flop on the bed like she'd just finished a marathon. "How the hell do you do it? How do you keep your cool when you're Patrick and being chummy with that asshole?"

"I try to keep my mind on the ultimate goal – busting him for pandering and hopefully the drug trafficking."

She sat up as he took a seat next to her. "I almost wet my panties when I saw you talking with Peter. I don't know how you got in there or how you got Peter to send me tonight, but here I am, so now what?"

"We wait for a while and send you back with our money. I'm going to put a transmitter in your purse. Will Peter look in there?"

"No."

"OK, we'll put it in there and record your conversation with him. Bring up something about sex with Patrick. We need to show he knew you were coming here for a sex for money agreement. How much is he expecting?"

"He didn't say, but I usually would get paid anywhere from one to two thousand. He will probably take half of that."

"Wow, two thousand. I think I'll send you back with sixteen hundred, OK?"

"That should work. What about the meth?"

"What about it?"

"He's given it to me and sold to me in the past after jobs. Would you like me to buy from him?"

98

"OK, if it feels natural at the time. Just don't do or say anything out of the ordinary. So, you use meth?" Travis asked with a disappointed tone.

"Not any more. I did a little before, about a year ago, but I was able to kick it."

"Good for you," Travis said as he smiled at her.

"Oh, shit. I have to call my driver."

"You have a driver?"

"Yeah, it's a new guy, Lawrence. He's waiting in the car," Jennifer said as she fumbled through her purse looking for his card.

"Is he the black guy that was working the gate?" Travis asked.

"Yes."

"He's the guy we saw in Hollywood talking with Peter," Travis told her.

Jennifer said, "I knew I'd seen him before. Hold on." She dialed her phone and then held it to her ear. "Hi, Lawrence, I just wanted to let you know I'm fine." There was a pause and she said, "I'll call you when I'm on my way down." She hung up and said, "He's waiting outside in Peter's Hummer." Travis called the guys in the lobby to let them know to watch out for Lawrence.

"So what do we do now, Travis? Peter won't be expecting me for another few hours."

"We hang out, talk, whatever."

"OK, well, you know all about me. Tell me about yourself," Jennifer said with a little laughter.

"Not much to tell. I was in the Army before becoming a cop. I've been a cop about nineteen years, I'm married and have two kids."

"Oh yeah? How's that working out?"

Travis told her about the distance between him and his wife, how when they went to bed at night it felt like there was an invisible wall between them, neither one making an effort to be close to the other. He began to open up as though he was with a marriage counselor. This went on for quite some time, as they both shared the most intimate secrets of their lives. He told her that he was thinking of moving out and thought he might be getting a divorce. Before they knew it, an hour had passed and they fell upon an awkward silence. Travis took Jennifer's hand in his, leaned in and kissed her for about five seconds. After the kiss they kept their lips about an inch apart and just stared into each other's eyes.

Travis said, "This time I kissed you, so you have nothing to be sorry about." After another kiss Travis told her, "Now we need to get ready."

He got up from the bed and picked up the plastic box Frank had given him. He unsnapped it and took out a black metal box that was a bit thinner and longer than a deck of cards. At one end was a thin wire with a miniature microphone at the end. "Jen, this is the wire I was talking about. Give me your purse." Travis opened a side pocket and took out the tampons she had in there. He turned on the wire and placed it inside the pocket. He then carefully closed the zipper until it held the tiny microphone in place. "There, can you see that?"

"No, I wouldn't notice that. Is that how you'll hear us?"

"Yep. Jesse will be recording everything. It's powerful, so don't talk loud or lean into it, that would just give it away." Travis called Joe's cell phone. He let him know they were ready and asked Joe where he was. Joe had changed into his plain clothes and was sitting in his Camry across the street from the hotel. "Terry told me about the driver, so I'm sittin' on him now. I can follow 'till they're back at Snake's," Joe said.

"Good. Do you have a fat wire receiver on board?"

"Yeah, it's in my trunk. Do you need it?"

"Jennifer's wired, I wanted to see if it's working."

"Give me a minute," Joe responded. When he came back on the phone he said, "Ok, it's on." Travis told Jennifer to say something.

"Hi, Sergeant Joe."

"I got it, Travis. She's loud and clear."

Travis hung up his phone and spoke into the wire: "OK, Joe, I'm gonna send her down now." Looking at Jennifer he said, "Don't be scared, we'll be able to hear you the whole time. When you're done, leave and drive to the Mobil station at Second and PCH. Here's the sixteen hundred, keep it in a different part of your purse so you don't hit the wire or expose it." Jen took the cash and put it in the main compartment of the purse. She then took out Lawrence's card and called him to let him know she was on her way to him. Travis walked her to the door and said goodbye. She hugged him and quietly blew him a kiss as she stepped backward into the hall. It was hard for Travis to stay in the room. He was sick with nerves, sending her back there to see Snake again. He paced in the room counting all the things he would have done differently if he only had longer to plan the operation. He never dreamed it would happen so fast, be so unpredictable. It was all in Jennifer's hands now.

Joe followed the black Hummer east down Ocean Boulevard. He didn't have to worry about passing off the follow because it was a straight shot on two major streets all the way back to Naples. When they were driving through Belmont Shore, Joe called Jesse and Frank to let them know that Jennifer was on her way back.

Travis jumped in Terry's car and put on an old shirt over his white tuxedo blouse. They headed out to Naples a few minutes behind Joe, but thanks to Terry's lead foot, they caught up as the Hummer turned right on The Toledo and headed toward some of the most expensive real estate in the city. Travis had Terry drive south on Velentia Drive and drop him off on foot halfway to the canal. He jogged the last block to the van, where Jesse and Frank were stationed. He tapped on the back door and softly said, "Jess, open up." The door opened and he jumped in quickly. The interior light went back on automatically when the door shut. "Holy shit, what's that smell?" Travis said.

"Your partner's wife packed him tamales and beans for dinner. So while you were drinking bourbon and looking at fine art I got a nose full of ass," Frank said while pinching his nose. Jesse had a set of headphones on and was intent on the wire but could hear Frank, as illustrated by his middle finger over his shoulder. Frank handed Travis the second set of headphones, and he quickly slipped them on his ears.

Jennifer was just walking into the house, and the party was still going in full swing. They couldn't hear any conversation until Jennifer told someone to let Peter know she was waiting for him in his office. That was followed by the sound of Jennifer's shoes on the wood floors and then a door closing, blocking out most of the background noise. Travis looked at Jess and said, "I think she's in his office now." A few minutes passed and they heard the door open and close.

"How's Mr. Sullivan doing?" Peter asked.

"Is that Snake?" Jesse whispered. Travis nodded his head.

Jennifer answered, "He was very nice."

"How much did you make?"

"Sixteen hundred."

"Let me have it," Peter ordered as he reached out his hand. That was followed by the sound of rummaging in the purse. It was so close to the microphone nothing else could be heard. When it stopped, Jennifer could be heard finishing a sentence, "...all he had." Peter counted the roll of hundreds and twenties and said, "Here's your share."

"Six hundred dollars? You normally give me half."

"You were gone less than two hours. You obviously didn't have to work very hard."

"That's bullshit. I fucked him *and* gave him head." Then an unmistakable sound could be heard: a tremendous slap, followed by Jennifer screaming for a second, and then a whimper. Travis began to get up from his seat, and Jesse grabbed his arm. "Stay here bro, she'll be all right." They continued listening as Snake went off on her. "Don't you ever tell me what you do for them. You do whatever they want and keep it to yourself. I don't care if he asked you to lick his fucking asshole. You don't complain about how much fucking you had to endure. That's your job."

"I'm sorry, it won't happen again. Really, I'm sorry, Peter!"

It was a tense moment in the van. Travis was terrified, thinking about the story Jen told him and Jess about how Snake had raped her. Jesse must have been nervous too. When Travis looked at him he was unlocking the rack that held the pump shotgun. The wire went very quiet, then, Peter could be heard talking calmly again.

"OK, go take a shower."

"I think I'm going to just go. My girlfriend wanted to go dancing tonight."

"Whatever, here's your money."

"Can I get a sixteenth of tweek?"

"I thought you quit."

"I did, but my friend wants some. If you don't have any, I understand."

The sound of a drawer opening and closing was heard and Peter said, "Here's a teener."

No more words were exchanged. The detectives listened while she made her way out of the house. Lawrence could be heard in the background calling to Jennifer; his voice got louder as he got closer to her. There must have been some worry on her face. All Travis had to go on was what he heard over the wire. "Miss Jennifer, are you OK?"

102

"I'm fine, Lawrence," Jennifer said, although her voice was shaky.

"I can drives you wherever you needs to go."

"That's OK, Lawrence. I've got my car here."

"OK, Miss Jennifer. You got my number if you needs anything."

The next sound was a car starting up and the dinging of a seat belt warning. Jennifer could be heard sniffling over the music on her radio. Travis looked at Frank and said, "She's out." Frank broadcast the developments to the other units who were waiting on Second Street. Jesse climbed into the driver's seat and started the van, then shut it off. Travis asked what he was doing, and Jesse explained. "We should stay a minute and make sure that black guy doesn't follow her. He seemed kinda concerned about her." Jesse was right; Travis got in the front seat next to him and watched as Jennifer's Explorer passed in front of them. They waited five minutes and then drove off in the same direction. By then, Jennifer was already calling Travis on his phone. When he answered she was scared. "Where are you guys? I'm at the gas station!"

"Don't worry, Jen, we're coming. We had to make sure you weren't followed. We'll be there in a minute."

"OK. Your sergeant is pulling up now," she said just before hanging up.

Pulling the van into the gas station, they saw Joe standing next to his car smoking a cigar. Jennifer was parked in the next stall and was still sitting in the driver's seat. Travis got out to go check on her. Her right cheek was red and swelling from Snake's backhand. Although she tried to hide it, Travis could see a small cut in front of her ear. She didn't look at Travis when she asked, "How was that? Did you get what you need?"

"You did great, better than what we expected. I need the money and the dope." She reached over pulled her purse onto her lap. She unzipped the main compartment and pulled out a small plastic baggie of meth and the $600 Snake had given back to her. She handed it to Travis and said, "I hope this hangs the bastard." Then she broke down and started to cry. Travis opened her door and put his arm around her, and she latched on to him like a scared child. He told her it was over and that it wouldn't be long before Snake was in jail. His words had little comfort for her, as she knew Snake could make bail. She let go and reached back into her purse. She handed Travis the wire that had transmitted the conversation that would prove Peter Mullen was a pimp and a drug dealer. "I need to go," Jennifer said while she started her car.

"Where are you going? Where are you staying?"

"With Cheryl."

"Does Snake know where she lives?"

"No, she lives in Redondo Beach. He doesn't even know her."

"Good. Call me when you get home so I know you're OK." She smiled, nodded and drove off toward the freeway.

Travis walked over to Joe, whom now had most of the team assembled. Jesse was filling him in on the conversation they had heard. Joe liked what they had so far but wanted to run it by the district attorney. Travis was ready to get search and arrest warrants and hit the door that night. Joe and he rarely disagreed on tactics or how to make a case, but Joe could see Travis was not thinking clearly. "OK, guys, it looks like we have a few days of follow-up work ahead of us," Joe told the crew.

"What are you talking about? Let's hit the house now, we got this prick," Travis argued.

"We need more, T.J. First we need to test the dope and transcribe the recordings. Then I want more than just a half an eight-ball of crank before I knock down the door of a guy who has the City Council on his speed dial." Travis was pissed. He felt Joe was being too coy, too concerned about the administration. He asked Terry to take him back to the hotel to pick up the Cadillac. As they were walking to Terry's car, Joe said, "This isn't like when we used to kick down doors in the Carmelitos projects, Travis. We need more to go on than a taped meeting between him and a whore."

"She's not a whore!" Travis yelled back as he quickly turned and approached his supervisor, getting to within six inches of Joe's face. "Sure, she fucked up, but she's not a whore." The team stood and watched, waiting to see Joe's reaction. He was as cool as the fog coming in from Seal Beach, still leaning on his car smoking his stogie. He never flinched once and just said, "OK, T.J., she's not a whore. She's also not what I would call a star witness. Now let's go home and pick it back up on Wednesday."

With that, Terry took Travis by the arm and led him away to collect the rental car. Joe pulled Jesse aside and walked away from the others. Joe sat on the hood of his car and took his cigar out of his mouth. "Jesse, this is a great case for you guys, but he's getting way too emotional about it, and he just can't make it personal. You know him and this isn't like him. You need to keep an eye on your partner, he's getting a little out of control."

Chapter Six

D.R.T.

The house was quiet when Travis woke up. His hunger was unbelievable, and it was keeping him from going back to sleep. He realized it was because of the scent of bacon and muffins cooking downstairs. He pulled on a pair of jeans that were folded at the end of the bed and grabbed a sweatshirt. Shuffling down the stairs he saw his two daughters sitting on the sofa, both quietly reading books. Nine-year old Tara was sitting up straight and was wearing her glasses. She had blonde hair and was almost an exact copy of Travis's wife, Sarah. Seven-year-old Lisa was sprawled out with one leg up on the armrest. Her red hair and freckles were obviously passed to her from Travis's mother, who came from Ireland when she was a small child.

Lisa caught sight of her father first. "Daddy's up!" she exclaimed. Sarah walked in from the kitchen, kissed her husband good morning and gave the five-minute warning for breakfast.

Travis said, "You girls were being so quiet."

"Mommy wanted us to be quiet because you were sleeping. She said you were working all night." Lisa said.

"Yeah, I was. Thanks, you girls were real good."

"Did ya catch any bad guys, Daddy?" Lisa asked. She was the tomboy of the two and loved the cop stories. Of course Travis had to clean the stories up before sharing.

"Well, we didn't arrest him, but we got drugs from the bad

guy."

"Why didn't you arrest him?" Lisa quizzed as her sister listened.

"We're hoping to get more drugs from him and then arrest him."

"I would have arrested him, Daddy," Lisa said as she got up and walked to the kitchen. Travis realized Joe was right, that they needed to build a stronger case against Snake. He followed Lisa to the kitchen and sat down at the table. Sarah was scooping the eggs onto plates and asked how Travis's night went. He avoided saying what exactly had transpired, but he said the team had made headway. While they ate, the girls talked about all kinds of things like television, school and a desire to get a pet rat. After they were done, the girls ran upstairs to get dressed for the day. Sarah started doing the dishes and asked Travis, "So what exactly did you guys do last night?"

"I went to a party undercover to try and get close to a pimp."

"Why does your tuxedo smell like perfume?"

"It must be from Jennifer, she's my informant. We had to hang out in a hotel room while her driver waited downstairs. I didn't realize it smelled."

"Is that the best you can come up with?" Sarah said as she stared out the kitchen window.

"That's what happened."

"Whatever," she said as she shut off the sink and walked away. Travis didn't want to expend the energy to fight, so he went to the back yard and started throwing the ball for his dog.

Sarah yelled out the bedroom window down to him, "Travis, your work phone keeps ringing."

He tossed the ball one last time and ran inside to his office. Looking at the screen, he saw it was Jen. He flipped the phone open and said, "Hello, Jennifer?"

"Travis, I'm scared," she said.

"What's wrong?"

"Peter called me this morning and told me that if I complained to him one more time he was going to make it so no man would want me. Travis, he's going to find me."

"He's not going to find you, Jennifer."

"Why didn't you guys arrest him last night? You had him."

"It's more complicated than that. We need more time, we need more evidence."

"Travis, I'm scared he's going to find me. I don't know how, but I just get this feeling he'll find me." The trembling in her voice concerned Travis.

"Where's your friend Cheryl?"

"I don't know. Travis, I don't want to be alone."

"Jennifer, it's my day off."

"I need you here with me. I don't know what to do. I'm so scared and alone."

"Hang on." Travis fumbled for a pen and some paper. "OK, give me the address there." He scribbled the address on the pad and said, "It will take me an hour to get there. Don't go outside or open the door."

When he hung the phone up he turned around to see Sarah standing in the doorway to his office with her arms folded and a shocked look on her face. "Are you kidding me? Who the hell was that?" she asked.

"It was my informant. She's all messed up and thinks this guy we're workin' is after her. She's afraid for her life, and this is a huge case. I can't let it all go down the toilet, not after all the work we put into it."

"And you're going over to her place, on your day off."

"Just 'till her roommate comes home."

"Don't bother coming back." Sarah turned around and walked away. Travis followed her down the hall and grabbed her by the arm. "What's your problem?" he asked.

"It's the God-damn job that's my problem. It comes first, it comes before the family. Don't you even remember? We were going to take the girls bowling today." Now he felt like shit. He had totally forgotten. "Just go, Travis, just go, but when you come back I want you to pack up. Maybe you can stay at your brother's." Sarah cupped her hands over her mouth and ran up to their bedroom. Travis thought about following her for a moment then grabbed his kit and got his gun out of the lock box in the office drawer. He started for the door and could hear Sarah telling the girls that Daddy had an emergency and had to go to work. He couldn't face his girls; he was letting them down again. He walked out without saying goodbye and headed for Redondo Beach.

Located on the west side of the Los Angeles basin, Redondo Beach was about 10 miles south of Los Angeles International Airport. It was a beautiful, quiet beach community with only one drawback. It was so damn far from the freeway that Travis spent more time driving surface streets than he did on the San Diego Freeway. Finally he arrived at the little beach house at Knob Hill Avenue and Esplanade. It was a yellow clapboard sided bungalow with white trim that probably had been built in the '20s when the Arts and Crafts era swept through Southern California. With the exception of the garage, it looked completely original and restored. It sat on the west side of the street and backed right up to the bike path on the beach.

Travis called Jennifer on her cell phone to let her know he was out front. She met him at the door, barefoot, wearing faded jeans, a baggy linen blouse and a big smile. He could tell that she had been crying. Jennifer said, "Travis, thank you so much for coming, I was so scared." He walked in and set his kit bag down by the front door. She shut the door behind him, took him by the hand and walked toward the back of the house. It had a grand porch on the west side that overlooked the beach. Seeing this, Travis said, "Wow, this place is great. How does your friend afford it?"

"She makes a lot of money. Besides dancing at The Powder Room she makes adult films. You wouldn't believe what they pay her."

"No kidding?"

"Yeah. She once asked me to do one, but I don't think I could do that. All those people seeing you having sex, I just couldn't." She sat down on a patio chair and Travis sat on a chaise next to her. Jennifer said, "I hope I didn't ruin your plans for the day."

"Well, my schedule kinda cleared up for the near future. Seems I have nothing to do and nowhere to be."

"Why's that?"

"My wife asked me to move out."

"Oh God, Travis, did I cause that?"

"No, I've been causing it for the last few years. Today was just the proverbial straw. It's not your fault." Jennifer moved to the chaise, sat next to Travis and wrapped her arms around him. They sat there holding each other in the warm sun. Jennifer ran her hand up and down Travis's back then up into his hair. He felt her lips on his neck, so soft and warm. He knew that going there would make his wife furious, and he would risk losing her love and his career forever. He went anyway. Deep down this was what he wanted; at that moment he decided to give in to his temptations and risk his whole world.

Travis fell back on the folding lounge and Jennifer followed him. The kissing was so passionate they began to sweat. Jennifer straddled him and sat up for a moment. She ran her fingers up under his sweatshirt to his chest, back down then under his back. She pulled his sweatshirt up over his head and tossed it onto the deck. She massaged his chest and arms. In turn, he slid his hands under her top and felt her breasts for the first time. With no care about beachgoers or neighbors, Jennifer crossed her arms, grabbed her shirt and lifted it over her head. Travis sat up with her on top of him. He cupped her soft white breast and began to kiss her nipples. Her breathing became deep and loud. She made moaning sounds the likes of which he had not heard in many years. Then a quiver vibrated through her body for just an instant. She gripped his hair and pulled his head back. She looked into his eyes and said, "Make love to me."

Not another word was spoken as she led him upstairs to her bedroom. They kissed and undressed each other as they climbed the stairs. A tall, king-sized sleigh bed with bright white sheets and a down comforter dominated the cozy room. It felt like a cloud to Travis when their naked bodies landed on it. The room, the bed, the house were all so foreign to his senses. It made him feel like another person. This was it; this was what he'd envisioned it would be like to be Patrick.

The hours passed, as witnessed by the light of the setting sun against the wall. The cool breeze blew the curtains into the room and the temperature began to drop, but neither of them wanted to leave the warmth of the bed to close the window. They just huddled their bodies closer and made love again.

Later, Jennifer was lying on her stomach while Travis caressed her body. As he studied the tattoo of the peacock on her lower back he said, "Snake has peacocks on his estate."

"I know. The tattoo was his idea."

"His idea?"

"He makes all of his street girls get a tattoo of a snake on their leg or ass. It's kinda his way of marking his property. What do you call it? Branding?"

"Why did you get a peacock?"

"I can't stand snakes. No way was I going to put one on my body, so since I love those birds so much he suggested it. I was so high when I did it, but I kinda like it." Travis slid his hand over it and noticed it covered two small circular scars.

"What's that?" he asked.

"I had a boyfriend back home who burned me with a cigarette."

"Are you serious?" he asked. She rolled over and lifted her right foot and showed him the bottom. It had three more similar scars on it.

"Oh, my God. Did you report him?"

"Yeah, I did, he was very sick. Please, let's not talk about that. Just hold me."

Cheryl came home around midnight and found the detective and his informant in bed. She just stood in the doorway to the bedroom for a while, smiling. As she walked toward the bed she said, "Jennifer, didn't your mother ever teach you that if you bring something sweet you have to share?" She sat on Travis's side of the bed and stared at him like he was an exhibit at the zoo.

"He's all mine, Cheryl, don't you dare."

Cheryl giggled, got up and headed for the door. As she walked down the hall she said, "Well, I can sleep safe tonight knowing there's a cop in the house."

***

The dresser was different, and the walls were not the right shade. Then Travis realized that the day before had actually happened. He rolled over to find that Jennifer was no longer in the bed. He got up, slipped on his jeans and went looking for her. In the hall he encountered Cheryl, who was walking by in her underwear. She cornered him against a wall, put her hand on his chest and said, "Aren't you married?"

"Yeah, but my wife just kicked me out."

"Don't hurt my friend. Don't promise her something you can't deliver."

"I won't," he said. She still had him pinned, stroking his chest with her fingertips.

"She's making you breakfast. I've never even seen her eat breakfast, let alone make it. She must really like you." She stopped teasing him and kept walking down the hall. Travis watched her nice little ass as she shook it. The reality of the moment was just too strange. He was sleeping with his informant, whom he had arrested for prostitution, and he'd spent the night in the house of her friend, who made porno movies and walked around dressed like a Victoria's Secret model.

He found his way to the kitchen, where Jennifer was busy cooking while wearing nothing but Travis's sweatshirt. Her face was glowing when Travis walked into the room. Jennifer hadn't been this happy for a while. She gave Travis a kiss on the cheek and had him sit at the small, whitewashed table. She said, "Here, I made you breakfast."

He looked at the plate put before him and saw that the eggs were runny and the toast was a little burned. He didn't say anything because he was starving; he hadn't eaten since the morning before. While he ate, he explained that he had to go home to collect some things so he could move into his brother's house. Jennifer sat silent on the other side of the table and watched and listened. Travis said, "Hopefully, by the end of this week we'll have Snake in custody, and you won't have to worry about him ever again."

"But I'll have to testify, right?"

"Yeah, chances are you will. If you do testify I can see about getting you money from the DA's office to relocate you."

"That's fine. Once it's over I'm going back home."

Once Travis was finished, he got up and put his shoes on and collected his kit bag. Standing at the front door, he just stared at Jennifer until she realized she was wearing the only shirt he had brought. They had a laugh together, and then Jen slipped it off and stood in front of him in just her panties. She handed the sweatshirt to him and hugged him tightly. She kissed his ear and whispered, "Call me tonight."

"So, is this normal? I mean, do you girls always walk around in various states of nudity?"

"Well, we're kinda free spirits," she said with a smile.

***

Back on the road, Travis knew no one would be home by the time he arrived. It was Monday; the girls had school and Sarah was at work. He was glad because he just couldn't face her knowing he had ruined the best thing that ever happened to him. He packed for the equivalent of a two-week trip and included his laptop, some books and some pictures of the girls. While he was packing the car, the reality finally hit him. He began to cry and just sat in his driveway for about 10 minutes. When he regained his composure, he headed for the port town of San Pedro just across the harbor from Long Beach.

Halfway there he called his brother, Paul. Paul Jensen was the older of the two brothers at fifty years old. He'd found his success as an entertainment lawyer in downtown Los Angeles but had managed to screw up the rest of his life pretty well. His first marriage lasted about a year and produced a son whom he'd not seen in several years. The second one broke up after he was caught repeatedly having affairs; the last affair had been with his first wife's divorce attorney. He wasn't Travis's first choice for a role model for his girls, but he had a nice pad and an empty guest room. Paul answered the phone: "Paul Jensen."

"Hey, bro."

"Travis, how's it goin'?"

"Shitty. I need to stay at your place for a while if that's all right."

"Yeah, of course. Dude, are you OK?"

"No, but I'll fill you in tonight."

"My place is yours, man. The back door is unlocked. Just make yourself at home."

"Paul, you're a fuckin' victim waiting to happen. You need to lock up everything."

"I know, I know. Hey, does Mom know about this?"

"No, and hopefully she won't need to."

"OK, I've got a deposition in 10 minutes, so I'll see you tonight. And Travis, it's going to be OK."

Travis hung up the phone. It would be nice to see Paul. They only got to see each other a few times a year, even though they lived only an hour apart. He pulled up to the modern three-story house at the top of Twenty-fifth Street overlooking Fort MacArthur. Travis relished this view of the old parade grounds surrounded by homes once occupied by Navy captains and admirals. He unloaded his things into the guest room and checked the fridge. As expected, there wasn't much in there, so he headed to the market on Gaffey Street. He stocked up on pasta, some fish, garlic bread, and a 30-pack of Coors Light. As the young kid rang up the sale, he said to Travis, "That's a lot of beer, mister." Travis just stared at the case on the counter and said, "God, I love beer." He and Paul drank half of the case that night as they talked about their mistakes in life and how much fun they'd had together as kids.

***

Wednesday started earlier than normal. Travis got called into court for a jury trial of a street hooker he had arrested about a year before. She'd picked up two more cases since, and they were all being combined into one trial. She was a nasty black girl about twenty-three or so, and she'd been hooked on crack for at least five years. After Travis testified for the prosecution, the defense attorney started asking him questions from way out in left field. He asked about statistics of streetwalkers related to race and other questions about how a vice detective chooses which women to attempt to pick up. Travis saw where this was going and was getting pissed that the city prosecutor was not objecting.

"Detective, isn't it true that the Vice Detail arrests a disproportionate number of black women as compared with any other race?"

Travis tried to be as middle-of-the-road as possible. "I've never kept track, sir, but most of our prostitution complaints come from predominantly black neighborhoods, so I guess it's possible."

"Detective, do you target black women?"

"No."

"Are you prejudiced?"

"Absolutely not." Now Travis was pissed, not only at this young asshole of a public defender, but at the judge and prosecutor who were both leaving him out there to answer these stupid questions. He was going to have to put an end to it himself.

"Detective, are there any groups of people, any segment of society you don't like?"

"Yes, sir." His answer shocked everyone in the courtroom, and the jury perked up.

"Do you care to expand on your answer, detective?"

"Yes, sir. I don't like people who can't handle driving and talking on their cell phones at the same time and lawyers who ask stupid questions." With that the jury started laughing. The judge quickly admonished Jensen for his comment, and then turned to the public defender in response to his objection motion and said, "Well, it was your question, Mr. Parks." Even the judge was trying to hold in his laughter. The defense rested, and after the jury reached its verdict, his client promptly went off to County Jail for six months.

***

Travis recounted his testimony for the guys, who had now gathered in the office getting ready for another week of sweeping the human wreckage off of the highway. Everyone was there except Jack Barnes, who was sick. After story time, Travis told Joe that he had been in the office for a few hours after court. He'd checked with the lab, and the baggie of dope Jennifer had gotten from Snake had tested positive. Debbie was about halfway through transcribing the wire recordings. He also told Joe how Snake marks his girls with a snake tattoo.

Terry spoke up. "Hey, I remember arresting a white girl with a snake tattoo a few weeks ago."

Joe actually looked pleased at the news, and then he began to play devil's advocate. He explained that the conversations and money transfers were great for a pimping charge, but if they could get Snake on some substantial drug trafficking, he could do some real time. Travis suggested, "Let's start with the dealer he supplies at the Gold Rush. It's local, and we could roll him over on Snake."

"Perfect. You and Jess figure that one out, and I'll have the guys hit the highway and we'll pick off as many white girls as we can. The ones with the tattoos we'll interview on Ben's little hidden camera. That way they can't testify differently if we call them. You know, if we prove that all these folks work for him and he's using the businesses to hide his profits, we could bring in the Feds and file a RICO case on him." The whole office went quiet as the detectives looked around at each other, then at Joe. Joe said, "Nah, fuck the Feds. They'll just screw it up and take two years to do the case when it will only take us two weeks."

When darkness covered the city, the plan was put into action. Terry and Ben both landed some white girls on the first loop around the prostitution circuit. Ben's was named Cherry, according to the name tattooed under the three-inch cobra on her right calf. Not an uncommon name for a redheaded hooker or stripper. Ironically, he arrested her at PCH and Cherry Street. Terry's little princess was a feisty gal named Pandora. Named after the first woman in Greek mythology, she gave a whole new meaning to the evils in her box.

Jesse and Terry booked the two girls in the basement booking area while Ben and Travis were upstairs setting up his computer and camera to record their statements. Jess brought Cherry in first and sat her in a chair next to Joe's large desk. While he cuffed her left wrist to the chair's arm, she looked around the room in amazement. "I've never been in here before. Whatchu guys doin' with me?" she asked.

Terry, the master bullshitter, said, "Detective Jensen here is doing his master's thesis on the factors that make women turn to prostitution. He'd like to ask you some questions. Are you good with that?"

"Sure, go ahead. You already caught me." Terry looked at the computer monitor that was facing away from Cherry and nodded to Travis that it was recording. Travis asked several questions about how long she had been selling her services and what had driven her to that point. After about five minutes he asked, "Do you work for anyone?"

"Yeah," she replied quietly.

"What's his name?"

"I don't wanna say."

"It's just us here, it's not like this is going into your police report."

She looked around the room and thought for a minute. Then she said, "His name's Snake. I don't know his real name."

"Do you have to share your earnings with him?"

"Yeah, at least half. But he takes care of us."

"You mean like bail you out of jail?"

"No, he said that's on us."

"So what does he do for you?"

"He has Araña keep us safe and hooked up."

"Who's Araña? Does he hook you up with tricks?"

"No, we do that. He gives us tweek or smoke when we need it." She went on and laid out how she worked in Hollywood most of the time but Snake had her and Pandora come to Long Beach when it was warm or there was a big convention in town. It almost sounded like ducks migrating.

"How do you get here from Hollywood?"

"Lawrence drives us. He works for Snake too. Hey, look, if you guys try to bust them I'll say I never said this. Besides, you never read me my rights."

"You're absolutely right, we can't use this against you," Terry said.

Travis continued, "What do they call Lawrence?"

"Lawrence," she said.

"He doesn't have a nickname?"

"No, just Lawrence." Travis thought the poor guy must have felt left out. He was the only one without a stupid street name. He let her know that she had better not discuss this with Snake or Araña for her safety. Then she was taken to the women's jail and put to bed for the night.

Terry came in a few minutes later with Pandora. She was a real treat from the get go. She wasted no time getting to the point. "What the fuck do you want?" she yelled at Travis.

He smiled and asked, "Do you kiss your mother with that mouth?"

"Get to the point, Jensen, I'm tired."

"How do you know me?"

"You arrested me last year for possession."

"Oh, yeah. You had a huge piece of crack and you tried to shove it up your snatch when we arrested you."

"I just got out three weeks ago, you're not going to violate my parole for hookin' are ya?"

"Not up to me, but it's just a misdemeanor, so…" Right then Terry held up a baggie of meth in his rubber-gloved hand. Travis asked, "Was that on her?"

"More like *in* her," Terry replied with a sickened look on his face.

"Ah, Jensen, cut me a break," she pleaded.

"OK, then tell me about your pimp, Snake."

"Snake? Why would you say he's my pimp?" Travis pointed down to the tattoo of a coiled rattler just above her ankle.

"OK, so he's my pimp. Why do you care?"

"Does he make you give him part of the money you make prostituting?"

"Yeah."

"Is this Snake?" Travis asked as he opened his folder and showed her Mullen's DMV picture.

"That's him. How the hell do you know about him?"

"We're the Po-Po, honey, we know these things. Don't contact him and tell him we talked."

"Are you kidding? He'd fuckin' kill me for talking to you."

"Would you testify in court that you work for him?"

"Fuck no! He's a nut job. He stuck his shotgun in my mouth once, I thought he was going to fuckin' blow my head off."

"Wow, it was probably the first time the 'F' word wasn't coming out of it every five seconds. So, why do you work for him if he's such an ass?"

"Cause I'm scared not to. If you knew what a sicko he was, you'd be scared too. There was this girl from Arizona working for him a few years ago, she started doing tricks that she got on the Internet on her own. Then one day she was gone. Snake said she moved back to Arizona, but like four weeks later when I got out of jail I was picking up my things from the motel where I was staying, and I saw her clothes in the storage area. The dot head Indian guy running the place said she just didn't come back one night. She wouldn't have left her clothes and things behind. Something happened to her. I tried to report her missing, but I didn't know her name."

"What did you know her as?"

"Gigi. Look, can I go crash now?" Travis quietly nodded to Terry, who took her to the jail while Travis and Ben put the interviews on a DVD. When Terry got back, he had a piece of paper he'd found on Pandora. It was from a note pad that said M&M Laundry Inc. A handwritten note read "Come to the LBC this weekend. If you need me call." It was signed with only an S and had a cell phone number on it. Travis called Jennifer and confirmed that the phone number was for Peter's cell phone.

They were collecting some great evidence to put together a solid pimping case. Travis was hoping Joe was having some luck on the highway with the dope angle.

Joe had gone out on his own to watch Flores at the Gold Rush. Flores came out of his room sometime after 10:00 p.m., just before Joe was going to hang it up for the night. Like clockwork the tweeks, freaks and whores came out of the woodwork. From Joe's vantage point on top of an abandoned furniture shop, he could see the customers trading money and probably stolen goods for their fix. He got on his phone and chirped up the team. "Get out here, this guy's slingin' big time," he said.

All the guys ran for their cars and headed for the highway. Terry made a call to one of his friends on the night narcotics team. Unfortunately, they were working a case outside of the city and didn't have any confidential informants to send in to make a buy.

Joe climbed down from his perch and met the crew at Seventeenth and MLK just a few blocks from the target location.

He described the action he was seeing and asked the guys how they wanted to run it. Terry let him know that Narco wasn't around, so they were on their own. Ben suggested picking off buyers then serving paper on the guy's room. Joe shot that down because they would need a positive lab analysis before a judge would sign a warrant.

Then Jesse spoke up: "It's obvious, I have to go make the buy. None of you guys look like tweekers."

"No offense, bro, but tweekers are normally skinny pukes," Travis said.

"Yeah, but when I put on my nasty jammies I blend right in."

Travis knew he was right. Jesse's nasty jammies were a set of filthy old pajamas that he kept in the trunk of his undercover car. They were wrapped up in a plastic trash bag to keep the smell contained. Every time Jess used them he would spill beer or mustard or something on them to add to the aroma of homelessness. He hadn't washed them in about a year. Jesse went behind his car and changed while the team put a plan together. It was a simple one. Travis would get himself as close as possible to cover Jess, and then Jess would go make the buy. Once he was clear, the team would roll in and snatch Araña. Then they could write paper on the room.

Travis put a beanie over his blonde hair and left right away. The problem with the Gold Rush was its layout. It was a deep, horseshoe-shaped building with the parking lot reaching 90 feet back from the street. It was also very narrow, making it almost impossible to get an eye from across the street where Joe had been. Some times the best hiding place is in the open, so Travis drove right in, got out of his car and rented a room. Flores was sitting on a three-foot-square chunk of concrete that was the stair to his room. It was all the way in the back of the lot. Travis got his key and drove 30 more feet to his room, No. 7. Flores was at No. 10, across the thin parking lot and one room further from the street. Travis carried in his backpack and a box he had in the trunk. He came back out and got the small cooler from behind his seat. He figured the props would make him look like an out-of-towner getting settled for the night.

Once inside, he attached an earpiece to his car-to-car radio and called Joe to let him know he was set. Joe told him to hold on; the team was going to let Flores resume his normal operations to make sure Travis hadn't spooked him. Joe had been around the department a long time and knew not to rush these things. It took about 30 minutes, but a shriveled-up, leathery Mexican rode in on a bike. Travis watched as he handed Flores what looked like cash. Flores took it and went over to a bush. He stuck both of his hands in the bush and fiddled around. When he came back, he placed a very small object in the Mexican's hand. The guy took off on his bike and was gone into the night rather quickly. Flores sat back down on his step and waited for the next customer. Travis told Joe what he had seen and the decision was made to send in Jesse.

A few minutes later, Joe called Travis on the radio and told him that Jess was inbound and about 30 seconds out. Travis always thought of himself as a good UC operator. He could fit in most of the time, but when it came to blending into the street scene of Pacific Coast Highway, Jesse Guerra was the king. Travis peeked out from the curtains and saw Jess walk up to the entry of the motel. He was dressed in the dirty set of blue pajamas and had matching slippers. Over the pajamas, he wore a Levi's denim jacket that he'd found in a Dumpster one night. He milled about the entrance for a while and talked to some passersby. Finally one pointed in the direction of Flores. This was a smart ploy, as Flores might have been hesitant to sell to a first-time customer who just walked right up to him.

Jesse made his way deeper into the parking lot and out of Joe's sight. Travis took over the play by play and let the rest of the team know what was going on. Jesse called to Flores, who was in the shadows. Travis couldn't quite make out the conversation, only that it was in Spanish and soft. Flores came into the open, and they talked standing about five feet apart. After an exchange of words, Jesse reached into his jacket pocket and took out a wad of crumpled bills and a handful of change. Flores put out both hands and cupped them like he was holding water, and Jesse dumped the money into them. The change was a perfect touch, as paying with a crisp $20 bill would be out of character for a bum.

Jesse was doing so well that no one expected what came next. While Flores went to get the drugs from the bushes, Travis started to turn his doorknob to get ready to take him down after Jess walked away. Flores had come back and had begun to hand Jesse a small baggie when Travis realized that his doorknob would turn, but the mechanism wasn't working. He couldn't open the door. A helpless feeling shot through his stomach, like seeing a car coming at you but not being able to move. Looking back out the window, he saw that the exchange was being done, so he radioed Joe that he was stuck and to have Ben and Terry roll into the lot. Travis began to struggle with the knob and accidently pulled his earplug loose from the radio. Unknown to him, Ben and Terry, who were parked at the motel next door, began to pull out and were cut off by a bus that had stopped to pick up passengers.

Joe began yelling over the radio to them to get in there. Without the earplug inserted, Travis's radio erupted with the unmistakable sound of a police radio. This alerted Flores, who looked over at the room and saw the curtains move. A perfectly executed plan turned to shit in the flash of a second. Flores realized it was a sting and that with his criminal record, it would be a multiple-decade prison sentence.

He turned toward his room and began to run for it. Jesse, who was already walking away, turned and gave chase. But Flores wasn't running to get away; he was trying to get to a large knife that was sitting on the step next to where he had been sitting. Jesse was at a full run when Flores bent down then came up turning to his left. Just as Jess lunged to tackle the dealer, he felt the pain under his rib. Burning, sharp, almost paralyzing, he knew he was hurt but had no idea how bad.

Only Travis could see the two fighting, and he'd seen the knife but was helplessly stuck in the room. He squeezed the push-to-talk button on his radio and yelled, "Nine-nine-nine, nine-nine-nine!" One of the most frightening things an officer could hear was the code for "officer needs assistance." The only thing more frightening was being the one who needed the assistance.

Travis placed his left foot on the wall next to the doorknob and yanked it with both hands. The latch tore through the jamb and took a huge chunk of 50-year-old plaster with it. He didn't remember covering the 25 feet across the parking lot, but when he got to the struggle Jesse was on top of the ex-con and still throwing punches. Flores had his left arm around Jesse's neck, preventing him from getting up. Underneath, Flores was thrusting the knife under Jesse's ribcage. Jesse was screaming like he'd seen a ghost. Travis tried to pull him off, but Flores's hold on him was too strong.

Travis later said he'd just reacted and didn't think. Like most officers, he had run scenarios though his mind, thinking up different situations and figuring out how he would react to them. The department's advanced training staff had put together a scenario similar to this, so it was no surprise to Travis to find his Colt .45 in his right hand. Reaching over Jesse's shoulder, he placed the barrel into Flores's left eye socket. He saw the scumbag look in its direction just before Travis double-tapped him.

Some people claim that when you die you see a bright light. In this case, a bright flash was definitely the last thing Flores ever saw. In an instant, Flores's brain stem had been severed, and he went limp. A life of crime was extinguished as his head began to ooze blood and some brain tissue. The deep crimson color of brain blood is a sure sign of death to a police officer. In his career Travis had seen it dozens of times but had never caused it. He stood there mesmerized, watching the puddle grow, then the tunnel vision went away and he turned to Jess. He had rolled over onto his back after the blast and was holding the handle of the knife lodged just under the left pocket of his shirt.

Terry and Ben had abandoned their boxed-in car and came running to Jesse's aid. Terry wasted no time in taking his shirt off, wrapping it around the knife and applying pressure. He told Jess, "Don't move, bro, we've got ya, just hold still."

Sirens could be heard coming from all directions because Joe had broadcast the triple nine on the west division's radio channel. When the first unit pulled up, Ben, who was wearing a raid jacket to identify him as the police, waved at them to drive to the back of the lot. As they rolled past him he yelled out, "Scoop and run, scoop and run."

The two patrol officers and Terry loaded Jess into the unit's back seat while Ben stayed at the street to make sure the next responding units didn't block the driveway. Travis stood in the middle of the chaos in shock, still holding his gun in his right hand. In less than a minute, the black-and-white was back on PCH headed to Memorial Hospital with Terry crouched over Jesse in the cramped back seat, holding the knife in place. Terry did his best to comfort Jesse, but he could see frothy blood dripping from the corner of Jesse's mouth. The responding units instinctively started blocking every intersection with a traffic light between the crime scene and the hospital. The two miles were covered in about a minute and a half.

Joe climbed off of the roof as fast as he could but didn't get to the shooting scene until after Jesse was gone. He asked Travis if he was OK, and Travis replied, "Yeah, I'm fine. Why?" Travis didn't know that he had a fine mist of blood splatter on his face. Joe told Travis, "OK, put your safety on and holster your gun." Travis hadn't realized he was still holding it. He looked down and saw blood on his hand and the gun. He holstered it and told Joe he needed to sit down. Joe called Ben over and said, "Stay with him, you're his peer officer. You go everywhere with him and make sure no one asks him a bunch of questions except homicide. Not even the chief. And get the blood off of him as soon as we get a picture of it."

"Got it, boss."

Joe was barking orders to the patrol officers who were arriving. He was in his element as a crisis manager. Travis watched in awe as Joe took control of the scene and all of the motel guests who had started to pop their heads out of their rooms. There was so much activity and noise spinning around Travis, but watching Joe calmed him. Joe was like a general on the battlefield and left no doubt as to who was in charge. Joe saw four firemen coming into the crime scene, and he stopped them about 30 feet from Flores's lifeless body. "Hold on, guys. This dude's dead, we just need one of you to pronounce him."

A paramedic stepped forward and said, "OK, I'll do it." He took a box from another fireman and walked to the body with Joe. As he was putting the electrodes on Flores's tattooed chest he asked, "So, what happened? We got an officer down call."

"This is the suspect. He stabbed one of my guys."

The paramedic paused and said, "No shit? Where's your guy?"

"He's at Memorial, we took him." The paramedic turned the machine on and let it run for about 20 seconds. He asked Joe, "How's your guy?"

"We don't know yet but it didn't look good."

The machine printed out an EKG strip with a flat line on it. The paramedic tore off the tape and handed it to Joe saying, "This is for the investigators. He's D.R.T."

Joe asked, "D.R.T.?"

"Dead right there," the paramedic said, pointing at Flores. He added, "Tell whoever shot him, nice grouping."

The emergency room at Memorial was ready when the black-

and-white showed up. A patrol officer had been close to the hospital when the rescuing unit had said they were en route, so he'd gone to the ER and told them a wounded officer was coming. Whenever an officer went down, the entire city mobilized to do what they could. The doctors and staff at Memorial had been saving cops' lives for decades, and the growing number of officers gathering outside were all hoping tonight would produce another miracle.

During Jesse's three-hour surgery, the rest of the team walked through the officer-involved shooting procedure. An OIS could take an entire day to process, even when it looked cut and dry. The shooting was investigated by the Homicide Detail and the District Attorney's Office in parallel investigations. The entire area was locked down, and every person who'd been in the area was interviewed. Even if they said they had not heard or seen anything, their information and statements were taken so they could not come back later and say they saw something they didn't. Every piece of brass in the chain of command of the involved officer showed up, including the chief of police.

After talking with the police union attorney, Travis was asked to walk the OIS teams through the events that led to the shooting. By now, news cameras were set up across the street trying to get a good story for the morning news.

Ben asked Travis, "Dude, should you call your wife? She might wonder where you are." Travis didn't want to tell him they had separated, so he pulled out his phone and called home. It was now 1:00 a.m. on Thursday.

Sarah answered, "Hello?"

"Sarah, it's me. Sorry to call so late."

"Travis? What's wrong?"

"I got into a shooting tonight. Don't worry, I'm OK, but Jesse got stabbed. I think he'll be OK but I can't go to the hospital right now, so I don't know for sure."

"Oh God, Travis, does Sandy know?"

"I don't know. Terry's at the hospital with him, I'm sure he's taking care of it. Look, I have to go. I just wanted you to hear it from me and not from the news while you're at work in the morning."

"Thanks. Call me when you know about Jesse. Thanks for calling, and Travis, I love you."

"I love you too."

He walked over to the group of investigators, command staff and crime scene photographers. The walkthrough took about 30 minutes. When Travis was showing the investigators the area where Flores would rummage in the bushes, they found a black water bottle, the kind bicyclists used. The lab tech recovered it with a gloved hand. Inside were about a dozen baggies of meth like the one Jesse had bought. That one was now stuck in the coagulated blood on the pavement. At the conclusion of the walkthrough, the chief took Travis aside, shook his hand and said, "You did a good job, son, I wish I could have shot that piece of shit myself."

Before heading in to the station to file his official report, Travis asked Ben to take him by the hospital. When they pulled up to the ER, they saw about ten black-and-whites scattered around the area, and twice as many officers waiting in the parking lot. When he got out of the car the officers came over and started to congratulate him for a job well done. He felt sick to his stomach, thinking that if he hadn't knocked his earpiece out then none of this would have happened.

He made his way into the emergency room and was told by the head of the nursing staff that Jesse was out of surgery and was in a recovery room. He was still asleep but was going to make it. She said, "It was a good thing your guys brought him as fast as they did because the knife nicked an artery; luckily, there was a vascular surgeon in the hospital for another patient." She led him and Ben to the family room, where Sandra and some of Jesse's brothers had gathered.

"Travis! Oh my dear Travis." Sandra grabbed Travis's hand as she sat in a chair. She held Travis's hand to her cheek and said, "You saved my Jesse. They told me you saved his life."

Travis began to cry as he knelt down next to her. He knew he had fired the shots that had stopped the suspect, but he couldn't help but feel responsible for the operation going sideways. He said to her, "I'm sorry I couldn't stop it earlier. I couldn't get to him right away."

"It's all right; you were there for him when it mattered." She put her arm around his neck and pulled him closer. She whispered in his ear, "We will make it through this."

Travis could not believe how strong she was. He and Ben stuck around for a few minutes comforting Sandra but had to go in and file their reports. They picked up Terry, who was now wearing a nurse's scrub top, and the trio headed back to the station. During the ride back, Travis said to the two of them, "You guys were great. Jesse might not have made it if you guys weren't so quick."

Terry reached forward from the back seat, put his hand on Travis's shoulder and said, "You did good too, bro."

They made their way to the homicide office to file their reports and found Joe waiting for them. He explained that the patrol officers who had searched the suspect's room had found a small brick of meth that had not been opened yet, along with a bunch of other evidence. Hopefully, some of it would point to Snake, considering that the opportunity to turn Flores was now gone.

It took until 8:00 a.m. for Travis and the others to finish dictating their individual accounts of the night's events. When it was all done, Travis had to surrender his gun to the homicide investigators. It wasn't a punishment; they had to take it to the range, test fire it, examine the ammo, and make sure everything was within policy.

Joe and the team went back to their office to put their things away. They all sat quietly for a while, numb from the lack of sleep and the general shock. Joe took a Polaroid picture out of his pocket and retrieved an ink pen from his drawer. He stared at the photo for a moment and then wrote something on the bottom border. Pinning it to the bulletin board next to pictures of the guys and news articles written about the squad, he said, "This is the first guy ever to be killed by the misdemeanor squad boys." They all looked up at it, and at the three uppercase bold letters written on the border that summed up the night: "DRT."

When Travis left the station, he grabbed his Walther from his car and stuffed it in his back pocket. He headed straight for the hospital to see if his friend and partner had awakened. Jesse was in the ICU ward and was not allowed visitors outside of his immediate family. What the hospital staff didn't understand was that every Long Beach Police officer had about 900 immediate family members.

Rudy Anderson was standing outside the hospital room in jeans and a raid jacket. Travis thought this was odd because Rudy worked in juvenile and hadn't seen the street in five years. "Rudy, what are you doin' here?"

"Jesse's from my academy class. We all decided to take turns at his room in case he needs anything and to make sure he gets his rest."

"Good deal, bud. Is he awake?"

"Yeah, go on in Travis. He asked for you."

The room was dark and full of machines that were all monitoring something. Jesse was in the bed and was propped up slightly. He had an oxygen tube in his nose, an IV in his arm and a drainage tube in his chest. Travis got a chill down his spine seeing his good friend like that. Jesse's body didn't move, but his eyes locked on Travis as he came into view. With a soft voice broken by the buildup of phlegm, Jesse said, "Why'd you shoot the guy? I had him right where I wanted him. I was kicking his ass." Jesse started to laugh at his own joke, and then began to cough.

He filled Travis in on the list of his injuries: a collapsed lung, a lacerated diaphragm, and the cut to the aorta. Travis sat down and said, "Buddy, I'm so sorry. My earplug came out while I was trying to get the door open. If he didn't hear my radio this wouldn't have happened."

Jesse said, "If I didn't chase him without my gun out it wouldn't have happened either."

From the doorway a voice said, "We are not defined by the mistakes we make but by how we react to them, overcome them, and then move on." They looked over and saw it was Commander Baker standing there with Joe. Baker continued, "You boys got yourselves in quite a pickle last night, but you got out of it. That's what matters. I remember my first shooting. I was working the west side when..."

Joe interrupted and said, "Commander, let's save that one for when Jess is feeling better."

"Yes, point well taken, sergeant. Well, Guerra, you let me know if you need anything," Baker said.

Joe added, "I'll be by tomorrow, Jess, you get your sleep." And the two left.

Jess asked Travis, "Did you call Sarah and tell her what happened?"

"Yeah, I did, and um, by the way," Travis paused, thinking he might not want to break the news at this time. He decided that Jesse would want to know, so he continued. "We split up on Sunday. I'm staying with my brother for now and I don't know what's going to happen."

127

"Dude, I'm so sorry."

"Don't worry about me, little Pico. You work on getting better. It's a good thing he got you on the left side. If he'd hit your liver 10 gallons of Budweiser beer would have spilled all over the asphalt." Jesse grimaced through the laughter.

"Travis, I'm getting tired. Can you close the curtain?" Travis looked over and saw that it was already closed. When he turned back, his friend was asleep; the morphine was kicking in to overdrive. He waited for a few minutes, and then left Jesse to rest. He wanted to tell Jesse about Jennifer, but now was not the time. Travis had been up for more than 24 hours himself, so he headed to his brother's house to crash.

When he got to Paul's house he took a shower. Even though he had placed his shirt into evidence and washed, he still felt creepy about the suspect's blood getting on him. After the shower he crawled into bed and began to drift off to sleep. Around 9:30 a.m. his phone began ringing. He ignored it at first but someone kept calling. He looked at the screen and saw it was Jennifer, so he answered it. "Hi, Jennifer."

"Travis, are you OK?"

"Yeah, why did you ask that?"

"I was watching the news and saw Sergeant Joe on it. They said an officer was shot."

"Nope, not shot, stabbed. The news always gets it wrong."

"Were you stabbed?"

"No, Jesse was, but he'll be all right. I shot the asshole that shanked him. It was the drug dealer we saw Snake with in the laundromat."

"Oh my God, if you need to talk about it, I'm here for you."

"Right now, Jen, I need to sleep."

"OK, Call me later. I want to see you."

"I'll call you in the morning – tomorrow morning. I can meet you for lunch then and fill you in on what happened."

"OK, I'll see you then. Sleep well."

Some men are haunted by demons when they take another man's life, but to Travis, the killing was necessary in order for good to triumph over evil. He remembered back to what an academy instructor had once said to him. During a training scenario in which a deranged man pulled out an axe and advanced toward the recruit, the recruit was graded on when he made the decision to shoot. The instructor explained to Travis, "A lot of situations can be negotiated, but now and again you'll come across people that just can't be fixed, and someday you may run across one that just needs killin'." Back then Travis thought those were harsh words, but now, Travis understood them all too well. He closed his eyes and drifted back to sleep.

Chapter Seven

The Big Island

Travis was sitting on the patio looking east and was well into his third beer by the time his brother Paul arrived home from work. After dropping his keys and wallet on the table, Paul grabbed a cold beer from the refrigerator and joined his little brother. They watched the setting sun reflect off of the buildings of downtown Long Beach across the harbor from San Pedro. The green paint of the Vincent Thomas Bridge glowed and made it pop out from the port. Not taking his eyes off of the view, Travis said, "From here Long Beach looks so beautiful, so peaceful."

"Don't you work tonight?" Paul asked as he sat in a big wicker chair.

"I got into a shooting last night. So, I'm on administrative leave for three days."

"No shit? Did you kill someone?"

"Yeah, some punk that stabbed my partner. We were buying dope from him when he got spooked and things went sideways fast."

"Holly shit, are you OK?"

"Yeah, no worries here. The guy just wasn't goin' back to jail, so I obliged his wishes and dispatched him to the afterlife." Travis tipped his beer back and took a sip.

Paul looked at his little brother with some disbelief. He had never seen him this callous or detached from such an emotional situation. "Wow, that's wild. Did you tell Mom?"

"Yeah, I called her when I woke up. Luckily, she didn't watch the news, so she heard it from me first. I didn't want her to think I was the one who got stuck."

"Who got stabbed?"

"My friend Jesse."

"The chubby Mexican guy?"

"Yeah, but he'll be OK."

"How did Sarah take it?"

"Well, I called her at about one in the morning and she was fine. I tried her again when I woke up but no answer. I figured she would have called back by now, but I guess she's too busy."

"Do you want to talk about it?"

"No. I kinda want to just sit here and feel numb for a while."

Paul got up, patted his brother on the shoulder and went in the house. Travis sat alone on the patio until well after sundown. He kept thinking about the earplug, the doorknob, the bus blocking the takedown team. Could he have changed the outcome? Could they have approached it differently? The questions continued to roll through his head until the beer stopped him from feeling anything at all.

***

Looking at the recessed lights in the ceiling of the ultra-modern bedroom, Travis could only try to guess how he'd gotten to bed. It was the third bed he'd slept in during the last week. While getting some orange juice out of the fridge, he noticed most of the beer was now gone. He thought, *Sarah might be right; I'm drinking way too much.* He sat at the kitchen table looking at his cell phone searching for the courage to call her. When he reached for the phone it rang just as he touched it. It startled him so much that he knocked it on to the floor. Fumbling around for it under his chair, he didn't take the time to check who was calling. He answered it, "Jensen here."

"Hi Travis, are you doin' OK?" It was Jennifer. Travis forgot he'd told her he would see her today.

"Hi Jen, I'm fine. How are you?"

"Fine. Are we going to lunch today?"

"Ah, yeah. I need to go by the hospital and see Jess first."

"I could meet you there and we could do lunch nearby."

"No. That wouldn't be a good idea. I'll come that way and meet

131

you somewhere."

"OK, call me when you're on your way. We can go to the Brewing Company. It's on Catalina by Cheryl's house."

"OK, Jennifer. Give me a few hours."

Travis headed toward Memorial Hospital over the two grand bridges that separated San Pedro and Long Beach. As he drove past downtown, he began thinking about the case with Snake. He was bothered that he might have killed the best link they had between him and drug dealing. While he drove the transition from the Gerald Desmond Bridge to the northbound 710 Freeway, he called Joe at home. He told his sergeant that he wanted to have the brick of meth that was found in Flores's motel room processed for fingerprints. "Joe, if we could find Mullen's prints on it, then we'd have him."

"I'm way ahead of you, T.J. I submitted the request yesterday and told them to test it for touch DNA also. Do yourself a favor and enjoy your time off. Mullen will still be here when you get back."

"OK, I'm going to the hospital to see how Jesse's doing."

"Take care, T.J."

Travis dropped his phone on the passenger seat and decided to take Joe's advice. After seeing Jess, he was not going to think about police work until he had to go back on Wednesday afternoon, five days away. He exited the freeway at Willow and headed east toward Memorial Hospital. As he passed the Dugout bar at Magnolia Avenue where the team had gotten into the brawl, Travis thought, *It sure has been a hell of a month for Jess.*

At the hospital, Travis parked in the rear and walked toward the Emergency Room entrance. As he approached the automatic doors, he was challenged by a uniformed security guard, so he pulled his badge from his shirt and let it dangle on its chain. He told the guard he was there to see the wounded officer in ICU. The guard let him pass and directed him to the service elevator, and from there, Travis made his way to Jesse's room.

Jess's folks were in the room, so Travis hung out at the nurses' station. He asked the nurse behind the counter how his friend was doing. She said, "He'll be OK, but it will be a longer than normal recovery time."

"Why's that?"

"His diaphragm was severed."

"How bad is that?"

"Well, combined with the injury to his lung, it could cause some breathing problems. Then there could be an infection to the thoracic cavity. The next few days are very important to his recovery. Right now he just needs rest."

"I'll make it short," Travis assured her.

When Mr. and Mrs. Guerra walked out of the room, an elderly Hispanic priest wearing his Catholic collared shirt and blue jeans followed them. Mrs. Guerra was a small, wrinkled woman, but could light up a room with her smile. Mr. Guerra was a rough man of many years with big, strong hands calloused from years of hard work. Mrs. Guerra came up to Travis and said with a heavy accent, "You must be Travis. Our Jesus has told us much about you."

"Yes ma'am. Is everything OK?" Travis was looking at the priest, puzzled by his presence.

"Jesus will miss Mass this Sunday, so we brought the Eucharist to him."

"Oh, of course. Can I see him?"

"He's expecting you." Mrs. Guerra gave Travis a kiss on his cheek before leaving. Mr. Guerra shook Travis's hand and stared into his eyes. The old Mexican immigrant never said a word, but his steely grey eyes communicated the father's gratitude.

Travis entered the room and was quite surprised to see his partner sitting up in bed, smiling. The chest tube that had been draining fluid from his left lung was now gone. "Crap, dude! I saw the priest and thought you were getting last rites."

"My mom had him come to give me communion. She thinks that if you have an illness or a serious injury that the Devil can easily enter your soul through the infection or wound. She's kinda crazy like that."

"No way. All the Devil has to do is hide inside a beer tap and you're as good as in Hell."

"Not a Mexican, bro, Budwieser is like holy water to us." After they both chuckled, Jesse asked, "So how are *you* doing?"

"I'm good," Travis said as he took a seat in the chair next to the bed.

"So tell me what happened with you and Sarah?" Jesse asked. "And why didn't you tell me?"

"Sorry, buddy, I thought I could get through it on my own. She just got fed up with the job and, I guess, me. I have to admit it, I haven't been the greatest husband in the last few years, but the last straw was the morning after Snake's party."

"Why, what happened?"

"Jennifer called me and she was freakin' out 'cause Snake threatened her, and she wanted me to come over and stay with her. Well, Sarah heard the conversation and that was it. She asked me to move out when I was done."

"Did you go over there?"

"Yeah."

"Who did you take with you?" Travis didn't answer the question. "You went alone, didn't you?" Jesse asked.

"You can't tell anyone about this."

"Don't worry, I won't."

"Seriously, Jess, no one, not even Sandy."

"Hand me my water," Jesse said as he grimaced in pain. Travis grabbed it from the tray and handed it to him. Jesse took a few sips and spilled some down his chin. Handing the cup back, he coughed violently for about 10 seconds. Taking a tissue from his right side, Jess spit into it and tossed it toward the trashcan in the corner of the room. It bounced off the wall and landed on a pile of tissues inside the can. Travis noticed they all had stains of blood mixed with mucus. Despite Jesse's upbeat mood, Travis knew his friend was still in bad shape. Jesse regained his composure and asked, "You slept with her, didn't you?"

"Yeah, that's why you can't even tell Sandy."

"Oh fuck, dude, you're in way deep now."

"I know, I know. It just happened, you know?" Travis got up and paced back and forth. He popped his head out of the room's doorway to make sure no one was listening to them. He turned back to face the bed and said, "In a way, I think I wanted it to happen. I gotta tell ya man, she's something else."

"You know if anyone asks, you never told me this," Jesse said, pointing a weak finger at Travis.

"I know. If I get called on it, you knew nothing."

They both were silent for a while, not knowing what to say. Then Jess asked, "So how was it?"

Travis smiled and said, "Better than you could imagine. It's like living a different life. There are no worries, no stress, just passion."

"I think we've all fantasized about it before, you know, hooking up with a hot hooker or stripper but shit, you're the first one to actually do it. Well, in our generation at least." After a few minutes Jesse changed the subject with a more serious tone. "Sandy and I were talking about the future."

"Are you guys OK?"

"Oh yeah, it's nothing like that. I don't think I'm going to stay in vice when I get back to work. I've had enough of it, and I know she has."

"What do you want to do?"

"I don't know, maybe a day job or at least something at a desk."

Travis gave his good friend a big smile and said, "Whatever you decide to do, bro, you've certainly earned it."

"But first I'm going to help you nail Snake."

"OK, bud. You just work on getting better for now." Travis could feel his phone vibrate but didn't want to answer in Jesse's room. They sat and talked for about 30 more minutes. They shared how they felt about the worth of their work and how they doubted sometimes whether they were making a difference. When Travis left, he instructed the officer outside the room not to let anyone in who wasn't Jesse's family or the brass. He knew Jess was getting a constant flow of visitors, and it was making him very tired, so he called the communications center and had them send out a message to all of the patrol units not to bother Jesse for a few days. When he hung up the phone, he saw that he had a voice mail from his wife.

Although she tried to hide it, Travis could hear the concern in her voice. She wanted to know how he and Jesse were doing and offered to talk with him if he needed. He called her from his car and left a message for her on her phone. This game of phone tag had become all too familiar in their busy lives.

***

The Brewing Company in Redondo Beach was a bright relief after the hospital. The dining room on the second floor only had a few customers, so Travis took a table near the open windows and felt at ease as the cool ocean air touched his face. A waiter came over and handed Travis a menu and asked how many would be in the party. Travis told him two, and the young man set another menu on the table. "Would you like a drink while you wait, sir?" he asked. Travis was craving a beer to take the edge off, but he thought about how he'd depleted the cooler at his brother's the night before, so he responded, "An iced tea would be great."

135

The metrosexual-looking waiter began to walk toward the bar and said, "I love your new hair color." Travis was looking out the window and smiled, figuring the guy was referring to his bleached tips. He turned and saw the waiter hugging Jennifer at the top of the stairs.

"Thanks, Philip, I just had some highlights put in," she said. The young man ran his fingers through the tips of her long, beautiful locks and said, "They did a wonderful job."

"Can you get me a water and lemon?" she asked.

"Sure thing, sweetie."

Jennifer made her way to the table. Travis stood when she approached as his father had taught him to do when he was a boy. He pulled her chair out, but she did not sit right away. She cupped his strong jaw with both hands and kissed him, then wrapped her arms around his neck and squeezed him tight. "Thank God you're OK, I was so frightened by the news." He reached around her tight waist and hugged her back.

"Thanks, it feels nice to have you worry about me." After the embrace they took their seats. Philip was back at the table with the water and tea. As he set the glasses on the table, he kept smiling at Travis. Jennifer asked him, "How's school, Philip?"

"Great, I'll be all done in three weeks, and I have a job lined up in Venice."

"That's so wonderful, but I'll miss having you here."

"I'll still wait tables on weekends 'till I have a set clientele."

When Philip went back to the bar, Jennifer told Travis, "He's in cosmetology school."

"Well, that explains a lot," Travis said.

"Stop that," she said as she slapped Travis's hand. "Hey, what are you doing for the next few days?"

"Nothing special, I'm off 'till Wednesday, why?"

"Come with me to Pismo Beach?" She was excited to ask him the question.

"This weekend?"

"Yes, tonight. I have reservations at a little place up there; it's right on the beach. We can go to Cambria or Hearst Castle, or just lay on the beach."

"I don't know, Jen," Travis said as he was looking into her beautiful eyes.

"You need this Travis. We need this."

136

"Let's eat lunch first and we'll talk."

Philip took their order, and they had their food quickly. During lunch, Jennifer told him how she'd taken a drive up the coast when she first came to California and had car trouble as she was pulling into Pismo. She'd had to spend the night, so the mechanic recommended this place at the south end of town. Right on the beach, with little one-room bungalows, it was a gem of a find for Jennifer and soon became her regular retreat from the world. This was the first time she had ever invited anyone to go there and share it with her. Travis was touched by the gesture, and although he knew there were a hundred reasons why he shouldn't, he could not resist the invitation, as his desire to be with her was too great. They decided to leave at 3:30 p.m. so they could enjoy the sunset as they drove north on Pacific Coast Highway. After they said their goodbyes, Travis headed for San Pedro to pack for the weekend.

On the drive to Paul's house, he took Palos Verdes Drive South and drove on the coast side of the Palos Verdes Peninsula. It was a longer drive, but very scenic. The size of the homes and their picture-book location always impressed him. When he was passing the Trump National golf course, his phone rang. It was Sarah. The guilt of his pending weekend lay heavy on his mind as he picked up the phone from his cup holder.

"Hi Sarah. How are you and the girls?"

"They're good. They miss you, of course."

"I miss them too."

"Are you doing OK? I didn't call yesterday because I knew you'd be asleep."

"Yeah, I was. I slept the whole day. We were up all night the night of the shooting."

"How is Jesse? Does Sandy need me to watch the kids this weekend so she can go see him?"

"She's doing OK, I think. I saw his folks this morning, and he was doing a lot better. I think they watch the kids, but you could call her and ask."

"What happened out there?"

Travis told her about the drug buy and the series of mishaps that led up to the shooting. The conversation took so long that Travis found himself sitting in Paul's driveway, parked and still telling the story. When he got to the part where he'd watched Jess get stabbed, he broke down and began to sob into the phone. The vision of his good friend almost being killed while he was helpless was haunting. He knew it would be for some time to come.

Sarah said, "I want to be there for you, but if we were to get back..."

Travis interrupted her: "I know. You need more time alone."

"Yeah."

"In a way, I do, too. I'm not sure what direction I'm going either."

"Whatever happens with us, Travis, I still love you."

"I know. I love you too."

***

The city's crime lab had made great strides in technology in the last few decades with DNA testing, better photography equipment, and the AFIS system that could get print results in minutes when it used to take days. Now housed in a state of the art building about a mile from the main police station, one thing hadn't changed at the crime lab, and that was the need for dedicated lab technicians to fulfill the varied and demanding requests from investigators and prosecutors. The staff at the crime lab was, like most of the department, expected to manage an overwhelming workload while underfunded and understaffed. The perfect oxymoron: *Do more with less*.

Sergeant Marino knocked on the secured door and looked up at the camera in the corner of the ceiling so that the police service assistant working the desk could see who needed to be buzzed in. Once at the counter, he signed the guest book and proceeded to the fingerprint lab. In the back corner of the room was a print scanner. Basically, it was a table with a macro camera lens suspended over it and two bright lights on flexible shafts mounted on each side. The lights could be maneuvered to highlight the composition of the latent print to be scanned into the computer. Sitting at the scanner was Tanya Boyd, a short, plump woman of thirty years with big eyes made bigger by the thick glasses she wore.

"Tanya, any luck on that brick of meth we found at the OIS?"

"I processed it with cyanoacrylate." She could see the blank look on Joe's face, so she used cop lingo: "I super-glued it in the tank."

"Oh, did you get any prints?"

"Yeah, a thumb and middle finger of the guy Jensen killed and a pristine index finger of William Felton."

138

"Why is that name familiar?"

"Because he's the graveyard patrol officer who booked it into evidence."

"Fuck, you're kidding me."

"I see more cops' fingerprints than you'd like to know."

"Nothing from Peter Mullen?"

"No, sorry." Joe sat there thinking for a moment, then asked, "Where is it?"

"Here in my desk locker. I was going to check it back into evidence."

"Can you take the tape off and print the plastic under it?"

"I guess, if the tape doesn't leave a big residue, sure." She pondered for a moment and said, "Yes, yeah, we can do that. I think it could work. Give me a hand."

The two of them put on some latex gloves and retrieved the brick from the locker. The tape on the outside was the brown glossy type used on boxes at the post office. As Joe picked it up, his glove stuck to it. Tanya explained that it was from the super-glue fumes. Using tweezers, she lifted the corner of the tape's edge while Joe gingerly held the brick like a Faberge egg. She stopped for a moment, went across the room and pulled off a three-foot section of butcher-block paper from a large roll on the wall. She spread the paper on her desk and continued to remove the tape. As each piece came off, she attached it to the paper. The sections of tape were all between 18 and 24 inches long. With each piece of tape removed, the contents became visible. After a few minutes, they were left not with a brick of meth, but with eight sandwich-sized baggies each a quarter-full with an off-white powder.

"Good call, sergeant, I'll get on these tonight. I won't go home until I have them all in the tank. Check with me tomorrow to see if I get anything."

"Will do, Tanya, and thanks for your help."

"Anything for Detective Guerra. He's such a nice guy."

Joe went about the rest of his night with the team minus Jesse and Travis. No matter how devastating or tragic something like this was, police work didn't take the day off. There were still whores on the highway, boys in the toilet and any number of illicit activities going on in this city once known as "Iowa by the Sea."

***

The note left on Paul's kitchen counter read: *Paul, I'm going to be gone for a few days up the coast, don't worry, I'm cool. Travis.*

Travis still had mixed emotions about going away with Jennifer because of how sincere Sarah had sounded on the phone, although she hadn't offered to see him or invited him home. He wasn't even thinking about the department policies he was breaking; those were the furthest things from his mind. He was consumed with his personal future and what he was going to do with his life. Once on the road, he felt calm again looking at Jennifer as she drove them north on the Coast Highway in her Explorer. The sunset came in through the driver's side window and warmed her face with a reddish glow. Travis was still tired, so he dosed off for a while when they got stuck in traffic south of Santa Barbara. He woke in time to see the entrance to Jennifer's hidden oasis.

The blue neon against the white stucco lit up the entire parking lot. "Big Island Bungalows," it read. The name was Hawaiian, but the architecture was definitely Art Deco with its curved corners and chrome trim over the eaves of the main entrance. Several varieties of palm trees filled the entry and courtyard. Lush plants filled every void in the planters, and a well-groomed Bermuda lawn separated the office from the 11 bungalows. On each side of the path was a set of plastic pink flamingos. The place was a mix of Hawaii, Jamaica and a cheesy trailer park in central Florida. Tapping one of the flamingos, Travis said, "You're kidding me, right?"

"I know it's kinda corny, but the owners like it. They're real sweet people."

"OK, I'll take your word for it."

When they walked into the office, the owners, Ralph and Emma, came to greet them. The old man was short but stout and had salt and pepper hair, and his wife was bent over slightly from the onset of osteoporosis. They knew Jennifer from her several visits to the "Big Island." Framed pictures adorned the walls as a tribute to the couple's 50-plus years together in nearly every state west of Nebraska. The old man was a retired railroad engineer, and they'd moved every couple of years. Their favorite place of all was the Big Island of Hawaii, where they'd spent a year while Ralph worked as a welder during the '70s.

"Welcome to the Big Island," Ralph proclaimed.

Travis put out his hand and said, "I'm Travis, sir."

Ralph shook it with the power of a 20-year-old. "Enjoy your stay Travis, you two will be in bungalow number eleven."

They took the key and headed down the path to their bungalow. It was the last one and farthest from the office. Jen explained that it was the best because it was separated from the rest. Travis slipped the key into the old mahogany door and turned the knob. The room that lay before them was dark, but Travis could see right through to the beach and the reflection of the moon on the water. Jen turned on the light to reveal a cute tropical themed room that had a small kitchenette next to the entry and a queen-sized bed in the middle of the room.

"This is nice," Travis said.

"This is just part of it. Come out here." Jen led him out the sliding glass door on the beach side. The covered patio was veneered in Spanish tile and had two oversized wicker chairs. It was enclosed on three sides and offered a lot of privacy. About forty feet onto the sand was a fire ring with more chairs. The bungalows were separated by about 50 feet, giving each one the feel of a private beach.

"Jennifer, this is awesome. How much did you spend?"

"Don't worry about that. It's the least I could do for you. Well, that and maybe this." She ran her fingers up the back of his neck. He turned to her, and she began kissing his neck ever so lightly and made her way to his awaiting lips. They spent little time getting back to the forbidden relationship they'd forged at Cheryl's house in Redondo Beach.

Later, the two of them cuddled under a comforter on one of the big patio chairs, watching as the moon glittered on the water and listening to the crashing of the waves. They were silent for a long time, caressing each other's backs and arms. Travis was the first to break the silence. "I remember when I was a kid and we'd go camping at this lake above Fresno. I used to walk out of the tree line at night to the edge of the lake with my dad and just look out at the water. I was amazed how bright the moon was in the mountains with no city lights to interfere. My dad use to say that, in a way, it was like life."

"How's that?"

"It's a metaphor. He told me that when you can set aside all the peripheral distractions in the world, like the city lights, you can easily find your way, even in the dark."

"He sounds like a smart man."

"He was. That was our last camping trip. He died later that year."

"I'm sorry, Travis," Jennifer said as she buried her head in Travis's chest and held him tighter. Travis couldn't help but think how he'd lost his path and wasn't sure how to find it again, or if he really wanted to.

"Since then, I've always been more comfortable at night. I love being up late and working in the dark, both when I was in the Army and now with the Police Department."

Jennifer looked up, stroked his chin and said, "You certainly did a good job tonight."

They spent the next two days going to antique shops, eating great seafood and making love. Travis was almost able to put work completely out of his mind, with the exception of worrying about how his buddy was doing. He called Sandy twice a day for updates and to make sure Jess was getting his rest.

On the drive back to the Southland, Travis told Jennifer about the investigation and the brick of meth they had recovered.

Jen asked, "Is it wrapped in brown plastic tape?"

"Yeah, how'd you know?"

"That's like the ones I saw in his secret compartment behind his stereo speaker."

"How many did you see in there?"

"Ah, six or seven, it's been a while."

"So it's big enough for more than one?"

"Oh yeah, and behind the other speaker he can fit a briefcase worth of money. I've seen that too."

Travis was starting to get back into investigation mode. He explained to Jennifer that he might not see her for a while because he would be busy when he got back to work. She told him that it was OK and that she wasn't going anywhere.

***

No one was in the homicide office when Travis walked in, knocking on the door and yelling, "Where's my gat?" Hearing no response, he looked at his watch and realized that his impatience to get back to work had put him there at lunchtime. He walked over to Trevor White's desk by the window and sat in his chair. White was an old-timer, a real relic. He was a gruff man in his late fifties with the same flat-top haircut he'd had when he'd joined the department thirty-six years earlier. Although he was maxed out for his pension, he stayed on, partially because he loved the job too much to leave it. The guys who knew him knew he also stayed because he was lonely. Eleven years ago cancer took his wife Gloria, and the couple never had kids, so now he worked 70-plus-hour weeks knee deep in the worst carnage the streets could produce. His experience and dedication to the job made him the perfect investigator to work on Travis's OIS.

Travis began to thumb through the set of accordion folders labeled with the name "Flores, Raymundo AKA Araña." Tucked inside was a stack of photographs of the scene. Most of them were of evidence on the ground like the shell casings, the knife, and a small baggie of meth stuck in dried blood on the ground. The next picture was of Flores's lifeless body. Travis just stared at it for a while in disbelief that he had taken a human life, although in the picture, Flores looked anything but human. The muzzle flash had burned the flesh around the left eye, and blood had pooled in the eye socket. By the time the pictures were taken it had been several hours and the blood had coagulated into a dark crystalline paste covering half of the face.

"Checkin' out your handy work, Jensen?" The voice startled Travis, and he dropped the pictures on the desk. He looked up and saw Detective White standing in the doorway. He was taking off his jacket and hanging it on the coat rack. He was wearing a short-sleeved white shirt with a wide brown tie and his gun in a shoulder rig. He was a real throwback to when the department was comprised entirely of very big cops that walked the Pike. "Sorry, Travis, you're a bit jumpy. Are ya ready to come back?"

"Yeah, you just startled me, White."

As White swaggered into the room he said, "The DA investigators said they liked the shoot. It's gonna be a few weeks, but you're as good as cleared, kid."

"Kid?"

"Hey, when you're my age, everyone's a rookie and a kid. Well, I guess you're not a kid anymore, but you'll always be a rookie to me, even though you've crossed over."

"Crossed over?"

"You know, there are those who have and those who haven't."

"You mean killed someone?"

"Yeah, it kinda changes you. I can't exactly say how, but it does."

"How about you, White, did you ever kill anyone?"

"Yeah, twice, a liquor store robber and a suicide by cop."

"No shit. How'd the suicide one happen?"

White grabbed a bottle of water from a small refrigerator in the corner then slid into a chair opposite Travis. He opened the water, took a few big gulps, and spoke. "I was working a one-man car and got dispatched to a domestic disturbance at the New Kennedy Hotel at Broadway and the Boulevard. Do you remember it?"

"Hell yeah, we used to snatch and grab hypes and rock dogs in that place before it was torn down."

"Do you remember the desk clerk?"

"Romi, the one-eyed Indian guy?"

"Yep. Well, I get to the place and Romi is standing out front. He tells me this guy on the second floor was beating the snot out of his gay lover. Like I gave a shit back then if two queers duked it out, but I had to do something 'cause you could hear the screams down on the sidewalk. It was during a blistering heat wave, so every window in that fleabag was open. People were sticking their heads out yelling for me to do something. By the time I got to the top of the stairs, the place had gone silent. I peeked into the hall, and the suspect was standing there with a shotgun at port arms. He said, 'Took you long enough,' and lowered the barrel right at me. I let loose with four rounds from my .45 Long Colt, hitting him with three."

"He waited for you?"

"The shotgun wasn't even loaded."

"What?"

White continued, "He had just been diagnosed with AIDS. Remember, this was back when AIDS was like a death sentence, so he took it out on the guy who infected him by slicing him up and smashing his nuts with a hammer."

"Holy shit, did that fuck you up?"

"Hell yeah, Gloria's folks were coming for dinner and she blamed me for not being able to make it."

"No, I meant the fact that the guy didn't have any ammo and tricked you into killing him."

"Fuck him! I never had a problem with it, and you shouldn't either, Travis. You're a hero."

"I don't feel like one."

"You are, you saved Guerra's life. At the chief's weekly briefing they were talking about giving you the Medal of Valor."

"They should give it to Jesse."

"Actually, they talked about that too."

White spun the chair around and walked across to the far end of the office. There he pulled Travis's gun from a large safe kept in the closet. It was unloaded with the slide pulled back and an evidence tag attached to the trigger guard. White pulled the tag off and had Travis sign it showing that it had been returned to him. He also handed Travis the magazine with only two rounds in it. Travis knew they would test-fire it and save a live round for evidence, so he pulled out a handful of .45 caliber rounds from his pocket. He loaded the magazine, inserted it into the gun and dropped the slide. He then removed the magazine and loaded one more round to replace the one he had chambered. Slapping the magazine back in the gun, he looked at White and said, "I'm back." As Travis walked out the door, he heard White yell, "Be safe out there, Travis."

Detective Jensen walked through the halls of the station and was greeted by a half-dozen cops all saying things like "Good job" and "Glad you're OK." When he made it to his office, he found it empty and dark. Turning on the lights, he saw there was a bit of mail on his desk. There were a few inter-office envelopes, one reminding him to see the department shrink before heading out into the field, but one envelope in particular caught his attention right away. It had his wife's handwriting on it. Travis sat down and just looked at the envelope for a while before he opened it. Inside was a card with a picture of a lone rose on the front. When he opened it a photograph fell into his lap. It was of him and Sarah in Jamaica on their fifth wedding anniversary. On the inside of the card was a note in Sarah's beautiful cursive writing. It read:

My Dear Travis;

I hope you are doing well. I guess our split didn't come at the best of times with the shooting and all. I went to see Jesse and Sandy today. They told me how it all happened. I am so proud of you and always have been. I am here when you want to talk about it. Please call me soon, I want us to start working on us. Perhaps we can have dinner this week or something. I know I bashed you when you left but I admit, I have not totally been there for you either. I hope to hear from you soon. I love you.

Sarah

Travis was a contradiction of emotions, excited about the card, guilty for his transgressions, and scared that he had caused irreversible damage. He slid the card into his desk and looked at the next envelope. It had been sent via inter-office mail from the Civil Service Department. Travis thought it was strange, but then it hit him. It was about the sergeant's exam. It was a form letter congratulating him for passing all of the eligibility requirements and tests required to make the list. The letter went on to explain that the final list of promotion candidates would be posted in the next few weeks. It was mixed news, considering the first people on the list would promote fast and the lower ones would wait. Travis was concerned about that because few people were expected to retire in the next two years due to a big raise that would take effect on the first of October. Those who were ready to go might wait an extra year to bump up their retirement. Right now, he was just glad to have passed everything and put that grind behind him.

Joe Marino came into the office and greeted Travis with a hug. "Welcome back, fucker!" he yelled into Travis's ear.

"Thanks, Joe. How are things going around here?"

"Same sick wackos as always."

"Good, I was afraid you guys would have arrested all of them by now."

Travis's comment triggered a thought in Joe's mind. "Speaking of arresting people, let me check this," Joe said as he started to dial his voice mail number on his desk phone. There was a message from Tanya Boyd at the lab. Joe put it on the speaker so Travis could hear.

"Joe, this is Tanya, I got some prints on the tape strips and one off of the baggies. I think you will be pleased, but I want to show you something. Call me when you get in today." Joe dialed the extension to the lab and was told that Tanya was in the restroom. He told the intern on the phone to let her know he was on his way. When he set the receiver down, Travis asked, "Is that about the brick of meth?"

Joe responded with "Yep," and started for the door. Travis didn't wait for an invitation. He grabbed his bag and followed. On the drive to the lab, Joe asked Travis how he was feeling about being back at work. Travis assured him he was fine, and then Joe asked what Travis had done with his time off. Travis felt a jolt through his body, thinking Joe must know what was going on with him and Jennifer. He sat silent for a moment to collect his thoughts and said, "Just fucked around." Joe just nodded his head approvingly.

Tanya was waiting for them on the front steps of the lab. When the detectives stepped out of the car, she said, "Hi Travis, you doing OK?"

"I'm good, Tanya, thanks." He knew everyone meant well, but it was starting to get annoying being asked constantly how he was doing.

"Come on in and look at this, you guys." Joe asked her as they walked down the hall, "Did you get a name?"

"Oh yeah. Oh, I got a name all right."

"Was it Mullen's?"

"Yes and no."

"What?" Travis and Joe said in unison. They all reached Tanya's desk, where she had several enlarged photos of fingerprints.

"OK, let me show you. I got a few prints from the tape, one on the underside and the other on the top surface. The third lift was a thumb on one of the little baggies. The thumbprint was perfect, so perfect that I decided to just put it into AFIS. Naturally, it came back to Peter Mullen, as you expected. I also ran it in the FBI system."

"So what's so odd?" Joe asked.

"Mullen's only arrest was for a DUI about five years ago, right? Well, guess what, he has another name out of Florida."

Confused, Travis asked, "How's that possible? I checked him out through DOJ and FBI."

Tanya explained, "It's very rare, but I've seen it before. His first arrest was back in the late '90s in Florida for distribution of cocaine, but he used a fake name at the time he was booked. Since he didn't have any prints on file back then, he went into the system as Peter Meyer."

"Why didn't California pick it up when he got popped for duce and connect the FBI rap sheet with the California one?" Joe asked.

Glancing up at the ceiling and hesitating to throw her colleagues under the bus, Tanya looked for the right non-technical words. "Chances are that when he got arrested here in California, he had his license on him. So since he had a California Social Security number, a California license and no previous arrests, someone in the system didn't run the prints in the FBI database. So, he got a California rap sheet as Mullen."

"Are you sure both names are definitely him?" Joe asked.

"Yeah, I had Florida send me his print exemplar card. He's also Peter Meyer. Here's the shitty part. He skipped bail in Florida before the trial, but they won't extradite him from California."

"We don't need them to extradite," Joe explained. "Mr. Mullen will be staying in California for the next five to ten years." He looked at Travis and said, "Time to write your warrant."

Travis was excited about writing the warrant. He hadn't done one in a while due to the nature of vice work. They had a much better case on Snake for drugs than for pimping, but Travis felt that if Jen testified about his pandering and they found more evidence of other girls at the house, his sentence could be enhanced. Travis's mind was all a buzz on the way back to the office; he was trying to organize the search warrant affidavit in his head. Joe was making suggestions, most of which Travis had planned on doing, but it was distracting listening to Joe interject his thoughts.

When they turned the corner, they saw Commander Baker standing in the doorway to the office talking to the other guys.

"Oh good, Marino, I'm glad you're here. You guys need to work the beach tonight at sundown."

"Why?" Joe asked as he walked in and sat on the edge of his desk.

"It's a complaint from the mayor's office."

"Can we work it tomorrow? We were possibly going to serve a warrant tonight."

"Nope, this is on the front burner. I guess a friend of the mayor is in town and was walking on the beach after sunset and saw a guy getting serviced by some cocksucker."

That's when Terry Knight spouted off from the back of the office, "Sure, you build a thousand bridges and do they call you a bridge builder? Nope, but suck one cock and you're a cocksucker for life." The comment got a laugh out of everyone, including Baker.

"Joe, just get some arrests tonight on the beach, OK?" He turned to Travis and asked, "How are you feelin' Travis?"

"Kinda like a bridge builder, sir." Commander Baker set his hand on Travis's shoulder and looked him in the eye. Travis could see the fatherly concern in his weathered face. Baker remained silent, but his gesture conveyed the pride he had for his surrogate son.

After Baker left, Joe instructed everyone to do a quick run on the highway, then they would hit the beach after code-seven. He told Travis, "You stay here and get started on the warrant for Snake's house."

Travis grabbed Joe's shirt as he walked toward the door and said, "Joe, to be honest with you, I think we should let SWAT handle serving this warrant. The house is real big and I'm sure there's gonna be some guns in it." Travis was all business on this one. He didn't want to take any more chances with this case or with his friends' lives.

Joe had known him long enough to know that if Travis wasn't ready to go charging in, then there was a good reason for it. "OK, let's get the paper done and we can work out the logistics later. Tomorrow we're hitting a few places with the bookmaking guys in the morning. After we serve their paper you can cut loose and work on yours. Go ahead and get started tonight, though."

And with that Travis found himself alone in the office again. He spent the first 30 minutes just organizing the arrest reports, the lab analyses and the statements made by the different girls who worked for Snake. Typing was never Travis's strong point, but it was better than handwriting the warrant without the aid of a computer to check his spelling. Two hours into his work, Jensen got a call from Ben. He and the team were meeting at a pizza joint down in Belmont Shore. Travis saved what he had so far, collected his bag and headed for the door.

Driving in his undercover car down Ocean Boulevard felt good to him. It was like being home, or in a familiar bed. He was beginning to wonder if he would ever experience normalcy again, but tonight was a big step. He was doing police work and that always felt right to him.

"How goes the paper, T.J.?" Joe asked as Travis sat down at the table.

"Not bad. I'm through my expertise section and most of the narco stuff. All I need to do now is tie in the pandering case. I think I'll finish it after the beach and take it to Judge Coy when I come in tomorrow."

"You don't want to try and get it signed tonight?" Joe asked.

"No rush, besides, I want to go to the beach with you guys."

Terry asked, "Is the office getting to ya?"

"Yep, I need to get out."

"OK, that works," Joe said as he devised the night's plan. "Travis, you, Ben and Terry walk out on the sand at Eighth Place and work anyone you find out there. Have Terry work 'em, he's never collared a lewd before."

Terry's face showed just how nervous he was. He had only been with the team for a short time and had only heard the strange arrest stories associated with lewd conduct. He was good at picking up whores, but boys were a whole different game. What made it even more fun to watch Terry's face was the fact that he was a decorated Marine; sitting on the moonlit sand looking for guys to masturbate didn't sit well with his macho image.

"Barnes and I will work the parking lot. If we're able to get two bodies tonight, then great, we're done," Joe said.

Eighth Place was one of about a dozen half-block streets that ran south from Ocean Blvd. and dead-ended at the top of the bluff overlooking the beach. Eighth Place had a flight of stairs that led down to the sand and the bike path. Located at the bottom was a bathroom structure made from cinder block that had historically been a problem for lewd activity.

As the three detectives stood at the top of the bluff under the streetlights, they could see a few silhouettes down at the shore break. Terry was fidgety like a kid on his first day of school. Travis tried to calm him down. "Look, Terry, there's nothin' to it. You just stand out there on the beach looking at the water. Just remember, you can't initiate any contact."

Terry's head snapped toward Travis and he said, "Don't worry, that's the last thing I want to do." Ben was sitting on the hood of his car laughing. It wasn't helping Terry any.

Ben said, "Come on, Terry, we've all done it. Besides, you're not truly a vice cop 'till you've had a guy grab your balls."

"What?" Terry asked. "Ah, Travis you didn't say anything about that. You said I might see two guys going at it or a guy wackin' his pud, but not grabbin' my package!"

"Relax, Terry, Ben and I will be right there. We'll go down there first like we are a couple. Give us five minutes, then you come down. Stay within 20 yards of us, and you'll be fine."

Ben took an old Army blanket from the trunk of his car, threw it over his shoulder and headed down the flight of stairs. Travis patted Terry on the back, gave him a nod and turned to follow

Ben. The two of them made their way out to where the sand sloped down to meet the small breaking waves. Ben began to set out the blanket and quietly told Jensen to take a look at the lifeguard stand. Travis could barely see it at first but then realized there was a person huddled in the shadow under the wooden structure. The two guys they saw from the bluff were about a hundred feet apart on each side of the detectives.

"Travis. Travis, lay down," Ben whispered. Travis laid down on the blanket next to Ben. "You look one way over my shoulder and I'll watch the other. That way we aren't spinning our heads around," Ben suggested. They were both on their sides propping their heads up with their hands and facing each other, Travis on his right side looking west and Ben on his left looking east.

"OK, Ben. This doesn't mean were dating."

"Here comes Terry, he's about 50 yards away."

Terry walked to the water's edge and stood there in silence, fidgeting with his hands in his pockets. The only sound on the beach was the lapping waves that were stunted by the breakwater offshore. Ben kept an eye on Terry and quietly whispered the play by play to Travis. It only took a few minutes for the shadowy figure to emerge from under the lifeguard's perch. He was a small black man, about five feet four with a tight Afro. He walked up to Terry and stood just to his left. It wasn't like he was being obvious or anything; there were seven miles of beach in Long Beach, and this guy picked a spot four feet from Terry on which to stand. The suspense was killing Travis. "What's he doing now?" He pressed Ben for an update.

"They're just standing there. Wait, I think the guy reached over and grabbed his package."

"Did he give the hit?"

"No, I didn't see it. Oh, shit, the guy did it again and Terry's just sittin' there."

Ben's phone rang and he quickly handed it to Travis and said, "Answer my phone." Travis was now desperately trying to hold back the snickers as he fumbled to flip open the phone before the next ring. Once the phone was open he said softly, "Ben's phone."

"Ben, is that you?" a female voice said on the other end of the line.

"No, it's Travis. Ben's busy."

"Hi, Travis, it's Donna." Donna Hutchens was Ben's wife and

one of the sharpest dispatchers in the Police Department. "So where is my husband?"

"He's here lying on a blanket with me on the beach."

"Why are you guys lying on a blanket together?"

"We're watching Terry Knight."

"What's Terry doing?"

"Well, we're kinda not sure. Hold on." Holding the phone down Travis asked Ben for an update.

"Dude, the guy put his arm around Terry and grabbed for his cock again, and still no sign. I don't get it, it looks like they're slow dancing."

Travis put the phone back to his ear. "It looks like he's slow dancing with a guy by the lifeguard tower."

"OK, you guys are way too gay for me. When my husband has a chance can you have him call me?" Travis closed the phone and was now lying on his face to contain the laughter. Ben wasn't making it any easier with his little comments. "Dude, he's the 'Dancing Queen' from that ABBA song." Then he began to sing its chorus quietly, "You are the dancing queen, young and sweet, only seventeen, yeah!"

Terry pulled out a lighter and a cigarette as the target began to walk toward the bike path. He flicked the lighter and lit the cigarette. He turned and nodded to Ben. Ben, in return, slapped Travis on the head and told him, "It's a bingo, let's go." They hopped to their feet and quickly caught up to the guy. Each detective grabbed an arm as they announced their true identities. The suspect was cooperative and in handcuffs within seconds, so Jensen headed back to Terry. Wrapping up the blanket in his arms as they walked together toward the bluff, Travis asked, "Dude, what took you so long?"

"He wouldn't give it up."

"What? We saw him squeeze your balls."

"Yeah, he did that quick too, what a fuckin' freak, but I couldn't get him to talk about sex *or* money for the longest time."

"You're kidding me, right?"

"No."

"You bonehead. You had the arrest for lewd conduct the minute he grabbed you. You were thinking of a prostitution arrest. Oh, this is too fuckin' funny, I gotta call Joe."

"Come on, Travis, don't do that."

"Shit, Ben's wife called while you were embracing that guy so the whole dispatch center already knows."

After they ascended the stairs to the cars, Ben sat the young would-be stranger in the night in the front seat. He shut the door and walked over to Terry. "Hey, Terry, your guy's a little confused. He was tellin' me how he just wanted to give you head but you insisted on paying him. I think you made him feel cheap."

"Screw him, he tried to molest me."

Down at the Junipero parking lot, Joe and Jack Barnes had rolled up on a guy and gal having sex in the bushes. It was a homeless couple and they were totally naked, doing it doggy style. Joe kinda felt bad for them as they had nowhere else to go, being homeless and all. They were just unfortunate to be in the wrong place at the wrong time. Three in custody from the beach for various sex acts in public would make the mayor very happy.

Travis, Ben and Joe took the trio to booking so the other two detectives could start on their arrest reports. West division patrol was running a parole sweep, so the basement booking room was packed with cops and crooks. Ben had the place in stiches telling the story and re-enacting Terry's slow dance on the beach. Travis was grinning as the story seemed to get funnier each time he heard it. He was glad to be back with the guys having fun, joking around, back with his brothers. By the next day the escapade would be spread throughout the department and Terry Knight would forever be known as the "Dancing Queen."

Chapter Eight

Gumshoe

Working 'till midnight and then coming back in at 4:00 a.m. to serve a few bookmaking search warrants made for some tired, cranky cops. The six hours of overtime that the team was going to make helped take the edge off, a little. Around thirty five cops were gathering in the patrol squad room for the briefing. A few patrol guys were sitting in the front row and were ready to go as Travis and some of his team walked into the room. More guys were scattered around putting on gear and getting their assignments. The room resembled a classroom with rows of desks facing a projection screen and a whiteboard. Just off to the side of the screen, at a podium, stood Collin Bates.

Bates was the sergeant in charge of the bookmaking branch of the Vice Detail. His crew worked primarily during the day and focused on gambling and alcohol laws, so they didn't do a lot of work with the night team except on occasions such as this one. Bates was a big man of six and a half feet with a thick frame. He was overweight, but you wouldn't want to call him fat, at least not to his face. His hair was as white as snow, making him look sixty years or more. His large, red nose marked the many years he'd spent in the bottle. He was the perfect guy to work bookmaking in the bars. He looked just like a bar rat, because he was one.

Commander Baker entered the room from the patrol sergeants' office. He was dressed in his uniform, but it was short sleeves, not the usual long sleeves and tie most command staffers wore. His loud, grumbled voice brought the room to order. "All right, let's get the ball rollin', gentlemen!" He then noticed two female officers sitting to his left and quickly added, "And you too, ladies." The stragglers in the hall made their way in and found seats or stood in the back of the room. The Gang Detail guys were all in raid jackets with POLICE in big white letters on the back. These guys were the department's type-A personality club, hard chargers and ball busters. Travis wasn't their biggest fan and thought they lacked in brains what they made up in brawn. But when serving search warrants or in a fight, he couldn't think of any better assistance.

The patrol officers were in their blue uniforms and the vice detectives were in jeans and a variety of tactical gear. Travis wore his favorite black T-shirt for warrants. On the back it read, "O-Jay's Bail Bonds, because jail house sex isn't an option." It had a cartoon of a scared little guy behind bars with a very large cellmate and hearts floating in the air. He liked to wear it and see if any of the crooks would think he was a bond agent and ask him to bail them out of jail.

Baker began his welcome speech when the last troops strolled into the room. "I want to thank everyone for being here and helping out today. I know a lot of you worked last night or will work tonight. Sergeant Bates will brief you on the three locations we are hitting this morning, but first I want to remind everyone to take their riot helmets. LAPD did a narcotics warrant last month and one of the bad guys got a round off at the entry team. Luckily, it glanced off the officer's helmet." He turned and began to walk away from the podium but turned back and said, "Oh, and if you're wondering, they smoked the jerk." That drew a round of cheers from the audience. Stepping to his right, Baker motioned with his left arm to Sergeant Bates and said, "All yours, Collin."

Bates got up from his chair, walked to the podium, and plopped down a large three-ring binder. He opened it and pulled a remote control from his shirt pocket. He waved it at the projector hanging from the ceiling and began his PowerPoint briefing. Travis was intrigued by the sophistication and detail being given to bookmaking warrants. He'd done them before on Super Bowl

Sunday and during March Madness, but they'd always been more casual in nature.

First, Bates showed the driver's license photos of his four suspects. They were running a good old-fashioned bookmaking operation, taking action on football, basketball and horse racing for guys who had been banned from the track and offsite wagering. Bates explained further that these four middle-aged guys had been running numbers through about forty bars from Long Beach to Torrance for the last twenty-five years. When Bates was a detective, he had tried to put a case on the patriarch of the group but his lawyer got him off on a technicality. Bates wouldn't admit it, but it sounded as if this were a personal matter. Travis knew a thing or two about letting a case get personal.

One of the members of the Gang Detail asked, "Hey, Sergeant Bates, why go after these guys? They seem like the kind of guys you'd share a beer with at The Tube."

Bates paused for a second, gathering his thoughts as the laughter died down, then responded, "That's a legitimate question. On the surface, this probably sounds like a victimless crime. The problem is these four schmucks have their hooks into hundreds of gamblers who are blowing their families' savings. Most of our tips come from the pissed-off wives. And that's just the tip of the iceberg. Several of their customers have been seriously assaulted for failure to pay up, and the arson fire that nearly destroyed that tweeker bar on Bellflower a year ago, we think they were responsible for that. So, you see, they are actually some crooked badasses. If you are worried about this being a misdemeanor, don't. After today, I will probably have enough on all of them for conspiracy and criminal profiteering." The crowd was silent. Bates had driven the point home and continued with his briefing.

When he put up the aerial photo of the main suspect's 5,000-square-foot house in Palos Verdes, several expletives rang out. "Holy shit, I'm in the wrong business!" one officer yelled.
Another added, "That must have taken a lot of Pick Sixes." Bates explained that the house had surveillance cameras, and due to its size, the gang unit would handle this entry.

Travis just couldn't resist saying something. "You Neanderthal gang boys better wipe your feet, that's not Snoop Dogg's pad."

After a few minutes of bantering back and forth, Bates finished up. They were going to hit three houses in unison, in three different cities.

The highlight of the briefing came when the lineup was read. It detailed every officer's job from perimeter to the order of entering at each target location. When Bates got to the Long Beach location, he smiled as he got to the "pick" and "ram" of the team. The pick was a five-foot-long pry bar specially designed for ripping security screens from doorways. A second officer would use the battering ram to tap the pick between the house and security door. Once the pick officer had cleared the screen, the ram officer would hit the door. Bates looked up and said, "Jensen, you'll be on the pick. Commander Baker is on the ram."

Baker stepped out of the sergeants' office with his Kevlar helmet on, holding the ram over his head like a Viking warrior. Someone belted out from the back of the room, "Get some!" and the room erupted in cheers and hollering. When it died down, Baker addressed the crowd again.

"I haven't told anyone yet, but I will be retiring in a few weeks, so today is my last chance to bust in a door and do some actual police work. It has been an honor to work among all of you, and I couldn't think of a better way to go out." The news was a shock to Travis. Baker had always been there for him, even before he became an officer. He knew this day would come, but not at such a critical moment in his life and career. When the briefing concluded, Travis talked to his mentor as they walked outside to their cars. "So, you think you can still swing that ram, old man?" Travis quipped.

"Hey, rookie, when you get the screen off, just get the Hell out of my way 'cause I'm knockin' that door in with one shot," Baker said as he tapped the metal ram into Travis's shoulder.

"I didn't know you were pulling the pin, sir."

"It's time, Travis. This is a different department from when I started; it's your department now. I'm not a 21st century cop. It's time for guys like you."

"What are you going to do with your time?"

"Well, you know that parcel of land I bought a few years ago above Bishop?"

"On the road to Lake Sabrina? Yeah."

"The foundation was poured last month and the log kit gets delivered next week."

"You're building your cabin? You've talked about wanting a

cabin since I was a kid. Good for you."

"Thanks, Travis. Now let's go give these bookies a wakeup call."

The parking lot of the station was buzzing with activity as the scores of officers made their final preparations in the darkness of the foggy morning. Like modern urban soldiers preparing for combat, they planned for the worst and hoped for the best. The first convoy of Ford Crown Victorias headed over the bridge toward Palos Verdes. The second shot up the freeway to head west to the city of Torrance. Travis loaded up in Joe's car with Baker in the back seat. It was close to 5:00 a.m. when the team members parked their cars in tandem, blocking the quiet and narrow East Long Beach street. Within a minute the officers were quietly walking around the corner toward the target. A few patrol officers broke off to cover the sides and rear of the house as the main body got to the front door undetected.

Sergeant Marino held the line while Jensen and Baker took up their positions at the door. Travis stuck the tip of the pick against the screen's frame. He leaned over to Baker, pointed at the strike plate on the pick and whispered, "Tap it two or three times as I pry, then go around me to get into your spot." Baker gave a quick thumbs-up as he held both handles of the ram.

The peaceful morning was abruptly transformed when Marino began banging on the screen, yelling the standard announcement: "Long Beach Police, we have a search warrant. We demand entry." He repeated it, and a voice came over the radio from a perimeter unit. "Someone just ran to the back of the house!"

Joe stepped back from the door and said, "Hit it!" Baker tapped the pick and sent it wedging between the metal frame and the stucco about an inch deep. Travis yanked on the handle and the frame budged a little. Baker gave it a second tap and the point of the pick went a few inches deeper. As Travis gave it a second yank, he yelled, "Switch sides!" Baker scrambled to get around the handle of the pick and had to duck out of the way as Travis pulled on it like an oar of a rowboat. The entire screen, frame and all, was ripping right out of the wall. Travis dropped the pick, grabbed the frame with his gloved hands and pulled it the rest of the way, clearing it from the path of the team. Baker took his first swing with the ram, hitting the door hard but too close to the middle to cause much damage. Travis said, "Hit it by the dead bolt." Baker did so on his second swing, and the result was spectacular.

Chunks of plaster and splinters of wood flew across the dark living room illuminated by the flashlights of the first two officers through the door. Travis and Baker stood to each side of the door as the strike force of helmet-clad detectives and officers stormed the house. They found their suspect in a back room trying to destroy his computer. He disappeared behind his desk under a blue fog of flailing uniformed arms and flashlights. Hearing the commotion, Travis and Baker rushed in to assist. Baker still had the ram in his hands so he tossed it to his right after he entered the house. It landed on a glass coffee table, shattering it into a dozen foot-long shards.

After the house was secured, Baker was looking at the damage to the doorframe when Marino made a comment. "Nice work, sir."

"Thanks, it was fun," Baker said as he turned around.

Marino was pointing to the destroyed table and said, "No, I meant that."

Baker smiled smugly and said, "Fuck him, he ran from the police. You don't run from *my* boys." Baker picked up the ram, slapped Travis on the back and headed outside as Travis followed him out through the damaged doorway. Baker sat on the steps and took his helmet off while Travis retrieved the pick from the bushes and tossed it to the middle of the lawn like a javelin. He sat next to Baker on the steps. Baker said, "You know, Travis, I always hoped that one day I would get the chance to ride in the same squad car with my son, David. Today kinda made up for not being able to do that."

"I feel the same way, sir."

Marino came out of the house and announced, "I just got off of the phone with Collin, sir. He got his guy and a shitload of pay-owe sheets at the big place in Palos Verdes."

"How about this guy, Joe?" Baker asked.

"He has some hand written records. We won't know for sure 'till computer crimes does their investigation, but it looks good. He has like four cell phones, three land lines and a little bit of meth. I think Collin nailed 'em this time."

***

After the warrants were all wrapped up, Travis took a long lunch to go see Jesse in the hospital. The fifth floor of the hospital was a nice change from the ICU. Most of the rooms were

159

semiprivate, but Jess was able to have his own room. When Travis entered the room, a nurse was changing the sheets on the bed.

"Hey, where's my buddy?"

"In there," she replied, motioning with her head to the bathroom door. Jesse was now able to get up from his bed and walk to the bathroom on his own. He emerged wearing a pair of doctor's scrub pants and a T-shirt from a legendary local bar called Joe Jost. As he towed a wheeled IV stand behind him, Jesse exclaimed, "I'm getting out of here tomorrow!"

"Dude, that's great news, are we still on for today?"

"Yeah, the game is behind that chair," Jesse said, pointing behind Travis. While Jesse climbed back into bed with a few grunts, Travis pulled a backgammon game from behind the chair. They occasionally played it at barbeques and sometimes at the bar, but with Jess laid up, it had become a daily ritual for the two good friends, who sometimes played half a dozen games before Travis had to go. Travis began to set the pieces on the board, and Jesse asked questions about the morning's warrants. "So did Bates get his crew?"

"Yeah, I think he got some good stuff on 'em."

"Bitchin. He'd been after that group for a long time. Now he can retire in peace."

Travis stopped setting up the board and said, "Oh, yeah, that reminds me, Baker's bailin' out too."

"What?"

"Yep, just a few weeks left. He came on the warrant with us. Dude, he had the ram and thrashed this guy's house without a care in the world. Those guys, Baker and Bates, are from another time, man."

"Yeah, like Trevor White in Homicide. That guy is right out of a crime novel. You know the kind we would read as kids. What was it they would call the old cops?" Jesse asked.

"Ah, 'flatfoot'?"

"No, no, it was 'gumshoe,' those guys are gumshoes. Shit, we better put a few of them in the Smithsonian before they're all gone. Those guys are good, they're the kind of detectives that get the job done when no one else can handle the pressure."

The two shared a few laughs and tossed their initial roll of the dice to see who would go first. Jesse changed the subject.

"Speaking of gumshoes, where are we with Snake?"

"I'm trying to get it done, but we keep getting pulled this way and that way."

"Well, at this rate, you might as well wait for me to get back to work and I'll do it for ya."

The rest of the midday chat was spent discussing kids, baseball and how they both missed the Army.

***

Blue jeans with tennis shoes and a black T-shirt wasn't what most people expected a street prostitute to be wearing as she strolled down a busy boulevard, but it worked for Dori Garnett. Dori was a white girl in her thirties. She took care of herself as best she could, but her features gave away the secret of her drug addiction. Any evidence of her former life when she'd been the cute wife of a biologist on the central Oregon coast was lost years ago. Until recently she'd lived in a 12-by-15-foot room and did whatever it took to get enough money to pay her expenses and buy her dope. Now she didn't even have the room, as she'd just been put out by the motel owner for failure to pay her rent. Although her pants covered it, on her left calf was a testament to how she'd gotten to this point in her life. It was a tattoo of a king cobra with the name Medusa written underneath it in script. She had been known by this name for several years now, but covered the tattoo because it reminded her of the man who'd made her get it in the first place. She only knew him as Snake.

Dori looked over her shoulder at the cars passing her on the highway in the late evening to see if any of the drivers were looking at her. Some slowed down but then sped off, getting cold feet or perhaps hoping to see a better-looking girl. Finally her tired eyes made contact with a driver, a white guy in a late '80s pickup. He was around 30 and had terrible acne scars, but she didn't care. Her arm was calling to her for more heroin. She hadn't shot up in two days, and she was getting desperate. His head followed her as he drove past, and she nodded to an empty parking lot at an auto repair shop. The language was unspoken, but in an instant they said so much. He was looking for it, she was selling it, and in her condition it was going to be at bargain pricing.

The passenger door opened as she approached. She climbed in and buckled up. "Drive," she instructed.

"Where to?"

"Just drive and I'll tell you."

161

He pulled back onto Pacific Coast Highway and drove west. She directed him to pull off onto some residential streets. With each turn she looked in the mirrors and spun her head around. This went on for about five minutes until he asked, "What are you doin'?"

"Looking to see if we're being followed." She turned around and said, "OK, you're not a cop, what are ya lookin' for?"

"Head."

"All right, ten bucks. Do you want it here or can you get me a room?"

"How about we do it by the flood control, it's quiet over there."

She agreed and he drove toward Twenty-fifth Way and San Francisco Avenue just south of the Willow Street Bridge. While they were driving, he began asking her questions about her life, where she came from, how she got to this point. It began to make her nervous, but he was no creepier than the rest of the perverts in Long Beach. They parked, and he suggested they walk to the bike path, pointing out that if they stayed where they were, cars driving by might see them and call the police. So, off they went into the darkness and through the pedestrian gate that led to a bike path atop the east bank of the flood control channel. They ducked into some bushes, and she had his belt open and his pants down within seconds. She got onto her knees and took his manhood in her hand. "Before I start you need a condom." She pulled one out from her bra and rolled it onto him.

She began her trade of pleasure and was only a few minutes into it when he said, "Take off your pants, I want to fuck you." She paused and said it would be $30. He agreed, and she lay on her back in the leaves and dirt and started to unbutton her jeans. She was excited because $30 meant two fixes and something to eat. It had been 24 hours since her last meal.

Just after she pulled both legs out of her pants everything went black and her head thrashed backward into the dirt. She thought she had been shot, but there was no blast, no muzzle flash. She fought to open her eyes as he hit her again with his fist. Before she could yell, he put his hand over her mouth and held a hunting knife to her neck. "Shut your fuckin' mouth, whore. If you scream I'll cut your heart out." She nodded, letting him know she wouldn't give him a problem. He positioned himself over her and began violating her. She closed her eyes and tried not to think of what was happening. She tried to think of nice things, like the 15-year-old daughter she hadn't seen in eight years. Now she thought she might never see her again.

"Look at me bitch! Look at me. I'm your new man; I'll protect you and feed you. I'm going to make sure you have all the junk you need." He said this as he was still forcing himself inside of her. Thrusting and grunting, he just kept slamming his pelvis into hers. She could feel the tearing of her skin between her legs and the point of his knife on the left side of her neck. It was so dark she couldn't make out his face, just the moon through the bushes over her head. And as soon as it started he was done.

The tears made her mascara run down the sides of her face to her ears. She thought that this was it, she was as good as dead, she was sure he would kill her. He stood up, then squatted down by her feet. He grabbed her ankle, twisted her leg inward and held it up so she could see her own tattoo. Placing the edge of his knife under the name, he asked, "Medusa, is that your name?"

"Yeah."

"Did Snake give you that name?"

"Who's Snake?" she asked.

He slapped her with the back of his hand and said, "Don't play stupid, the guy I'm replacing." He then slashed her leg through the cobra tattoo and back the other way, making a large, deep X through the artwork. As Dori began to scream, he backhanded her again, splitting her lip. She placed her own hands over her mouth and cried as quietly as she could. Still holding her ankle, he leaned up to her ear and asked, "What's the name of that bridge?" as he motioned over his shoulder using the knife to point.

"Willow, Willow Street," she whimpered.

"OK, then your new name is Willow."

Another slash of the knife and the artful script writing on her ankle was now completely unreadable. Dori rolled onto her side, now muddy from the mix of blood, dirt and sweat, still naked from the waist down. Moving back up next to her ear, he said, "You're mine now. You work for me."

Through her sniffles and whimpers she was able to ask, "Why? Why are you doing this?"

"Because he took something from me, so I'm taking what's his. Now get your shit on and keep quiet."

She pulled her pants on over her bleeding leg and got to her feet. He actually helped her up the hill and back down the path to his truck. There was no one around. She was hoping she could make a run for it, but she now knew he had chosen this location for a reason. He reached into the bed of the truck and pulled out a towel. "Here, wrap your leg in this," he said. Sitting on the curb, she rolled up her pant leg and saw the damage under the street lamp for the first time. It made her sick to her stomach and she almost passed out from the sight. She fumbled with the towel, so he squatted down and helped her wrap it. She couldn't understand why he was now trying to help her. After tucking the end of the dirty rag in on itself, he said, "Let's get you a room for the night."

He drove her back to the area of Pacific Avenue and P.C.H. There he let her out in front of a motel just off the main drag. She began to open the door and he grabbed her arm. "Don't even think about calling the police. I'll know if you do and I'll find you." She just nodded her head up and down quickly. "Do you need a fix?" he asked.

"Yeah, I'm messed up real bad."

"Do you shoot smack or speed?"

"Heroin," was her enthusiastic reply.

"You got a kit?" he asked.

"Yeah, in my purse."

He reached down into a hole in the broken panel of his driver's door and took out two round black balls. They were balloons of heroin, and the second Dori saw them her urges took over. She needed them. She didn't feel her leg throbbing anymore, she didn't care that she'd been raped. She just needed those balloons. He took out a roll of cash and split off $50. He held the money and the drugs and said, "Here, you had a rough first day on the job so take the rest of the night off and enjoy yourself. Now you stay in this place. I'll be around to keep an eye on you. Make me a C-note a night and the rest is yours, got it?" As she began to reach in for the stash, he jerked it back and snapped, "Got it?"

"Yeah, yeah, I got it."

She grabbed the greenbacks and tossed the dope in her mouth. She scooted off to the office window of the motel, slid $30 through the slot and began frantically tapping the small bell to alert the night clerk. She couldn't fill out the registration slip fast enough. The balloons in her mouth were calling to her; she could feel her arm getting warm.

164

Room number four was just like all the other crappy, cheap motels that dotted the central area of the city. The queen bed in the middle of the room was so worn it had a large depression in the middle. The sheets were faded, the bedspread had cigarette burns, and the pillowcases didn't match. A single ceramic lamp stood on a nightstand next to the bed. At the foot of the bed was a six-drawer dresser, at least it had space for six drawers. One was gone, and another was missing the face.

Dori didn't care about how well the place rated with the Auto Club. She went right for the bathroom. She dumped the contents of her purse on the floor and sifted through them looking for the bandana. Neatly rolled inside were a syringe, a metal bottle cap, some cotton and a lighter. She placed the blackened bottle cap on the edge of the sink and emptied the contents of one balloon into it. With her right hand she flicked the lighter until it lit and then held it under the corner of the cap that was hanging over the edge. She watched in anticipation as the powder slowly became a liquid. She began to salivate like a refugee seeing food for the first time in weeks. Once it was melted, she pinched a piece of cotton and rolled it tightly between the thumb and index finger of her left hand. She set the cotton in the cap and set the lighter down. She quickly flung the bandana around her left bicep and tied it in a tight knot using her right hand and teeth. She squeezed her left hand a few times to raise her veins. Taking the syringe, she drew the melted liquid into the needle through the cotton ball.

Five seconds, she thought. I only need to hold on for five more seconds. Sitting on her knees in the bathroom with her feet tucked under her butt, she slowly inserted the needle into her pale arm. She felt the effect right away and it got better with every millimeter she pushed the plunger. When the syringe was empty, she pulled it out and dropped it to the floor with the bandana. She finally felt calm and OK. She curled up on the bathroom floor and tried to enjoy her high. She even tried to convince herself that the horror she had just endured was worth it to have a room, money for food and, of course, some heroin. She cried herself to sleep right there on that dirty, cold floor.

***

Travis grew increasingly concerned because he could not reach Jennifer on her cell phone for several days. He had finished the warrant after visiting Jess, and it had been sitting for three days, ready to be signed by a judge, but Travis wanted to run Jen through Snake's house one more time to be sure there would be dope there when they hit it. Finding Jennifer would have to wait, though; Travis received a call from dispatch to meet with a traffic unit at the East Division substation. Intrigued, Travis high-tailed it out there from the team's downtown eating spot. He found Rudy Kelley sitting in the empty squad room handwriting an accident report. "Rudy, did you call for me?" Travis asked.

"Yeah, Jensen. I was on a traffic stop and this woman walked up and asked for you."

"Cool. Was she hot?"

"Not this one, bro. She was a nasty old thing. She said her name was Aunt something."

"Aunt Mary?"

"Yeah, that's it. Oh, dude, I'm sorry. Is she your aunt?" Rudy looked concerned that he might have just insulted the Jensen family.

"No. Everyone calls her Aunt Mary because she tries to help the hookers on the highway. She gives 'em condoms, food certificates from the mission and even clean needles if she can't get them to kick dope."

"Oh, she looked nasty."

"She *was* a hooker for a long time, and as you can see, it took its toll. What did she want?"

"She wouldn't say, she just asked me to have you meet her at the Blue Bird Motel. When I went to call for you on the radio, she freaked and told me not to air it. Whatever it is, I think she's scared."

"Thanks Kelly. Hey, it's starting to drizzle outside so keep the rubber side down."

They shook hands and Travis headed for his car and straight to the Blue Bird. This motel was a bit farther east and cleaner than most of the cheap places on PCH. It was on the north side of the street, putting it in the city of Signal Hill. In a situation reminiscent of West Berlin during the Cold War, the city of Signal Hill was completely surrounded by Long Beach. Mostly a city of commercial and industrial properties, it was quite a bit slower in the action department than its imposing neighbor, but the police there were every bit as hard-charging as any. On a slow night they worked the highway like sentries guarding a walled city. It was no wonder they kept the Blue Bird free of repeat riffraff with all the pressure they put on the area.

When Travis parked he saw a little black kid riding his tricycle in the long, narrow driveway. The rain had started in earnest, but this kid just kept doing a figure eight. As Travis got closer, he could see the kid was only around six or seven. *Where the hell is this kid's mom?* Travis thought. "Hey buddy, where does Aunt Mary stay?" The little guy stopped and looked Travis over like a seasoned streetwise teenager.

"She lives in number eight, are you her new boyfriend?"

"Nope, just an old friend." Travis started past the kid deeper into the motel lot when the kid asked, "Hey mister, why's your hair white like that? Are you a bi-no?"

"A bi-no?"

"Yeah, you know the people with white hair but aren't old yet like my nana."

"Oh, you mean albino. No, I'm not an albino. I bleached my hair."

"Wow that's cool, and you didn't get any on your shirt. That's good, 'cause I spilled the bleach once and my mom's dress got white spots all over it."

Travis thought he could stand there all night and listen to this kid ramble on, but the rain and his curiosity told him to find Mary quick. He trotted the rest of the way to the room, pulling his coat closed to keep the rain out. He knocked on the door and saw the curtains move a bit. After unlocking the door, Mary opened it and said, "That was quick, Jensen. I figured you would come by tomorrow." Travis didn't wait for an invitation; he just walked into the room. It was small and toasty inside. The heater was working overtime, and the leaky window added a musty smell to the scent of several candles burning on the nightstand.

"What's up with the drama, Mary?"

"Hey, do you want a beer?"

"Mary, I'm kinda busy on a case right now." Travis leaned against the dresser and folded his arms, waiting to hear what was so important.

"Travis, some of the girls have been talking about a guy roughing them up."

"Why don't they call the police?"

"You know that wouldn't do any good. A hooker reporting

getting slapped around, they would just say it's a business dispute. Besides, a few of them think it could be a cop."

"Whoa, wait a minute. Why do they say that?"

"Because he keeps pumping them for information about a girl named Liz or Elizabeth. Don't worry, I told them he's not a cop."

"How do *you* know, Mary?"

"You vice guys are tricky and mean sometimes, but I've never known any of ya to hit a girl unprovoked. This guy can't be one of you."

"So what does he want with this Liz?" Travis asked.

"I don't know, but he's taking it out on every working girl he sees. And Travis, the word is he's making some of them work for him."

"Do you know his name?"

"No."

"White guy, black guy, what are we talkin' about?"

"He's a white guy with acne scars. That's all I know. I guess he sounds like a redneck."

"OK, Mary, I'll look into it. I might have some patrol guys work it, I'm about to do a big case."

"Thanks, Jensen."

Travis opened her little refrigerator, pulled out a can of beer and asked, "Mind if I take one for the road?"

"You can't drink and drive," she said.

"Call the police," he replied as he popped the tab and headed out the door into the rain.

Travis drove the main streets checking the hot spots for any action, but the rain was keeping everyone inside. He drove PCH, Anaheim Boulevard, Seventh Street and Alamitos Avenue. He was about to call it a night when he saw Lawrence Washington pull in to the Gold Rush, the same place where Travis had shot Raymundo Flores just a few weeks before. Travis parked across the street and watched. Washington was in a long trench coat and had an umbrella over his head. He knocked on a door and spoke to a girl who answered. They only talked a few seconds, and he was off to another door. A black girl answered there and talked to him for a minute or two. When he left the parking lot, he walked down the street and spoke to some crack-heads hanging out in front of the liquor store at Martin Luther King and PCH. While Lawrence was talking with them, one of the crack-heads pointed down the street.

Lawrence was interviewing these guys like a cop would. He was looking for someone or something, and Travis knew it couldn't be a coincidence that they were both out on a rainy night asking questions and searching, both beating the bushes.

Travis did his best to follow Lawrence but eventually lost him near the freeway around midnight, so Travis headed in for the night. While driving back to the station, Travis noticed he had missed a call from Jennifer. It was late, so he decided to call her when he came back to work the next day.

***

Lawrence stuck around the highway and found himself at PCH and Pacific Avenue in the heart of central Long Beach, a busy crossroads that never slept. In this city, renowned for its diversity of people and culture, there existed some areas where they just didn't all get along. This was one of those places, the intersection of Crime and Chaos.

Lawrence approached a few panhandlers in the gas station on the southeast corner. He was driving his pristine '97 Firebird painted black with gold trim all around. The first panhandler came over and offered to wash his windows even though it was raining. She was a small black woman with dreadlocks under a floppy hat, pants that were way too big, and skin wrinkled beyond her age. It took a while for Lawrence to figure out that she was a woman. "Hey bro, come here, I've got a question for ya," Lawrence said.

"I'm not a bro, my name's Carla."

"Oh, I's sorry. Can you tell me if you've seen any new white guys around here? Like, say, in the last few weeks or so?"

"Yeah, the cowboy guy. I don't know where he stays, but he's been down here a bit."

"What's da white boy drivin'?"

"I've seen him in a truck and a small car like a Toyota or somethin'. The last time I saw him he was at the Boardwalk Motel." She pointed over her shoulder down Pacific toward Seventeenth.

"Here, thanks for da help," Lawrence said as he handed her a couple of five-dollar bills.

When he got to the motel, he pulled his car into the back of the lot and sat there for a while in the darkness to see whether the mystery man would show. Through the pounding rain on his windshield, he could only make out figures as they darted back and

169

forth through the night. One in particular caught his attention, so he turned on the wipers. With the glass clear for a second, he could see it was Dori Garnett running to her room with a grocery bag in her arms. Lawrence left his car and followed her to the door. She never saw him until he pushed her through the open door and quickly closed it behind them.

"Holy shit, Lawrence, I thought I was getting jacked. What the hell are you doing?"

"Where you been, Medusa? Snake doesn't like it when he doesn't hear from his girls."

"I'm not one of his girls, Lawrence, he turned me out."

"He cut you off, but you still belong to him."

"All he did for me was make me a dope fiend. I don't owe his ass nothin'."

Just then the door burst open and Lawrence turned to see the flash of a figure silhouetted by the lights of the parking lot. The rain-drenched figure slammed Lawrence against the wall, reached back and punched him in the left eye socket. Lawrence was on the floor looking up at the redneck through his one good eye. He took another hit and was struggling to hang on to consciousness.

"Listen, nigger, she works for me now, so stay the fuck away."

Lawrence grimaced as he spoke. "You fucked up cracker, Snake's gonna kill your ass."

"Get your shit, Willow, we gotta fly," the cowboy instructed as he kept an eye on Lawrence rolling on the floor. Dori dashed back and forth, grabbing what few possessions she had and stuffing them into her purse and a trash bag. When Dori headed out the door, Cowboy reared back and delivered a kick into Lawrence's ribcage with his boot before walking out himself. The snapping sound confirmed what Lawrence felt. His ribs were broken, and he still couldn't see out of his left eye. He couldn't believe someone could get the jump on him like that. He was pissed, and in his mind it wasn't over.

Getting to his feet and then to the door, Lawrence was just in time to see the two about to turn the corner of the building headed to Pacific Avenue. He let one fly into the night. The shot from his .357 Magnum was tremendously loud, and the bullet zipped past the heads of Cowboy and Dori, who were now running north on Pacific trying to get to their car. Cowboy flung open the door to a Toyota Camry and shouted, "Get in, Willow!" He jumped into the driver's side and jammed a shaved key into the ignition of the stolen car. *Kaboom, Kaboom,* was followed by the shower of glass flying through the passenger compartment of the car. Lawrence was staggering behind them, holding his side with his left hand and shooting with his right.

Cowboy put the car in reverse and hit the accelerator, sending the small car up onto the sidewalk and striking Lawrence as he tried to step to his right to avoid it. The impact sent him tumbling through a hedge of bushes in front of an abandoned dental office. He came up firing two more rounds, but the Camry was already to Pacific Coast Highway turning east.

Lawrence knew that the shots would bring the police, so he climbed out of the hedge and made his way to his own car. Soaking wet and now bleeding from his eye, Lawrence fumbled for his keys, dropping them in the parking lot. Once he made it into the car he took a moment to wipe his face so he would be able to see. He started the car and drove out the motel's rear driveway into the dark alley and headed south. When he got to Sixteenth and Long Beach Boulevard, he saw the first patrol unit rolling code three toward the motel. Lawrence headed for Naples and the safety of Snake's house.

As the patrol units descended on the motel, the rain began to lift. They couldn't find any victims of the shooting but did notice that the door to room number four had been kicked in and that the room was a total mess. Officer Vu Tran went to the office to ask the manager about the occupants.

Tran was an intelligent cop, kind of a timid guy, but a real thinker. He'd come to the United States from Cambodia as a 3-year-old kid. Most of his accent was gone, but his fluency in his native language was a huge help in a city with nearly 40,000 Cambodians. His linguistic skills would be of no help to him tonight, as the motel owner, like most in Long Beach, was a member of the Patel clan, a large group of immigrants from India who had gone into the motel business. "Mr. Patel, did you see what happened?"

In a heavy Indian accent, he answered, "Oh no, I heard boom boom and got under da table."

"Can you tell me who's supposed to be in number four? The door's been kicked in."

"God damn it, it was dat little whore Dori. I see her and her boyfriend running out just before da boom boom."

"I thought you said you didn't see anything."

"I don't see da person shooting, but I see Dori and her new man run just before d'ey were shot at."

"How do you know they were the ones being shot at?"

"'Cause d'ey were running like dis." Patel hunched over and demonstrated how someone runs while crouched.

"OK, Mr. Patel, we'll let you know when you can secure the door, you'll need some plywood or something 'cause it's split down the middle."

Tran and the other officers canvassed the area but found no witnesses, or at least no willing witnesses. It had been an hour and still no victim had come forward, and no gunshot victims had shown up at any of the hospitals. Tran ended up filing a crime report anyway, just in case this Dori gal ended up in a ditch someplace. When he was done with the report he shot an email off to the sergeants of homicide, violent crimes and vice, figuring they would all be interested in the evening's events.

***

The fog, combined with the raindrops, made it hard to drive. Add the fact that Lawrence's eye was now swollen shut, and it was a miracle that he could drive at all. While driving through the shore area he became nervous, terrified that someone saw him or got his license plate. Driving east on Second Street, it seemed his was the only car on the road. The bars had closed an hour before, and only a few stragglers were left at an all-night coffee shop. As he saw a squad car going the other way, he thought he would have to make a run for it if they tried to pull him over. He watched intently in his mirror as the black-and-white kept heading west.

He made it to the island and drove to Snake's house undetected. He got out of his car and entered the code to open the gate on a keypad that was hidden by the ivy on the wall. Mullen was awake and heard the modified exhaust of Lawrence's car. He went downstairs to see why Lawrence had come by so late.

After parking his car on the side of the garage, Lawrence made his way to the front door, where a robe-clad Peter Mullen met him. "What the fuck happened to you?" he asked as he tried to get a closer look at his enforcer's injuries.

"I gots jumped by a mother fuckin' psycho. How bad is it? I can't sees nothin'."

172

Mullen stepped aside and took Lawrence by the arm. "Come in here so I can turn on the light." Once inside the house, Mullen turned on the chandelier of the grand entry. Only then did he see the damage. The eye had swollen to the size of a baseball, red and seeping blood from the enlarged slit. Mullen said, "It looks like a baboon's ass and just about as big. Who got ya?"

Lawrence began to tell the story as Peter helped him to the bar so he could get some ice. "Well, I been lookin' all night for the girls that haven't been payin', I found Medusa at the Boardwalk on Pacific." Peter was filling a wet bar towel with ice. Frustrated that Lawrence had stopped telling the story, he asked,

"And? What, did she kick your ass?"

"No. I forgot about my ribs, I think they're broke." He grimaced as he sat in a low chair. "So I had her cornered in da room when dis white devil broke in and put a wup on my ass. I didn't have a chance, dat motherfucker took a cheap shot then he kicked me in da ribs. But I took a few shots at them."

"What do you mean by a shot?" Peter asked.

"I popped a few caps on 'em."

"Did anyone see you? Did you hit one of them?" Peter was getting more concerned about his operation than the health of his lieutenant.

"No, it was rainin' like piss, so no one was out. And boss, dis guy said she works for him now."

"So it's true. Someone's trying to cut in on us."

"Why don't we just cut da street girls loose, Snake? Dem bitches are just a pain in da ass as it is."

"Them bitches, as you call them, are important to us. They bring us easy money for one, but they perform a more important role. Because every pervert, college kid and housewife that comes down to *your* hood to score crank will ask a white hooker for a connection long before they'll talk to a Negro or a Mexican. And those girls send them to our people. You see? They're like the fuckin' Wal-Mart greeter of the ghetto, so we need them to be loyal even if we need to beat it into them."

"So what's we gonna do?"

"We're gonna find this asshole and show him his place on the food chain. First we need to get you fixed up."

Lawrence made his way to the couch while Mullen went to the garage and pulled his Hummer out into the driveway, allowing him to put Lawrence's car in the garage and out of sight. By dawn, a doctor had arrived at the estate to take care of Lawrence's eye and give him something for the pain. House calls were mostly a thing of the past, but a married medical professional with a $3,000 a month habit for call girls could be very accommodating when called upon.

***

Travis got a call from Joe the next day as he was driving to the station. "T.J., how late did you hang around last night?"

"'Till 2:30 or so."

"There was a shooting last night at the Boardwalk at 2:00 a.m., and I guess a whore named Dori was involved, but she's in the wind. Doesn't she work for Snake?"

"I think so. Yeah, she goes by Medusa, I think."

"Well, someone was gunning for her and her boyfriend last night."

"You know, last night I talked with Aunt Mary and she was telling me about a new white guy roughing up the girls on the highway looking for a 'Liz,' and I saw Lawrence Washington out pounding the bricks looking for clues. I bet he had something to do with it. Shit, I had just logged off the radio and went ten-seven."

"Well, according to the report the guy *she* was with was white, so that would make Washington the shooter if he was involved."

"Wow, this is getting bigger."

"I want the warrant for Snake's place signed today. Also, we'll be handing it to SWAT like you suggested. There's just too much of a chance for guns on this one."

"OK, I was hoping to run Jennifer through one last time, but you're right, we need to take this guy off quick."

When he hung up the phone, Travis immediately called Jennifer, remembering he'd missed her call the night before. When she picked up the phone she greeted him with, "I miss you."

Travis said, "I tried calling you last night. I was getting a little worried."

"I'm sorry. I was out with Cheryl dancing and didn't hear the phone."

"And the previous three days?"

"Sorry. I've been dancing a lot at The Powder Room lately. I want to get some money together before I head home after this is all over. Can I see you tonight?" she asked.

174

"I miss you too, but things are getting crazy around here. There's some guy on the loose roughing up the girls on the street. I think he's trying to horn in on Snake's territory or something, and he's looking for a girl named Liz. Do you know her?"

"What was her name?"

"Liz or Elizabeth perhaps." Jennifer was quiet and did not respond to Travis. "Jen, does that name mean something?"

"No, I don't remember hearing that name. She's not a call girl that I know of, she must be a street girl. Who's this guy?"

"I don't know yet, but I'll be busy with this for a while." Travis heard the call waiting buzz on his phone and took it away from his ear to look at it. His wife Sarah was calling. "Well, what does he look like? Is he from Long Beach?" Jen asked. Travis had to let his wife go to voicemail.

"Jen, I don't know yet. Boy, you sound like a reporter."

"Sorry, I was just wondering."

"He's probably from out of town 'cause he's been described as a redneck. Why so many questions, do you know someone who has it in for Snake?"

"No, no one but the girls that he's used, but they're all too afraid of him."

"OK, just stay clear of Long Beach for a few days. This should be over soon."

"Be careful, Travis."

As he hung up and pressed the auto dial for his wife's number, he couldn't help but wonder how he'd functioned back when he didn't own a cell phone. Sarah was calling with news of the girls' accomplishments in school and to tell Travis about a burned-out light she needed him to replace the next time he was over. Then she asked, "Can I see you tonight after work?" *Holy crap*, Travis thought. He was glad she wanted to see him, but with everything going on, this was the last thing he needed at that moment. He was going to have to let her down easy, but then his heart took over and he said, "Sure, do you want me to come over?"

"I have a sitter lined up. Why don't we meet in Seal Beach?"

"OK, I'll call you when I get close to getting off. I worked a lot last night, so I can take off early I think, but no promises. Things are busy. Oh, by the way, Jesse went home a few days ago."

"That's great. I'll wait for your call, Travis. I love you." Her voice was different; something was going on, he thought. Did she find out about Jennifer? Did she want him back? Was she serving him with papers? So much stuff was happening all at once, so much pressure was building up. When he crested the last bridge to downtown Long Beach, he could see a cruise ship docked in the harbor. He fantasized about jumping on board and heading to Mexico. But he remembered what Jesse had said about a good gumshoe being able to take the pressure when most couldn't. The thought of making a run for the border quickly faded from his mind and was replaced by thoughts of the task at hand.

Chapter Nine

Death Tape

Travis's day was spent in the courthouse getting his search warrant reviewed by the Honorable Judge Walter Harrison. The 30-year veteran of the bench was a graduate of Oxford University and Harvard Law School. He was known as a difficult jurist to work with when it came to a warrant, but Travis went to him just for that reason. If it passed muster with him, it would stand up to any defense attorney. Besides, Travis's favorite judge, Judge Coy, wasn't available. "This is well-written, son, you have plenty of probable cause for the search and arrest, but you haven't illustrated why you want night service." Travis felt like a schoolboy who knew the right answer but had forgotten to put it on the test.

"You're right, sir, I forgot to explain the security systems and the likelihood for us to encounter armed suspects. I'll go fix it and be back in 30 minutes."

"OK, I'm here 'till four o'clock, Detective."

Travis reached across the large mahogany desk and took the warrant from the judge. "Thank you, sir. I'll be right back." He left the judge's office and passed through the courtroom to the main hall. The police station was just across the parking lot, so he was at his desk in minutes adding the forgotten details about the possibility for gun violence and the sophistication of the estate compound's security. Travis printed out a new copy and took it to the team secretary, Debbie, to proofread. Once she gave it her blessing, he signed his affidavit and was off to the court. When he got to Harrison's courtroom, the judge was on the bench hearing an evidentiary motion.

Travis took a seat in the gallery and watched the proceedings. The defense attorney was trying to get evidence thrown out from a pat-down search, but it was clear he hadn't done his homework. He cited some case law, and Judge Harrison stopped him in mid-argument and slammed him for citing a case that was not relevant. Travis thought, *How the hell can he remember all those legal decisions and procedural laws off the top of his head?* The motion was denied with the speed of Wild West justice. As Harrison stood to go to his chambers, he waved to Travis to follow him. After a few minutes reading the additions to the document, Harrison took his fountain pen from its desk holder, signed it and said, "Good luck, and be safe."

Now with the paper in hand, the team could get rolling on hitting the house with the assistance of the SWAT team. Detective Jensen made a few copies of the warrant and took one to Sergeant Dale King. Dale had been one of Travis's first training officers when he graduated from the academy. A tall, thin man with a chiseled jaw and arms to match, King was the tactical guru of the department and the senior sergeant in charge of the SWAT team. When Travis began to give the background on the case, King interrupted him and said, "Marino gave me the heads-up last night. We can go in two days if that's good for you."

"Yeah, that's great."

"Do me a favor, Travis. Can you diagram the layout of the house?"

"I can do most of the first floor, but if you give me a day, I can get the whole house from my informant."

"Perfect. Get it to me by tomorrow night if you can."

"Sure thing, Dale, and here are some pictures Guerra and I took of the outside." Travis gave him a few 8-by-10-inch prints, shook hands and headed for the door. As Travis was opening the door King said, "Jensen, you sure have come a long way from that first night when you left your kit bag on top of the cruiser as we drove out of the station." Travis didn't look back, but dropped his head in shame and continued for the parking lot. In police work, a training officer would never let his rookies forget their mistakes or embarrassing moments, not even two decades later.

When Travis got back to his office, the guys were already in the field except for Joe. He'd sent them to keep an eye out for Dori and this mystery cowboy. Joe was getting ready to head off to Jesse's house to give him some worker's compensation paperwork from personnel. Although they were friends, Travis always felt guilty about asking for time off or to get out early. "Hey Joe, Dale King has the warrant, and I was wondering if I could head out early tonight. If I can't, I understand, but my wife got a sitter and, well, I wanted to..." Without hesitation, Joe said, "Get out of here. Go on, family comes first."

"Thanks, Joe. Say hi to Jess for me."

***

The page of his notebook was still blank. Travis had been staring at it for 10 minutes as he sat alone at a small back table of the pub. All of his thoughts about what had gone wrong in their marriage bounced around his head like a pachinko ball, but he wanted to write them down so as not to forget them when Sarah arrived. With his head down over the book, he never saw her walk over to the table. "Just the facts, ma'am," a female voice said in a terrible impression of Jack Webb. Travis looked up to see his beautiful wife. She smiled down on him as their eyes met. "Taking field notes, Detective?" she kidded. He stood, and they embraced tightly for about a minute, each of them hurting inside for different reasons but both ready to move forward. Travis pulled out her chair and asked to take her coat. She was touched by the gesture and obliged. "So what were you working on?" she asked.

"Well, actually, on what to say to you."

"Ha. I had the same problem at work today."

The first half-hour of dinner was spent discussing the girls and their schedules for soccer and school. Travis filled her in on the sergeant's exam, Jesse's progress, and the case he was working. That's when the conversation got more serious. Sarah set her fork down and asked, "Is that the case with the woman informant who called you?"

"Yeah, it's also tied into the guy I shot." Travis did his best to get the focus off of Jennifer.

"Travis, did you sleep with her?" Sarah asked softly. The feeling hit Travis quickly, like the jitters you got when you came within inches of being hit by a truck. Right now, Travis was thinking he liked his chances better with the truck. He didn't answer her right away and she said, "I know. A woman just knows."

"Now what then?" he asked.

"We're both to blame, Travis. You drove me away with the drinking and I drove you away by turning within. Besides, I faltered too." The revelation that they'd both had affairs paralyzed Travis's thoughts. He didn't know what to say or do. Sarah continued, "It was a one-time thing with someone from my old work, a mistake, and I hope you can forgive me." He couldn't believe it; she was asking *him* for forgiveness. After everything he had put her through, she wanted forgiveness. Travis still didn't know what to say, so he reached across the table, took her hand and squeezed it. "Do you still love me?" Travis asked.

"Of course I do, I always will."

"Then I can forgive you, if you can forgive me." They sat there holding hands and both shedding tears as they looked at each other. When their waitress came to the table, they both snapped out of it and eventually finished their meal. They silently strolled Main Street toward the pier holding hands and stopping to kiss on occasion. Arriving at Sarah's car, Travis told her that he would be working this case for the next week and wanted to take some time off when it was over. She looked at the ground; she'd heard it before. She looked back up and brushed his hair with her fingers and said, "We'll talk." They kissed goodbye, and she drove off for home. Travis headed in the opposite direction toward his brother's house in San Pedro. On the way, he called Jack Barnes to see if there was any progress.

"Hello, Jack here."

"Jack, Travis. You guys get anything?"

"Nope. Are you coming out?"

"No, I went to dinner with my wife, and I'm not in the workin' mood right now."

"I hear ya, brother. Take care and we'll see you tomorrow."

Travis then tried to call Jennifer but got her voice mail. He left her a message about needing her to diagram Mullen's house and told her to call him back. He figured she must be dancing.

***

Thirty minutes after talking with Travis, Jack moved from watching the area of PCH and Martin Luther King and headed for the highway and Long Beach Boulevard about a half a mile away. He grabbed a soda from a gas station and got back into his car. While he was sitting there, he noticed a guy standing on the ramp that led to the Metro train's platform. He was a black guy about six feet three inches tall with ripped arms. He was wearing a wife-beater tank top and baggy black shorts. The guy was yoked up and probably fresh from the joint. He just stood there looking around as though his head was on a swivel. Jack figured he was going to wait for the train to pull in, run up the ramp and jump on to avoid a citation for being on the platform without a ticket. The train came and went and he remained. When the last few people had left the platform, his intentions became clear. He pulled some bolt cutters from a duffle bag and began to work on cutting a chain that secured a commuter's bike to the handrail. This was the kind of stuff you never got to see working in uniform.

While the guy worked the chain and kept looking around, Jack went into action, grabbing his radio, switching over to the patrol frequency and calling to the dispatcher. "David-Victor-Six, can we get a unit rolling toward PCH and the Boulevard, I'm watching a guy who's tryin' to steal a bike from the Metro platform." The dispatcher began calling for a unit to assist, but there was no response. About 10 minutes prior, there had been a gang shooting in the north division and a fatal accident at the traffic circle, so most patrol units were tied up. The dispatcher repeated the request on each division frequency. Jack gave her an update as to the suspect's description and actions as he patiently waited for a uniformed officer; taking action by himself while in plain clothes could be risky. The suspect might not believe he was an officer and the fight would be on.

Ben Hutchens came on the radio: "David-Victor-Nine, I'm en route to assist. Be advised I'm plain clothes also and rolling from Anaheim and the Boulevard." It eased Jack's mind to know that if he had to take action on his own, Ben was only a few minutes away.

The suspect finally snapped the chain, pulled it off of the bike and tossed it into the bushes. After stuffing the bolt cutters back in the bag, he hopped on the white mountain bike and began riding it eastbound. "David-Victor-Six, he's crossing to the north side of the highway heading eastbound, are there any black-and-whites rolling?" Before the dispatcher could answer, another unit spoke up. "Four-Sam-Twenty, I'm almost on scene with the vice units, I'm coming from Atlantic."

Any unit with a "Sam" designator was a sergeant; this one was Sergeant Denny Burke. A former vice detective, he didn't want to leave his old unit hanging, so he'd left his dinner to assist. He was headed straight for the suspect, who was riding toward him. In the glow of the yellowish streetlights, he could see the suspect riding in the gutter of the north curb. Denny maneuvered his sergeant's Chevy Tahoe into the parking lane and turned on his spotlight. The already hinked-up ex-con turned the bike north and pedaled up Pasadena Avenue. The chase was on.

"Sam-Twenty, suspect's fleeing northbound Pasadena." The inflection and volume of his voice was enough to get Ben Hutchens moving faster. He was stuck behind a van at a red light at Sixteenth and the Boulevard. He drove over the short curb-like barrier between his lane and the Metro tracks and drove through the red light when the intersection was clear. Sergeant Burke continued his transmission: "He's now westbound in the parking lot of the old Taco Bell." Jack was driving east on the highway when he heard the suspect was doubling back. He shot his car across the westbound lanes and into the alley on the west side of the parking lot. The lot was open to the alley, and the suspect was headed right for it. Jack could see him pedaling like crazy because he hadn't had a chance to learn the gears on his newest acquisition. The parolee kept looking back as the lot flooded with bright lights from the supervisor's Tahoe. The blue and red overheads, the spotlight and the high beams flashed off of the other cars and the walls as the large SUV bounced into the lot in pursuit. While the suspect looked back at his pursuer, feeling like a fox running from the hounds, he never saw Jack's car crossing his path.

The impact was a shock to Jack, even though he saw it coming. The bike tire made contact with the car just in front of the passenger door, leaving a one-foot vertical dent in the fender and concaving the bike's front rim. The would-be Tour De Ghetto rider was flung through the air, true to Sir Isaac Newton's law that a body in motion tends to stay in motion. It also tends to make contact with the windshield, hood and finally a block wall clear on the other side of the alley. Ben had pulled into the alley behind Jack just in time to see the aerial show. Denny Burke still had the button pushed in on his microphone when he saw the collision and yelled,

"Holy shit!"

Concerned for his safety, the dispatcher asked, "Four-Sam-Twenty, are you code-four?"

"Ah, Sam-Twenty here, yeah, we're code four, taking the suspect into custody now. He just fell off his bike."

Ben and Jack jumped from their cars and grabbed the bike thief by the arms. Bloody and dazed, he still put up a fight. It took all three cops to get the cuffs on him even though he had suffered a broken collarbone in the crash. Kicking and squirming, the guy wasn't going to give up just because he was injured; he knew it meant going back to prison and this guy was one tough buck. When the dust settled and the crook was sitting in the back of a black-and-white cruiser, Denny Burke took a closer look at him. "Hey, this is Rufus Bryant," the sergeant yelled out to the other officers.

"Who's that, Denny?" asked Ben.

"We arrested him for armed robbery like three years ago. He's an Insane." Referring to the Insane Crypt Gang of central Long Beach. Opening the door to the police car, Burke asked Bryant, "Hey, Rufus, when did you get out?"

"This morning."

"You got paroled this morning?"

"Yeah."

"Who's your PO?"

"I don't know, I'm supposed to report tomorrow," he said with his head hung in defeat. With a straight face, Burke told him, "I think you're gonna miss your appointment."

He shut the door and had the patrol unit take Rufus to the hospital to have his collarbone set. Ben and Jack headed to the station to trade their plain cars for a black-and-white. They would relieve the patrol unit because Bryant would have to be transferred to the County USC Hospital jail ward in Los Angeles. This was their arrest, and as the saying went both in fishing as in police work, "You catch 'em, you clean 'em."

Weeks later, Bryant would plead guilty to petty theft with prior felony theft convictions. He took a 30-month sentence rather than face trial and a possible seven years if convicted. The theft of the bike wasn't that big of a crime, but his record in California made any theft a felony. He was back in prison so fast, he probably got back to his old cell before the sheets had been changed.

***

"Travis, wake up. Travis. Travis, wake up!" When Travis came to, he saw his brother Paul standing above him in his underwear. "Dude, your phone has been ringin' for the last 15 fuckin' minutes."

Travis sat up and squinted at the numbers on the clock next to his bed. 12:47 a.m., who in the hell would be calling at this time of the night? He took the phone from Paul and rubbed his eyes. The number on the missed call log was a department cell phone, but not one of the guys from the squad. He dialed his voicemail and listened to the message.

"Jensen, this is Trevor White from homicide. Call me as soon as you can, we had a shooting and I need your help with it." This greatly intrigued Travis. Homicide was the *crème de la crème* for detectives. Why did they need him? Who got shot? He hit the call back button on his phone and listened as it started to ring. Trevor answered the phone, "White," in a grumbled, pissed-off voice. It was apparent he had someplace better to be than investigating a murder at one o'clock in the morning.

"Hey, sir, it's Jensen. You were trying to call me?"

"Yeah, sorry to wake you, kid, but the dispatcher seems to think your team was out here looking for a new pimp tonight, a white guy, kind of a good ol' boy type."

"Yeah, we were, but the guys were all EOW at midnight."

"Well, I think we found him for ya."

"Where is he?"

"Seventh and Alamitos. He's just laying here on the sidewalk waiting for the coroner. Can you come in and give me a hand? Since you guys were looking for him it might help. Besides, my partner is tied up with a gang shooting in north town."

"Yeah, I'd be glad to help, I'll be there in a half an hour."

When Travis hung up the phone, Paul said, "What's the matter, is the city getting run over by a bunch of hookers?"

"No, this guy we were looking for just got killed."

"The guy with the big house you told me about?"

"No, a different one, but we think they're related somehow. It's too much of a coincidence. I gotta run."

Paul shook his head in disbelief and said, "Man, you've got a fucked up job."

As Travis pulled up his pants he said, "Me? You're the one that has to work with lawyers all day." Paul was already heading back to bed when he yelled from the hall, "Good point. See you later little bro."

***

The yellow police tape closed off Seventh Street from Alamitos Avenue to Olive. This section of Seventh Street was a one-way street headed west toward the freeway. Travis parked his plain car at the gas station at the corner where the tape began. He could see White and a few officers gathered on the other corner just west of MLK. Several more officers were taking measurements, knocking on doors and talking with street people. He bent under the yellow tape and showed a patrol officer his badge. When he got to the crowd of officers, a rookie with a clipboard asked for his badge number and unit designator. The youngster was the scribe, and it was his job to document everyone who entered and exited the scene and the times of major events in the investigation. It was a crappy job, but an important one. Travis said, "Detective Jensen, 5-2-0-1 unit David-Victor-Thirteen." The officer thanked him and walked off to his squad car.

The shooting victim was flat on his back at the northwest corner of Seventh Street and MLK. His head was to the west and the feet to the east. His right arm was under his body, behind his back, and his left arm was over his head. As Travis looked at him he thought, *Now that looks uncomfortable, but then again, when you're dead, comfort's not really an issue.* The most notable thing was the huge hole in his chest. It looked like a morbid salad bowl with tossed bloody flesh, pieces of jacket and shirt sprinkled with muzzle blast burns. There were also a few pellet holes in his legs. A red, spent shotgun shell was in the gutter, marked with a yellow evidence placard. He had been there a while because the three-foot pool of blood under him was dark and starting to dry, and some small cockroaches were beginning to probe the area looking for a meal. Trevor White came over and jokingly asked, "Do you know what he died of?"

Travis said, "Yeah, lead poisoning."

"Damn, you heard that one."

Travis looked around and asked, "How can I help Trevor?"

185

"The clerk at the gas station said this guy's been coming in to buy tobacco for the last few weeks. Supposedly he bragged to him that he had girls working for him. If this guy is related to your deal, do you know who might have done this?"

"If it's him, and judging by the acne scars I think it might be, he got shot at last night at the Boardwalk in west division, but no witnesses or victim on that deal. The shooter might be Lawrence Washington, a guy I tried to tail just before the shooting. It could also be his boss Snake, or even a hooker he roughed up. Did you say he's been going there for a few weeks?" Travis asked as he pointed to the gas station where his car was parked.

White answered, "Yeah, he's probably staying right around here."

"Well, there's only two motels on this street," Travis said as he pointed them both out. One was on the south side of Seventh about a block east of Alamitos, and the other was on the north side just west of MLK.

White looked at them both and said, "Well, he's half way between the gas station and that one," and pointed to the latter of the two. "I'll go wake the manager and see if he knows him."

Travis said, "OK, I'm gonna go talk with the clerk at the station. Hey, I'll bet you five bucks the manager's name is Patel."

"You're on," White said.

Travis knocked on the clerk's window at the all-night gas station. The guy behind the thick bulletproof plexiglass woke up and hopped off of his stool. He came over to the door and unlocked it. The young Mexican guy said, "You're a detective now." Travis didn't recognize him but figured he must have met him while he was in patrol. He had worked this area for several years, so it was likely because this station was a hot spot for trouble and a popular pop-spot for sodas.

"I actually work vice, I'm just helpin' out on this homicide. You told the other detective that the dead guy came in here for smokes a lot?"

"Not smokes, tobacco, chewing tobacco. He chewed Redman®, we almost never sell that stuff." Travis figured this had to be the guy. The only person he ever saw chew that stuff was a roommate in the Army, and he was definitely a redneck. While talking to the clerk, Travis noticed that there was a monitor in the cashier booth showing several camera views outside the store. The station was sandwiched between Alamitos and MLK where the streets made a wedge shape at Seventh, and that was almost a 180-degree view.

"Hey, do those cameras work?" More times than not, surveillance cameras in the central area didn't.

"Yeah, it's a 24-hour looped tape, but I can't get it. It's in the office and that's locked. The owner will be in at six."

"It's tape, not digital?"

"My boss is real cheap, it's like twenty years old." Travis pulled out a business card and handed it to the clerk. "Have him call me tomorrow so I can pick up the tape."

"Sure thing, Detective. Come by and get a soda sometime."

As Travis stepped out of the mini-mart, he was approached by a woman who looked to be domestically challenged. She was wearing at least three layers of clothing and was pushing a baby stroller and pulling a red wagon. There must have been 200 pounds of crap in the stroller and another hundred in the wagon. When she spoke, her voice was scratchy, and she sounded like a man who had throat cancer. "Hey, officer. Who died?"

"Why do you think someone died?"

"'Cause you guys never put up the yellow tape unless someone dies. It's like the Death Tape of the Long Beach P.D. When it goes up, some poor bastard died." Travis chuckled at her comment, and then realized that for a bag lady she was quite observant. They really did only put it up when someone died or was about to die.

"Well, you got that right, lady."

"Can I go in to da store, officer? I kneed to use the bathroom bad, the puss is howlin'."

"Yeah, go on in and it's been a pleasure meeting you," Travis said with a smile as he walked away snickering. Trevor was coming out of the motel office holding a plastic bag with a piece of paper in it. The two met at the hood of Trevor's car. He tossed the bag across the hood and said, "William Adams was his name, and look at the driver's license on the registration card." Travis looked it over and noticed the number sequence was odd, and then he saw the abbreviation for the state, "OK." "Oklahoma? This guy's from Oklahoma?" Travis asked rhetorically.

"Yep, and here's your five bucks, asshole," White answered as he tossed a crumpled up bill across the hood. Travis picked it up, smiled at White and shoved it in his pocket. "Let's go toss his room, rookie," White instructed.

They knocked on the door, but there was no answer. White inserted the key the manager had given him and turned the knob. He pushed the door open and it stopped suddenly. The chain was still on the door and could only be put on by someone from the inside. Both detectives drew their weapons and stepped back to each side of the door. The young scribe officer saw this from his car and ran over to back them up. White yelled out, "Police officers, come to the door now." There was no answer. Again: "Police, come on out now or we're comin' in there so there won't be any witnesses to see what we do to you." Travis laughed at the demand because if a younger guy said it, even as a bluff, he would be in I.A. Not White, though, and he wasn't bluffing.

A woman's shaky voice cried out, "OK, OK, I'm coming." The door closed, followed by the sound of the chain coming off, then it opened all the way. In the doorway stood Dori Garnett, barefoot in a pair of shorts and a tank top. White grabbed her by the arm and pulled her from the room. The patrol officer took her, and not knowing exactly what to do, put cuffs on her just to be safe. White and Jensen went inside and cleared the room, making sure there were no more surprises. Dori had been the only one inside. When the detectives came back outside Travis recognized her. "Medusa, right?"

"I don't use that name anymore," she said.

"But you used to, didn't ya?" As he pointed down to her ankle, he saw the scabbed-over cuts that distorted her tattoo. Looking back up, he saw how frightened she was. "Go ahead and uncuff her," he instructed the patrolman. Travis asked, "Is your real name Dori?" While the uniform was unlocking the handcuffs she said,

"Yes sir. You arrested me a few years ago."

"That's right. You took me to the parking lot behind the old Doolies Hardware in north town. Did you know they tore it down and built a school there?"

"No kiddin', guess I can't use that spot anymore."

"Hey, you don't have any guns in the room, do ya?" Travis asked.

"No, you can look," she said. White and the rookie officer went in to toss the room. "What's this about?" Dori asked as she rubbed her wrists.

"You don't know?"

"No sir."

"It's about the guy who rented the room."

"Cowboy? He left like an hour and a half ago to meet someone." Travis figured he would get as many answers as he could from her before breaking the news. "Do you know who he was meeting?"

"Nah, he don't tell me shit."

Looking down at the scabbing scars on her tattoo, he asked, "How'd you get all cut up, Dori?"

"It's nothin'."

"Why don't you have a seat on the steps," Travis said as he motioned to the stairs of the next room. "So who's Cowboy?"

"He's my man."

"Really, and he didn't tell you who he was seeing? Or is it more like he's your pimp?"

"Hey, I turn tricks, I'm not gonna lie. Cowboy just takes care of me, it's dangerous out here." She couldn't make eye contact with Travis, and he figured even she wasn't buying her own bullshit.

"Would your answer be different if you knew he was dead?"

"He's dead?" she asked, as she looked up with her eyes wide open. Her face told Travis that she was glad he'd been killed, or so he thought. She then dropped her head on her knees and began sobbing. Travis looked in at White and shrugged his shoulders as if to say, *Oh well, there's no good way to tell them.* "Hey, I'm sorry, I didn't mean to be so blunt," Travis said. Dori was mumbling something so Travis bent down to listen. Dori was repeating, "It's over, it's finally over."

"What's over, Dori?"

"The hell. I was so scared of him. That fucker raped me and made me whore for him." She cupped her face with her hands and cried. "Who killed him?" she said as she looked up.

"We don't know. We were hoping you might have an idea."

"I wish I'd done it. Oh God, I can't believe it's over. That bastard did this to me." She said as she stuck out her leg and turned her ankle to show his butchery. Travis was sickened by what he saw, so he went inside the room and spoke to White. "Find anything, Trevor?"

"Nah, there's nothing here. Just a few needles under the bed."

"Man, this guy was an asshole. Did you hear what she was

saying?"

"Yeah, do you know why she didn't know he'd been shot?" Trevor asked.

"No."

"Her pupils, man. See how dilated they are? She's so strung out I'm surprised she knows who she is." The rookie officer was listening intently as the conversation went back and forth like a tennis match. White added, "Far as I'm concerned she left herself open for it by getting so loaded."

"No one deserves that shit," Travis argued. White thought for a moment about Travis's statement and realized that perhaps he had become a bit too jaded over the years. He said, "You're right Travis, sorry." Then he looked at the rookie, who was getting a glimpse into the softer side of the old investigator. The moment was short-lived. White yelled at the rookie, "Don't you have a fucking log to keep or something?" The rookie ran from the room and headed to his unit.

Travis led Dori back to her room and had her sit on the bed. She was shaking, her thin fingers trembled as she tried to wipe her hair from her eyes. Travis took her hand and said, "Dori, I need you to tell me who might have done this. I know you got shot at over on Pacific last night, was this 'Cowboy' guy with you?"

"Yeah, but it wasn't him." Dori just stared at the floor and stopped talking. Her less than cooperative demeanor was frustrating Travis.

"Hey, the suspense is killin' me. Who shot at you last night?"

"It was Lawrence."

"Lawrence who?" Travis asked. Even though he knew the answer, he had to have her say it.

"Lawrence Washington, he works for the guy who used to pimp me out, but we got away. Do you think it was him?"

"Well, it could be. Dori, I'm going to have an officer take your whole statement including what happened last night. Do you need anything?"

"No, I'll be all right."

Back out at the command post, an officer had brought a potential witness for the detectives to talk with. She was an old Hispanic lady, very short with dark leathery skin. She only spoke Spanish, which just pissed off Trevor White. The officer who'd found her had to translate. She had seen a large black car pull up to the corner. Cowboy approached it, placing his hands on the passenger door like he was going to lean in and talk to the driver. Cowboy quickly stood up and stepped back, and then the blast came from inside the car. The barrel of a long gun came out and blasted him again while he was on the ground. The car sped off eastbound and nearly collided in the intersection with a truck going south on Alamitos. Trevor interrupted the story. "What did she say about the two cars?"

The patrol officer explained, "Before I brought her over here I had her show me which way each car was going. She said the shooter was eastbound and a work truck was southbound, and the truck had to slam on its brakes to avoid the crash."

"That means one of them had to run a red light. My guess, it was the suspect. Look." The seasoned detective was pointing to the traffic signals.

"What?" Travis asked.

"Red light cameras," the patrol officer said with excitement. "They just put them in like a few months ago." Trevor grabbed his radio and instructed the communications center to wake up the on-call accident investigator and have him respond to the station. Only the accident investigation detectives had access to the system, and it possibly had a picture of the suspect's car and hopefully his face and license plate number. "Can she tell us anything else about the car? Was it new, old, license plates, anything?" White asked. The officer exchanged some words with her in Spanish, turned to White and said, "She said it was nice and shiny like a limo."

The coroner's team arrived to take custody of the body. An investigator arrived in a Crown Victoria, and his assistant was driving a van they called the meat wagon. The first thing the investigator did was to check in with the scribe and get all of the call and crime report numbers, the investigating detectives' names and the name of the person who had pronounced the victim dead. Then the investigator and the assistant began to examine the body. It had only been about three weeks since the last class had graduated from the police academy, so for a few rookies on scene this was their first homicide. It might have been the first dead person some of them had ever seen. The coroner investigator sensed this and decided to have some fun. "Detective White, do you have all of your photographs?" he asked. White looked over at the crime scene tech, who gave him a thumbs-up. He relayed the yes answer to the coroner who was squatting down next to the body as he pulled on his rubber gloves.

The investigator reached over and began to roll the now stiffening corpse toward him. He began feeling around the victim's back with one hand and called the two wet-nosed cops over for a closer look. He asked them, "Do you know what he really died from?" The one officer that was on scribe duty stuck out his chest and said with an all-knowing grin, "Lead poisoning, sir." The investigator pulled his gloved hand from the stiff's backside holding out a crimson chunk of meaty tissue and said, "Nope, a broken heart, get it?" The scribe who thought he'd answered correctly blurted out, "Oh, fuck!" The Hispanic officer who'd been translating was now at a loss for words. He just turned around and hurled his lunch into the bushes. Trevor White was laughing hysterically and said to the coroner, "That one always gets me, Sid."

The dispatcher called for White and let him know that the accident investigator was responding to the station from the traffic circle where he had been working on the fatal accident from earlier in the night. Trevor turned to Travis and asked, "Can you go to the station and look at the pictures while the coroner wraps this up? I'll join you in about 30 minutes."

"Yeah, ten-four. If he can print them out I'll meet you in your office."

White said, "Our secretary should be in by now, so I'm going to start sending some of the patrol guys in to file their reports."

Travis checked out with the scribe who was still a little shaken from the coroner's prank. While he drove to the station, he couldn't help but feel good about how White trusted him to help with a homicide investigation. Most detectives didn't consider the vice guys to be true investigators. Travis began to think about what it would be like to be a homicide detective, and then he realized that if he made the sergeant's list he would never get the chance to find out. Once you promoted, you became a supervisor and you were not a worker bee any longer. Then he thought about his own sergeant and realized he needed to call him and let him know about the evening's developments. Travis called Joe at home. It took Joe a while to answer the phone, as he'd been asleep and wouldn't answer the phone at first when his wife nudged him. When you're a cop and the phone rings after midnight, you might as well answer it, because chances are it won't be for anyone else in the family. Travis filled Joe in on the night's developments after the team went ten-seven.

"Shit, everything good happens after our shift," Joe said. He instructed Travis to help out Detective White however he could and to call him back if it turned out to be related to their investigation. Travis was so tired he sat on the floor in the hallway of the second floor of the station. He had arrived before Devin Rogers, the accident investigation detective. Travis was just about to nod off when the elevator door opened. Rogers stepped out and headed for Travis. A thin black guy, Rogers walked with a limp. He'd been a motor officer for years until a car made a left turn in front of him. That was six years and three surgeries ago. Now he was relegated to desk duty until he retired.

"Hey Travis, how you doin'?" Rogers asked.

"Tired dude, thanks for comin' in tonight."

"No worries, I was already called in for a fatal. A drunk hit the traffic circle, literally. He was going east on PCH down the hill and must have passed out. He went straight into one of the big trees in the center of the circle."

"Bummer for him."

"Yep," Rogers said as he began to unlock his office and started to explain the camera system to Travis. "The Communication Center told me what you needed so I called our vendor from the field."

"Vendor?" Travis asked.

"Yeah, we don't run the cameras, it's an outside company. They screen the pictures and forward them to us if the driver and car are identifiable."

"So are we going to have to wait for them to get to work?"

"Nope, the guy I called can access the system from his house," Rogers said as he turned on the light at his desk and logged onto his computer. When he got to his email he saw one from the vendor that read in the subject line, "*Only activation on that camera in last six hours.*" Rogers opened it and saw the first picture. It was of the entire intersection and showed a black Mercedes headed east and a white work truck going south, just missing the rear end of the Mercedes. "Is this what you're looking for?" he asked as he turned the monitor so Travis could see it better. Travis looked at the time stamp in the upper right corner: 12:37 a.m. "Yeah, that's it. What about the driver?" Travis asked. Rogers went on to the next picture in the set. It was a split image, one of the license plate and the other of the driver. Travis was expecting to see Washington in the picture, but a raised hand and a baseball cap shielded the driver's face. Not only could you not see the face, but also the hand was from a Caucasian person, not a black man. The license plate proved to be a much better clue. Travis knew he had seen it before, but where? While Rogers was running the plate through the Department of Motor Vehicles, the answer came to Travis. "Peter Mullen, the plate will come back to a Peter Mullen," Travis said. When the response finally popped up on the computer, Rogers looked at Travis in astonishment and said, "You're right, Peter Mullen on Naples Island." Rogers pointed to the printer across the office. The pictures were almost done printing.

Travis called Joe and alerted him that things had changed dramatically. Joe was going to call the team in to work and told Travis to have White make the call as to what the next step would be. Travis grabbed the pictures and his kit bag and bolted from the office. He didn't wait for the elevator, opting to run the stairs instead. Reaching the fifth floor, he yelled out for White. One of the officers from the crime screen pointed to the bathroom. Travis flung the door open in excitement and held up the pictures. White was standing at a urinal and looked over slowly. "Let me guess, it's your Lawrence Washington guy, right?"

"Nope, Peter Mullen. Well, I think it's him. It's his car and it's a white guy drivin'." As White zipped up his fly and moved to the sink to wash his hands he looked at the pictures as Travis held them for him. "That's enough for a search warrant," White said as he wiped his hands with a paper towel. Travis opened his kit and pulled out some paperwork. "I already wrote one," he said.

"What? How did you write a warrant that fast?"

"We were going to serve it in the next few days."

"What's it for?"

"Possession, sales and pimping."

"Perfect, that will get us in so we can secure the place and him. I'll write another one to cover the murder investigation."

This was it, time to put an end to Mullen's little crime ring. Travis had mixed feelings about the fact that it was now going to fall under the umbrella of homicide, but he was glad that it was going to be over – over for him, over for the city and over for

Jennifer. Trevor and Travis decided to split their efforts. Trevor would stay at the station and oversee the filing of reports and make the proper notifications. Travis would suit up and head to Naples to lock down the house until the SWAT team could be summoned. Travis raced along Ocean Avenue past the tall buildings of downtown. Passing the Museum of Art, he accelerated along the straight deserted stretch of road that ran along Bluff Park. He could see the horizon was getting brighter and daybreak would soon be at hand. He called for a patrol sergeant to meet him at the corner of Second Street and Siena Drive. Unit Two-Sam Twenty answered the call. Travis's phone rang and he flipped it open without looking at the Caller ID. "Jensen here."

"Travis, it's Ben. Jack and I are on our way. We're at the 405 Freeway and Lakewood, we've been at County Jail with a prisoner from earlier."

"Great, meet me at Second and Siena in the bank parking lot. Do you guys know what's goin' on?"

"Yeah, Joe called and so did my wife, she's dispatching on channel one tonight."

"Cool. I'm glad you guys are here. All we have to do is secure the place 'till SWAT takes over. See ya in a few."

Travis pulled into the lot and Denny Burke was waiting for him with a two-officer patrol unit. Denny was leaning against his supervisor's SUV with his arms folded, holding a large cup of coffee. When Travis opened his door, Denny said, "You vice boys have been tearing it up tonight. What do you have now?"

"What are you doing here? Aren't you a swing shift guy?" Travis asked.

"Yep, but they needed a sergeant on a call-back and I need the overtime."

"I guess it's not a crime 'till it's overtime," Travis said, referring to the department's latest tightening of the purse strings.

Travis explained the situation and the target to Burke and the two officers. He explained how the rest of the team would be arriving soon along with the SWAT team. Burke took charge as the incident commander and told the dispatcher that all responding units needed to check in with him for their assignments. He then opened the rear of his rolling command vehicle and pulled out a whiteboard map of the island from an array of maps of different neighborhoods. Travis marked the target location with an X and told Burke that he was going to go on foot to see if the Mercedes was still at the house. Burke insisted he take the patrolmen with him. Travis went to the trunk of his car to get some extra gear. While he put on his tactical vest, he told the two officers that he would walk up first and head down the side access alley toward the canal. He would be able to see the driveway and garage from there. Then he would cover the house from the waterside. He instructed them to wait until he was out of sight and then to pull up to where they could see the front gate of the property. He cautioned them, "Look, if this guy's there, I seriously doubt he's asleep because he just blasted a guy with a gauge, so stay out of sight." The officers nodded in silence that they understood.

Travis finished putting his equipment on his vest and attached his radio microphone to a strap on his left shoulder. Reaching into the right belly pocket, he pulled out an elastic bandoleer holding five shotgun rounds. He walked over to the patrolmen's black-and-white and hit the release switch for the shotgun suspended over the headrests of the front seats. Holding the weapon at port arms, Travis released the slide action and pumped the gun, sending a round into the chamber. He then pulled an extra round off of the bandoleer and slid it into the tubular magazine, then slid the bandoleer onto the butt stock.

Rather than walk, Travis rode on the hood of the black-and-white to cover the few hundred yards or so. He hopped off and motioned with his hand to hold back. After passing a few houses, he got to the alley. He took a right and crossed the alley to hug the perimeter wall of Snake's little fortress. When he reached the side gate, he slowly crouched down, then slid to a prone position and inched his head forward for a look. He saw the Hummer but not the Mercedes. The house still looked dark, so he got up and darted across the gate. From the other side he could see the Mercedes parked in the driveway by the large entry gate. He read the license plate to himself and then looked at the letters and numbers he had written on the back of his hand in haste at the station. It was indeed the same car as the one in the red light camera picture.

Travis reached up with his left hand, squeezed his microphone and spoke with a soft whisper, "David-Victor-Thirteen to Sam-Twenty."

"Sam-Twenty here, go."

"OK, the suspect vehicle's at the house inside the gate. I don't see any lights on from here. Your guys have the front, so I'm going to make my way to the canal side."

"Ten-Four Travis, David-Victor-Six and Nine are here now, I'll send them your way."

"Send them up the walkway on the canal side; I don't want anyone else going by the house until we are ready to call him out."

Travis let himself through a neighbor's gate and dashed across the lawn to get to the canal walk. He took the walk about 20 feet to the corner of Snake's property. The sea wall made for perfect cover, and Travis could see the entire backside of the house and garage. Now all he had to do was wait.

The sun was now bouncing across the canal off of the widows that faced east, but Travis was still in the shadows. Travis loved the night but hated the dawn because that was when the air was the coldest and it was hard to see your target. Intently staring at the house, Travis could see his breath blowing across the shotgun barrel. The sweat under his vest began to cool. The chill in the air combined with his racing heart made him shake, but he wouldn't have long before things would get hot in a hurry.

Chapter Ten

Wake-Up Call

Travis thought that the patio that overlooked the canal and Mullen's private dock seemed a lot smaller in the daylight than it had when he'd been there for the party. While he waited, he scanned it looking for areas of cover he could use if he had to move. Like any good cop, he constantly examined the "what-ifs" of the situation. *What if Mullen surrenders? What if there is a shooting in the house, what if he tries to run?* As these scenarios played out in Travis's head, he came up with plans for each of them. His concentration was broken by his call sign on the radio.

"David-Victor-Thirteen this is Six. Travis, we're comin' up behind you." He knew the voice; it was Jack Barnes. When Travis turned and looked back toward the Second Street Bridge, he saw Jack jogging along the canal walk with Ben Hutchens right behind him, dressed in their tactical gear and helmets. They slowed down to a walk about 40 feet away, drew their weapons and made a stealthier approach as they got closer to the target location. Travis was surprised but happy to see his two teammates. He said, "I'm glad to see you guys, but what the hell were you doin' at County Jail?"

"Dropping off a prisoner," Jack said.

Ben added, "You should have seen it, we were chasin' a parolee on a bike and Jack here played bumper cars with this dude. It fuckin' rocked." Even a righteous use of force sounded funny when Ben told the story. Jack asked, "So, who'd Snake kill?" Travis knelt down and turned to face his friends. "He shotgunned that guy that's been on the highway. You know, the Cowboy guy."

"No shit, so this is like a misdemeanor murder?" Jack responded.

"Yeah, something like that," Travis said. He continued, "So we're gonna hit the place with my dope warrant and get him in custody, then homicide will take over." Ben and Jack looked around at the grounds with the finely cut lawn, the sculptures and the fountain. They started to assess the environment, as did Travis. Ben pointed to the south corner and asked Travis, "You got anybody on the south side?" Travis just shook his head no. Ben tapped Jack on the knee and the two of them moved to the south side of the property, walking in a crouched position behind the sea wall. Once there, Ben continued south for about 50 yards to make sure they had an escape route while Jack kept an eye on the house. When Ben returned, he gave Travis a thumbs-up.

The chatter on the radio began to increase as more units were rolling to the command post. Travis listened intently as each unit logged on and reported in. He heard units with Y designators, pronounced as "Young," meaning that some of the SWAT members were beginning to show up. When Young-Eighteen logged on giving his badge and radio numbers, Travis knew it was his academy mate Fred Crackers, as his badge number was one digit lower than Travis's. He figured it would be about 30 minutes before they were relieved by SWAT, but the pressure in his bladder couldn't wait that long. Travis knelt down on both knees and set his shotgun down on the walkway. He unzipped his pants and began to urinate against the wall. It was a very uncomfortable position, but he couldn't stand up and risk being exposed. Glancing over at Ben and Jack, he saw them making rude gestures simulating masturbation and holding up an index finger and thumb about two inches apart to equate Travis's manhood with that of an eight-year-old boy. Travis had to physically hold in his laughter by putting his free hand over his nose and mouth.

The laughter and the morning silence ceased with the loudest shriek of a blood-curdling cry that any of them had ever heard. It echoed through the neighborhood and across the water. Ben and

Jack hunkered down behind their cover. Travis dropped to his side and fumbled with his zipper as he lay on the walkway. A voice over the radio said, "What the hell was that?" Another voice came on, shaken and shocked: "It was a bird, a huge ass bird jumped out of the bush as we walked by it." Then Travis realized it was the damned peacocks. Grabbing his mic, Travis broadcasted, "David-Victor-Thirteen, they're peacocks, the suspect has pet peacocks in the yard." He felt bad that he'd forgotten to tell the patrol guys about them. Jesse had told him they looked like turkeys, and Travis was about ready to serve one up for Thanksgiving.

The radio broke again: "Light's on upstairs." The voice was Terry Knight's; he hadn't had time to log on. He'd been running up the street to back up the two uniforms when he saw a light come on in a window on the east side of the house. Travis was back to his position with his twelve-gauge pointed at the rear of the house. He could feel that in the excitement he hadn't completely finished relieving himself before he put his package away. He reached down and felt a large wet spot on the crotch of his pants. He thought, *Great, now the guys will think the bird made me piss my pants.* The area was quiet for a minute, and then yelling could be heard on the front side of the house. The detectives in the back yard could only make out the words "Hands up." A frantic police officer's voice came over the radio, but he did not hold the press to talk button long enough. All that could be heard was, "...Suspect in the ..." The other officer and Terry could be heard in the background on the radio yelling, "Get your fuckin' hands up." This played out for what seemed like a minute to Travis but in reality was probably ten seconds. To hear the confrontation, both on the radio and on the other side of a house, and to have to stay put was extremely difficult and took a lot of discipline. Although he wanted to run to their aid, he and the others had to remain in their positions and they did.

It wasn't Peter Mullen who was causing the commotion out front, it was Lawrence Washington. He had emerged wearing a pair of boxers and holding a gym bag. He dropped behind a large terracotta pot and pulled his .357 Magnum from the bag. All four men on the east side of the house, Lawrence versus the three officers, began to fire at the same time. The different caliber sounds could be made out by Travis, even though the shots were so close together they sounded more like a pack of firecrackers.

Pings and clacks could also be heard as the bullets struck the house and the cars parked out front. Jack Barnes let the command post know what was happening. "Nine-Nine-Eight, Nine-Nine-Eight, front of the house." Then the back sliding glass door shattered as a bullet zipped through the open front door and passed through the entire house. Then another made it through and hit the handrail on the walkway about 20 feet from Jack and Ben. Everyone in the back tried to make themselves smaller as the rounds continued to fly in their direction. "Travis, get down!" Ben yelled as if Travis needed some type of motivation to keep from getting shot.

The shooting suddenly stopped followed by another transmission. It was garbled, but the point was clear. "...Back in the house..." The officer on the other end was now screaming into the radio. Lawrence had run back into the house after the exchange of fire. He knelt down behind a large column in the entryway and reloaded with a speedy-loader he'd pulled from the bag. He fired twice more blindly out the front door and then dashed toward the back of the house.

With the situation evolving quicker than expected, Fred Crackers assembled four other SWAT members as quickly as he could. They threw on their entry vests over their civilian clothing, grabbed their MP5s and M4 carbines and loaded onto the running boards of a K-9 Suburban. Fred told the driver to get them as close as possible as fast as possible.

Washington emerged from rear of the house through the broken slider. He never saw the trio of detectives 70 feet away at the seawall until Ben and Jack let loose with a volley of rounds that peppered the side of the house on each side of the former football star. Lawrence dove back through the opening that still had some broken glass hanging from the top of the frame just as Travis got off a round of buckshot. The nine pellets pulverized the rest of the glass and took out the window next to the slider. Lawrence had been hit by one of Ben's bullets but did not feel the effect yet. Two muzzle flashes came from the darkened living room followed by a ripping sound in the trees about five feet above Travis's head.

Crackers came on the radio. "Young-Eighteen, we're inbound, where do you want us?"

"Fred, take the north side in the alley. There's a gate there," Travis instructed. The K-9 officer pulled over at the mouth of the alley, and the tactical team headed down the narrow egress in a conga line, each with his weapon pointed at a different danger area. Fred set two officers on each side of the gate covering the grounds and a third to cover their backs. He took the last officer, Grant King, to the neighbor's house across the alley. Grant was the younger brother of SWAT Sergeant Dale King and a veteran of Afghanistan, where he'd served with the Army Rangers. King's training and scope-mounted M-4 made him a good substitute for a sniper, as none of the sniper teams had yet arrived. Crackers pounded on the neighbor's kitchen door and announced, "Police, this is the police, we need to get in your house!" A voice could faintly be heard yelling back, "OK, come on in." Sure enough, the door was unlocked like most in this wealthy enclave. Stepping into the expansive kitchen, Fred told Grant, "Find the high ground."

Grant broke off and scooted up the stairs. Fred was met in the living room by the elderly homeowner and his wife. They were in robes and shaking with fear. As he pointed toward the passage door to the garage on the north side of the house, Fred said, "Go get in your garage and wait there to be evacuated. The south side of your house isn't safe." The homeowners ran down the hall and through the door.

Washington was now somewhere in the middle of Snake's house firing an occasional round out the front door or out the back slider. Sergeant Burke checked on everyone's well being. "Four-Sam-Twenty to Jensen, you guys OK back there?"

"David-Victor-Thirteen, yeah, we're all good back here."

"Sam-Twenty to Knight, what's your status?"

"I'm good, sir, and I'm with the patrol unit in the front and they're OK too."

"Young-Eighteen to Sam-Twenty, my guys are in place but we're going to need to do some evacuations from the neighborhood," Crackers instructed.

By now the sirens could be heard rolling to the quiet island from every division in the city. Even some Seal Beach units were rolling along with a Highway Patrol officer who'd heard the call on his scanner. Sgt. Burke would have plenty of help at the command post and he would need it. Long Beach's most expensive neighborhood was now experiencing its worst and most violent wake-up call.

***

Lawrence Washington sat on the floor behind the bar in the living room trying to figure how his life had gone so terribly wrong. He'd been just a few years away from playing in the NFL, then he'd thrown it all away and it had spiraled down to this: working for a pimp drug dealer and now wanted for attempted murder of several police officers. To him, there was no choice: Escape now or face prison for the next few decades, or life. He could reach his car in the garage through the house, but the Hummer was parked directly behind it on the driveway. The Hummer would be his only way out. He crawled to Mullen's office just a few feet away and slid open the middle drawer of the desk. In the tray along the front of the drawer he found the key ring he was looking for and something extra: a Smith and Wesson nine-millimeter pistol. He took both and headed for the garage.

Through the small stained glass window in the center of the garage door, he could see one of the patrol officers outside the front gate. The officer's attention was on the front door of the house and not the garage. So rather than triggering the door opener, Lawrence disconnected it and slowly raised the door just high enough for him to crawl out. He slowly let it settle back down behind him. When he got to his feet he could see that the officer at the front gate had not detected him. He made it about five feet away from the driver's door when he heard the crackles of MP-5s on three-round bursts combined with the thuds of the bullets hitting the other side of the Hummer. Lawrence had never seen the officers at the side gate, but it was too late to consider another plan let alone a new line of work.

The resumed gun battle caught the attention of the officer at the front gate. At his angle from the Hummer, he was completely exposed as Washington made his way to the driver's door. Washington fired a continuous volley from the nine-millimeter, and the young patrol cop returned it bullet for bullet. Lawrence made a lucky shot, hitting the officer in the right kneecap and toppling him over onto the driveway.

Travis could see the SWAT officers shooting and their rounds hitting the Hummer, but he could not see Washington. He moved farther to his left to get a view of the driver's side of the SUV. The first movement his eyes caught was coming right at him so he instinctively fired his twelve-gage. The unlucky peacock dropped right there with a cloud of feathers above him. His mate ran across the yard and headed for the shrubs along the wall. Travis still could not see Lawrence but could hear him shooting.

Terry Knight was on the north side of the front gate from the downed officer and had no idea where Washington was other than in a position to shoot the young officer again. Terry yelled at the wounded officer's partner, "Cover me." Without hesitation, Terry ran across the driveway while Lawrence was still shooting. He reached under the armpits of the wounded officer, who was hunched over. He lifted the officer and dragged him to the far side of the driveway. He did this while the second uniform stepped out, placing himself between them and the threat, and exchanged rounds with Washington. Terry and the wounded officer tumbled into the ivy, falling to the ground behind the estate wall and wedged behind a large eucalyptus tree. The officer screamed as Terry landed on his wounded leg. Neither one of them could move much, but they were now safe.

Travis moved farther to his left in time to see the Hummer driver's door open as Washington started to climb in amid the flying glass and whizzing bullets. Travis leveled his shotgun, putting the front sight bead in the center of the door that blocked his view of Washington. He squeezed off a round, sending nine more pellets down range. By the time they reached their target, the spread of the impact was enough to hit the front headlight, the door and the window, which shattered.

Lawrence stumbled and grabbed the door to steady himself. Some of the lead pellets had hit him through the door, but Washington was still climbing inside the cab. Travis pumped and fired again, hitting the windshield as Lawrence dropped behind the dashboard. Travis fired one more time into the grill.

Even with all of the hits it took, somehow the peppered Hummer started. As it backed up, Travis had to take cover below the sea wall as the shifting fire from the SWAT officers was getting too close to him. The big black SUV began to slowly back up, and then it turned slightly, angling the back end in the direction of the side alley gate. The engine roared and the tires spun on the decomposed granite and gravel drive. The officers on each side of the gate could not see the driver, so they unleashed, on full auto, at the tires. This had little effect in the short run, and the vehicle barreled down on them.

Grant King couldn't see the driver from his sniper's nest as he had the same line of sight as the officers on the ground, but he was 15 feet higher in the neighbors' window. Falling back on his military training, he took aim at a point on the roof of the car that he felt was in line with where the driver would be. He chose a spot about seven or eight feet back from the windshield and two feet from the driver's side. He was able to get off four rounds before the truck reached the gate. The three officers at the gate dove out of the way to avoid being crushed. The driver's side tail end smashed into and through the brick wall, sending the gate hurling through the air, off of its hinges and onto the back of one officer. Fred Crackers was just reaching the alley when the Hummer came into view. He fired his MP-5 at the passenger side as the bullet-riddled behemoth smashed into the wall on the other side of the alley. The engine was still running and the tires spun, but the car was stuck. Fred fired another three-round burst at the slumped-over driver, thinking he was trying to drive off.

Travis and Jack had run over to where the alley met the canal to see the last few shots. Then the lifeless Lawrence Washington fell to his left and out the damaged door, pulling his foot from the accelerator. The officers scrambled to their feet and drew down on the suspect, but he was obviously dead. King's shot placement had worked, and one of his rounds went through the back of Washington's head, probably killing him instantly. His body had some 16 holes in it with no way of telling how many were entry or exit wounds.

Terry, having heard the crash, the shooting, and then the sudden quiet, climbed off of the officer he had just saved and tuned to look at what had happened. There before him, lying flat on his back in the middle of the main driveway was the patrol officer who had laid down cover fire for him. Terry could see the blood on his chest and figured he'd been hit in the exchange with Washington. As he got up to go to him, the wounded officer quietly said, "Don't come near me, sir." His voice was garbled from the fluid collecting in his lungs. He continued, "Another shooter in the doorway." He slightly lifted his left index finger in the direction of the front door. Terry slowly looked around the wall to see Peter Mullen about 10 feet inside the front door, pointing a rifle at him. Just as Mullen fired, Terry pulled his head back behind the cover. Chunks of brick popped off the wall as a small cloud of red brick clay powder filled the air from the pulverizing bullet strike. Several

205

officers out on the street, who were just arriving, took cover, as they didn't know where the shot had come from. Everyone in the alley also dove for cover behind the wall or the suspect's blasted vehicle.

Terry was the last one to see the suspect, so he grabbed his handset and broadcast, "There's another shooter in the house, he has a rifle and we have two officers down at the front gate. Two officers down at the front gate." The six or so officers who responded to the front gate along with Sergeant Joe Marino put everything they had into the front door of the house, sending Mullen retreating toward the back of his house seeking cover. Terry and a few other officers dragged the mortally wounded patrolman to the lawn on the north side of the gate. Terry didn't know who he was, so he wiped the blood from his nametag. It read, "A. Jimenez."

"Hang in there, Jimenez, we're gonna get ya to an ambulance in a minute." Terry tried to reassure him as he held both hands on the officer's chest, but the blood kept seeping through his fingers. Jimenez reached up with his left hand and grasped Terry's arm. "Sir, all I wanted to do was be a good cop," he said with labored breath. His eyes looked around at the commotion around him and then back to Terry. "I don't feel it, I can't feel my legs."
Terry told him, "A good cop? Are you kidding me kid? This morning you saved my life and your partner's life. Today you're the best cop ever." Jimenez smiled and said something in Spanish that Terry could only guess was a prayer. The grip of the young officers hand let go and his arm dropped to his side as he died.

He was gone that quick. An officer Terry Knight wasn't even sure he'd met before died in his arms. Jimenez was a 26-year-old local Hispanic kid who'd dodged the gangs growing up so he could concentrate on school and baseball. A graduate of Wilson High School and Cal State Long Beach, he'd chosen to serve his community to make it safer for his little sisters and his mother. One of Long Beach's true hero sons was now gone at the hands of a greedy, ruthless criminal.

On the backside of the house, Peter Mullen could see a lone officer on the canal walk. From the shadows of the living room, he took aim with his AR-15 and fired just as Ben Hutchens ducked down. Travis, Jack and Fred Crackers were just getting to the walkway about 40 yards north of Ben as they saw his head fling backward. His body followed as he fell off the walk into the water below. Stunned, Travis stood in disbelief until Fred pulled him down behind cover. Mullen was running across the patio toward the canal shooting at them. The wet lawn and pieces of the stone path were kicking up all around the pimp from the shots being fired at him by King, who was still perched in the neighbors' window. King was an expert shot, but the trees obscured his aim. Mullen leaped off the wall to the walk and ran down the gangway toward his boat, The Cottonmouth. As he reached it, his rifle was out of ammunition, so he tossed it aside and boarded the vessel.

Travis said, "I'll get Snake, you guys get Ben." The three of them ran to the wooden ramp that connected the boat slips with the walkway. Travis was trying to load his extra rounds into the tube of his Remington 870 shotgun but dropped them, so he tossed the gauge on the walk and drew his .45 as he made the turn down the ramp. He could hear the engine start up but didn't see Mullen on the flybridge. Travis figured he must be somewhere down below.

The buzz of the department's helicopter could be heard overhead now, as Fred updated everyone on the situation via the radio: "Suspect on a boat in the canal, notify the port unit and lifeguards. We also have an officer in the water, we need medics here, now!" The air unit took over the radio play-by-play. "Unit Fox, we're on scene. We see the officer at the boat but don't see the suspect. Wait, wait, he's at the bow untying his line."

Hearing this, Travis jumped onto the rear of the boat and took aim along the dockside. Mullen appeared on the waterside and dashed for the wheelhouse. Travis fired two rounds in haste and missed, and then the boat lunged forward and jerked to a stop. Mullen had forgotten to cast the stern line. Travis moved to a better position and took aim as Mullen floored the throttle again. A rip and a pop were all the warning Travis had that something was wrong. The tie-down on the deck of the boat held tight, but the cleat on the old rotting dock ripped loose with the force of a catapult. The 10-pound metal cleat's point of impact was just below Travis's right shoulder blade, breaking two ribs and knocking him flat on his face. When he looked up, Travis couldn't find his gun, and he could feel the boat turning sharply to the left. Getting to his knees, Travis looked up just in time to see Mullen's foot striking him in the face and whipping his head back. Mullen scrambled by Travis and up the steps to the flybridge as the boat was building speed.

Back on the walkway, Fred and Jack jumped into the water to get Ben, who was sinking under the weight of his gear. The water was about 10 feet deep, but just a few feet away was the steep rocky sea wall. When Jack plunged into the water right next to Ben, he was surprised to see his friend moving – not just moving, but trying to swim to the surface. They were all able to get to the rocks together. Jack gave his good friend and partner a hug and said, "Shit, I thought you were dead man." Ben still had a stunned look on his face and wasn't sure what had happened. He said, "Fuck, my head hurts, am I hit?" Fred pointed to Ben's helmet, which had a small hole dead center about three inches up from the brim and another oval-shaped one on top. "Look at this shit," Fred said. "It creased your helmet. You're gonna have a headache and whiplash, but that's it, bro." The three of them clung to the rocks and each other until some other officers could pull them out of the chilly water.

The boat rocked back and forth while Travis tried to get to his feet. He looked inside the cabin and saw the wheel of the boat turning on its own, and he realized Mullen was up top driving from the flybridge wheel. Travis went inside the cabin to look for his gun. He could hear Peter walking back and forth above him along with some banging sounds. Peter was lifting and closing the storage lockers under the bench seats. In the third one he found the object of his search, a small twelve-gauge flare gun with three signal flares attached. He loaded the first flare with one hand while he maneuvered the speeding boat through the canals with the other. Travis was unable to locate his gun, and in the rush to secure the house he had forgotten to take his Walther PPK with him. Now, unarmed and alone with Snake, who had control of the craft, Travis decided his only option was to try and rush him.

He ran from the safety of the cabin and ascended the ladder toward the bridge. Just as Snake came into view, Travis saw the blaze orange pistol in his hand. It was just enough warning to put his head down before the blast. The flare passed about a foot over Travis's head, pierced the fiberglass of the bench at the rear of the boat and lodged in a stack of life jackets. Mullen tried to reload before Travis could reach the top rung and close the distance on him. He let go of the wheel, opened the breach and dumped the expended round. He took another round that was attached to the handle and slid it into the tube.

Travis grabbed for the gun just as Mullen closed the breach. Travis's momentum pinned Mullen to the dash as the boat ran out of control. Both men struggled for the gun as it pointed skyward.

Running at around 30 knots, The Cottonmouth glanced off of the stern of a moored sloop. The impact jolted the boat, sending it back to the center of the canal and Peter and Travis to the floor. Rolling around, Travis caught a glimpse of the helicopter following them about 80 feet off of the water. He knew he wasn't alone and that help would be coming soon.

Mullen was able to fire the flare, but it shot harmlessly into the morning sky. Peter dropped the gun and gave Travis a knee to the groin. This was enough distraction to allow Mullen to get to his feet. He turned the wheel slightly to avoid another collision before grabbing a six-foot-long gaff that was lying on top of the bridge's dash. He whipped around, swinging the hook end of the stick as though he was trying to hit a home run. Travis ducked under the attack and lunged at Mullen, grabbing him around the waist. The two of them crashed into the captain's chair and the wheel.

Now the craft was headed directly for a point where the canal split into two channels. Travis yanked the wheel to the left, sending them back into the smaller canal and not into the main channel. The back end of the boat was now in flames as a result of the first flare. Travis released his hold on Mullen and took hold of the gaff. They each pulled and pushed, trying to gain control of the improvised weapon. Mullen saw an opportunity, and he pushed Travis down the ladder and let go of the gaff. Travis tumbled backward off of the bridge and landed hard on the main deck. The pain from his ribcage was so sharp he struggled to breathe. He could see Mullen up top looking for and finding the flare gun on the floor. Mullen loaded the last flare as he guided the boat around a sweeping curve in the tight waterway. Travis was trying to get to his feet by using the gaff like a crutch.

Something caught Travis's eye through the front windows of the wheelhouse as Mullen looked backward over the railing for the injured officer. It was a bridge that connected Naples to the smaller islands. Although the bridge arched up to allow boats to pass under, this particular canal was not designed for a vessel the size of The Cottonmouth. As Mullen took aim, he saw the startled look in

Travis's eyes and turned in time to see the bridge just as his prized fishing boat hit it. The momentum of the boat was great enough to rip the top five feet of the flybridge clean off, sending debris flying everywhere. Mullen was thrown to the lower deck and landed on top of Travis, with his body impaling itself on the gaff that Travis was still holding upright.

The impact drove the hook end through Mullen's sternum and into his heart. He landed on his side facing Travis Jensen. They were both covered in shards of fiberglass, wood and metal. Snake's eyes were fixed on Travis as blood trickled from his mouth and oozed from his chest. He struggled to get a few words out. "Patrick Sullivan? You're a cop?"

Travis replied, "Yeah, I'm a cop, asshole, and guess what? I'm the cop who just killed you." Travis twisted the gaff and shoved it deeper into Peter's chest. The final convulsion of Snake's body signaled the end for the drug-running pimp.

The boat's engines had stopped when the collision tore the controls out, and the vessel drifted under the bridge. Travis crawled forward to the wheelhouse that was still mostly intact and made his way through the V berth and out a deck hatch to the bow of the boat. The stern was now fully engulfed in flames, sending a dark black plume of smoke skyward. Within seconds, a lifeguard boat pulled up bow-to-bow and Travis was able to leap over to it as the flames began to claim the *Cottonmouth* and the body of Peter Mullen.

***

Most of Naples Island was closed down for the next 24 hours as the Homicide Unit and the District Attorney's Officer Involved Shooting team tried to piece together what had happened. In just a matter of minutes, over 100 rounds had been fired, two officers had been wounded, three more were injured, two suspects were killed, and one officer paid the ultimate price. One of the finest neighborhoods in Southern California now looked like a war zone. Snake's house was riddled with holes and broken glass. The garden wall and gate had been destroyed by Lawrence in the Hummer, and the Fire Department was putting out the burning boat about a half-mile away.

Paramedics were treating Travis and Ben, who were reunited at the command post, when a voice said, "Dude, I'm gone a few weeks and you blow up half the frickin' city." Travis sat up from the gurney, shielded his eyes from the morning sun and saw Jesse standing in front of him. "What are you doin' here?" Travis asked.

"Frank Tillbak called me and told me what happened, so I figured you could use some help."

"Well, thanks for comin' bro."

Travis refused to be taken to the hospital. He had broken some ribs years before and knew there was nothing a doctor could do for them. He figured he could be of better help if he stayed at the scene. Ben had to be taken to the hospital where doctors could keep an eye on his concussion. The ER was a zoo, with the media scrambling for a story and family members of the injured officers arriving, some in shock and others in tears. The family of Officer Jimenez was taken to a private room where a Catholic priest gave them the terrible news. Ben's wife, Donna, had been brought to the hospital by a squad car that had picked her up at the communications center. Working as a dispatcher, she had listened to the chain of events over the radio. Her professionalism had kept her composed through it all, until she saw her husband sitting in a wheelchair in the ER hallway. She burst into tears, grateful that he was not seriously hurt. When she saw Jimenez's mother step into the hallway, she felt guilty that by chance she had her husband but Mrs. Jimenez had lost her son.

Back at Snake's house, the rest of the SWAT team cleared the residence to ensure there were no more suspects. As they came out, Travis thanked each one of them for their time and hard work. He had already walked through the shooting events with the Homicide Unit and the District Attorney's investigator, but there was still the issue of executing the search warrant and searching the house. So he set about it with the help of Jesse, Frank Tillbak, Terry and some patrol officers. The patrol guys searched upstairs while Jesse and Frank looked for the computers and surveillance equipment. Travis headed directly to the office, the place where Jennifer said she had seen the hidden compartments of money and drugs.

The office was paneled from floor to ceiling in a dark cherry wood and had matching built-in bookshelves on two walls. On one set of shelves, there were two large stereo speakers. The large partners' desk in the middle of the room had a laptop on it and a stack of papers. Around the room, there were a few spots of white powder and books on the floor. This minor damage was from stray bullets ripping through the walls. By now, Travis was having a hard time bending his knee after hyperextending it on the boat. He also had trouble seeing out of his left eye, thanks to Peter's right foot in the fight. He told Terry, "Hey, pull out one of those speakers and see what's behind it." Terry climbed up and stood on the desk. He pulled the two and a half foot tall speaker off of the shelf, pulled out the wires from the back and sat it on the desk. He stood there looking into the empty cubbyhole and said, "Nothin' here, dude."

"Is it made of wood in the back?" Travis asked.

"Yeah, same as the other walls."

"Tap on it. See if it's solid." Terry reached in and knocked with his knuckles and immediately recognized the hollow, loose rattle. His face beamed with excitement as he punched the wooden panel in the lower corner. The panel twisted and fell forward onto Terry's arm. He reached in and pulled it out. Behind the false panel there was a void about eight inches deep and the same size as the speaker. Inside, Terry saw two bundles of meth with the same type of packing as the one found on Flores at the motel. Terry pulled them out, set them on the desk and quickly moved to the other speaker. He pulled it out and tossed it on the floor in haste. Making a fist, he punched the back panel and it too fell away, but that compartment was empty.

"Where's the money?" Travis asked rhetorically. Joe Marino walked into the room and said, "Chances are he was getting ready to make a buy from his supplier, so he moved the money to another location. It's not good to keep the money and dope in the same place." Joe was right, Travis figured. He had worked a lot of narcotics cases in his prior assignments, and it made sense. At least they'd found the dope that Jen had told them about. They didn't need it for prosecution now, but it would help shut up all the activists and naysayers when the inevitable complaints came in about how the L.B.P.D. had killed a prominent member of the community and a former football star.

Terry took care of the contraband, and Travis continued to look around the grand house. He hadn't eaten for almost 18 hours, so he grabbed a bagel from the kitchen and a bottle of water from the big refrigerator. When he shut the door, Jesse was standing there looking at him with disapproval on his face. Jesse didn't say anything, but Travis figured he'd better explain. "I'm fucking hungry. Besides, it's not like he's gonna miss it or complain."

"Whatever," Jesse responded. "Hey, we found security cameras and a monitor, but no recording device. We even looked in the attic for a hard drive, but no luck. I think Snake took it out for some reason. You don't have a system like this and no way to record it."

"Well, thanks for lookin', bro. We could have used you on this one, *mi amigo*," Travis said as he placed his left hand on Jesse's right shoulder. Jess pointed with his thumb toward the garage and said, "We did find something I think you should see." The two of them walked down the hall past the paintings Travis had talked with Mullen about at the party. The house was now crawling with personnel taking photographs of the damage and documenting the locations of shell casings and bullets. Some were just there to look at the mess and try to figure what this was going to cost the city.

When the two got to the garage, Jesse motioned to the black Firebird as it was being hooked up to a tow truck. "What do ya make of that?" Jesse asked.

"It's Lawrence's car. When I followed him the other night he was driving it."

"No, not the car, under it." When the truck pulled the black car outside, Travis could see a three-foot-by-five-foot patch job of concrete on the floor.

"Yeah, looks like he had a slab leak or something," Travis said.

"Nope, it wasn't a slab leak. I looked around the house. There's no plumbing in this part of the house, and the sewer goes out from the front to the street. Besides, a plumber or, say, a contractor would've used a concrete saw. This is a hack job."

"So, what are you saying?"

"I think there's something under there."

"Like what?"

"I don't know, but I'd like to find out."

"Well, we kinda did a lot of damage already, if you didn't notice," Travis said.

"I know, so I called my cousin. He works for the Sheriff's Department. They've got a machine called ground penetrating radar, it's like an X-ray machine. If there's something under there it can tell us what it is, or at least if we should dig or not."

"Is everyone in the Guerra family a gadget freak?"

"Oh, yeah and He's worse than me. Why don't you head to the station and get some sleep while we wrap this up. You look like I did a few weeks ago."

Travis limped back to the command post and got an ice pack for his knee from one of the paramedics before they left. The medic wrapped it with an Ace bandage over Travis's jeans. The mood around the small armada of police cars and support vehicles was somber. The loss of Officer Jimenez was weighing heavy on everyone's minds. The chief was there; he gave Travis a hug and said, "God, I'm glad you're OK, son." Travis addressed the group of command staff and officers gathered around a folding table. "If you folks don't mind, I'm going to head back to the station for a little rest." They all nodded or just smiled at Travis. Commander Baker said, "Let me drive you, Jensen." After checking out with the crime scene scribe, the two of them walked down Second Street to Baker's plain Crown Victoria. Travis fell asleep before they ever left Belmont Shore.

Once in the office, Baker opened his locker and pulled out an old Army cot. "I keep this here for occasions just like this," he said with pride. "Why don't you just crash here for a while? I'll have a unit bring your car back from the scene."

"Thanks, sir. These last few weeks have been kinda crazy for ya, I bet."

"Yep, you guys are definitely sending me off with a bang."

Travis took off his gear while Baker unfolded the makeshift bed. Travis didn't care that it was a cot; when he lay down, it felt like the Ritz Carlton. About two hours into his slumber, Travis heard Jesse's excited voice and woke up. He sat up quickly and looked around, but he was alone in Baker's office. He figured it was a dream and plopped back down. He heard it again, but it was preceded by a beeping sound. It was his direct connect mode on his phone. He picked up the phone from the floor and called back to his partner, "Yo, Jess, what's up? I was asleep."

"Guess what was under the concrete." Pausing to collect his thoughts and rub his eyes, Travis said, "I don't know, Jimmy Hoffa?"

"No, but close. It's a body."

"What? There's a body under his garage?"

"I told you there was something under it."

"You were right, bro. I owe you a big cold beer for that one. Hey, who is it?"

"They don't know yet, the coroner is slowly uncovering her.

Well, we think it's a her 'cause she's in a dress, but who knows in this town? I'll call you back if we get any more, I've got Sandy on the other line."

When Jess hung up to talk to his wife, Travis realized he hadn't called home. When he reached Sarah, she had already heard the news from Sandy Guerra. She cried at first and then they talked for a few minutes about how they missed each other. Sarah had already called Travis's mother and brother to let them know he was all right. When the news of an officer being killed hits the media, family members could find it hard to cope until they were reassured that it wasn't *their* loved one. So, wives, husbands and friends would spread what news they had as quickly as possible to help alleviate that fear. Before Travis could lay his head down again, Jesse called back. "What do you got for me, Jess?" Travis asked.

"The body was on top of a purse. Does the name Gina Duran ring any bells?"

"No, how'd you get her name?"

"It's on the driver's license in the purse."

"Does she have a Long Beach address?" Travis asked.

"Nope, it's from Prescott, Arizona."

Travis thought for a minute and wondered why Arizona seemed important to him. He got up from the cot and left the commander's office. "Jess, hang on. I need to look at something." He went across the hall to his office and unlocked it with the key on his badge chain. He sat down at his desk and pulled Snake's case file out of the top drawer. He studied it for a while as Jess rambled on about the crime scene. "Man, T.J., you should see this place. The fuckin' mayor's here giving a press conference like he's running the show. Snake only had one skeleton under his garage; I bet the mayor has a few in his closet."

Travis interrupted him. "I found it! Do you remember when we interviewed Pandora in the office?"

"Yeah."

"She said a girl named Gigi went missing after pissing off Snake."

"Yeah, how do we know this is her?"

"Gigi was from Arizona. Plus the name is too close. Not much of a stretch to get Gigi as a nickname from Gina," Travis explained.

"Wow, this guy was a coldblooded motherfucker." Jess paused and said, "Hey, Fred Crackers wanted me to tell you they found your gun on the boat and he'll bring it down to homicide when he comes in to file."

"Great. We'll see ya in a while. Thanks again for comin' out, Jess."

Travis headed to the homicide office to put the morning's events on paper. There were officers sitting in the hallway, in chairs and on desks. A stack of pizza boxes and soda cans was on the secretaries' credenza like a makeshift buffet to feed the two dozen officers milling about. Every homicide detective had been called in, plus some of the violent crimes detectives. Today made Travis's shooting at the motel look like a simple use of a baton. While he waited for a secretary to dictate his report, Travis tried to call Jennifer to give her the news. The recorded message said her cell phone was no longer in service. Travis looked through her snitch file for her bio sheet and realized it was the only phone number he had for her. Travis wondered, *Did she not pay her bill? Did she have to change the number for some reason? Why didn't she call me to let me know?* He would have to wait until after the job at hand was done to find out why.

Chapter Eleven

Life Rolls On

Travis didn't think he would be able to sleep after the adrenaline filled day and the draining investigation that followed, but after his shower, he fell asleep on top of the covers and didn't wake for nearly 16 hours. He would have slept more, but the doorbell kept ringing. He got to his feet and pulled on some gym shorts and a tank top. He couldn't figure who it could be other than one of his brother's romantic rejects stopping by to see whose car was parked in the driveway. Travis peeked through the curtains of the window next to the door and saw Sarah standing there. He opened the door and quietly stared at her. She simply gazed back at him until she squinted her eyes and two tears ran down her cheeks.

"Oh God, Travis, it could have been you," she said as she began to shake. Lunging at him, she wrapped her arms around his neck, laid her head against his shoulder and said, "I don't know if the girls and I could survive if ... well, you know."

"Don't talk like that, honey. Hey, where are the girls?"

"Your mom took them to a movie today so I could come see you."

"Why aren't you at work?"

"It's Saturday."

"You're kidding. It's Friday, Paul's at work."

"No, he's with your mom and the girls. He called me and told me you were asleep all day. They all love you very much, Travis, and I do too."

"Come on in," Travis said as he stepped back, still holding his beautiful wife. He shut the door behind her, took her hand and led her to the living room. When he passed the bar he looked at the clock on the wall and saw it was now four in the afternoon. Somewhere along the way, he'd lost a day or it lost him. Sarah sat on the couch, and Travis sat on the ottoman facing her.
She took his hands in hers and asked, "Are you OK?"

"Yeah, I'm fine."

"Fine? That's the one word that tells people that you're not OK. Do you want to talk about it?"

"It was so fast. I'm still not sure of everything that happened. There was something like 14 or 15 shooters and two bad guys. It must have sounded like Baghdad, there were so many damn shots going off. We're lucky some of the rounds didn't hit any civilians." Travis went on about how the event had evolved and his part in it. When he got to the part about the patrol officer being killed, he choked up. Sarah asked, "Did you know him very well?"

"No, I remember him from when I taught at the academy, but that's it. It just reminds me of ..." Travis hesitated, so Sarah finished his sentence.

"Of Derrick?"

"Yeah," Travis said. His lip began to quiver, and he cried out, "I miss him so much." Travis put his head down and cried harder than he had since he was a child. Sarah did her best to comfort him in his pain. It had been seven years since Derrick Brown, an academy classmate of Travis's, had been killed by a gangster's bullet under the Hill Street Bridge at Orange Avenue. They thought Derrick had stopped the kid for riding a bike without a light, and the kid had decided to run. Unknown to Derrick, the kid had just robbed a lady on Willow Street in Signal Hill. Derrick was found with his unfired gun in his hand, face down among the tires and trash on a dirt trail under the bridge where railroad tracks used to be. Derrick Brown died alone that night, and Travis took that hard because he'd been on vacation and likely would have been working the same beat. He always felt he could have done something or that they might have been partnered up in the same car.

Times like this tore at Travis from the inside. The prospect of attending another cop's funeral made his stomach ache. He had been to several, but they all reminded him of Derrick's and of his own father's, watching his grandfather play the bagpipes as the flag-draped casket was brought out of the church with hundreds, sometimes thousands, of police officers saluting. It didn't matter if the officer was black, like Derrick, or white, or this time Mexican; the pipes were always a reminder of the early Irish roots in American law enforcement. They were a reminder of a time when no one else except the Irish immigrants would do the job.

Soon Travis and Sarah were lying on the couch holding each other and talking about the case, the future and their marriage. Sarah ran her fingers through Travis's hair and made fun of the way it was standing up because he'd fallen asleep with it wet. Soon Travis and Sarah were consumed by passionate kissing and petting. As they drew deeper into the moment, Sarah said, "I told Paul not to come home 'till we called him." The two left the confining couch and headed for the bedroom.

Later, as they were getting dressed, Sarah asked, "So what happens with the case now?"

"Well, it's kinda done. You can't prosecute a dead guy."

"No, I know that. What about your snitch? I mean, do you still use her for other cases?"

"No. Not this one. She was just for this guy, but I still have to find her and let her know what happened." Travis could see the disappointment in Sarah's face. She looked toward the ceiling and said, "Do what you need to do, but when it's done, and I mean done, I want you to come back home." She looked back at Travis to see his reaction. He smiled, nodded his head and said, "I understand, and Sarah, I'm willing to go to counseling."

Sarah smiled and asked, "So do you have plans for tomorrow?"

"I think I'm going to go see my Daideó, it's been a long time."

"That would be nice. Perhaps you could invite him over to the house. I don't think he's seen the girls since Christmas." The time with Sarah gave Travis a sense of hope for their future. It was his recent past that he had to deal with now.

***

Sunday brought more rain and a lighter than normal turnout at Saint Anthony's Church at Sixth and Olive. It had been years since Travis had set foot inside the beautiful church where his parents

219

were married and he'd been baptized. He genuflected and made the sign of the cross before sitting in the half-empty pew. Feeling fidgety, Travis tugged at his wet sweater like a schoolboy dying to take off his uniform. Travis thought that because his lifestyle hadn't been exactly Christian-like lately that he didn't quite fit in with the church anymore.

As the pews began to fill, he saw his grandfather seating an elderly couple. For as long as he could remember, his grandfather – or as Travis called him by the Irish term for grandfather, Daideó – had been volunteering at the Mass as an usher, lector or whatever the Monsignor needed. The real Patrick Sullivan was into his nineties and was now starting to show the signs of Parkinson's. His hair had turned from reddish brown to pure white, but his eyes were still as green as the emerald island he called home. When he saw Travis sitting there, the old man slapped his leg and said in his Irish brogue, "Travis, my boy, so good to see ya. Your mum has been prayin' overtime for ye soul."

"I know, Daideó, I've been kinda knee deep in the crap lately," Travis said as he stood to give his grandfather a hug. Travis stayed for the Mass but did not take communion. This fact was not lost on his granddad. At the end of Mass, Travis waited outside the church in the misty drizzle and watched as the parishioners milled about. His grandfather made his way down the front stairs while holding the railing. As he approached, he said, "Why didn't you accept the Eucharist, son?"

"I haven't been to confession in a long time, Daideó."

"Father Bill could have taken you."

Travis looked down and snickered, "I think it would take all morning to confess my sins."

"Right, in that case I know what you need, fella."

"Oh, I don't know, Grandpa."

"Drive me there and I'll be your earpiece." Travis opened the passenger door to his SUV and helped his grandfather as he struggled to get into the raised seat. As they drove to the pub on Broadway, Travis suggested it might be a bit early to start drinking. "Gee, Daideó, its only noon. Don't you think that's kinda early?"

"Noon? That makes it eight at night in Ireland. So we missed happy hour boy, step on it." They took a cozy booth in the corner and were greeted by a cute blonde waitress who handed them two menus. "Hi Sully. Who's your friend?"

"Why, my dear, this is my grandson Travis. He's an inspector with the local morals police, so you'd best be runnin' a square house, love." Travis was embarrassed by his grandpa's crass description of the Vice Unit, but that was what they'd called it in his day. Mr. Sullivan continued, "Would ya be a darlin' and bring us two pints and a snort each of your best single malt." If Sarah thought Travis had a drinking problem, it wasn't a mystery which side of the family it came from.

"I've had a rough go of it lately, Daideó. I almost lost my partner and had to kill a guy, then Friday we had a huge shootout and a young copper was killed."

"I know, Travis, and you're askin' yourself if it's all worth it or not."

"Yeah, I mean, I don't know."

The waitress set the drinks on the table. She gave the old man a peck on the cheek and said, "It's nice to see you, Sully." Patrick held his shot glass up to eye level and slowly rotated it, examining the dark amber liquid inside. He held it up to Travis and with one word he toasted the old police force with which he had served for 20 years after the war: "Garda." Travis raised his glass, tapped Patrick's and repeated, "To the Garda." Patrick took a gentle sip of the whiskey with his eyes closed, licked his upper lip and said, "Like being kissed by the angels." He set the glass down and picked up the beer and raised it. "Here's to cheating, stealing, fighting and drinking. If you cheat, cheat death. If you steal, steal a woman's heart. If you fight, fight for a brother. And if you drink, drink with me." And with that they both tipped their glasses. "Travis, you know the job hasn't changed much in 50 years."

"Are you kidding, Daideó? It's totally different now. We have computers, helicopters and the Internet. It's nothing like when you worked in Limerick."

"Oh, it's not, is it? Sure, you have the technology stuff now, but take that away and it's the same. A bunch of overworked, underpaid constables and inspectors trying to keep the fringe elements of society from running amok. And we both know there's no greater trill than chasing down a robber or sneak thief and workin' him with the business end of your bludgeon. Let's face it, Travis, the public wants you to do this job because they won't or can't. Take care of business just as long as they don't have to see it. You see, police work is the same on both sides of the pond, my boy. That's why I knew your dad would be right for my little girl. He was a cop's cop, but he put the family first. Perhaps that's what you need to do now."

"So, you know Sarah and I have been living apart?"

"I may be old, Travis, but I'm not dead." The two shared a few drinks and more than a few good cop stories before they left the bar. The rain had stopped and the sun was now breaking through the clouds. Travis drove his grandfather the few blocks to the small two-bedroom house he had lived in for nearly forty-three years. While they were walking to the door, Patrick said, "I suspect I will be getting a call to play the pipes at the funeral, so I will see you then, my boy. This will be my last time, son."

"Why's that?"

"I'm finding it hard to work my fingers on the chanter and my lungs can't fill the bag like they used to. Oh, and Travis, call your mother."

"Thanks Daideó, I will."

***

It was now Tuesday, and Travis still had not been able to reach Jennifer. By now she had to have heard about the shooting because it had been on the news for four days straight. Her phone was still shut off, so he drove to Cheryl's beach house. The house was locked, and there were no cars in the driveway. The only other person he could think of who knew Jennifer was the strip club owner, Antranig. It was late afternoon when Travis got to The Powder Room and the place was already packed. He parked in the employee lot, and that drew the attention of the parking lot security guy. Travis was pretty well frustrated by this time, so he flashed his badge and told the guy it was official business. After being let in the back door, Travis paused to let his eyes adjust to the darkness. He stopped a waitress as she passed by and asked, "Where's Antranig?" Without saying a word she motioned with her head toward the bar.

Antranig was sitting on the last stool with a bottle of water in front of him. His fat butt hung over the stool, and the rear tails of his shirt were pulled out, making him look like a slob. He was slouched over, looking at bar receipts and writing down numbers on a pad of paper. *He may be a slob*, Travis thought, *but he's a rich slob*. Travis tapped him on his shoulder and said, "I'm looking for Jennifer." Antranig spun around and looked Travis up and down and said, "I not know a Jennifer."

Travis replied, "Yes you do, she goes by Summer."

"Ah, yes. You are that fellow she brought here."

"Yes, that's right."

"She's not here."

"Do you know where she is? It's real important."

"No. Look around, there's plenty more girls to see." Travis showed the bar owner his badge and said, "I'm not here to watch tit dancers. Do you know where she is?" Antranig stared at the brass badge that hung around Travis's neck, then back at him. "No, I don't know, I swear, but she did come by a few days ago. Ask her friend Bunny, they talked. Hey, I didn't know you were the police." Antranig pointed to Cheryl, who was sitting in a booth with two Asian businessmen. She was dressed in a red two-piece bathing suit that had more strings than a quartet. She was running her fingers through one guy's hair while her other hand was on the second guy's leg. She sure had these guys shellin' out the money thinking it might get them laid.

Travis walked up to the table and said, "I'm sorry, gentlemen, I'm with the management and I need to talk with Miss Bunny for a moment." He put his hand out, and she took it with a stunned look on her face. She led him to one of the changing rooms behind the main stage. She sat down in front of a vanity and asked with a smile, "Is this a personal or professional call, detective?"

"Cheryl, I'm looking for Jennifer, and her phone is out. Do you know where she is?"

"Not exactly."

"What does that mean?"

"She came by here on Saturday and was real upset. She said there were people dead because of her and was just jumpy like she'd seen a ghost."

"Yeah, there was a shooting, but it wasn't because of her."

"She said she wanted to get away for a while and that was the last I've seen of her. She'll come back soon. She has to, her stuff is at my place." Travis reached into his shirt pocket and pulled out a business card. "Here's my number. Can you call me if you hear from her?"

"Sure thing, sweetie." As Travis headed for the door, Cheryl said, "Don't be a stranger, detective." Travis looked over his shoulder to see Cheryl blowing him a kiss. It looked tempting, but

Travis figured one adult entertainer in his life was enough.

Heading back to San Pedro on the San Diego Freeway, Travis felt a bit of relief come over him. It looked like Jennifer knew about Snake's demise. Now he could concentrate on his own problems and not hers. He started by calling his wife. He talked with her for half an hour about their problems and about going to counseling. When he was done, he felt good. For the first time in a long while, he actually believed they could save the marriage and that it was what they both wanted. Like Daideó had told him, it was now time to put family first.

***

When Wednesday came around, the team met in the office at 2:00 p.m. The mood was somber, because the talk was about the upcoming funeral for Officer Jimenez. Ben was there, but his neck was still a little stiff. Jesse was also back to work but was on light duty and therefore could not go into the field. Terry showed up a little late because he'd been at the home of Jimenez's mother and little sisters. He was taking it very hard that Jimenez had died in his arms. He felt that he owed a debt to the late officer for giving his life to lay down cover fire for him and his partner. He had gone to the Jimenez house every day since the shooting, helping with chores and cooking; whatever they needed, he took care of it. The only one missing was Sergeant Joe Marino.

The phone rang and Jack Barnes answered it. "Vice Squad." This was followed only by, "Got it." He placed the phone on the receiver. It was Marino. He was in the homicide office and was letting the guys in the squad know their guns had all been processed and were ready for them to pick up. All of them except Jesse quietly shuffled out the door and down the hall to pick up their guns. When they got back to the vice office, they were shocked to see Commander Baker and Chief Robbins of the Detective Bureau sitting in the chairs that they had taken from Baker's office. They were talking with Jesse, and it looked like a serious topic.

Chief Robbins was a nice guy but had climbed the ladder way too fast. How could anyone command all of the detectives for a major police department when he'd never worked as a detective himself? Some of his decisions left the detectives scratching their heads, but this one was heartfelt and reassuring. Robbins stood up and said, "You guys need to plan Guerra's party. He has two more weeks in vice, then he's going to computer crimes to help out Tillbak." Everyone looked around wondering what to say. Travis spoke up. "Is he getting special detailed or is it permanent?" Jesse answered the question. "It's permanent. I was going to tell you guys last week, but it wasn't official 'till now." The chief shook everyone's hands as he and Baker left the office.

When the door closed behind them, everyone began protesting to Marino about Jesse's transfer. Then Jesse quieted everyone down by saying, "I asked for it." The room went silent. He continued, "I asked him a few weeks ago if there was a desk job I could have. Look, Sandy is real freaked about me goin' back out there right now, and frankly I'm not so sure I'm good with it either. Frank's absolutely swamped in computer crimes, so Robbins actually created a new position just for me." Travis walked over to his best friend, put his hand on his shoulder and said, "Well, if anyone deserves it, it's you, bro," and embraced him. Marino brought back some normalcy to the group when he said, "OK, stop the bromance, enough hugging. Let's hit the beach lots and arrest some boys before dinner. Jess, ride with me, and no getting out of the car except to eat."

Ben said, "That's the *only* time he ever gets out of the car, boss." Joe knew the best thing for the team was to get them back in the field and not lament the tragedy of the prior week. The guys all grabbed their kits and radios and headed out to the elevator. Everyone was back together, laughing and joking, for the first time since Jess had gotten hurt. It gave Travis a feeling of a new beginning – a new beginning for Jess, for Jennifer, and hopefully him and Sarah.

As the elevator doors were closing, Commander Baker stuck his hand in and stopped it. He said, "Marino, I need you to get out the watch report on the pending detective openings tonight so we can start collecting resumes." Joe replied, "OK boss," as the doors closed. Terry Knight asked Marino, "Hey, did he say openings, as in plural?" Marino said, "Yeah, there could be one in narcotics or something. Why, are you afraid we're gonna cut you from the team, Terry?" The group went back to laughing and headed out for a night's work.

The weather was still damp, so the guys gave up on the beach and went to dinner at their favorite burger joint on Atlantic Avenue. While they were chowing down, Joe made an announcement. "Since you guys put in so much work last week, I'll go in on the first whore we see, so Jess, jump in T.J.'s car." Terry, being the newest member, asked nervously, "Is it true that when you get a girl in your car you always get her nake-nake?" The salty sergeant smiled and said, "Yep, and the fatter the better." Terry responded, "No way."

Jesse said, "He's not kidding," and began to tell the group about an arrest they had made long before Ben, Jack, and Terry had joined the unit. "OK, we were workin' an outcall one night at the Hilton and Sergeant Bates was there talkin' about how you're not a real vice cop until you get your cock grabbed by a lewd and get a call girl naked. Well, Joe had set up a girl for himself to work but told Collin if he was such a stud he could have her and show us. So, Collin goes in the room and waits for this chick. We were all in the booking room and Joe pulls out her picture from her website. This gal was close to 250, maybe 270 and like only five feet tall. Apparently Collin didn't know that Joe orders 'em big. This fat chick shows up and gives Collin a massage and then starts a strip show for him, while we were all just bustin' up next door. Now, to Collin's credit, he made the deal in the first five minutes, but after talkin' so much shit to us he wasn't gonna give the hit sign 'till this chick got full nake-nake. Then she pulls out a riding crop and starts smackin' Bates on his ass while he's on the bed." By now the guys were in stitches with the image of Bates being ridden by a gal who was five foot tall and five foot wide. Ben asked, "So what did he do?"

Jess continued, "So now he's got to give the hit, which for some reason he picked the phrase 'happy day,' I have no clue why. He says it a few times but it's kinda muffled into a pillow so he blurts it out. We start headin' for the door and now we hear her yelling, 'Oh, happy day, oh, happy day.' We get in the room and she is straddling Bates who is face down on the bed in his underwear and can't get up. This nasty chick had big-ass pimples on her legs, and the only thing she had on were a pair of torn stockings. There she was ridin' Bates like a pony, whipin' his ass yelling, 'Happy day, happy day!'"

Ben said, "No shit?"

"Oh yeah, Joe has a Polaroid of it. It's in his desk."

Terry said, "We gotta see that."

Joe said, "You will next month at Bates' retirement party, I'm

226

getting it blown up like a poster."

Surfer boy Ben said, "Epic, that's wicked epic."

Joe made good on his promise to go in on the first girl of the night. She wasn't a fatty, but he did get her halfway to nake-nake. She was a young black girl with super-long fingernails and big hoop earrings like a movie hooker from the '70s. Nice, clean skin and young. She was definitely a 'Downtown Ten," nothing special in the real world, but on the streets of downtown, at the top of the food chain. She had just taken off her pants while reclining in the passenger seat when she caught a glimpse of Terry sitting in his car under a street light. She bolted from Joe's car like a steer out of the gate at a rodeo, naked from the waist down and running barefoot through the darkness toward Linden and PCH. Joe got on the radio and said, "She's good to go, boys. Get on it." Terry was hot on her heels when she made it to the highway. In a flash, she crossed the six lanes of traffic without hesitating. Terry had to wait for the cars to clear. When the rest of the team caught up, they had lost her in the night. Terry kept searching around on foot while the other guys went back and got their cars.

It wasn't long before Terry heard a commotion at Eddie's Liquor at MLK and PCH. A lot of wild stuff went on in this neighborhood, but a half-naked woman hiding behind the counter was out of the ordinary. Terry made it into the store just in time to see the little Asian cashier take a broom and whack the cowering crack whore, who was curled up on the floor. Joe's slippery date ended up being wanted on a parole violation, which explained her motivation to run. After she was rescued from the crazy broom-wielding clerk, she was much more cooperative with the team. Jess got back in Joe's car to keep an eye on his hooker just in case she got froggy again. The crew resumed rolling the circuit looking for more targets. After Ben closed a deal at the corner of Eighth and Olive, Travis headed to the gas station at Seventh and Alamitos to take a leak. When he walked in, the store clerk recognized him from the night Cowboy was shot.

"Hey, Detective, I got that tape," he said as he set down the cigarettes he was stocking.

Travis asked, "What tape is that?"

"The one from the night of the shooting," he said as he pointed to the intersection. He continued, "My boss pulled the tape out the next morning, but I lost your card. Hang on, I'll get it." Travis headed for the back room and said, "Great, I'll be right out, I gotta piss." Travis didn't care about the tape now. All he wanted was to do his business and hit the road. When he came back out, the clerk had the VHS tape wrapped in a large manila envelope, and he had a big grin on his face. He was so proud to be able to help the police that Travis felt bad about telling him it wasn't needed anymore. Before Travis could say anything, the clerk said with excitement, "I hope this helps you guys catch him." Travis just took the envelope and said, "I hope so too, thanks for all your help." The kid offered Travis a free soda or water, but he declined.

Travis went to his trunk and tossed the tape into his kit bag. After getting in the car, he made contact with the other guys over the radio, and they were back on the prowl. The team racked up four arrests for prostitution and headed back to the house to book them in for the night. Travis hadn't made any arrests, so while the guys were filing their reports he began to read over the case file on Snake. He'd wanted to see it through to prosecution, but justice came early. In the back of the folder was Jennifer's snitch file. Travis opened it and looked at her mug shot taken the night he'd arrested her. He couldn't believe he had actually been with her. She was so beautiful and young. He definitely felt he was playing up a league or so. He looked over her booking slip that Jess had filled out that night. He read what was written in each box: name, date of birth, and so on. At the bottom Jess had listed her belongings as "condoms, massage oil, keys and vibrator." He loved doing that just to see the uptight secretary in booking blow a gasket. As Travis studied the entries on the page, something looked odd or possibly familiar to him.

The team sluggishly entered the office. It was late, and the first night back on swing shift was always the hardest. Travis couldn't concentrate with all the noise, so he decided to walk down the hall and get a soda from the break room. He grabbed enough quarters from his desk drawer and left the office. At the far end of the dark hall, a light was on in an office. It was almost midnight, so there shouldn't have been anyone on the floor but vice and narcotics. Travis dropped his change in the slot and opted for the most caffeine he could get for a dollar and a quarter. When he went back in the hall, he headed for the open office where he could see the light. The sound of typing could be heard as he got closer. When he reached the Homicide Unit's door, he saw Gwen, the unit secretary, typing away feverishly at a computer terminal. Her back was turned to the door, and Travis didn't notice the earphones under her long black hair. When Travis stepped into view, Gwen shouted and jumped out of her chair. "Holy crap, Jensen, I was transcribing and didn't hear you come in."

"Sorry, Gwen, I was just lookin' to see who was here so late."

"Just me. I'm transcribing the interviews from the big OIS last week. I need the overtime. My son's college tuition is coming up next month."

Travis looked around the office for a second and said, "Hey, I need to take a look at the 187 from Seventh and MLK, I was helping White with it."

"Sure, go ahead. It's probably on his desk."

Travis walked over to the senior investigator's corner desk and sat in his chair. He began to look at the various brown accordion folders placed neatly along one side of the desktop. Each had a name written in thick black pen along the top edge. Some had the names of two or three victims. Travis was impressed with the organization and dedication White put into his work. Finally he came across the one labeled, "Adams, William." Travis sifted through the file looking at the crime scene pictures and the sketches. He read some of the statements collected by the patrol guys, mostly from people who'd heard the shots but hadn't seen much. Travis wasn't sure what he was looking for until he came across Adams's rap sheet. There were several arrests listed from a town called Catoosa, Oklahoma. The charges became more serious with each new arrest. At first he was a shoplifter and a car thief, but he progressed to drugs, alcohol-related offenses and domestic violence. His last arrest got him five years in prison for aggravated assault and kidnapping. The one thing that caught Travis's attention was that the rap sheet was faxed to White from the Tulsa sheriff's office in Oklahoma.

He took a pen from his pocket and jotted down the state rap number for Adams and the name of the town where he'd been arrested so many times. Travis made sure to put the file back as he'd found it and thanked Gwen on his way out.

As he approached the vice office, the door opened and Jesse stepped out. "Hey, where've you been?" Jesse asked.

Travis looked at his watch and noticed he had been gone for almost 30 minutes. He said, "I was talkin' with Gwen down in homicide. She's working late on the OIS."

"Well, hurry up, we're all headed to The Tube. Joe's buying the first round."

"OK, I'll catch up. I need to put some things away."

Jesse headed for the elevator and Travis went into the empty office. He opened his desk drawer and pulled out a street guide for the city. A little book the size of a deck of cards, it listed every street in the city and some surrounding jurisdictions. Taped to the back cover was a list of states and their corresponding Social Security prefixes. Travis had used this tool in patrol when he'd questioned people about their identity. To avoid detection, crooks would often claim to be from another state, so Travis would ask them for a Social Security number. If it didn't match with the states index, then he figured they were probably lying about who they were.

He looked at Jennifer's Social Security number and there it was, the prefix 441. It was from Oklahoma, which made sense as Jennifer had said she'd lived in Tulsa with her grandmother. But what was her connection to Adams, or was it just a coincidence? To find out, he needed more detail on Mr. Adams's life. Travis got on the Internet and found a phone number for the Catoosa Police Department. When he called the number, all he got was a dispatcher. As with many small departments, it was closed for the night. The young lady with the cute country accent transferred Travis to the detective sergeant's voicemail. Travis left a message asking that he fax over the actual arrest reports for William Adams, explaining how Mr. Adams would no longer be a problem for the little town of Catoosa, Oklahoma.

The Tube was more crowded than usual for almost one o'clock in the morning. The entire vice squad was there as were some guys from north patrol. Jesse and Terry were arguing about which service was more important, the Army or the Marines. Terry got heated when Jess joked, "Do you know what M.A.R.I.N.E. stands for? It means, My Ass Rides In Navy Equipment." Jess loved pushing Terry's buttons. The place was poppin' like old times, Travis thought. He saw Joe sitting on a stool to the side, so Travis pulled an empty keg over from the corner and used it for a seat. "It's nice to have everyone back, isn't it?" Travis asked.

Joe looked over at the crowd and said, "Yep, kinda like going home for Christmas, but I'm gonna miss Jesse's humor in the unit." Travis took the schooner that Tommy the bartender had set in front of him, held it up to Joe and toasted, "To the morals police." Joe looked confused and asked, "What's the morals police?" Travis smiled and said, "That's what my grandpa calls the Vice Squad." Joe looked at the rest of the guys who were in a booth across the way and nodded in approval of the elder Sullivan's nickname for the unit. "To the morals police," Joe repeated as he tapped Travis's glass.

***

The next morning, Travis called the station and spoke with Debbie. He wanted to know if he'd received any faxes. Debbie told him, "Yeah, there's like 30 pages here, all reports from a department in Oklahoma." Travis explained that he was looking into the background of the guy who Snake had killed. He asked her if she would put them in the top drawer of his desk. The curiosity was driving him nuts, so he headed to work right away.

The office was dark, as he was several hours early and the day crew had taken the day off. Travis dropped his kit bag on the desk and turned on the small stereo that Joe kept on top of the file cabinets. While the music filled the room, he made himself comfortable in his chair and opened the top drawer. There was a manila envelope with his name in Debbie's writing. He pulled out the papers inside and looked them over.

The first page was a facsimile cover letter from Sgt. T. Vella of the Catoosa Police Department. Handwritten on the sheet was a note that read, *Sorry to hear that Willie Adams came to your city, but I'm glad he won't be coming back here. He was a real pain in our butts for many years. Here are all the reports on him, I hope they help.* Under the cover sheet were 32 pages of arrest reports beginning with the oldest one. Travis began reading the narratives that detailed the plunge that Cowboy took into the world of methamphetamine and crime.

While he was reading, he noticed that the message light on his phone was lit, so he took a break to check the messages. One was from the department shrink reminding him that he should make an appointment to meet and discuss the events of the last few weeks. The second call was from Cheryl. She said that Jennifer had called her and was coming by the house today to collect her things and then would be flying home. Travis called her back at the number on the caller ID.

"Hello," she said in a seductive voice.

231

"Cheryl?" Travis asked. "It's Detective Jensen."

Her voice changed to a more serious tone. "Oh, I'm glad you called back. Jennifer will be here in a few hours and she said she's flying back home for good. Is everything alright?"

"Yeah, I just need to talk with her before she goes. How is she?"

"She sounded upbeat on the phone."

"Good. Tell her I'm going to drop by and see her off."

Travis went back to reading the reports from Oklahoma and finally found the connection he was looking for. Cowboy's last arrest was for beating and torturing his girlfriend, Elizabeth Bennett. Travis read on and knew he had heard this story before. One of the witnesses in the case was Jennifer Bennett. Now it was clear. Jennifer and Elizabeth were sisters. So why was Cowboy looking for Elizabeth in Long Beach? Did she come out here with Jen? Travis seemed to have more questions than answers, so he called Sgt. Vella.

"Investigations, Sergeant Vella here," the voice answered.

"Sergeant Vella, Detective Jensen, Long Beach P.D. out here in California. How are you, sir?"

"Fine, Jensen, call me Tom."

"OK, Tom, I wanted to thank you for your quick response. I do have another request though."

"No problem, we're just glad to be rid of Adams. What can I do for ya?"

"Do you have anything on Elizabeth Bennett or her sister Jennifer?"

"Let me take a look," Vella said. Travis could hear the sound of a computer keyboard over the phone. Then Vella said, "Well, it looks like Elizabeth had a few run-ins with us for possession of a controlled substance and then as a victim on the domestic violence report I sent you."

"How about Jennifer?" Travis asked.

The sergeant began looking through his computer database, and then said, "She is listed as a witness on the same report with Elizabeth and once as a driver on an accident report, both like six years ago. Do you want the accident report?"

"No, that's cool."

"So, how did Adams get whacked?" Vella inquired.

"I think he came here looking for Elizabeth and he crossed this pimp I was working. Well, the pimp found Adams first and shotgunned him in the chest. We ended up killing the pimp and his muscle guy the next morning."

"Nice work."

"Jennifer Bennett is my informant on the case, and we were about to take the guy down for dealing when he capped your guy."

"Well, if there's anything else you need, call me," Vella said before he hung up the phone.

Travis figured he would grab a bite before he headed out to say goodbye to Jennifer. He opened his kit and took out his gun in a concealment holster. He tucked it inside his pants under his shirt and put his badge around his neck and dropped it inside the collar of his shirt. He left the bag there on his desk and walked across the street to a taco stand. The smell of the carne asada on the grill was alluring. The little stand always had a line of customers from when it opened at noon until it closed around midnight. He got his tacos and a drink and took them back to the office. He unrolled each taco from the foil and added a splash of hot sauce. It was like a little Mexican picnic there on his desk. One of the great pleasures of working in this city was the variety of ethnic food.

Travis was indulging his taste buds when he heard a knock on the door. With his mouth full, he walked over and opened the door. Debbie had another fax in her hand. "Here, Travis, this came for you," she said as she handed it to him. He tried to say thanks but he could only make a muffled sound or risk spitting chopped meat and onion on her. He took the papers and closed the door.

The fax was from Sgt. Vella. The note on the cover sheet read, *"I pulled that accident report anyway, and I'm glad I did. I think you need to read it."* Travis looked at the accident report and sat down. He continued to eat as he read the narrative. It told the story of a horrific accident on a farm road caused by a drunk driver. He set his taco down as the information in the report dumbfounded him. When he finished reading it, he sat there looking at his desk and his opened kit. He pulled out the envelope that was sticking out and removed the VHS tape that had been given to him the night before. He walked over to the television mounted on the wall above Collin Bates's desk, and slid the tape into the VCR. As the tape rewound to the beginning, Travis looked at his notes from the night of Cowboy's murder. The witnesses all put the time of the shots around 12:20 a.m. Travis stopped the tape and backed it up until the time stamp said 12:05 a.m. He let it play from there as he sat on the edge of Bates's desk. The time-lapse style of tape took a frame a second and played them back at normal speed. It was like watching it in fast forward.

The camera angle showed the propane tanks in a cage on the west side of the building, but the camera was pointed north so it didn't show the intersection. Travis watched and then paused the tape when he saw movement. First, he saw a homeless man walk up and piss on the wall. A few minutes later a black Mercedes backed up to the wall and stayed in the frame for about three minutes before pulling out. It was a great shot of the driver's side window. He played it back and forth several times and then backed the tape up to where the Mercedes came into view and removed it from the machine. He placed it, along with all the reports and Snake's file, in his kit bag, put his remaining taco in the refrigerator and headed out to take care of some unfinished business.

Chapter Twelve

The Send Off

There were still a few hours before the team would be in to work, so Travis headed to the basement of the police station. The hall was filled with the remnants of large cardboard boxes and Styrofoam packaging, and Frank Tillbak was on his back under a new desk. "It looks like Christmas came early, Frank," Travis said. Frank slid out from under the desk and said, "This is going to be Jesse's new workstation." Frank was beaming with joy that he wasn't going to be alone anymore in the computer lab. Finally he would have someone to talk with who understood him. For Travis, it was bittersweet. He was giving up the best partner he'd ever had, but he was happy for Jesse at the same time. "How can I help you, Travis?" Frank asked.

"I need to make a few copies of a VHS tape. Do you have that equipment down here?"

"Yeah. If you want to put it on a CD I can do it."

"A CD would be perfect. Can you show me how and I'll do it so you can get back to work?" Frank led him over to a rack that had several electronic components on it like a CD player, VCR, cassette decks – the works. He turned on the VCR and television, inserted the tape that Travis gave him, then sat down at a computer terminal. Frank opened a video editing program and set it up for Travis. Frank then instructed Travis, "OK, just click the mouse on record, then play the tape. When you're done, just click the stop button. It will prompt you to save to disc or file. Click the D drive and it will save it to the disc. Then it will ask if you want to make another. If you do, put in a new disc and click yes. Then when you're all done just close the program."

"Thanks, Frank, I've got it from here." Frank went back to work in the other room. Travis made two copies of the tape and slid them into some small paper jackets. Then Travis typed out a note on the computer and printed it out. He folded the note and tucked it in with one of the compact discs. He put the tape back in the envelope and tucked everything inside his kit. On his way out, Travis said, "Thanks, Frank, that was easy. You take care of my little buddy now." From underneath the half-assembled desk, Travis heard, "So long, Travis."

The air was turning cold as an armada of grey clouds blowing in from Northern California blocked the midday sun. It felt like winter, Travis thought. He liked the cold air; it made him feel alive and gave him a sense of progression of the seasons. He loved the winter because he would take Sarah and the girls to Big Bear and stay in a rented cabin for three or four days. The girls would play in the snow all day and then they would shop in town. When nightfall came the girls would be so tired they would fall asleep by eight o'clock, then Travis and Sarah would just hold each other in front of the fire. He was hoping it would be like that again soon, but knew he needed to find closure with Jennifer first.

Two trustees in orange jumpsuits were standing at the gas pumps when Travis pulled up with his undercover car. He had them fill it up and pull out all the trash on the floor. They filled half of a trashcan with burrito wrappers and a lot of beer cans. While his car was being tended to, Travis called Jesse to bring him up to speed on what was going on. "Jess, Jennifer is leaving town. I'm headed out now to see her off, but I may need you to meet me."

Jesse responded, "Whatever you need, bro."

"Let Joe know I'll be late. If he asks, tell him what I'm doing but tell him you're gonna hook up with me, ten four?"

"OK, but is there something wrong?"

"I don't think so. I'll give you a call soon."

When his car was ready, Travis jumped in and headed for the freeway. Normally it would take around 30 to 40 minutes to get to Redondo Beach from the station, but Travis covered the distance in about 20. He was eager to see her again and frustrated by the questions in his head. He pulled his car into the driveway and was met at the door by Cheryl. She was dressed in jeans and an off-white pullover sweater with her red hair draped around her face. She didn't look like a porn actress but more like a beautiful young Irish girl.

"Hi Travis, she's out back on the deck," she said as she opened the screen door. He walked through the beach house to the back door and saw Jennifer sitting on the same chaise where they had shared that incredible moment. She looked up with her eyes as blue as the ocean and said, "Travis, I'm sorry I didn't call. I was scared and confused." She sprang to her feet and threw her arms around him. Travis knew a little about being confused. His emotions were playing mind games with him. He was excited to see her, even aroused, but at the same time he wanted to see her leave his life forever so he could get back on track. "Jennifer, we need to talk," he said.

"I know. I saw it on the news. I'm so sorry about the officer that got shot," Jennifer said.

"Let's go for a walk, Jen."

They walked down the wooden stairs of the deck and crossed over the bike path and onto the beach. They took their shoes off and left them on the wall that separated the sand and the bike path. Jennifer took Travis's hand and put her head on his shoulder as they walked along the deserted beach. "Travis, I'm going home today. I sold my car and I'm letting Cheryl have my other things. I want a new start. I think home would be the best place."

"Who are you going to stay with?"

"My grandmother."

"You're not going to stay with your sister?"

"My sister?"

"Yeah, don't you have a sister named Elizabeth?"

"Yeah, but she doesn't live at home anymore."

"I know, Jennifer; she lives right here in Redondo Beach." Jennifer let go of Travis's hand, folded her arms and drew silent. They kept walking side by side and she said, "How did you know?"

"I got all the police reports from Oklahoma. The one about how William Adams tortured Elizabeth with cigarettes like you told me the night we made love. And I read the report from when Jennifer died in the car accident. Why, Jen? Why did you take your sister's name?"

"It was just a few months after William was sent to prison when Jen was killed. She was my strength through the ordeal of the trial and everything. Without her there, I was scared that somehow he would get out and find me, so I left but I took her ID with me. We looked a lot alike, so when I landed here in California, I took her name in case he tried to search for me. You wouldn't believe how easy it was to get a driver's license, and then after that I lived as Jennifer all through school and everything. Cheryl doesn't even know my real name is really Elizabeth."

Travis stopped walking and turned to her. "So when I told you there was a new guy moving in on Snake you knew it was William, didn't you?" Jennifer looked at the sand and said, "I figured it was probably him, that's why you couldn't reach me. I went up to Santa Barbara to hide from him. I even changed my cell phone number."

"Why didn't you tell me?" Travis asked as he placed his right hand on her shoulder.

"I thought about it, but I thought you would hate me if you found out I had lied. I couldn't live with that. Don't you see? I love you, Travis." She tried to kiss him, but he turned away. He never responded to her statement, and quietly they started to walk back to the house. Travis quickly changed the subject. "When is your flight?"

"In about two hours."

"LAX?"

"No, I'm flying out of Long Beach." Travis smiled at her and asked, "Can I drive you? I'm headed back to the city anyway."

"Thanks, I'd like that."

They made their way off the sand and back to the house. Jennifer's bags were sitting by the front door, so Travis picked them up and took them to the car. He told Jen to take her time saying goodbye to Cheryl and that he would wait in the car. He set the bags in the trunk and saw Jen's itinerary sticking out of her carry-on bag. He pulled it out and opened it to see the flight time. Folded inside the boarding pass was a receipt from FedEx for an overnight package sent to an address in Oklahoma. Travis glanced over the open trunk and could see Cheryl and Jen through the kitchen window, sitting at the table talking. He took his phone out of his pocket and pressed the auto-dialer. Jesse answered after the first ring. Travis said, "Bro, you got a pen handy?"

"Yeah, I'm in the office."

"Take this number down quick."

"Hold on," Jesse said as he scrambled for some paper. "Alright, shoot." Travis read him the tracking number on the receipt, 18 numbers in all. When he finished, Jesse asked, "What's that about?" Travis stuffed the receipt back in the itinerary and placed the papers back into her bag. He then said, "It's a tracking number for a FedEx package. Does your cousin still work there?"

"Yeah, why?"

"I need you to call him and have that package intercepted; we need to look at it." Jennifer and Cheryl walked out the front door and hugged one last time. Travis started to climb into the driver's seat, still listening to Jesse ask what it was all about. In the few seconds Travis had alone in the car as Jennifer was walking toward it, he said, "I can't explain. Just have him try to get it and call me back." Travis slapped his phone shut as Jennifer opened the door.

During the drive, Jennifer talked about the relief she felt knowing she could go home and see her grandmother without fear of running into William or being followed by Snake. She held Travis's hand part of the way but he remained fairly quiet. She asked if anything was wrong, and he explained how he was trying to get back together with his wife. His cell phone vibrated as it sat in the cup holder between the seats. He saw it was Jesse and opened it. "Talk to me, bro," was all he said. When Jess was done, Travis said, "Well, that's convenient. Why don't you meet me at the airport? I'm seeing Jen off. She's going home today." Travis hung up the phone, looked at Jen and said, "Jesse's going to meet us there and say goodbye as well."

"I like him. How is he doing?"

"He's back to work, but he won't be going back in the field."

When they got to the airport, Travis pulled up to the curb in front of the Art Deco terminal that had been featured in so many movies, including the closing scene in CASABLANCA in which Humphrey Bogart said his famous goodbye to Ingrid Bergman. That was Hollywood; this was a real goodbye, and a difficult one at that. Travis got out, set Jen's bags on the curb and flagged a skycap for her. She asked, "Is this it?"

Travis said, "No, I'm going to park the car and be right back." She smiled at him as he drove off to the airport police parking area. Jess was already there with his undercover car, and he was talking with an airport officer. Travis parked next to them and got out of his car. The uniform began to walk off as Jess said, "He didn't recognize me with the beard. I told him we were just going to be a few minutes."

"Cool, so you got ahold of your cuz?"

"Yep, he said it entered the system in Torrance this morning and should be here by now. So, what's in it?"

"To tell you the truth, I'm not sure, but take a look at these reports real quick." Travis stuck his arm in the car and grabbed his kit bag, pulled out the reports from Oklahoma and handed them to his friend. "When you're done, meet us in the terminal to say goodbye."

Travis slung his bag over his shoulder and went to find Jennifer. She was already in the security line, so he told her he would see her inside. He made his way to the exit doors and showed his badge to the TSA employee standing there. She was a fat, dumpy lady of about 50 and talked like she'd just escaped from a trailer park or carnival. He explained that he was seeing a witness onto a plane. The poor old gal didn't know what to do, so she called over an airport police officer. The officer knew Jensen and told the screener to let him through. Travis told her there would be another officer coming through and described Jesse to her so he wouldn't have the same trouble.

Travis was waiting for Jennifer when she came through the security-screening checkpoint. She looked at him with amazement and said, "How'd you do that?" He gave her a quirky look and said, "You're kidding, right? I'm the PO-LICE in this town; I can do whatever I want." She looked past him and yelled, "Jesse!" She ran over and gave the chubby detective a big hug and a kiss on the cheek. "I'm so glad to see you're doing better, you look like you lost some weight."

"Yeah, a liquid diet for two weeks will do that to ya, and it wasn't the kind of liquid diet I like." The three of them made their way to the gate to find her plane was already beginning to board. Jesse said goodbye and left after getting one more hug. Travis and Jen just looked at each other, not saying a word until Jen said, "You may not believe me but I do love you, Travis, I do."

"You don't love me. You used me to get the result you wanted."

"Don't say that," she protested.

"It's true. If you loved me you wouldn't have lied to me. Instead you let things get out of hand."

"I had no idea it would turn out the way it did." Travis was angry inside, but he didn't want to cause a scene. He took a deep breath and said, "Well, it did. Look, go have a good life as Elizabeth and just forget about these last few months."

"I'll never forget you, Travis."

"Goodbye, Jennifer." He leaned in and kissed her one more time before turning and walking away. He never looked over his shoulder, so he never saw the tears in her eyes as he passed through the exit doors.

Jess was sitting on the hood of Travis's car as he approached. Travis asked, "You got any quarters?"

"Yeah, in my ashtray." As Travis fished for the quarters Jess asked, "So how'd you figure she wasn't who she said she was?" Travis came out of the car with two quarters and said, "I didn't right away. I was trying to locate her and I kinda stumbled on to it." Travis walked to a newspaper machine a few yards away and dropped the coins in the slot. He opened the door and grabbed the entire stack of papers and shoved them into a gym bag that was on the back seat of his car. Jesse was now thoroughly confused about what Travis was doing. He asked, "Why are you taking all the papers?"

"I have a hunch, *mi amigo*. Let's see what your cousin has for us."

They drove in tandem to the far side of the airport where the cargo carriers were handled. While on the way, Jess called his cousin Enrique to let him know they were almost there. Enrique was a big fellow with a thick mustache and goatee. He stood well over six foot four and his arms filled the sleeves of his uniform shirt. He was waiting in the parking lot when the two detectives arrived. Jesse introduced Enrique and Travis. Enrique said, "It's here. I put it in the security office for you guys and there is packing tape to seal it back up."

Travis said, "It sounds like you've done this before."

"Oh yeah. We've done it for the DEA a bunch of times and for your sex crimes people when they intercept kiddy porn." Travis took his gym bag with him, and Enrique led them through an employee entrance and to the security office. The office was a bare room. On the lone desk sat a box a little bigger than a briefcase. It was addressed to Elizabeth Bennett of Catoosa, Oklahoma from Jennifer Bennett of Redondo Beach, California. Enrique left the room and shut the door behind him. Jesse asked Travis, "If she was mailing this to herself it has to be something you can't take on a plane, right?"

"Perhaps. Well, there's only one way to find out." Travis took out a boot knife from his belt and slit the tape on the bottom side of the box so he wouldn't disturb the labels. When he was done he put the knife away and paused for a moment. He tucked his fingers inside the flaps and pulled them open. The two detectives stood there in total shock. Jesse asked, "So, how in the hell did you know?"

Travis smiled and said, "You gave me the answer. You wrote it on her booking slip the night we arrested her."

"What?" Jess asked.

Unzipping his gym bag Travis said, "Let's finish up here and I'll fill you in later."

***

Friday morning was bright and sunny but the temperature was in the low 60's. A strong wind overnight had blown all of the smog out of the Los Angeles basin, making the local mountains look closer than they normally did. It was a gorgeous morning and it was cool enough not to sweat in a wool class-A uniform. It was the perfect morning to say farewell to a young hero. The detectives' locker room was elbow to elbow with guys from every detail shedding suits and ties for their long-sleeved uniform shirts and the old-school eight point hats that, in the Southern California area, only the Long Beach Police Department used. The funeral for Officer Jimenez wasn't for a few more hours, but everyone had to be in place early. The service was expected to draw more than 2,000 officers from all over the state, so it was going to be held at the Terrace Theater next to the arena. This also had been done when Travis's friend Derrick Brown was killed. An officer's funeral was one of the most awesome, and at the same time horrible, things to witness in police work.

Travis and the rest of the Vice Squad drove to the theater in a pair of plain detective Crown Victoria's and parked on Ocean Boulevard. As they made their way toward the theater, they could see officers from other agencies walking up from the parking structures. The shoulder patches were like an almanac of law enforcement. Every agency in Southern California was represented, and there were some from as far away as Kern County and Las Vegas. They didn't come for Jimenez; none of them knew him. They came for the family to let them know he would never be forgotten. They also came to support the agency as if to say, "Whether you wear green or tan or blue, we are all one family and we will always be there for each other."

The squad was almost to the entrance when Ben's phone rang. He answered it, spoke for a moment, then said, "Hold on guys. My wife is walking over here and she wants us to wait for her." They stepped to the side of the entrance and fidgeted with their ties and gun belts while they waited. Travis fixed the black band on his badge, and then looked at his reflection in the big windows. He hadn't seen himself without a mustache and goatee in almost three years. The entire team had shaved and cut their long hair. Jesse stood next to him and said, "I look good in a uniform, don't I?" As Travis turned to make a funny comment, he saw Sarah walking toward them with Donna Hutchens. She walked up to Travis and hugged him without saying a word. He whispered in her ear, "It's over, she's gone forever. I'm ready to start over if you are." She simply smiled at him and nodded her head.

Donna said, "OK, you all, I've got some breaking news. Just before I came down here they posted the results for the sergeant's test." The whole team looked at Travis, who was looking at Donna in suspense.

"Well?" Travis asked.

Donna said, "You're number three out of twenty-seven." The guys all hollered and slapped Travis on the back and began shaking his hand. "So who was number one?" Joe asked.

"Fred Crackers," Donna replied. That was no shock to anyone, as he had demonstrated time and time again his proficiency as an officer and a leader. Commander Baker walked up to the group and said hello. He shook hands with all his boys and gave Sarah a kiss on the cheek. She said, "Hi Al, it's nice to see you again."

"You too Sarah. Well, I was going to break the big news to you all but it looks like I'm a few minutes late."

Travis said, "I'm number three, sir."

"I know, Travis, I've known for two weeks. Why do you think I had Joe advertise for more than one opening? The second one was for your spot." The old man had an all-knowing smirk on his face.

"Now look, I have something for you. I've been holding on to this for a long time." Baker reached into his back trouser pocket and pulled out a small brown cardboard box about the size of a deck of cards. It was old and the tape on the corners had yellowed terribly. Baker held it out in one of his big hands. The lid had a handwritten address on it but the ink had faded many years ago. Travis took the box and carefully opened it. Inside was a police badge. It was the older style of Long Beach badge, all brass and without the city seal in the middle. Instead of the seal, a silver screw on a disk with blue enamel numbers was attached to the center of the badge. It was his father's badge number but not his rank. It was a sergeant's badge. Baker said, "That was the badge the department ordered for your dad's promotion that he never got to see."

"Where did you get it sir?"

"When I promoted the next year I saw it in the safe in the personnel office, so I took it. I knew one day I'd see it get pinned on a Jensen. I figured between your brother and you, one of you would strap on the blue suit. It's been in my desk drawer at home for almost three decades, Travis. They are promoting four sergeants right away, probably within a few weeks. Congratulations, son." Travis put out his hand expecting a handshake. Baker gave him a hug and then said, "Oh, and if you're wondering, it's OK to wear it with your dad's badge number on there. The chief put a memo in your personnel file authorizing it."

"Really? That was nice," Jesse said. Baker smiled and said, "When you've been around as long as I have, Guerra, you have dirt on everyone so little favors like this come easy."

Travis gave the badge to Sarah to hold during the ceremony. The girls went to the upper balconies to sit with the other wives while the guys filed into the lower level of the theater. The team all sat together except for Terry. He was asked by Mrs. Jimenez to sit with her and her family. She even asked him to go up to the podium and talk. First the chaplain spoke, followed by some family members and Jimenez's high school baseball coach. When Terry took the stage the place grew tensely quiet. Everyone who knew the details of the shooting waited with anxiety to hear what he would say. He began by thanking everyone who came to support the family and explained that he had never met Officer Jimenez before the morning of the shootout. His words were profound and from the heart.

"I never met him before, but I didn't have to. He wore the same uniform and swore the same oath we all did, and for that reason he was my brother as you all are. And in his darkest hour, my brother, knowing he was seriously hurt, thought of me first and by doing so saved my life." Terry paused for a moment to collect his thoughts and wipe the tears from his eyes. He continued. "I have a wife and an infant son. Every day I get to spend with them is now extra. Every kiss and hug I get is because of Jimenez. I will have the joy of taking my boy to his first day of school because of Adrian Jimenez, and God willing; I will grow to be an old man because of Adrian. For whatever reason, God sent me an angel that morning, an archangel to watch over me. He now stands at the side of God, a protector of the heavens as he was here on earth."

When he finished there wasn't a dry eye in the building. When the service ended, all the uniformed personnel headed outside and got into formation in front of the theater. When the casket was brought out, they were all were called to present arms. They all held their salutes until the casket reached the hearse. The command of order arms was given by the lieutenant in charge of the Honor Guard, who then dismissed everyone to go to their cars for the long procession to the cemetery.

Sarah found Travis in the crowd before she left. She took his hand and walked with him to his car. She said, "I want you to come home Travis."

"Are you sure?"

"Yes, I'm sure. You know, while I was sitting up there I was holding your dad's badge and listening to Terry and it kinda helped me to understand."

"Understand what?"

"Why it's not a job but a way of life for you guys. You know, the way Al kept the badge all these years waiting for the day he could give it to you. You were meant to take his place. You were meant for this job. You all are, in your own ways."

"I'll be home tomorrow, my love." Travis leaned over and kissed her on the cheek before she left to get back to work.

On the slow drive to the cemetery, citizens lined the street to watch as the procession of several hundred police cars quietly drove by with their lights flashing. The farther they drove north on Cherry Avenue, the bigger the crowds became. Some were holding signs saying things like *Thank you Officer Jimenez.* Terry Knight, who was sitting in the front seat, turned around and said to Jesse and Travis, "This is where Adrian grew up. His mother still lives at Sixteenth and Gaviota. I still can't believe he made it out of this neighborhood just to die this way."

***

While the line of police cars made its way through the city, a FedEx truck was making its way to a farmhouse outside Catoosa. Jennifer, who'd gone back to the name Elizabeth the second she landed in Oklahoma, met the carrier at the door. She signed for the box and took it to her room. Before she could open it, her grandmother came in and asked her to get something off of the upper shelf in the kitchen. Jennifer slid the box under her bed until she could get to it later.

***

Once at the gravesite, it took nearly an hour for everyone to get parked and in formation, while the guys in the Honor Guard stood at parade rest waiting for the time to show their respects. When everyone was in place, the chaplain said a few more words and turned it over to the Honor Guard Lieutenant. Travis's grandfather started playing "Amazing Grace" on the bagpipes. He was about 50 yards away on a small hill overlooking the grave. Dressed in a kilt in the Black Watch tartan and his uniform tunic from his days with Garda, he was a striking sight to behold. When the pipes were silent, the casket detail marched in to fold the flag.

***

Jennifer returned to her room and closed the door behind her. She retrieved the box from under the bed and began to open it. She slit the top with a pair of scissors and peeled back the flaps. She felt her heart miss a beat when she saw that the $265,000 in cash she had taken from Snake's hidden compartment was now gone and had been replaced with a stack of newspapers. She dug through the papers hoping she might find some of the money or that it was just a bad dream. All she found was a compact disc and a typed note.

***

Back in Long Beach, the flag was lifted off of the beautifully crafted wooden coffin. The seven members of the firing detail snapped their chrome shotguns to port arms waiting for the command. "Ready, aim, fire," the sergeant belted out. The blast was so tremendous it set off car alarms in the parking lot. They repeated twice more in unison. The Honor Guard lieutenant gave the order of present arms and everyone saluted for the last time as white-gloved hands folded the flag. The flag was passed to the chief, who presented it to the mother of Officer Adrian Jimenez. And with that the formation was dismissed.

Travis and Jesse were walking together when Frank Tillbak came up and told them that an anonymous donor had sent a homeless man into the Police Officers Association office early that the morning with a bag. He gave the bag to the secretary, who found a quarter of a million dollars in cash inside and a note that said it was for Jimenez's family so they could move to a better neighborhood. Jesse looked at Travis knowingly and said, "No shittin', I wonder who did that?" Travis remained silent as Frank took off to catch his ride back to the station. Jesse looked around to make sure he could talk to Travis in confidence. He said quietly, "I think I figured it out."

"What's that?" Travis asked.

"The clue on the booking slip. The keys. It was her keys, wasn't it?"

"Why do you say that?" Travis quizzed.

"Because she was worried about her car being in the hotel lot when we arrested her. I looked through her stuff and found her keys, Mercedes keys to be exact. But she didn't own a Mercedes, we only saw her drive an Explorer. She had a set of keys to Snake's car."

"Very clever, Jess, very clever."

"So how do you know she'll never come back and snitch you out?"

"Because, my friend, I have an insurance policy for that."

***

Sitting alone in her room, Jennifer read the note, which was typed and not signed. *If you are reading this then by now you know I know your secret. I think once you play this disc you will see why you must never talk about what happened. I will keep the original for my protection until which time it is needed or until the day I die.* Jennifer turned on her laptop and waited impatiently for it to warm up. She put the disc in and it began to run. Jennifer cupped her hands over her mouth in startled disbelief when she saw the first few frames as she recognized the gas station parking lot in the video. When Snake's black Mercedes backed into the view of the camera, she began to cry as she watched herself in the driver's seat tucking her blonde hair under a big hat so she would not be identified as a woman. She had thought of everything – the car, the money, even making sure the plates got captured on the red light camera while hiding her face. But thanks to a minimum wage gas station attendant, all she had left was a box full of newspapers and there was nothing she could do about it without going to prison for the rest of her life.

***

Jess asked Travis, "So you're good with letting her go?"

"Yeah, I mean let's face it, the cowboy guy she killed probably would have killed her first if he'd found her, right? And no one cares about Snake and Washington. What happened last week could have happened if we just served the warrant for pimping. Either way, it was Snake who killed Jimenez, not Jennifer. Besides, it looks like Snake was already a murderer with that girl under his garage. The way I look at it Jess, everyone got what they deserved". Travis paused for second, grimaced and said, "Except Jimenez, of course."

As the two detectives reached their car, Patrick Sullivan walked up holding his bagpipes under his left arm. He said, "So did I ever tell you fellas about the time I played for Prince Edward when he visited our station house in Limerick?"

"No, Daideó, but I think you're about to. Why don't you hop in our car and we'll give you a ride home," Travis offered.

"Home? Like hell yer gonna. Once you boys get out of them monkey suits you can take me to the pub so's we can toast your brother officer proper like."

"OK, OK, you got it Daideó," Travis said as he smiled at the rest of the team, whom were all chuckling at the tenacity of the old policeman.

The End

Made in the USA
San Bernardino, CA
07 April 2016